KINGFISHER

OTHER BOOKS AND AUDIOBOOKS
BY CLAIR M. POULSON

I'll Find You
Relentless
Lost and Found
Conflict of Interest
Runaway
Cover Up
Mirror Image
Blind Side
Evidence
Don't Cry Wolf
Dead Wrong
Deadline
Vengeance
Hunted
Switchback
Accidental Private Eye
Framed
Checking Out
In Plain Sight
Falling
Murder at TopHouse
Portrait of Lies
Silent Sting
Outlawered
Deadly Inheritance
The Search
Suspect
Short Investigations
Watch Your Back
Fool's Deadly Gold
Pitfall

KINGFISHER

A SUSPENSE NOVEL BY

CLAIR M. POULSON

Covenant Communications, Inc.

Cover image *Majestic Image of Horse Silhouette with Rider on Sunset* © Standret / Shutterstock.com

Cover design copyright © 2020 by Covenant Communications, Inc.
Cover design by Aleesa Parsons

Published by Covenant Communications, Inc.
American Fork, Utah

Printed in the United States of America
First Printing: August 2020

27 26 25 24 23 22 21 20   10 9 8 7 6 5 4 3 2 1

ISBN 978-1-52441-257-9

For Yankee Hit Man's Eliminator P. (better known as Tator), the beautiful black stallion owned by my son Alan and me and trained as a show horse by my nephew Roy Poulson.

CHAPTER ONE

KINGFISHER WAS A MAGNIFICENT HORSE. Jet black with a white star on his forehead and four white socks, he stood at sixteen hands. He was built to run, and he loved to do it. With the firm but loving guidance of twenty-two-year-old Kit Troxler, Kit's twin sister, Paizlee, and Kit's ranch foreman, Andy Boyse, Kingfisher was fast becoming one of the top quarter horse racehorses in the West.

Kit and his twin sister were natural riders. In fact, Kit was one of the best jockeys around. When in a race, Kit and his horse were as one. He rode smoothly, and his horse responded to every command. He seldom touched Kingfisher with a whip, but when he did, it was soft, just a reminder to the horse to pick up speed. And Kingfisher always responded to that gentle reminder. Paizlee was not far behind Kit in ability and rode their other horses in races from time to time. Both loved the sport.

Kit contemplated the events of the day with a frown as Andy led Kingfisher to the trailer. He'd just finished second in a major race at Albuquerque Downs. That wasn't bad, but Kit knew, as did his foreman and his sister, Paizlee, that he should have won easily. He'd stayed about four horses behind the leader until the next-to-last turn of the race. At that point, Kit leaned forward until he lay almost on the black stallion's neck, spoke words of encouragement to Kingfisher, and touched him ever so gently with his whip. The horse shot forward like a cannonball.

Within seconds, he'd passed all but the lead horse. There was room between that horse and the rail, so Kit had slipped Kingfisher into the space. He was quickly neck and neck with a bay stallion by the name of Sharpshooter. Kit was forging ahead when the other jockey, Sam Overmyer, reached over and gave Kit a shove, nearly unseating him.

Sam was riding a horse not favored to win. Kit knew Kingfisher, who was the favorite in this race, had what it took to beat Sharpshooter and every other horse on the track. No horse in Sharpshooter's category came close to being a favorite when pitted against a horse like Kingfisher. There was no question that Kingfisher was about to take the lead when the shove occurred. By the time Kit had regained his seat, he'd fallen behind by eight or ten lengths, and two of the other horses had passed him.

Kit had leaned forward, told Kingfisher to run his best, touched him lightly with the whip again, and the big stallion shot forward once more, passing the third- and second-place horses, leaving them in the dust. He was running beautifully and was soon just a neck behind Sharpshooter and his jockey, Sam. Unfortunately, it was too little too late. They crossed the finish line at that point. At the rate Kingfisher was running, he'd have taken the lead in a couple more seconds. Had it not been for the shove from Overmyer, he would have easily won by ten or twelve lengths.

Andy and Paizlee had both been in a position to see the push, but the officials had apparently been looking at other runners or were simply not in a positon where they could clearly see the activity at that point. They complained angrily to the officials, but they let the results stand. Kit still couldn't believe what had happened as he and Paizlee watched Andy lead the big stallion into the trailer. When Andy came back out, his face, which was already ruddy by nature, had turned beet red. The race had been over for two hours, but Andy still fumed with anger.

"You had him beat," Andy said through clenched teeth as the three of them headed for the cab of the truck. "Kingfisher was still full of energy, and Sharpshooter was winded. I could see it from where I was standing. It was a rotten trick that guy pulled. I wish there had been an official where I was at. He should have been disqualified and banned from racing for the rest of his life."

Kit nodded but said nothing. Paizlee also did not remark. They'd already said enough, and the three had a long drive ahead of them. Other trucks and trailers were also headed for the exit, which brought the traffic to a standstill, and Kit waited impatiently. A horn honked behind him. He looked in his mirror and recognized the leering face of Sam Overmyer. Sam honked again, and Kit got out of his truck. He marched back to Sam's, his anger stirred up all over again. He didn't even hear his twin sister tell him to let it go.

Sam rolled his window down. "Get that ugly horse of yours out of my road. You're as slow at driving as your worthless black nag is at racing on the track."

"I would have won by several lengths if you hadn't cheated," Kit said, barely holding his anger in check. "And you know it."

"I didn't cheat. You just can't stay in the saddle very well," Sam said. "You're a poor excuse for a jockey."

"The line is moving again," Paizlee called to him from the back seat of their truck, and Kit relented.

"Get out of my road, you loser," Sam shouted, shaking his fist.

Kit looked back. "We'll meet again. And when we do, Kingfisher and I will win." He confidently trotted back to his truck, calling over his shoulder as he went. "I won't fall for any of your dirty tricks again."

Kit had barely started to drive forward when he felt a light jar. He looked in his mirror and could see that Sam's truck was right up against his horse trailer. He was sure Sam had intentionally bumped him with the big, heavy-duty grill he had on the front of his silver one-ton Dodge Ram. He and the fellow with him were laughing like it was some kind of big joke.

They bumped him twice more before he was finally able to exit the parking lot and pull onto the street. He hadn't gone more than a block when Sam roared around him with that big Ram of his, his horse trailer swaying dangerously. His passenger made an obscene gesture at Kit, Paizlee, and Andy as they passed.

"Don't worry about Sam Overmyer, Kit," Andy said as the Dodge completed the pass without rolling the horse trailer. "He'll get his one day."

"I wish I didn't have to race against him again," Kit said. "But I'm sure I will. Kingfisher can beat him every time, but Sam sure takes the fun out of it."

"One thing we've learned from today," Andy said, "is that you won't want to come up on the inside of him another time. You won't need to. Kingfisher is so much more powerful that you can overtake him on the outside, just like you did after you recovered from the push."

"Yeah, that was my mistake," Kit admitted. "But I didn't know that another jockey would do something like that. There was plenty of room. I've been thinking about it, and I'm sure he planned it that way. He should have been disqualified."

The next night, Sam Overmyer and a bunch of rowdy young men were drinking and generally being obnoxious in a smoke-filled Tonopah, Nevada, bar. Sam was celebrating his Albuquerque win on his racehorse from the day before. "I've trained my horse so he responds to me on the track so well that no one has a chance of beating me. That horse of mine is worth a million dollars. He proved that yesterday. He is without a doubt the best racehorse in the West." Sam's friends responded to his outlandish bragging with cheers and back slaps. "The next round of drinks is on me. So everybody drink up."

Not all the people in the barroom were fans of Sam Overmyer. In fact, some badly disliked him. One fellow, who was drinking with his wife, shouted above the din, "Hey, folks, don't believe everything you hear. Kit Troxler from Utah has a stallion he calls Kingfisher. He's twice the horse Sharpshooter is."

"You don't know anything, Bob." Sam laughed drunkenly. "Sharpshooter is in a whole different league above that nag of Troxler's. And you know what else? Someone needs to teach that loudmouth kid how to ride. He nearly fell off his horse." Sam's friends laughed loudly along with him.

Bob Sims and his wife, Annie, both looked at Sam with disdain. "Hey, big mouth, Annie and I were at that race. The officials didn't see it, but we did."

"See what?" Sam asked with a sneer.

"See you try to push Kit from his horse and over the rails. If an official had been sitting where we were, you would have been disqualified and banned from riding again."

"I don't know what you're talking about," Sam said. "Troxler wasn't even close to me. You need to keep your fat mouth shut and quit making stuff up."

"He didn't make it up," Annie said in defense of her husband. "It's just like he said. Kit lost because you cheated."

"You shut your trap," Sam said. "If you had half the brains you have fat, you'd know I won fair and square."

Bob Sims was six feet tall and was 195 pounds of pure muscle. He worked as a mechanic. He loved his wife dearly—no one made fun of her and got away with it. He charged across the barroom floor and swung a huge fist at the little jockey. Had it connected, it could well have knocked Sam through the wall, but even after he'd been drinking, Sam was quick; Bob had not seen Sam pull a pair of brass knuckles from his pocket. He ducked under Bob's powerful swing and hit him with his right fist, the one holding the brass knuckles. His fist connected with Bob's right temple, and the big man went down, blood gushing from his head. Bob did not get up.

With an angry scream, Annie rushed toward Sam, moving faster than anyone would have thought she'd be able to. She didn't throw any punches; she just lowered her head, hit the jockey square in the chest, and kept going. She carried him toward the wall, knocking chairs over as she went. Sam, his breath knocked out of him, sank to the floor.

In moments, the fight turned into a full barroom brawl, and as sirens could be heard approaching outside, Sam finally got back to his feet. He spotted Annie standing in the middle of the brawlers. No one else was paying any attention to her but Sam. He ran toward her, knocking his way through the other fighters, and punched her in the face. She flew backward, breaking a chair as her body hit it, and fell unconscious to the floor.

Bob had regained consciousness in time to see what Sam had just done; he surged to his feet and roared like a bull, charging toward Sam. But Sam once again managed to deliver a blow to Bob's face, cutting his eye and drawing blood. Once again, Bob fell unconscious to the floor.

Cops crashed through the door, but Sam, paying no attention to them, kicked Bob fiercely in the side. Then he was tackled by a couple of deputies. He hit one of them with the brass knuckles, and down he went. The fight didn't let up. The police just added more bodies to the melee. One of the deputies, Sergeant Vince Hodson, grabbed Sam by the arm, pulled him away from the fight, and dragged him from the building. Once outside, he shoved Sam against the closest car and stripped him of his brass knuckles.

"Sam, how many times have I told you not to fight when I'm on duty?" Vince said. "It puts me in a bad light with my men. I'm going to let you go because you're my cousin, but don't keep doing this. I'm not always going to be able to protect you, as hard as I've always tried. And if anyone asks where you are, I'll tell them you got away."

"Bob accused me of cheating to win that race," Sam bawled.

"He must have seen what you did. Don't worry about it. I'll make sure he learns to keep his mouth shut," Vince said as he dragged Sam toward his big silver Dodge Ram pickup. He helped him in, and as soon as Sam had managed to start the truck, Vince slammed the door. "Go home and go to bed. And don't let your dad see you."

Vince watched as the pickup left the lot and started down the road, weaving back and forth. "You better not wreck that thing," he shouted. "I might not be able to cover for you if you get arrested for drunk driving."

Of course, Sam couldn't hear him, and Vince knew it. Vince headed back to the bar. The fight was still going on inside, but when Vince shouted, pulled his pistol, and fired a shot into the ceiling, everyone stopped fighting and looked for where the shot had come from. Vince slipped his sidearm back into its holster. "That's it. Let's all calm down now."

Someone asked who'd fired a gun.

"How would I know?" Vince said. "Now, all of you, line up against that wall there and stand still." The other deputies stood back, all but the unconscious one on the floor. He was in pretty bad shape, having been stepped on several times by the battling drunks. One of the officers pulled him back just as more officers poured through the door.

Someone had also called an ambulance, for three paramedics entered, stopped, looked around, and then headed for the unconscious deputy. While two of them tended to him, the third, Artie Webb, called out, "Anybody else need an ambulance?"

Someone pointed Bob and Annie out, but they were both stirring again and refused help. "You're both bleeding," Artie said. "Come out with me, and I can at least bandage you up."

They reluctantly agreed to that and followed him to the ambulance, where he went to work on their battered faces.

Inside, the unconscious deputy was strapped to a gurney and hauled out. Sergeant Vince Hodson took charge as the bar patrons were questioned. "Who started this?" he asked, and several men told him it was Bob Sims. None of those who had been against Sam and his friends dared say a word, even though it was clear Sam had disappeared.

"Okay, Bob goes to jail as soon as he's patched up. The rest of you, find sober drivers and go home."

The bartender, Clark Drene, protested loudly. "Somebody's got to clean up this mess and pay for it."

"I'll see that Bob does," Sergeant Hodson said, glaring at Clark.

"He can't clean this up," Clark said. "You saw him. He can hardly stand up."

"You get it cleaned up, Clark. Keep track of what it costs. I'll see that Bob pays for it all."

"But he—" Clark started again, but Hodson shut him up with a glare.

At some point, someone finally asked where Sam Overmyer was. "Didn't see him," the sergeant lied. "He must not have been here."

"He was here all right," the bartender said.

Hodson stepped over to him and said with his eyes narrowed, "He must have left before all this got started." No one disagreed with him. Hodson was an officer no one wanted to be on the bad side of, and that included his fellow deputies.

Ten minutes later, the barroom was cleared of patrons, and Clark had shut and locked the door. Bob Sims was taken into custody. His wife screamed at Sergeant Hodson, so she was also arrested that night. "Not fair!" Annie shouted as handcuffs were fastened onto her wrists. "You need to find that weasel, little Sam Overmyer. He's a dirty liar."

"He isn't here, now is he?" Hodson said nastily as he shoved her in a patrol car. "When you sober up, maybe you will remember what really happened here tonight."

"Yeah, I'll remember all right," she said, and Hodson slammed the door.

CHAPTER TWO

ANDY, PAIZLEE, AND KIT HAD spent the night in a motel, keeping Kit's horse at the ranch of a friend. It was early afternoon when they had finally pulled into the yard of their thousand-acre ranch near Fillmore, Utah. Kit raised horses and cattle on the ranch with the help of Andy, another ranch hand by the name of Greg Gerard, and Kit's sister, Paizlee. At times, it was necessary to hire additional help, and it seemed like Andy never had trouble finding that help when it was needed.

Kit had been home for about a month after serving a mission for The Church of Jesus Christ of Latter-day Saints when both of his parents had perished in a plane crash. If it hadn't been for Andy Boyse and Greg Gerard, Kit didn't know what he would have done. That was a little over a year ago, right after Kit and Paizlee had turned twenty-one. Their father had been a successful rancher, and he had very little debt when he passed away. So financially, the two Troxlers didn't have any worries. But they had a lot of grief to overcome and a lot of work to do. The first few months had been difficult, but the two had eventually been able to settle into a routine and move on with their lives.

Kit had worked with his father from the time he was big enough to help, and he knew the ranching business inside and out. But being in charge of such a big operation was another matter. That's why Andy and Greg were so vital to him.

They had dozens of horses, but Kingfisher was a huge cut above the rest. Kit's father and Andy had started training him before Kit left on his mission. Several offers came in from prospective buyers shortly after the death of Mr. and Mrs. Troxler, but Kit and Paizlee had no desire to part with him. They'd loved that horse from the day their father bought him. The teenagers and the horse had been inseparable right up to the day Kit left on his mission.

Andy, Kit, and Paizlee continued to work with Kingfisher after Kit's mission, and he had developed into everything they had hoped for and a lot more.

The ranch ran smoothly despite Kit's young age. Money was not a worry as long as he didn't make some costly mistakes along the way or run into disasters. He missed his parents every single day but was determined to do everything he believed his father would have wanted him to do. Kit was a responsible, hardworking man. He was dedicated to keeping the ranch running well in memory of his father.

Trouble came in the most unexpected way. A half dozen deputy sheriffs from Nye County, Nevada, drove into the yard about three weeks after the Albuquerque race and announced that they were there to arrest Kit. The charge was causing the death of Sam Overmyer's star racehorse, Sharpshooter. Moments later, several local Millard County deputies joined them.

"When did this happen? I've been in Wyoming for the past week looking at young bulls," Kit protested.

"So says you," the sergeant in charge said with a sneer. The name Hodson was embroidered on his uniform above a shirt pocket. "Sharpshooter's owner, Sam Overmyer, saw you near his ranch early in the morning of the day he found his horse dead in his stable. That was the day before yesterday, as you well know, since you were there."

"I was not there! I was on my way home from Wyoming," Kit protested.

"One of the other deputies will stay with you while we search," Sergeant Hodson said, ignoring his protests.

"Search for what?" Kit demanded.

"Evidence," the sergeant said as he handed a copy of the search warrant to Kit, who looked at it for a moment and then handed it to Andy.

"What are you searching, my house?" Kit asked, his voice trembling with barely suppressed rage.

"Not just your house. This warrant covers all the buildings on your ranch and all the vehicles as well as you and all the people who work here."

"That's kind of broad," Andy said, his face flaming with anger.

"It's not every day someone kills a million-dollar horse," the sergeant said.

"A million dollars! That horse isn't worth half what ours is, and Kingfisher is probably only worth a half million," Andy said.

Kit was listening, but he suddenly felt faint. He didn't kill that horse, nor would he kill any horse unless it was to put it out of its misery. And he hated to do that, so on the rare occasions it was needed, he and his father had always had a veterinarian do it for them.

"How was the horse killed?" Kit finally asked.

The officer snorted. "You tell me. You're the one who killed it."

"What happened to innocent until proven guilty?" Andy asked, his anger simmering right at the surface.

"Are you kidding? I don't arrest innocent people," Sergeant Hodson said with narrowed eyes. "I never have. Stick your hands out here. You're under arrest, Kit Troxler."

Kit felt his freedom slip away and for no good cause. The handcuffs bit into his wrists, but he said nothing, fearing that would only make it worse. The sergeant ordered one of his men to stay with Kit while they searched. Paizlee came running from the house, screaming, "You let him go. What do you think you're doing?"

"Stand back, Miss Troxler," Sergeant Hodson said with a scowl. "Your brother is a horse killer."

Paizlee's mouth dropped open and her eyes grew wide. "He is not!" she shouted.

A Millard County deputy who Kit and Paizlee both knew stepped over to where Paizlee was now clinging to her brother. "I'm sorry, guys," Sergeant Jason Anderson said. "He claims he's got evidence. I'm not convinced. I know you folks too well to believe you would do something like that."

"Deputy, keep your mouth shut," the sergeant ordered brusquely. "If you can't be objective here, then you can leave. I don't need anybody like you on my team."

"We are not a team," Sergeant Anderson said with an icy stare. "This is my jurisdiction. I am the ranking man from my department here. Your rank means nothing to us. So don't go telling me what to do. This man asked you a question, and he deserves an answer. When was this horse killed, and how was it done?"

"Very well, although you should be asking the killer here, since he knows exactly what happened." He threw a hateful glance at Kit. "Sometime the day before yesterday. My cousin found him dead in his stall that evening."

"Your cousin?" Andy broke in.

"Yeah, that's what I said."

"Are you saying that the hotheaded Sam Overmyer is your cousin?" Andy said. "This isn't right. No wonder you're denying my boss his constitutional rights. Your cousin is a first-class jerk."

Sergeant Anderson stepped beside Andy. "Calm down, sir. We'll get to the bottom of this."

Kit was thinking about what the Nevada sergeant had just stated. "I was on my way back from Wyoming the day before yesterday. I left Lyman late, so I didn't get here until around noon the next day. I couldn't have done it even if I'd wanted to, which I didn't."

"Says you," the sergeant said nastily. "Let's get on with this. You've stalled all I'm going to allow."

They started the search at the house. Andy and Paizlee trailed along, staying as close as they could to Kit and the Nevada deputy who was assigned to keep an eye on him. The Millard County deputies mostly observed, for it seemed that not a single one of them thought that what the Nevada officers were doing was right. Sergeant Hodson and his officers were practically tearing the house apart, leaving it a mess.

Sergeant Anderson was outraged and slipped outside to call his boss. When Sheriff Marc Ledford arrived a few minutes later, he bailed out of his gray Expedition and listened while Anderson filled him in. Then he followed Anderson into the house. He was outraged, and with his face in Sergeant Hodson's, he said, "This is not the way we work in my county. I will not stand by and allow you to make a mess of these young people's home."

Hodson said a few words that made Paizlee put her hands over her ears. Then he added, "I have the search warrant, and I will search until I find what I'm looking for."

"What are you looking for?" Sheriff Ledford asked, poking his face even closer to the sergeant's.

"Evidence, you idiot. What do you think I'd be looking for?" Hodson unwisely said.

"Hey, I'm the sheriff of this county. You don't talk to me like that," Ledford said, his voice soft and deadly. "I asked you a question. Answer it right now."

For a moment, Sergeant Hodson stuttered. "Proof that this hoodlum rancher of yours killed a million-dollar horse."

"Let me see that search warrant." The sheriff waited while the sergeant picked it up from a table where Andy had dropped it when they first came in the house. "Tell your officers to quit searching. I'll decide when it's okay to resume."

"I don't need your permission, Sheriff. I have a judge's order." The sneer on the sergeant's face was the straw that broke the camel's back. "Out of this house, all of you!" the sheriff thundered. "Sergeant Anderson, go with them and make sure no one touches anything until I say they can." They left with Sergeant Anderson, the other Millard deputies, and Andy following them.

As soon as they'd all gone, the sheriff instructed one of his deputies who had stayed behind to take the handcuffs off Kit.

Sheriff Ledford took his time reading the search warrant and the affidavit that supported it. "Kit, I'm sorry about this." He waved the search warrant.

"This seems to be in order. It was signed by a judge in Washington County. I would have thought they would have gone to one of our judges, but there's nothing I can do about that. It seems to be valid."

"I see," Kit said, but he was angry, mostly because he knew he was innocent and was being treated like a common criminal. "How do they justify it? I haven't been in Nevada for a long time. And I have never been to Tonopah. I don't even know for sure where that is, except that it's north of Las Vegas. I was just returning the day before yesterday from a trip to Wyoming where I'd been looking at some yearling bulls I'm thinking about buying."

"Were you alone?" the sheriff asked.

"Yes, everyone else was needed here," Kit responded. "They can search all they want, but they won't find anything because I didn't hurt that horse."

Sheriff Ledford glanced again at the papers in his hand. "Kit, it says here that you were seen on a ranch belonging to Randall Overmyer in Nye County, Nevada, early yesterday morning. It says you were on foot and sneaking around the outbuildings. It also says you threatened Sam Overmyer a few days earlier, that you told him he would wish he hadn't beaten you in a horse race."

"I said no such thing," Kit retorted angrily.

"We'll get to that. It also says that they found a glove belonging to you in the stall where the horse was killed."

Kit's blood pressure spiked. "I lost a glove at the race grounds in Albuquerque. Paizlee and I searched all over for it before we left. We couldn't find it."

"Did it have your name on it by any chance?" the sheriff asked.

Kit couldn't believe what was happening. A neat trap had been laid for him. He felt helpless. "Yes," he said at last. "It was sewn on the back of both gloves. My sister gave me those gloves for my birthday."

"Well, I'm guessing that Overmyer must have found the one you lost at the racetrack. Where's the other one?" the sheriff asked.

"It's in my shop in a drawer where I keep spare gloves. It's of no use to me without the other one. But if Overmyer found one, he found it at the racetrack. He must have picked it up while we were looking for it. That would explain why I couldn't find it."

"That is the claim in the affidavit that was used to justify the issuance of the search warrant. An affidavit is the document used by law enforcement to convince a judge to issue a warrant," the sheriff explained.

"He lied on it," Kit said.

"That may be, but the judge has no way of knowing that. Now, let me ask this: do you know a man by the name of Randall Overmyer?"

"I know Sam," Kit said. "He tried to put me over the rails at the race in Albuquerque three weeks ago to keep me from beating him. The officials didn't see it, so Sam got away with it. I suppose that Sam could be Randall's son."

"So Sam doesn't like you?"

"That's for sure. Let me tell you what else happened." Kit then told the sheriff about the problems he'd had with Sam after the race. "I can show you the dents on my horse trailer that he made with the big steel bumper on the front of his truck."

"I would like to see that, but let's get this over with first. Let's go outside for a minute."

Kit trailed after the sheriff, wondering if he was in a lot of trouble even though he was totally innocent. The sheriff called Sergeant Hodson over as soon as they stepped off Kit's porch. "Let's go back inside and finish up in there. And while we are doing that, you might like to explain to me who claimed to have seen Kit at the Overmyers' and why you got this search warrant in Washington County. The way we work in this state, if we have a case on someone from another jurisdiction, we meet with the officers there and then work together on the matter and use a local judge."

Hodson sneered. "I'll finish the search, but you can stick your head in the mud before I tell you anything else."

Kit could not believe how the sheriff kept his cool. He had to admire him. He trailed back inside with the others, and to his surprise, as soon as they were all there, the sheriff ordered everyone to listen to what he had to say. "This place is a mess. You officers from Nevada are to put things back the way you found them before any more searching is done. And when everything is in order, my deputies will conduct the rest of the search."

"No way will that happen," Sergeant Hodson said with narrowed eyes. "You don't even know what we're looking for."

"That's why, in our area, we sit down with officers from other jurisdictions and go over everything," the sheriff responded. "If you have something specific you want us to search for, you can tell me. But that can wait until you've cleaned up in here. So get to it."

"And if we don't?" Hodson asked with a growl.

"Then you will be spending some time in my jail. I would suggest you don't push me any further."

They finally went to work. Kit sat at his kitchen table with his head in his hands and his twin sister's arm around his shoulders.

The house was nowhere near as neat as it had been before the officers began their search. Paizlee may have only been twenty-two, but she kept the house clean just the way her mother had always done. And when he had time, Kit helped her. There were still a couple of rooms to be searched, and Sergeant Hodson announced that he would do them.

"You will watch while my officers search," Sheriff Ledford said firmly. "I will not allow you and your officers to make any further messes in this house."

The sergeant laughed. "It would be a waste of time for us just to watch, and we both know it, Sheriff."

"Not if you tell us what to look for," Sheriff Ledford responded. "The search warrant does not specify exactly what you're after, only items that have to do with the death of the horse. That's pretty vague. So what exactly are we looking for?"

"We'll watch. If we see it, we'll tell you," the sergeant said stubbornly.

"Have it your way," the sheriff said.

A very thorough search was conducted, but at no point did any of the Nevada officers point out something they were looking for. The group then went outside and began on the other buildings. For the next couple hours, a careful search was conducted. In Kit's shop, Sergeant Hodson suddenly said, "I'll take that," when a deputy thumbed through some gloves in a drawer. "That one with the horse killer's name on the back. I'll take it." The deputy picked it up, and Hodson snatched it from his hand. "You'll find it hard to explain why you still have this, Mr. Troxler. You lost the other one, didn't you? And unluckily for you, we found it. It was in the stall where you killed the million-dollar racehorse."

Kit said nothing. He knew it would do no good to point out the lies. Sergeant Hodson had to have known where that glove was actually found—likely at the racetrack and certainly nowhere near Sharpshooter's stall—but he would never admit it.

The search continued. Kit, at one point, noticed Sergeant Hodson snooping around his truck. He wished he'd left it locked, but he never locked it here at the ranch. He trusted everyone here. Too late now, he thought. He followed the officers to his large barn. Suddenly his twin sister came running up to him and said, "Kit, I just saw something." She put her mouth to his ear and whispered, "A policeman opened the door to your truck. It was only for a minute or so that he was leaning inside, and then he shut the door very quietly. I don't think he knew I was watching him. What do you think he was doing?"

"Good question. Which officer?"

"The nasty one," she said. "You know, the sergeant. I couldn't see him very well because he was at the far door, the side of your truck that was the farthest from me, but he was definitely leaning inside, far inside."

"The driver's door?"

"Yes."

"That's not good," Kit said. He caught the eye of the sheriff who walked over to him where he stood just inside a large door to his barn.

"I saw your sister telling you something. She seemed pretty upset. Do I need to know what it was?" Sheriff Ledford asked.

"Yes. She saw the sergeant open the driver's side door to my truck," he said.

"What did he do after he opened it?" Sheriff Ledford asked with a slight shake of his head.

"She couldn't tell exactly what he was doing because it's on the far side, but he was leaning inside of my truck."

"Okay, maybe I'd better go take a look," he said. "Come with me."

The sheriff led the way, and Kit and Paizlee followed. Unfortunately, so did the sergeant, who caught up with them and said, "I looked through the windows of that truck, the one I believe belongs to you, Mr. Troxler." He glared at Kit. "There's something in there that we will need to seize."

Sheriff Ledford made no response. But when they reached the truck, Sergeant Hodson pointed with hands that had latex gloves on them. "Right there in the consul," he said. "I will need to take that syringe and the bottle as well."

"Tell me what you think it is before I pick it up," the sheriff said, his voice filled with suspicion.

"I won't know for sure until I see it. But if it's an insulin bottle, I will need to seize it and the syringe."

"That isn't mine," Kit said. "Someone put it there. You put it there, Sergeant, when you got into my truck."

"Now don't get carried away with your imagination, Kit. I did not open your truck. But I did look in. Do you have the keys? It's probably locked," Sergeant Hodson said.

"It's not locked. I never lock it here at the ranch."

"I saw you open the door," Paizlee said accusingly. "Why are you lying to us?"

"Now, young lady, you need to be careful what you accuse people of. I did—"

Paizlee cut him off. "You are the one that needs to be careful what you accuse Kit of. I did see you open the door of his truck, and I did see you lean inside."

The sergeant plastered a sad look on his face and said, "You are mistaken, little girl. Sheriff, let's see what that is." The sergeant tried the door, but it was locked. "We'll need Kit to give us the keys since it's locked."

"It was not locked earlier," Kit said. "You locked it when you'd finished snooping and putting stuff in there."

The sergeant shook his head. "Try the door, Sheriff."

"It's locked, Kit," Sheriff Ledford said. He gave the key to the sheriff.

Kit was afraid the sergeant was right about what was in the truck. If it was insulin that the sergeant was after, then that's what he would find, after placing it in the truck, of course.

The sheriff retrieved the bottle and syringe. Kit could tell from the look on the sheriff's face that it was insulin. He showed it to the sergeant. "So why is this important?"

"That million-dollar horse of my cousin's was killed with a very large dose of insulin. If you know anything about horses, you will know that too much insulin can be fatal to a horse just like it can be to a human." Hodson reached his gloved hand out, and the sheriff let him take the bottle and the syringe. He held it up and said, "Almost empty. That was a stupid thing to do, Kit. I would have thought you would have been smart enough to throw such damaging evidence away." He shook his head. "Very stupid of you."

"I did not put that insulin there, and you know it. You did that yourself," Kit said angrily. "And I did not kill that horse of Sam's."

"I think a jury will believe you did."

"What did I ever do to you?" Kit asked as he fought back some threatening tears. "Are you just crooked by nature?"

"I'm a whole lot more honest than you. You made some very serious and false accusations against my cousin Sam. And you threatened him." He turned to the sheriff. "I think we can call off the search now. We have found the evidence I was looking for."

"The evidence you put there!" Paizlee screamed. "You are a horrible man."

"Now you be careful what you say, little girl. Making those kinds of false statements can get you in a lot of trouble. Sheriff, I will need the handcuffs back. This man is under arrest and is going with me."

CHAPTER THREE

RANDALL OVERMYER WAS SITTING IN the large office of his ranch house thinking worrisome thoughts. He'd worked hard for the wealth he now possessed. He owned a prosperous cattle ranch in Nye County, Nevada, not many miles from the Humboldt-Toiyabe National Forest and something like two hundred miles north of Las Vegas.

When he had first inherited the ranch upon the death of an uncle, it had a large debt. He was a young man in his late twenties when he took over the ranch. Everything he now had he'd earned through the sweat of his brow and smart business management. He'd just finished balancing his books, which he did regularly. For the most part, things were good. Though he missed his wife, who had passed of cancer nearly a year ago, and had endured a difficult few months, he was finally adjusting.

What was causing him the most concern now was his son, Sam. He regretted being too generous to him as he was growing up. Sam did as little as he could get away with on the ranch. He was irresponsible and ran with the wrong crowd.

Outside of wasting his father's money on riotous living, Sam's only real interest was riding racehorses. At that sport, Randall had to admit Sam was reasonably good. He honestly believed that Sam loved riding Sharpshooter more than he loved his own father. Randall had paid a hundred thousand dollars for the stallion, and he'd felt like it was money well spent. He'd given the horse to Sam in the hopes that it would bring the two of them closer and that it would cause Sam to take more interest in the ranch. Sadly, neither had happened.

Sam seemed to barely tolerate his father. Just that very morning, he'd sworn at him when Randall accused him of not helping the way he'd asked him to a couple days before. Sam had said, "Dad, I did exactly what you asked. Why do you take the word of those scummy guys who work for you over me? It isn't fair to treat me like that. I think the reason you do is because I inherited Mom's DNA instead of yours. That's why I'm so short, you know. You despise me because I'm not big like you."

"That's not true. Size isn't important, Sam," Randall had said. "It's what kind of person you are inside, not how tall or how strong you are."

The conversation had gone downhill from there. When Sam had stormed out of the house, he'd offended his father yet again when he'd said, "You are a selfish old man." It hurt Randall deeply, for he had always tried to be anything but selfish.

What hurt him even worse was remembering the way Sam had treated his mother. He'd repeatedly made fun of her petite size and then blamed her that he was so small. The older he got, the ruder he was to her. When she became ill, he berated her for not taking better care of her health. In the last desperate weeks of her cancer, he had totally avoided her. Randall couldn't help but think that the way Sam treated her had helped accelerate her illness and her death.

Other than the racehorse, Sam still took no interest in the ranch. Randall had asked him a number of times lately to help the hired hands on one thing or another. He'd always say, "Sure, Dad," then get in his truck and drive off. He didn't even help much with Sharpshooter. "I'm the jockey," he would say. "It's not my job to train him—it's Bruce's."

Sharpshooter was trained by Bruce White, Randall's ranch foreman, a former jockey himself, who had done an excellent job. Yet Sam, once he realized that the horse was a decent runner, bragged to his friends and anyone who would listen that he'd trained the horse himself. Randall knew that only because a couple of Sam's rowdy friends' fathers told him what Sam was saying. It hurt to hear the lies.

Since the death of Sharpshooter, Sam had grown angry to the point that he frightened Randall. He demanded his father buy him a new racehorse, but Randall told him he'd have to think about it before investing more money on one.

Sam blamed the death of Sharpshooter on a young fellow from Utah. "That guy falsely accused me of cheating when I beat him in the race in Albuquerque," he'd told Randall. "I did not cheat. I just have a better horse. Besides, I am a far more skilled jockey. That's why I won. I didn't need to cheat. Kit simply couldn't accept the fact that he was a loser."

Randall had never met Kit Troxler, nor had he seen a picture of the young man, so he wouldn't know him if he saw him. Sam claimed he'd seen the young fellow sneaking around the ranch buildings several hours before he'd discovered that his prize horse was dead in his stall. Not one of the ranch hands could confirm that Troxler had been there, but Sam stubbornly insisted that he'd seen him. A blood test had shown that the horse had died from a large insulin injection. Randall didn't doubt that, but he wondered if it was really Kit Troxler who, seeking revenge for losing to Sam, had given the fatal dose to the horse. Was it someone else Sam had angered? He knew there were plenty of people he'd hurt to go around.

Randall booted up his computer, and then he did a search for Kit Troxler. Everything he learned was positive. He couldn't find an instance of the young man ever being in any kind of trouble. He'd lost his parents in a plane crash about a year ago, shortly after he'd returned from a two-year mission in Mexico for his church. He'd apparently taken over the ranch and, together with his twin sister, had kept it going.

Like Randall's ranch, the one Kit and his sister had inherited was a successful one. Kit still raised cattle, but he also raised high-blooded quarter horses, some that they raced. Kit's horse—the one he had lost to Sam on—was called Kingfisher, a black stallion. Randall ran the pedigree on the horse, and it came back with blood lines that were among the best in the nation. It appeared Kit and his father had purchased the horse as a yearling just before Kit had gone to Mexico. Randall knew horses, and Kingfisher was without a doubt a better horse than Sharpshooter had been if his pedigree and pictures meant anything. To Randall, they most certainly did.

He searched some more and found that Kit also had highly bred Hereford cattle, another animal Randall was an expert on. The pictures of Kit's cattle were impressive. It looked to him like Kit knew what he was doing, and that impressed him. On Kit's twin sister's Facebook page, she had written about his recent trip to Wyoming to look at some prize yearling bulls that he was considering purchasing. Randall looked more closely at the dates she mentioned. He shook his head when he saw she had written that Kit had returned to Fillmore, Utah, the day after Sam's horse had been killed. He didn't see how Kit could possibly have been here at his ranch that same day. Kit being the killer of Sharpshooter just didn't add up. He wasn't sure what to think. He had expected to find something damaging about the young rancher, but he had not found anything.

Randall finally shut down his computer and leaned back in his chair with his eyes closed. He had a hard time believing that the young rancher and jockey had killed Sam's stallion. But Randall's nephew Vince, who was a deputy sheriff, swore it was Kit Troxler and claimed they had the proof.

He thought for a moment about his nephew Vince Hodson. He might be a sergeant with the sheriff's office, but he was one of Sam's closest partying pals, and from when he was a small boy, he'd done questionable things, illegal things, but was slick and never seemed to get caught. Randall often wondered why and how he had ever got into law enforcement. Randall didn't like the way it looked, and frankly, he didn't like Vince. But Sam had put Vince on a pedestal. To him, his older cousin could do no wrong.

Was it possible that someone else had it in for his son and had killed the horse? Sam was an angry little man. Randall could imagine him offending people, making them angry. And yet, Sam was his son. He had to support him until evidence proved that Kit Troxler hadn't killed Sharpshooter. He had a feeling that, in the end, that's exactly what would happen. All he could do was let things take their course and hope that an innocent young man wasn't convicted because of his son's dishonesty.

Kit spent the night and part of another day in the jail in Fillmore. The sheriff had explained that they could not take him to Nevada without extradition papers signed by a judge. That was completed by early afternoon the next day, and Kit was hauled to Nevada by Sergeant Hodson.

Only a few hours after the sergeant had delivered Kit to the Nevada jail, Kit's foreman, Andy, and his sister, Paizlee, arrived to bail him out. Kit was given his property, but his cell phone was not with his other things. It was already getting dark, but none of them wanted to spend the night anywhere in Nevada, so they started home. As they drove, Kit told the others about his phone. "Did I leave it at home? I was pretty sure I had it when I was booked in the jail in Fillmore. But as upset as I've been, I could be wrong."

"I'll bet it's at home," Andy said. "Don't you have that Find My iPhone app? We can use it when we get there."

"Yeah, I do. I hope it's at home," he said. "Another thing, I've been thinking a lot about Sergeant Hodson. I was sure I'd seen him before when he was at our place stirring up trouble. I finally figured it out as I was sitting in jail in Fillmore."

"Tell us about it," Andy said.

"Do you remember when Sam was bumping the back of my trailer? He had someone with him."

"Yes, I do. But all I remember was that it was someone in a black cowboy hat."

"That's right, Andy. I could see his face in my mirror when they first came up behind us as we were waiting to get out of the parking area. He was grinning and pointing at us. It was the same guy that was helping Sam in the ring. I know it was him," Kit said.

"He probably had your glove when they passed us," Paizlee said angrily. "He shouldn't be a cop."

"You've got that right," Andy agreed. "But he is, and we've got to figure out how to beat him at his crooked game. We can't let him and that Overmyer guy win."

"How do we do that?" Paizlee asked doubtfully. "We aren't cops and don't have any close friends who are."

"We may have to hire a private detective to help us," Andy suggested.

Kit, who was driving, looked over at Andy and said, "Do you really think that would do any good?"

"Yes, I do," Andy said. "An investigator could backtrack where you were on the bull-buying trip and get proof so we can show that you couldn't have been in Nevada when Sam's horse was killed, that you'd only just got back to the ranch around noon the next day. He'd know how to use the GPS feature on your phone to prove where you were. He would be experienced at things like that and would know how to put the evidence together so it would stand up in court."

Kit thought about that for a moment, and then he said, "First, let's see if we can find my phone. If you don't mind me leaving again for a few days, I could backtrack to the places I'd been myself. The only thing I would have trouble with is the GPS thing, and unless I find my phone, that won't help anyway. I know where I went and what I did each day."

"I could go with you," Paizlee volunteered.

"Well, that might work," Andy said. "Greg and I will take care of things while you're gone."

"Are you sure you want to go, Paizlee?" Kit asked. "It could be boring."

"Yes, I'm sure," she said firmly.

"Okay, then we'll do it. We'll leave in the morning."

They rode in silence for a while after that, but Kit suddenly had a horrible thought. "Andy, I'm worried about Kingfisher."

"You don't need to be," Andy said. "We'll take good care of him while you're gone."

"That's not what I'm worried about," Kit said. "Sam Overmyer might actually believe I had something to do with his horse dying. Would he try to kill Kingfisher in revenge?"

Paizlee leaned up from the back seat and said urgently, "Kit, we can't let him hurt Kingfisher. We need to hide him."

"Where?" Kit asked.

"Somewhere Sam or his cousin wouldn't know to look," Paizlee responded.

"Let me take care of that," Andy said. "We have lots of friends. I'll find someone who will be willing to keep him for us for a while."

"Like who?" Kit asked.

Andy was thoughtful for a moment. "How about Norm Smith? He's a good friend, and he could keep Kingfisher in his barn. I'm sure he'd do it for us. He and your dad were friends all your dad's life," Andy said.

"That's a good idea," Kit said. "It will be really late by the time we get home, but we might call him now. He'd probably go get him if we asked him to."

"You really are worried, aren't you, Kit?" Paizlee asked.

"Yes, I am. Sam Overmyer and his cousin are rotten to the core. With what they're doing to me, the lies they are telling, I wouldn't put anything past them."

Andy pulled out his phone. "I have Norm's number. I'll see if I can reach him." Ten minutes later, after an intense conversation, Andy put his phone back in his shirt pocket and said, "It's all set. Norm will pick up Kingfisher within the hour. He didn't think it would pay to wait until tomorrow. He said it was no problem at all."

Kit relaxed some after that. They rode for several minutes in silence. Then Paizlee finally spoke. "Andy, I've been thinking."

Andy turned and looked back at her. "I think we all have," he said with a grin. "Tell us what you have on your mind."

"If those guys are so bad, would they hurt something else if they sneak onto our ranch and can't find Kingfisher? You know, like other horses or some cattle or even our equipment."

Andy's smile faded away. "I would hate to think they would, but who knows. Now you have me really worried, Paizlee."

"Andy, I wonder if we should hire some extra men for a few days. You could spread them out around the ranch and have them keep their eyes open for any trespassers," Kit suggested.

Andy took a deep breath. Then he said, "You kids know how to worry a guy, don't you? But you have a valid point."

"I hate to think that anyone would do something like this, but Sam Overmyer and his cousin seem to really have it in for me," Kit said.

"I'll see if I can get three or four guys to come tomorrow. Also, Kit, we need to hire an attorney."

"I've been thinking about that," Kit told him. "Sergeant Hodson tried to make me confess on the way to the jail in Tonopah, but I told him I wasn't saying a word without the advice of an attorney."

"I'll bet that went over well," Paizlee said snidely from the back seat as she leaned forward again.

"He told me that if I had nothing to hide, I didn't need an attorney. I felt like telling him that I needed one because I was being framed for something I didn't do. But I kept my thoughts to myself and didn't say anything else to him. He was fuming by the time he finally gave up on me."

"Was it just him questioning you?" Andy asked.

"Yes, I don't think he dared use anyone else. I have a feeling that not many of the deputies are crooked like he is, and he doesn't want them to know."

"Do you have any idea who to hire?" Paizlee asked.

"I think maybe I do," Andy said. "We want only the best. And that means we need to look beyond our own area."

"Who are you thinking of?" Kit asked.

"There's a defense attorney in Salt Lake that I've seen on the news quite a few times. He seems to be unafraid of anyone and takes very tough cases. His name is Lawrence Heslop."

"Is that the white-haired guy with a deep voice?" Kit asked. "I've seen him on the news. If nothing else, he looks and sounds pretty formidable."

"That is exactly the kind of attorney we need. We want someone who will tear that lying sergeant and his cousin to pieces in court. I think he would be our best bet," Andy suggested.

"If we can get him," Kit said doubtfully. "And if we can afford him."

"Kit, even if we had to put off buying those bulls for a while, I think we need to do it. I know you have money in savings, but you may need some of that to pay off the rest of your debt on the machinery. Let's see if we can get him to help you without having to dip too deeply into your savings."

"Will you call him?" Kit asked.

"If you want me to," Andy said. "But it's your decision."

"I don't want to go to prison," Kit said as he felt a shiver of fear rush through him. "Please call him."

"I'll get him, Kit. You take care of proving you were where you were when that horse was killed. I'll take care of retaining Mr. Heslop and keeping the ranch secure."

"Thanks, Andy. I don't know what we would ever do without you," Kit said as he thought about how hard it was to prove he hadn't done what he was accused of doing. An attorney would know how to go about things. That was what they were for. Kit felt hiring an attorney was the best way to go. But at this point, he didn't think they needed a private investigator.

CHAPTER FOUR

IT WAS EARLY EVENING WHEN Kit and the others returned to the ranch. Kit helped Andy with some chores. He was mentally exhausted and very tired when he got to the house. His sister had a light dinner ready. "I need to get to bed after we eat," he said. "Let's look for my phone in the morning. Wherever it is, it won't be going anywhere."

"Let me just try to call it," Paizlee suggested as she began to gather up the dinner dishes. "If it's here, it will ring."

The call went to voice mail, and they hadn't heard it ring. "Okay, the battery is probably dead. Let's try in the morning. If we don't find it, we still have yours," Kit said. "We can replace mine later."

They failed to find it the following morning. Kit simply could not imagine where he'd misplaced it.

Lawrence Heslop loved to take on sensational cases, ones lots of opposing attorneys didn't think he could win. He also took on a lot of cases that were neither sensational nor ones that he thought would be hard to win. Such a case was one he had just accepted. It was one where he hoped he could keep an injustice from prevailing.

After a lengthy phone conversation with a ranch foreman by the name of Andy Boyse, he had agreed to defend Andy's young boss, Kit Troxler, against what Lawrence suspected were false charges. Luckily, he was licensed to practice law in Nevada, where the case would be tried. He was anxious to meet the young Troxler fellow and his twin sister.

When Mr. Boyse had explained that Kit and Paizlee had left Fillmore an hour or so earlier and what they were intending to do as they traveled to Wyoming,

Lawrence asked that they meet with him. Andy had given him Paizlee's cell phone number after explaining that Kit's was missing, and he entered it into his phone and then made the call.

"Hello," a young woman's voice answered a moment later.

"You must be Paizlee Troxler. My name is Lawrence Heslop. Your foreman, Andy Boyse, has asked me to represent your brother in a legal matter in Nevada," he said, his voice deep and resonant. "Are you agreeable to that? Is Kit with you?"

"I'm right here. Her phone is synched to our truck, so we can both hear you. And yes, I need your help," Kit said. "I'm in a mess right now. I could end up in prison for something I didn't do."

"So I understand," Lawrence said as he detected a note of fear in the young rancher's voice. "Since you're driving north today, I think it would be a good idea if you and I met in person and discussed your case. It will take us an hour or so, but I would like to get to work on your problem right away, so it would be beneficial for both of us if we could meet."

"Thank you, Mr. Heslop. That would be great."

"I would like to call you Kit and Paizlee, and you may call me Lawrence. Do you object to that?" Lawrence asked, a smile creasing his face.

"Not at all," Kit said. "I sure appreciate your willingness to help us. We're both frightened about what could happen."

"I'll try to alleviate some of that fear. Where are you folks at right now?"

"We've just about reached Provo," Kit said.

"Perfect. Let me give you the address of my office. I'm actually in Sandy." He then gave an address and added, "I will expect you around nine."

The two siblings entered the plush office of Lawrence Heslop a few minutes before nine. Kit's stomach was upset with nervousness. He had a check in his pocket made out to Lawrence for $5,000 as a retainer. Andy had suggested he take him the money when they met so that Lawrence would know they were serious.

They were greeted by a middle-aged woman. She was a trim, attractive woman with a bright smile, short red hair, and sparkling green eyes. She stood and offered her hand to both of the siblings. "I am Jenna Hubbard. Please call me Jenna. I am Lawrence's legal secretary. He filled me in on your problem. I'm sorry you have so much trouble. But rest assured that Lawrence will fight for you for all he's worth. And I can assure you, he's worth a lot. In my opinion, he's the best at what he does."

"Thank you," Kit said nervously. "I'm Kit Troxler, and this is my sister, Paizlee."

"Let me buzz Lawrence and tell him you're here," she said. After a short conversation with her boss, she put the receiver down and said, "He's on the phone right now, but he'll be free in about five minutes. Would either of you care for a drink of water?"

They both shook their heads. Kit said, "Thanks. I'm sorry if I seem a bit rattled, but I am. I've never been in a situation like this before."

"Again, I'm sorry. Tell me a little about yourselves," she said, smiling so sweetly that Kit couldn't help but feel more at ease.

For the next few minutes, Kit and Paizlee told Jenna about how they had lost their parents and how hard they had both worked to keep the legacy of their father and mother alive.

"I understand you are also a jockey," Jenna said with a smile.

"I try," Kit said modestly.

"Don't let him kid you," Paizlee said with a grin. "He's really, really good."

"Paizlee's not so bad herself," Kit said.

Just then the outside door of Lawrence's office opened, and Kit was struck dumb. A young lady entered the room, a big smile on a gorgeous face with deep dimples and a sparkle in the prettiest green eyes Kit had ever seen. Her hair, long and wavy, was as red as Jenna's. "Hi, Wiona," Jenna said. "You are just in time to meet Lawrence's newest clients. Kit and Paizlee Troxler are from Fillmore. They have a ranch down there." She turned her head to Kit and Paizlee and said, "Wiona is my daughter."

"I would have never guessed," Paizlee said facetiously with a grin.

"I do look a lot like my mother, don't I?" Wiona responded. Not once had the smile on her face faded or the sparkle left her eyes. "It's nice to meet you guys. I hope you aren't in trouble."

Kit was so overwhelmed at the sight of this pretty girl that he still couldn't speak. Paizlee did not have that problem. "We are in a lot of trouble," she said. "At least, Kit is. But he didn't do anything wrong."

Those sparkling eyes lost their sparkle then, and Wiona looked directly at Kit. "I'm sorry, Kit. You sure don't look like some of the clients of Lawrence's that I've met. I hope he can help you."

"He's got to," Paizlee said. "This is so awful."

Just then, a door down a short hallway opened, and one of the most impressive men Kit had ever seen strode toward them. "Sorry to keep you waiting. I'm Lawrence Heslop." He held out a hand to Kit and said, "You must be Kit." His voice was deep and rich.

"Yes, sir," Kit said, finally finding the voice that he'd lost when Wiona walked in.

"It's a pleasure to meet you. And you, young lady, must be his twin sister, Paizlee." Paizlee grinned at him. He also shook her hand. "You've both met my legal secretary, Jenna."

"They've been telling me a little about themselves," Jenna said. "They are fine young people."

"Not what I always have for clients," Lawrence said with a gleam in his intelligent gray eyes.

"I hope you can help us," Kit said.

"I will do my best, and not to brag, but my best is better than a lot of my colleagues." He looked toward Wiona. "I guess you've also met Wiona. She comes in regularly and helps us out. She's very efficient and totally trustworthy. I'm glad for her help. Wiona and Jenna, I hope you'll excuse us, but I need to spend some time with Kit and Paizlee."

"Of course," Wiona said. Her smile was back in place, and the sparkle in her eyes had returned.

"Right this way," Lawrence said. For the briefest moment, Kit's eyes met Wiona's, and despite all the trouble he was carrying around, he was able to smile at her. She smiled back, those dimples getting even deeper. *Wow!* he thought. But then the short euphoria faded, and he followed his sister and his attorney down the hallway.

"I can't believe he's in trouble," Wiona said to her mother. "He seems so nice."

"And so handsome?" her mother said with a smile on her face.

"Cute, yes. Very. What did he do?" she asked.

"From what little I know, he apparently made an enemy of someone who's not a good person. He's been accused of killing a champion racehorse, but of course he denies it. And from what little we know, and all of that from their ranch foreman, he may be totally innocent."

"He looks innocent," Wiona said. "Not that looks mean much when it comes to people's lives. There is often so much hidden that we don't see. Why isn't their father with them?"

"Their father and mother died about a year ago in a plane crash and left the ranch to the two of them. We'll learn more later—if Lawrence wants us to."

"Oh, Mom, that's so sad. I hope he . . . they will be okay," Wiona said wistfully.

"You have stars in your eyes, my dear," her mother said. "Remember, he is a criminal defendant. We don't think he's guilty, but then again, he could be a great actor, and he might be a very bad person."

Wiona shook her head. "I'll never believe that," she said firmly.

"I hope he isn't bad," Jenna said, "but let's not be too sure until we learn more."

"What have you got for me to do today, Mom?" Wiona asked. "I'm all caught up on that online class I'm taking. So I can work for as long as you need me."

Jenna allowed herself a laugh. "You just want to be here when they come out of Lawrence's office so you can see Kit again. Well, honestly, I don't blame you. I sure hope he turns out to be what he looks like and not what he's been accused of being."

"Mom, what do you need me to do?" Wiona repeated. "And if they come out while I'm still here, that's just a bonus."

Jenna pointed to the computer that Wiona often used. "You can do some typing for me today. There are some handwritten statements there from witnesses on the Kirby case. Lawrence would like them typed and then wants us to have the Kirbys come in and read over what you've typed to make sure it is what they meant and then sign the statements. I hope you can read the handwriting on these. It's not very good."

Kit was impressed with the size and opulence of Lawrence's personal office. He was particularly encouraged by the oil paintings on two of his walls. They depicted scenes that could have come straight from the Troxler ranch. One was of a black stallion. It was pure black, no white socks like Kingfisher's, but every bit as impressive.

"You like my paintings?" Lawrence asked. "I am a cowboy at heart. I was raised on a cattle ranch in Montana. Even after all these years, I still miss the cattle and the horses, not to speak of the beauty of the ranch. But for some strange reason, I was drawn to the law. And I haven't regretted it, although at times it's very stressful."

"That horse," Paizlee said, pointing at the portrait of the black stallion, "is gorgeous."

"We had a horse a lot like that one when I was a youngster. He wasn't quite as striking as the horse in the painting, but he was pretty, and I loved to ride him."

"He looks a lot like Kingfisher," Paizlee said as she continued to gaze at the painting.

"Is that the horse your foreman told me about?" Lawrence asked.

"Yes, and he is as pretty as that one," Paizlee said.

"Let's start at the beginning. I want you to tell me everything you can about your conflict with, let's see, your foreman called him Sam Overmyer," Lawrence said. "Actually, let's go back further. I heard this from your foreman, but I'd like you to tell me how you two came to own a large ranch."

Kit took a deep breath and tried to will the churning of his stomach to stop. Finally, he told Lawrence, "Like Andy must have told you, our parents were killed in a plane crash about a year ago. I hadn't been back from my mission for very long, so it took me a few months to figure out how to manage a ranch. I could never have done it without Andy and Greg. They have been great."

"I know who Andy is, but who's Greg?"

"He worked for my dad and stayed on with us after we took over."

"So he's a hired hand, so to speak?"

"Yes, and a great guy and hard worker."

"Okay, so let me ask you this: did your folks leave you a lot of debt that you have to deal with?"

"No, Dad had very little debt, and we are paying it off. There's no way we could have kept the ranch running this past year if we'd inherited a lot of debt. I am so grateful for that," Kit said.

"The reason I asked is because my services aren't cheap," Lawrence said.

"Oh, yes, I almost forgot. I have a check here for your retainer. Five thousand dollars is what Andy said," Kit told him as he extracted the check from a pocket of his western shirt.

"That will get us started. But I need to warn you both that it may cost a lot more than that before we're through," Lawrence said as Kit rose from his chair and held the check out to him.

"Thanks. But why don't you take that out to Jenna or Wiona. They'll give you a receipt. While you do that, Paizlee and I will talk some more about the house and domestic chores. You can leave that door open until you get back."

Kit simply couldn't help the way his heart sped up at the thought of seeing the pretty red-headed girl again. Thinking of her made him feel tongue-tied, but strangely, it settled the rolling of his stomach.

Kit left the room as Lawrence was saying to Paizlee, "Do you take care of the house, or do you hire someone to help you?"

As he walked down the hall, he could hear her say, "I do it myself, and Kit helps when he can."

"Can I help you, Kit?" Wiona asked as he entered the reception area. She was busy typing something on a computer that was on a desk near her mother's. He couldn't see Jenna. As if reading his mind, Wiona said, "Mom had to step out." She grinned. "So I guess that leaves me in charge of the office. So you're a cowboy and a jockey?"

Kit had to untangle his tongue. He didn't usually have such a hard time talking to young women, but this girl, well . . . she had thrown a spell on him that had him bound up tight. With an effort, he got his voice to work.

"I am. My sister rides in races as well."

Wiona's green eyes grew wide, letting the sparkle shoot out in every direction. "As in really fast horses?"

"That's right," Kit said. "You'll have to come visit our ranch sometime. I am supposed to give this to you." He held out the check.

Wiona stood up. She was several inches shorter than his five foot eight and had to look up at him as she took the check from his hand. "Why thank you, Kit. Is this really for me?"

That threw him. "Well, it's . . ." he stuttered.

Wiona chuckled, a pleasant sound. "Just kidding," she said. "I know what it's for. He probably told you I'd give you a receipt, didn't he?"

"Ah, yes," he said.

"Then I'll write you one. It will take me just a minute."

She didn't write it; she sat at her computer, minimized the document she was working on, and started a new one.

She stood up. "It'll come out of that printer over there. I'll get it and sign it for you."

He stepped back to let her by, but she paused just a moment and looked up at him. "I sure hope you are not guilty of what you've been accused of, 'cause I kind of like you."

He blushed. She grinned, stepped over to the printer, and waited for a moment for the receipt to come out. He watched her. She was certainly not shy. How he wished he were meeting her under different circumstances. If he were, he would try to muster up his courage and ask her out.

She retrieved two copies from the printer and brought them back across the room. He was still standing near her desk, feeling the worry begin to dominate him again. "Are you okay?" Wiona asked as she slid past him and sat down.

"I've been better," he said honestly.

"I'm sorry." She hesitated for a moment, looking up at and into his eyes. He could almost feel the intensity of her gaze on him. She suddenly asked in a straight voice, the smile gone, "Are you afraid of me?"

Yes, he was, he thought truthfully, but he wasn't about to admit it. "I guess I'm just—"

"Shy?" she asked and started to laugh. "I'm sorry, but I'm not shy. I must make you uncomfortable."

"It's fine," he said. "You're a very nice lady."

"And I hope you are a nice guy, because I want to come visit your ranch. I really mean that," she said. She dropped her eyes, picked up a pen, signed both copies of the receipt, and then stood up and handed one to Kit. "Here you go. Good luck, Kit."

"Thanks, Wiona. You are so . . . so . . . sweet." He couldn't believe he'd actually said that, but he had. And she was. "I'd better get back in there."

She wiggled her fingers at him and turned back to her work, a smile planted firmly on her face.

CHAPTER FIVE

"Your sister has been telling me about how hard the two of you work to keep the house up and the ranch running and still do some racing," Lawrence said as soon as Kit had entered and shut the door. "I'm impressed. Now tell me what happened in Albuquerque."

For the next hour, Kit explained, with some help from Paizlee, everything that had happened from the beginning of the race in Albuquerque up to his release on bond from the jail in Tonopah, Nevada. Occasionally, Lawrence would insert a question, but mostly he listened.

When they were through, Lawrence said, "One thing I want to tell you right now, Kit, is that I believe everything you've told me. I don't say that to many clients. I will do everything I can to prove your innocence."

"You don't know how relieved it makes me to have you on my side," Kit told him, and he meant it.

"Rest assured that I am totally on your side. Now, you have a receipt for the retainer, don't you?" Lawrence asked.

"Yes. Wiona typed it for me and signed it," he said.

"She's a doll, isn't she?" Lawrence asked with a grin.

"She's . . . very nice," Kit said.

"She's a tease; that's what she is. I'll bet she gave you a hard time, didn't she?"

"Well, sort of," Kit admitted.

"Get used to it. Her mother keeps the office running and smooths things out with some of my clients. And believe me, I have some tough ones. It will be refreshing working for you, and that is what I'm doing. If at any time you question what I'm doing, don't be afraid to tell me so. I'll either explain or I'll modify my approach," he said.

"Thanks," Kit said.

"You're welcome. Now as I was saying, get used to Wiona's teasing. She's not a shy girl. And she will be going with me when I need someone along so her mother doesn't have to. And as soon as you get back from this little trip you two are going on, I want you to call me. I'll find the time to bring Wiona and visit your ranch. I want to get a feel for the place, for your employees, and possibly even interview a few of your neighbors. And I sure look forward to meeting that horse of yours."

"You'll like him," Paizlee spoke up, and as she did, she glanced at the painting of the black stallion on Lawrence's wall.

"Now, I don't want to offend you, but when I meet with you at your ranch, I will go over everything you have garnered on your little investigating trip. If I'm not satisfied, I'll have a private investigator go over it all again."

"I won't be offended," Kit assured him.

"I will be using a PI for a number of things as we move forward with your case. It will be his job to learn everything he can about Sam Overmyer and his crooked police officer cousin. I use a man by the name of Brandon Phelps. He's a former Navy Seal. He's smart, dedicated, and as honest as the day is long. You'll like him. I warn you, he'll cost us quite a bit, but he's worth every penny."

Kit and Paizlee exchanged glances, and then Paizlee said, "We'll spend what we have to. Whatever it takes to save Kit from this trouble Sam and his cousin have caused."

"Do you agree, Kit?" Lawrence asked.

"Yes. We've got to do whatever it takes."

"All right then, that's it for now," Lawrence said.

As the three of them stood up, Lawrence suddenly asked, "Kit, when and where do you race again?"

"In Santa Anita, California, a week from Friday."

"Are you going, Paizlee?" he asked.

"Of course," she said. "I always go, and when I race, he goes. We help each other with the horse. I never race in big races though, and I haven't raced on Kingfisher. That's for Kit to do."

"Very good," Lawrence said with a smile as he extended his hand to each of the twins. "Let's keep in touch. And I will try to get down your way sometime after your race next week. And I'll bring Wiona with me." He winked, and despite himself, Kit blushed. "And you two try not to worry so much. I'll do the worrying, and we will get you out of this situation."

Kit and Paizlee went back to the reception area, where Jenna and Wiona both looked up from their work. "You two stay safe and trust Lawrence," Jenna said.

"We'll try," Kit said as his eyes met Wiona's.

She gave him one of her thousand-watt smiles and said, "It's been good to meet you, Kit. You too, Paizlee. See you guys soon."

Outside, as they headed for their truck, Paizlee grinned at Kit and said, "She likes you."

"Who, Jenna?" Kit asked with a sober face.

Paizlee punched him lightly on the shoulder. "Wiona's pretty," she said and then added, "and Lawrence inspires confidence."

Sam Overmyer was fuming. He'd just renewed his demand that his father buy him another horse to replace Sharpshooter, and Randall had flatly refused. He shook his fist in his father's face. "You can afford it. I'm the best jockey in the West, and with a good horse, I can win every time I race. Why are you being such a jerk to me?"

"Sam, sit down and listen to me," Randall said. "I know you're a good jockey, but I also know that you let your temper control your actions. If you want another horse, there are some things you need to do first."

Sam did not sit down but glowered instead. "What do you mean?"

"I mean you will carry your weight on this ranch. If you can do that for the next year, then we'll see about finding a replacement for Sharpshooter. But you will help pay for him."

"And how do you propose I do that?" Sam asked, his nostrils flaring.

"I'll pay you for the work you do, and you will save the money instead of drinking and gambling it away like you've been doing with my money," Randall said.

"Okay, fine. How much will you pay me?"

"I'll give you twenty dollars an hour," Randall said. "And I will have our foreman keep track of your time."

"You don't trust me!" Sam shouted.

"No, I don't," his father agreed. "But you must do what I say if you want another racehorse. It's time for you to earn my trust."

Sam swung around and headed for the door, but his dad stopped him when he said, "I've canceled your credit and debit cards. You will pay your own way from now on. So get to work and prove that you really want a new horse."

"You're no kind of father," Sam said angrily without turning around. "No one else treats their sons like you do me."

"Sam, I do love you, certainly enough to stop giving you money for you to blow on booze and gambling and I don't even want to guess what else. This is the end of that," Randall said firmly. "Now, go get to work. Bruce will tell you what to do."

"And if I don't do what that jerk tells me to, then what?"

"You can pack up and leave, Sam. If you want to continue to live in my house, you will earn your own way. Otherwise, go find a job somewhere else. I'll give Bruce a call and tell him you're coming out to work."

Sam left, slamming the door so hard the windows rattled. Randall shook his head sadly. He called Bruce. "Sam's coming out to work. Keep him busy and keep track of his hours. I'm through letting him just come and go as he pleases. He can work with the other guys at your discretion."

"Randall, you know that Sam resents me," Bruce said.

"He resents me too, but he will either do what you tell him to or he can go find a job somewhere else. I'm through coddling him."

"Whatever you say, Boss," Bruce said.

"If he doesn't work or if he causes problems with any of the other men, let me know," Randall added.

"Okay, but he's not going to like this."

"This is my ranch and my money, and even though he's my only child, I'm not going to continue to let him act the way he does and still live here."

"Randall, there's something you need to know," Bruce said. "And if you want to fire me for saying it, then so be it."

"I would never fire you, Bruce."

"We'll see after you hear what I have to say. That Troxler kid didn't kill Sam's horse. He hasn't been around here like Sam and your nephew claim. And it wasn't Sam who found him dead; it was me. Sam came in right after I found the horse lying there."

Randall felt a wrench in his gut. "What are you saying, Bruce?"

"I'm saying Sam lied about that young fellow being here. I just don't believe it."

"Sam found his glove in the stall with Sharpshooter's body," Randall reminded him.

"That's what he claims, but he didn't mention it until Vince came out, representing the sheriff's department. Honestly, I don't think there was a glove in there. I certainly didn't see it if it was."

"Then where did it come from?" Randall asked.

"I don't know."

"Bruce, you do realize what you're saying, don't you?" Randall asked as he pressed his free hand to his forehead.

"Yes, and fire me if you want, but I think Sam's lying and Vince is backing him up on it," Bruce said.

"All right, put Sam to work, and, Bruce, thanks for telling me this. I wish you'd told me sooner."

"Sorry, Boss. I didn't want to upset you, but this has gone too far. An innocent young man could go to prison," Bruce said. "Oh, here comes Sam now."

"Bruce, you're not fired. Nor will you be. Now put that boy to work," Randall said and ended the call.

Randall sat back and stared at the wall. Could Bruce possibly be right? He'd never known the foreman to lie to him. He tried to find some way to believe that Bruce had been mistaken about the glove, but he just couldn't see it. That meant, as much as it hurt, that Sam had falsely accused the young rancher from Utah of a crime that could send him to prison. He wanted to believe his ranch foreman, but at the same time, he wanted to believe that his son was not that bad.

He debated with himself for some time before he finally decided to just let things play out. Unless he found something more solid to convince him that Sam was lying, he would let the courts decide. He didn't want an innocent young man to go to prison, but he also didn't want his own son to be convicted of falsely accusing Kit. Sam was, after all, his son, his only child.

An hour later, Randall was still sitting at his desk. He was in anguish. Finally, he decided that rather than sit there worrying about the situation, he had to do something. And that something was to talk to Kit Troxler face to face.

Wearily, Randall got to his feet. He put his hat on and headed out to his truck. He was going to find Kit. His phone said it was about a three-hour drive to Fillmore, Utah. It was almost ten in the morning, which would put him in Fillmore around one in the afternoon. He left and was a half hour from his ranch when he got a call.

"Hey, Boss, it's Bruce. I hate to bother you, but Sam left a few minutes ago. He told me he'd be back tomorrow or the next day to work some more, that he didn't have time today. I told him that you may not like that, and he said something to the effect that you . . . well, that you could stuff it, sir."

"Thanks for telling me, Bruce. I will deal with Sam when I get back. I'm headed out of town," Randall said as his gut churned.

"Sorry, but you said to let you know," Bruce said. "I'm not trying to get the kid in trouble. I hope you know that."

Unfortunately, Randall knew that only too well. Sam was a big boy. He would have to make his own decisions, and if he kept making the wrong ones, the ranch would never be his. "Don't worry about it. Sam is my problem. Keeping the ranch going is yours. And I appreciate the way you do your job."

As Randall drove, he thought about how he should approach Kit Troxler when he got to his ranch. How the young rancher reacted to him would help him make a decision about Sam and how he should handle him in the future. Randall felt like he was a pretty good judge of character, and he hoped he could form an honest opinion of the young rancher by spending a little time with him.

Sam came back a short while later. He passed the house and noticed that his dad's truck was gone. That gave him an idea. He went in the house and straight to Randall's office. He knew that office about as well as his dad did. He'd made it his business to know where his dad kept things. He even knew the combination to the safe.

He spun the dial a few times, and the safe opened. As expected, he found a bunch of cash there. He didn't know why his dad kept money in there, and he didn't care. He helped himself to a couple thousand dollars and even found two credit cards. They both appeared to be current, so he took one of them. Then he closed the safe.

He went into the kitchen, where he made some sandwiches and took several bottles of water from a cupboard. Then it was off to his room, where he packed a bag that included some black clothing and a pair of sneakers. That done, he left the house, got in his truck, and drove out of the yard.

He had no idea where his father had gone, but Sam knew exactly where he was going. He'd talked to Vince about it. He planned to make a late-night visit to Kit Troxler's ranch. He'd teach the guy a thing or two about making accusations of cheating. After tonight, Kit would have a lot more to think about before he met his date with the Nevada State Prison.

CHAPTER SIX

THE TWINS HAD MADE THREE stops by the time they reached the Wyoming border. It had not been fruitful. Kit had not seen one person he recognized. To Paizlee he said, "I don't think I'm cut out for this detective kind of work. Unless we can find someone who remembers me and is willing to sign a statement to that effect, I'm sunk. That was so stupid of me to lose my phone."

"Hey, don't be so gloomy," Paizlee said. "You always keep receipts of your expenses. Didn't you keep receipts for the things you bought at the places you stopped?"

Kit looked over at her. "Sis, you're a genius! Of course I did. That will show not only that I stopped at those places, but also what date and time. It will even show that I was in a motel the night they claim I was in Nevada killing Sam's horse. Maybe this trip is a waste of our time since I have those receipts. We could go back, I suppose."

"No," she said. "It still wouldn't hurt to get statements from the guys whose bulls you looked at."

"That's true," he agreed.

"Where are the receipts?" Paizlee asked.

Kit pointed to the jockey box. "In there," he said. "I was going to take them in the house and file them, but I hadn't got around to it yet."

She opened it, and Kit heard her gasp. "Kit, there's nothing in here. Not even the registration papers."

"What? That can't be," he said as he looked over at her.

"Sergeant Hodson," she said with a hiss. "He must have taken them when he put that insulin in here. That's why he was leaning in so far. He could have dropped the insulin without leaning in the way he did. What do we do now?"

Kit felt his face going red as anger built up inside. This was just too much. Was there anything Sam and his cousin wouldn't do to destroy his life? He looked over at Paizlee and said with a helpless feeling, "I don't know. That sergeant is a crook. He's as bad as Sam or worse. I'd like to punch his face in."

"Kit, that's not who you are, and you know it. I think we should call our attorney," Paizlee suggested.

"I guess it's worth a try," Kit said. "It's more than I could think of."

She got out her cell phone. "He gave us an office number and a cell number. Which should I use?"

"I hate to bother him with this on his cell. Just call his office," Kit said.

She did that. Kit kept driving, but he listened to the conversation his sister was having on the synched phone. "Hi, Jenna. This is Paizlee Troxler. We've discovered a problem and need to talk to Lawrence about it."

"I'm sorry, but he's out right now. I can have him call you back," she said.

"Okay," Paizlee said. "That would be great."

Kit spoke up. "We're both on the phone, Jenna. Would you tell him that we just discovered someone stole everything in the jockey box of our truck while the cops were at our ranch? We think we know who did it."

"Hi, Kit. It's Wiona. I just borrowed the phone from Mom. She got a call on her cell phone. If you'll please give us a minute, I'll let you talk to Mom."

It was not a long wait before Jenna said, "Hello, Kit. Sorry for the wait. What did you need to talk to Lawrence about?"

"Someone stole some papers from my jockey box," he said.

"You mean like your registration and important papers or something?" she asked.

"Yes, stuff like that," he said.

"What kind of things were taken besides your registration?"

Paizlee spoke up then. "What we're missing are some receipts that would show where Kit stopped on his trip to look at young bulls and where he bought things and what dates and times and where he was staying the night the horse was killed in Nevada."

"Ah. The receipts would prove that you couldn't have been in Nevada when those men say you were."

"Exactly," Paizlee said.

"I'll tell Lawrence. He should be back before too long. He had to make a short appearance in court, but it's here in Sandy, so at least he's close," Jenna said.

"Thanks. Maybe he'll know what to do," Kit said. "I sure don't. I am so angry. It was Paizlee's idea to call Lawrence. I could hardly think when we saw they were missing."

"He will know what to do. He will want to contact your credit or debit card company and get the information from them. If you used a credit or debit card, that is."

"I used a debit card," Kit told her.

"Piece of cake. Don't worry about it. Other than that, how are you guys doing?" Jenna asked.

"Okay," Kit said.

"Here, Wiona wants to talk to you for a second," Jenna said.

"Cheer up, Kit. It'll all be okay. You can trust Lawrence to make sure things are taken care of. And just so you know, I have your back too. See you later, Kit," she said. Then after a short pause, she added, "And you too, Paizlee."

"I think you have a girlfriend," Paizlee teased after the call ended.

Kit frowned at her. "You know better than that."

"I do? Hey, I'm a girl too. I can tell by the way she talks to you that she is smitten." Paizlee chuckled. "You could do worse, you know."

"Yeah, I could go to prison," he said gloomily.

In less than half an hour, they got another phone call. "Hi, my name's Brandon Phelps. I have been retained by Lawrence Heslop to do some investigating for you. He told me you guys wanted to talk to him, but he asked me to call you."

"Hello," Kit said. "I'm Kit and my sister, Paizlee, is with me. The phone is synched, so you'll be talking to both of us."

"Great. So Lawrence asked me to find out what your debit card number is so I could get the information that you've lost," Brandon said.

"Not lost," Paizlee said angrily, "stolen!"

"Sorry, my mistake. Can you get me the number, and I'll go to work on this for you?"

Kit continued to drive while Paizlee gave Brandon the information he needed, including the dates of the receipts. "So those dates are from the beginning to the end of the trip, Kit?"

"Yes, but the most important date is the last one from where I spent the night and fueled up before leaving the next morning."

"I understand that, but I might as well get a complete record while I'm at it. I could also use the GPS feature on your cell phone, you know."

"If I hadn't lost it," Kit said.

"How did you lose it?" the PI asked.

"I wish I knew. I thought I had it with me at the jail in Fillmore, but when I was released from the one in Tonopah, it wasn't with my other property," Kit said.

"You sound stressed, Kit. Don't worry so much. We've got your back. I'll be doing some in-depth research into both Sam Overmyer and his cousin Sergeant Vince Hodson. I'll also call the jail down in Fillmore and make sure you had your cell phone with you when you were booked there. Now, if you don't mind, I'd like you to briefly go over the case with me. I've heard it from Lawrence, but I also want to hear it from you guys."

They talked for several minutes. When they had finished, the PI said, "It sounds like we're up against some crooks. Don't worry. By the time Lawrence and I get through with them, they'll be wishing they'd never messed with you."

"I hope so," Kit said.

"I understand you're racing your horse next week in California," Brandon said.

"That's the plan," Kit responded.

"Do you mind if I come?"

"You can if you want, but I don't expect any problems from Sam since he doesn't have a horse anymore," Kit said.

"That's the very reason I think I need to be there. Sam can still cause problems for you if he shows up. I'm betting he will, and I'll bet that crooked cop cousin of his will be with him," Brandon said.

"I honestly hadn't considered that," Kit said as he began to worry that those guys would show up there to cause trouble.

"I'll be there. I'll be contacting you again soon."

After that call ended, Kit said, "Paizlee, it's going to cost us, but I think we have some good people on our side."

"We sure do," Paizlee agreed with a smile. "So why don't you cheer up? Let's be positive about this."

"I'll try," he said, "but what if Brandon is right? What if those guys try to do something to cause us trouble at the race?"

"We'll just have to keep our eyes open," she said.

"I know, but Paizlee, this worry is getting to me. It could even affect my ability to ride well."

"You'll be okay. You are strong."

"I don't feel very strong," he said, trying to smile but not having much success at it. No one knew how hard it was, not even his sister.

Andy and Greg were walking toward the barn when a black Chevy pickup pulled into the yard and stopped in front of the ranch house. They were expecting a couple of the men they had hired who would be patrolling the ranch that afternoon and during the night to watch for intruders. But it wasn't either of them—they both drove older pickups.

Andy and Greg watched as a well-built man with a large gray cowboy hat climbed out of the black truck and looked around. When he spotted the men, he waved, but then he turned away and walked through the gate and up to the house, where he rang the doorbell.

"There's no one home," Greg shouted. Then in a normal tone he said, "He'll come meet us now."

"I wonder who he is," Andy said. "Guess we'll find out in a minute." The man was now walking toward them.

They continued to watch from where they were standing in front of the bunkhouse. When he got close, Andy said, "Howdy. If you're looking for Kit, he's not home."

"Hello, gentlemen," the stranger said. Andy could tell from the clothes he wore that he was well to do. He walked with confidence, his head held high. He stopped in front of the men and said, "You're right. I'm looking for Kit Troxler."

"I'm sorry. He's not here," Andy said. "I'm his foreman. Maybe I can help you."

"No, I need to see Kit. I suppose he'll be back in a little while?" The stranger posed the sentence as a question.

"Nope, he's out of state," Andy said as an older pickup drove into the yard and toward where the men were standing.

"I really need to speak with him," the stranger said.

"I'm Andy Boyse. I don't think I caught your name."

"Sorry, my name is Randall Overmyer."

That caught Andy's interest. "I don't think Kit will want to speak with you. I'm guessing you're related to Sam Overmyer."

"He's my son," Randall said.

"He certainly didn't get his size from you, did he?" Andy said. "Greg, will you take care of that fellow?" He waved toward the old pickup, and Greg walked away.

"No, and he resents me for it, I'm afraid. My late wife was just a little gal. Sam resented her too," Randall said. "He always blamed her that he was so short."

"What exactly do you want to see Kit about?" Andy asked.

"I just want to talk to him. I don't mean to make more trouble for him," Randall said.

"What do you want to talk to him about?" Andy pressed.

"I've heard Sam's side of both what happened at the race in Albuquerque and with the death of his horse. I've also heard from my nephew, a sergeant with the Nye County Sheriff's Office," Randall said. "I'd like to hear your boss's side of things."

"Of course. He and his twin sister own the ranch together. I can tell you some of Kit's side of things, if you'd care to hear it from me," Andy said.

"Well, first I wanted to talk to him about his accusation about my son trying to push him off of his horse in the race in Albuquerque."

"It's not just an accusation; it's a fact," Andy said firmly. "I was there. I saw it and so did his sister." Andy went on to describe exactly what he'd seen. "If the officials had seen it, Sam would have been disqualified, stripped of the win, and probably barred from racing."

"I see," Randall said, and to Andy, he looked very uncomfortable, his eyes darting around and one hand rubbing his forehead just below his hat. "You know that Sam found a glove with Kit's name on it, I suppose."

"I know he has it, and I also know that Kit lost it at the race grounds. Kit, his sister, and I all searched for it. The gloves were a gift from his sister. He felt terrible about losing it," Andy said.

"I see," Randall said again. He shifted his feet, took his hat off, and ran his hand through his hair. "So I guess it will be Sam's word against Kit's and my nephew's on those matters."

"And mine and Paizlee's. I'll testify to what I saw, and so will she." Andy was getting angry now. "I'll also testify to how the damage on the back of Kit's horse trailer occurred. I'm guessing your son and your nephew didn't tell you about that."

"What are you talking about?" Randall asked.

Andy proceeded to tell him what Sam had done as they were leaving the race grounds. "Would you like to see it? The horse trailer is right over there." He pointed toward their large red barn.

"If you don't mind, I would," Randall said.

They walked that way as yet another pickup pulled into the yard, another older one. Andy waved the driver toward where Greg was now talking to the first man. The young fellow nodded and passed them. When Andy and Randall reached the trailer, Andy took him to the back of it. "Right there," he said. "It's easy to see. We have photos of it. If you were to measure the height of Sam's big bumper, it would be exactly this height. We intend, of course, to see that that happens."

Randall had gone quite pale. But he still had another question. "The deputies from Nye County found an almost empty insulin bottle and a large syringe in Kit's truck. Did you know about that?"

"It wasn't just any deputy; it was that cocky nephew of yours. And he probably didn't bother to tell you that he had opened the door and leaned in for a minute. Paizlee, Kit's twin, watched him do it. You'd be welcome to talk to Sheriff Ledford. He was there. And I'm sure if he needs to that he will also testify in Kit's defense," Andy said. "I'm sorry, but your son and your nephew are not being honest with you. We have an attorney and a private investigator working for us now. I'm sure you won't want to hear what else they learn about those two."

Randall simply stared at Andy for a minute. Andy stared right back. Finally, Randall said, "I appreciate what you've told me. I'll give it some thought. But I'd still like to hear it from Kit's mouth. You surely won't object to that. When will he be back?"

"I don't know. A couple of days, maybe."

"Give me his number, and I'll call him and set up a time to meet with him," Randall said.

Andy shook his head.

"You don't trust me?" Randall asked, his face going red with anger.

"Why should I? Your son is trying to destroy one of the finest young men I know," Andy said forcefully.

"I'm sorry you feel that way," Randall said. "But please, let me call him. I don't want more trouble. I'd just like to get to the bottom of things."

Andy thought for a moment and looked toward Randall's shiny black truck. "I'll call him and let you talk to him on my phone. You are not getting his number. Well, I should say his sister's number. Kit's phone seems to have disappeared."

"I guess I'll have to live with that, won't I?" Randall said.

Andy made the call, speaking as soon as Kit picked up. "Kit, Randall Overmyer is here at the ranch. He wants to arrange to meet with you. He's Sam's father."

"I have nothing to say to him," Kit said. "Why would I want to talk to him? Would you please tell him to get off our ranch and stay off?"

Andy relayed that to Randall, whose face turned dark. "I mean him no harm. I'm not my son. Tell him that. And ask him if he would like my number so he can call me."

Andy spoke again to Kit.

"Tell Mr. Overmyer that if he wants to talk to someone, he needs to call my attorney. You have his number, so go ahead and give it to him."

"Kit says you can have his attorney's number and that you are welcome to call him. But he doesn't want to speak to you," Andy said. "Kit is really hurt by all this, and he's angry, which I understand."

"You really don't understand," Randall said, a pleading note in his voice breaking through the anger. "I just want to get to the truth. If my son is in the wrong, I'll see to it that he makes things right."

"Kit, I'm going to have you talk to Mr. Overmyer for just a second. I'd like you to hear from him what he just said to me," Andy said.

"Okay, but if I don't like what he's saying, I'll end the call," Kit said.

"Hi, Andy," Paizlee joined in. "I'll make sure he hangs up if the guy gets smart with him."

"Hi, Paizlee. Okay, I'm handing my phone to Randall, but I'm putting it on speaker now so I can hear what you guys say."

Randall spoke immediately. "Mr. Troxler. My name is Randall Overmyer. Thank you for talking to me. I sincerely do not want to cause you any more trouble. I've only heard my son's side of things. Well, I've now heard your foreman's side as well. I know my son, and frankly, I'm not so sure he's been honest with me."

"I'm sure he's lied to you," Kit said with a bite to his voice.

"I can see that may be the case," Randall admitted. "Please, I want to get to know you face to face. I've heard and read nothing but good things about you, except of course from my son and nephew. I will even come to where you are to meet you and your sister. I've come a long way and feel strongly that if you and I can get together, we can come to some kind of an understanding."

Andy spoke up then. "I think if you agree to this that I should be there with you, Kit, either me or your attorney."

Then Randall and Andy both heard Paizlee say to Kit, "Let's see if Brandon would be willing to be there. If he is, I'd be in favor of meeting Mr. Overmyer."

"Who is Brandon?" Randall asked.

"He's a private investigator who's working for us," Kit said. "If he can be there, we'll make arrangements to meet you. But it will mean another long drive for you, because I'm not coming back to Fillmore until I finish what I'm doing."

"I'm fine with that. Tell me where I need to go, and I'll go there."

"Stay there with Andy, if you can, and I'll call you back," Kit said before ending the call.

"I suppose he's calling the PI," Randall said.

"I would guess that or his attorney, or both."

"Who is his attorney?" Randall asked, and when Andy told him, his eyes went wide. "I've heard of him. That guy's a heavy hitter. He must be expensive."

"Very, but to Kit and Paizlee, they'll do whatever it takes to clear Kit's name," Andy said, "even if they have to go into debt to do it."

In only three or four minutes, Kit called back. "Okay, let's set a time and a place."

CHAPTER SEVEN

Kit was apprehensive about meeting Randall Overmyer, but he'd committed to do it, and he was not the kind of guy to back out of something once he'd promised. He and Paizlee had just checked into a second-floor room at the Gateway Inn in Lyman, Wyoming. They'd driven south while Randall was driving north. They agreed to meet in Lyman with their PI present.

"Our PI should be about here," Kit said, looking at his watch. "Let's look out for him from the balcony." They had barely stepped out of their room onto the balcony when a Ford Bronco—a tan late model—entered the parking area. The man who got out was well dressed, had a stocky build, and very short blond hair. He looked up at them and waved. They waved back. They met him a few moments later in the lobby.

"Brandon Phelps," the PI said and shook both their hands. "And you must be my clients, Kit and Paizlee."

"We are," Kit said.

"I'm glad to meet you two," Brandon said as he looked from Kit to Paizlee and back to Kit again. "Why don't we sit down in the lobby. You can fill me in a little more while we wait for Mr. Overmyer."

The three of them hit if off very well. Like their attorney, Brandon inspired confidence.

"I think I have a pretty good idea what we're up against here," Brandon said after a few minutes. "What time do you expect Mr. Overmyer to arrive?"

"It could be anytime," Paizlee said. The PI smiled warmly at her, and Kit did not miss the tinge of red that appeared on her face as she smiled back.

A minute later, Randall showed up. He looked nothing at all like his son, Sam. He was around six feet tall, well built, and tan. His boots were shiny, and he wore a gray cowboy hat. He looked every bit the well-to-do rancher he was. The hand he held out to Kit was callused and his grip strong. He assessed Kit with clear brown eyes. "I'm Randall," he said. "You must be Kit."

For privacy, they moved to the motel room, where Randall and Paizlee sat on chairs facing Kit and Brandon, who were seated on one of the two beds. Kit wasn't sure how to begin, but Randall made it easy. "I understand you have been looking to buy some new bulls."

"We were, but that's changed. We're spending the money I'd earmarked for bulls on an attorney and Mr. Phelps." He couldn't keep the frustration he felt from coming out in his voice.

"I'm sorry about that. Like I told you on the phone, I simply want to get your side of what happened. My son isn't always honest with me, and frankly, I don't trust my nephew as far as I could throw him."

That surprised Kit. Maybe Randall was an okay guy. He could certainly hope. "Then I'll tell you, Mr. Overmyer."

"Please call me Randall. I'm just a cowboy like you, and I don't much take to being called mister."

Kit nodded, but before he could say anything, Brandon spoke up. "I am going to record our conversation so I can refer to it later. I trust you have no objections, Randall."

"No, go ahead," he said.

After the small recorder was running and Brandon had mentioned who was in the meeting and the time and date, he turned to Kit. "Go ahead, Kit."

"Let me begin with the race in Albuquerque." Randall did not interrupt once as Kit and Paizlee recited in some detail the events that had occurred. "Have we forgotten anything, sis?" Kit asked Paizlee when they'd finished.

"I don't think so," she responded.

"For my benefit, Randall," Brandon said, "would you mind telling me what your understanding of the events that have occurred is?"

"I can only tell you what Sam and his cousin, Sergeant Vince Hodson, told me," he said. It didn't take him long to relay the information he'd heard.

"That's certainly nothing like Kit and Paizlee told us," Brandon said, his face serious. "But all of you can rest assured that I will look into things very thoroughly."

For a moment, no one else said anything, but then Randall, looking a bit nervous, said, "My ranch foreman said he did not see the aforementioned glove in the stall when he found Sharpshooter dead in there. But he also said he could have missed it."

"Wait a minute," Brandon said. "I thought you told us that Sam was the one who found the horse dead in his stall."

Randall shook his head. "I told you what Sam told me. Now I'm telling you what Bruce said to me this morning. Bruce is my foreman, and he's a good man. He would never lie to me. But I also have to consider what my son said, even though he's capable of lying." Randall turned his eyes on Kit. "So just because Bruce said that, it doesn't mean you weren't there that morning. That's something I need to figure out, that maybe you can help me figure out."

"I was not there," Kit said rather strongly. "I was in this very motel that morning, and I drove back to Fillmore after breakfast."

"But I understand you don't have any receipts to prove that," Randall said.

"Who told you that?" Kit asked suspiciously.

"Sam did. My nephew told him."

"And how does Sergeant Hodson explain how he knows that?" Brandon asked. He knew about the missing receipts from Kit's truck, but they had not mentioned that to Randall.

"I'm not sure, but Sam says he's positive about it," Randall said. Kit noticed how Randall was no longer looking him in the eyes.

Brandon stood up. "Kit and Paizlee, do you mind if I leave for just a moment? I'll leave the recorder going. I'll be right back."

Kit and Paizlee looked at each other. Paizlee nodded. "That's fine."

Brandon left the room with no explanation of what he was doing.

"Is it true?" Randall asked. "Are you not able to produce receipts? If you could, it would make it a lot easier to believe you."

"I kept them in my jockey box, and now they're gone. I'm not a liar. I'm also not the kind of person who would kill an innocent horse, no matter how evil its owner is."

"Are you calling my son evil?" Randall asked as his eyes began to show some signs of anger.

"You'll see," Kit said.

"I think we're through here," Randall said as he stood from his chair, his face dark. He started for the door but stopped before opening it. "At least you had the decency to talk to me. I thank you for that. I thank both of you. Now I'd better get going. I'd at least like to drive for a while before I have to stop for the night."

"Thanks for listening," Kit said, though he was afraid it had done no good. Randall trusted his twisted son, and that was that.

Randall left. Five minutes later, a tap came on the door. "I'll get it," Paizlee said before jumping up and hurrying to the door. "It's probably Brandon."

It was. "Did Randall leave?" he asked.

"Yes. He doesn't believe us," Kit said mournfully.

"Let me shut the recorder off, and then I have something to show you." He waved a paper at them and then laid it on the table beside the chair Randall had vacated. He spoke a few words to end the recording, then shut the device off.

"I think Randall has serious doubts about his son and nephew," Brandon said with a smile. "He should have hung around for a few minutes so I could show him this." He picked up the paper. "I got this from the folks downstairs. This is proof that you were here on the day the horse was killed."

"I never thought of that," Kit said sheepishly.

"I'm a detective. You're a rancher. It's my job to know about things like this," he said. "Now, let's talk about those missing receipts. It's pretty clear that the deputy stole them from your truck."

"That's why we're up here," Kit said. "I was hoping I could find someone who would remember me and give me a statement to that effect. But so far, I've struck out."

"Do you mind if I give it a try?" Brandon suggested. "I'd be glad to do that. This Sergeant Hodson could have more nasty tricks up his sleeve. I've already got a request in to your bank about your debit card, but so far they haven't responded. So what I need now is a list of places you stopped. But even if I don't do any better than you've done, there are other ways of proving you were at the places you stopped besides receipts."

"Like what?" Kit asked doubtfully.

"Most businesses have time- and date-stamped video recordings. Also, good businesses can get on their computers, find the information, and print out proof of any purchases you made."

"It sounds like Kit and I need to let you do that kind of stuff. We really don't know what we're doing," Paizlee said sheepishly. "And we have no way of knowing how much proof we need to get."

"In a case like this, there can never be too much. That's why I will keep digging. Oh, and I also called Sheriff Ledford's jail like I told you I would," Brandon added.

"What did they say?" Kit asked.

"You did have your phone there, and it was handed over to Sergeant Hodson with your other personal property," he responded.

Kit said nothing for a minute. He looked at his sister. "Could Sergeant Hodson have taken it?"

"I would have to say that that is a strong possibility. He would know what could be done with the GPS and likely didn't want to take a chance, so he probably took it," Brandon said. "But we will prove where you were without the phone, and you should think about getting a new one."

"He's a crook!" Kit said angrily.

"Probably so. It's after my dinnertime, and I don't know about you guys, but I'm hungry. Should we find a place to eat?" Brandon asked.

"I guess we should," Kit agreed.

Randall stopped in Evanston and booked a room. He was hungry, but his stomach was a bit upset. He desperately wanted to believe his son, but his doubts had grown after listening to Kit and his sister—they had given him a lot to think about. One of the things that had disturbed him most was the matter of Kit not having any receipts from his trip up here to look at bulls. Randall had always kept receipts when he was on ranch business. It was needed for income tax purposes. He gave that a lot of thought as he lounged on the bed.

How could his nephew have known that Kit had no receipts unless Kit had told him? From their conversation today, Randall was almost certain that had not occurred. This was very disturbing. Another thing that really ate at him was the fact that Kit's twin sister claimed to have seen Vince open Kit's truck door, lean in, and then close it after a moment. Vince claimed she was lying, but Randall was having a hard time believing that. Miss Troxler seemed like an honest young lady. Why would she lie about that? From her account, she had seen Vince do that before the sheriff of Millard County found the insulin bottle and syringe in Kit's truck.

He was still running all he'd learned today from Kit, his sister, and his ranch foreman through his mind when his cell phone rang.

"Boss, it's Bruce. Have you heard from Sam? He never did come back to work after he left."

"He didn't tell you where he was going?" Randall asked suspiciously.

"No, sir, he did not," Bruce said. "He did come back a few minutes after he left, but he didn't come out and work. He just went in the house. He was only there for a half hour or so, and when he came out, he left again, carrying a small bag. I haven't seen him since."

"I'm sorry he's giving you so much trouble," Randall said, and he truly was, for doubts about his only child continued to find fertile ground in his brain.

"I can't imagine what he's doing," Randall said to Bruce. "I canceled his credit and debit cards and closed his access to my bank accounts. I can't imagine that he has enough cash to last him very long."

"Boss, I hate to suggest this, but does he know the combination to your safe?" Bruce asked. "I mean, you know, he left without any funds. Who knows? He may need money for something right now. Do you have money in your safe?"

Randall felt a jolt. "Yes, he does know the combination." And Sam had come back long enough to go in the house. What had he been doing there during that half hour Bruce mentioned?

"I also have a couple of active credit cards that I haven't used for a while. I'm afraid you've answered my question for me," Randall said. He thought about asking Bruce to check, but he'd have to tell him the combination. Not that he didn't trust him. He had to admit that the real reason he didn't ask Bruce to check was because he didn't want to know that Sam had stooped that low.

He tried calling Sam, as he had done several times before, but once again, he got no answer.

His heart was heavy as he got ready for bed.

CHAPTER EIGHT

"Dad keeps calling me. He thinks I need to slave away on the ranch all the time just because he did before he started having heart trouble," Sam complained on the phone to Vince as he closed in on Fillmore. "He says he'll find me a replacement for Sharpshooter only if I work full-time for him for a year. That's a bunch of bunk. If I had another good horse, I could win a lot of money. It's racing that I want to do. He knows I'm good at it but won't help me by finding another top horse. He can afford it!"

"I agree that he's pretty stingy. He should help my mother out more, but he doesn't," Vince said.

"If somebody hadn't killed Sharpshooter, I would be racing in California next week," Sam complained. "I know Kit's going to be there. I sure would hate for him to win. He doesn't deserve to win."

"Kit killed Sharpshooter, Sam. You're being negative. Remember what you're doing later tonight. You take care of Kit's horse and that will end his racing, not to mention any winning in California," Vince reminded him.

"But if Kit was in Wyoming, then how could he have done it? I don't get it."

"He's lying, Sam. Use your head. And if he didn't do it, he could have hired someone to do it for him," Vince said.

"I never thought of that; so it's still Kit's fault. You sure are a lot of help to me," Sam said. "I don't know what I'd ever do without you."

"That's right. I always clean up your messes and take care of you. Now go get the job done and let me know when you're finished. And make sure you don't let anyone see you. Apparently, they don't have a dog. At least, I didn't see one the day I was there. Well, actually, there was a tiny black-and-white puppy. But that doesn't count—it won't cause trouble. You have time to take care of that horse of Kit's and get away before morning. Call me when you're done."

"Okay. You're sure you got his cell phone when he was in jail?" Sam asked.

"I told you already. It didn't even make it into his property. I got it, I disabled it, and then I ditched it. So he can't prove he was in Wyoming, if he even was, which I doubt," Vince said with a chuckle.

"Okay, I'll be in Fillmore before long. This old truck I borrowed is a piece of junk. I wish I could have brought my Ram. But I understand why you told me not to. Anyway, I need to scope things out there. I'll park far enough away that I'll have to walk for a while. I just hope the horse is in the barn when I get there and not out in a corral or pasture," Sam said.

"I'll bet he'll be in the barn. That's where he was when my guys and I searched the place," Vince assured him. "But Sam, don't get in a hurry. It needs to be the middle of the night before you do this. So go hide out somewhere for a few hours."

"I know. I'm not stupid. Oh, one more thing," Sam said. "Tell me exactly what to do when I give it the shot."

"Sam, Sam, my boy, you live on a ranch. You've done it lots of times," Vince chided.

"Not much," Sam said. "I don't want to mess this up."

"That's right. You usually manage to keep busy somewhere else so you won't have to help your dad," Vince said. He then reminded Sam how to do it and once more told him not to get in a hurry. Then their phone call ended.

Vince had gotten off a late shift earlier and was sound asleep when his phone rang. He answered and mumbled something into it.

"I couldn't find that stupid horse," Sam said. "There were some guys hanging around, driving all over the ranch, and then every so often, one of them would look in the barn and around the ranch yard. I finally found a chance to sneak into the barn, but Kingfisher wasn't there."

"Did you look in the corrals?" Vince asked as he became more alert.

"Yeah, but I couldn't use my flashlight too much because of those guys. I couldn't see him. He must have been in a pasture, but I didn't dare spend more time looking."

"That's too bad," Vince said. "Even though you failed, I hope you didn't leave any signs that you'd been on the ranch."

"I was careful where I walked, like you suggested. Since the yard is all asphalt and the floor of the barn is cement, there's really no danger of them figuring out I was there. And I know those guys didn't see me."

"Okay, well, we'll have to try another time," Vince said. "I'm tired. You woke me up. I need to get back to sleep."

"Maybe they've hidden him somewhere," Sam suggested. "But I've been thinking, and I have an idea."

"What's that?" Vince asked.

"What would it take to get Kit thrown back in jail?"

Vince thought for a moment. "He'd have to do something that would convince the judge he should revoke Troxler's bail."

"Like what?" Sam asked.

Vince rubbed his eyes, trying to wake up more. For once, his not-so-bright cousin had hit on a good idea, even though he knew he could never take it further than he had. So Vince worked it over in his mind before he said, "I think I've got it, Sam."

"Okay, tell me."

Vince told him, and Sam said cheerfully, "Let's make it happen!"

Kit and Paizlee were back on the ranch, following their Wyoming trip, when Lawrence came down on Monday, and to Kit's delight, Wiona was with him. She sure did seem like a good gal, and he wanted to get to know her better. She chattered and teased excitedly as he and Paizlee showed them around the ranch. There were several colts that came right up to them. She was delighted.

Lawrence was mostly interested in how the ranch operated, and with Andy's help, Kit explained things in detail. After a while, Wiona said, "I want to see your racehorse."

Kit's face darkened. "He's not here. He's at another ranch."

"Why don't you keep him here?" Wiona asked innocently.

"I'm racing him in California on Friday. I want to make sure he stays healthy," he said.

"What? I don't get it." But before Kit could explain, her eyes grew wide and she said, "Oh, I think I know. You're afraid those guys from Nevada might do something to him."

"Yes, and it would already have happened, but he was gone," Kit explained.

"Already have happened?" Lawrence asked with a frown. "Maybe you'd better explain."

Andy spoke up. "I hired some extra men to come keep an eye on things for us. They tried hard, but they couldn't be everywhere at once. The night

Kit and Paizlee stayed in Wyoming, one of them saw someone running from the yard around three in the morning. He followed him but didn't catch up. The intruder got away in an old truck of some kind. The man who spotted the intruder called me, and we searched all through the barn. Nothing was hurt, but a couple of doors were ajar that shouldn't have been. If Kingfisher had been here, I'm sure something would have happened to him."

"Did you call the sheriff?" Lawrence asked.

"Oh yes, and a deputy came right out, but there wasn't really anything he could do. Our man didn't have enough of a description of either the trespasser or the truck to give them anything to look for."

"I assume you've continued your surveillance," Lawrence said.

"Yes, but like we said, Kingfisher is not here."

"There could be other things they might do," the attorney suggested. "Believe me, I deal with crooks all the time. Don't count out something else happening."

"Like what?" Wiona asked with a stricken face.

Lawrence shrugged his shoulders. "Who knows? But I would guess that they might destroy something just for the sake of causing Kit trouble even if they can't get to Kingfisher."

"Are you sure he's safe?" the pretty redhead asked, looking directly into Kit's eyes.

"Not really, but I don't know what more we can do," he said.

"It makes me angry!" she said as fire lit her eyes.

"It makes us angry too," Paizlee said. "The way they've harassed Kit is appalling." She then turned to Lawrence. "Would you guys stay for lunch? I'll go fix some sandwiches if you'll stay and eat with us."

"So if we go, Kit and these other guys don't get anything," Wiona kidded, the fire gone from her eyes, sparks of humor replacing it.

"We'll stay," Lawrence said. "I was hoping that you, Kit, would let me look at your records."

"Of course," Kit said. "And then later, if you want, we'll go see Kingfisher. Andy and I need to give him a good workout."

"That will be fun," Wiona said. "I'll go help Paizlee." And away the two young women went.

After lunch, they drove to Norm Smith's ranch. Kingfisher was looking and acting as healthy as ever. Kit got on his back and rode out to Norm's track. It wasn't great, but it was better than nothing. He did a slow lap on Kingfisher and then let him go faster on the second one. As Kingfisher came back toward where

Andy was waiting with a stopwatch, he was almost flying, with Kit leaning right over his neck.

Andy signaled for Kit to go around again, and once more his time was incredible on the lap. Kit pulled him up, walked him around for a couple of minutes, and then approached Andy, where he dismounted and began to pet the big stallion's neck.

"He'll be ready," Andy said as Wiona ran toward them, laughing with excitement. "He's looking great. Without Sam there to try to mess things up, you'll have a real shot at winning."

"I've been studying the other horses that will be there. Kingfisher and I have our work cut out for us." Kit paused and glanced at the beaming Wiona. "Kingfisher will be fine. It's me I worry about. I need to be focused, and right now, I'm a long way from it."

An hour later, back at Kit's ranch, Lawrence was very encouraging as he and Wiona got ready to leave. "You've got a good place here. You and Andy manage it well. As for the case against you, I can knock that apart easily. Brandon has already found some things about Sam and his cousin, the deputy, that will make a judge and a jury look twice before believing anything they say. Actually, I doubt it will even go to trial. I believe I can get a judge to throw it out before that happens. So don't stress so much. You focus on getting ready for the big race. I'll take care of the legal problem."

That evening around eight o'clock, two burly men knocked on the door to the ranch house. Paizlee was busy cleaning the living room.

"My name's Rick, and this here's Arturo," one of the men greeted her. "We need to see Kit."

"I'm sorry. He's still working," Paizlee said as her stomach took a tumble. These two looked like trouble. "What do you need him for?" she asked, her voice suddenly weak.

"That's none of your business," Rick said. "This is between us and Kit. Take us to him."

"I'm not sure where he's at. He could be anywhere on the ranch," she said as she felt panic set in.

"He must have a cell phone. Call him," Rick ordered.

"I'll go get my phone," she said. "It's in the kitchen."

She started to shut the door, but the one named Arturo stuck his foot in it. "We'll come with you," he said. "We don't want you telling Kit to make a run for it. We just need to speak with him about a little matter, and then we'll be on our way."

Paizlee could see that she didn't have a choice. She led them to the kitchen on legs that felt like jelly. But she knew she needed to get a grip. She took a deep breath and felt strength flow into her body, calming the shaking. She got the phone. She dialed Kit's new phone number, but as soon as Kit said, "Hi, Paizlee, what's happening?" Rick grabbed the phone from her hand.

"Kit, my name's Rick. Meet me at your barn. We need to talk. My buddy Arturo will stay here with your pretty sister. Don't try to go anywhere. You don't want anything to happen to your sis, now, do you?"

He slapped the phone on the counter and said, "Keep her right here, Arturo. I'll let you know when you can rejoin me." He stomped from the house.

"What are you guys doing?" Paizlee asked as anger built and her fear increased.

"Already told you. We need to talk to Kit. Now shut up and sit down." He clearly had nothing more to say, so she didn't ask any more questions. Stubbornly, she remained standing.

She had the terrible feeling that they intended to harm Kit. But she was helpless. She wished she could at least call Andy, but there was no way she would be allowed to use her phone. All she could do was pray, and she did that.

Kit called Andy. "Some guys are here to talk to me. Call the sheriff's department, and then meet me at the barn. Bring Greg with you. And grab a gun but keep it out of sight," he said.

He'd been checking on some cattle about three miles away on the west side of the ranch. He jumped on his four-wheeler and drove like mad for the yard. Something was terribly wrong. He swung into the yard and drove toward the barn, where a burly guy was talking to Andy. By the time he reached them, Greg had also joined them.

"Kit Troxler, I'm Rick. You're going to have to come with me," the big man said.

"Greg, I don't see Paizlee. She must be in the house with the other guy. Go check on her," Kit said as he felt the anxiety that Lawrence had helped him shed a few hours earlier return with a vengeance.

"She's fine. Give me your hands," he said. "You are under arrest."

"Show me your credentials," Andy said as his hand slipped behind his back where Kit had already seen a 9mm Colt pistol stuffed inside his belt.

"I don't have to do any such thing. We have a warrant for your arrest in the truck. Come on, Kit, don't make this harder on yourself," Rick growled.

"Step away from him," Andy said as he produced his 9mm and pointed it straight at the big man's chest. "You aren't taking him anywhere. I've called the sheriff, and he'll deal with you."

Rick's face went purple with rage. "I'm on legal business. I'll see you in jail along with Kit here for threatening me with a gun. I'm a legal bounty hunter, and this wimp here is wanted in Nye County, Nevada."

"I haven't seen any ID or any warrant," Andy insisted, holding his gun steady, his eyes never wavering from the big man's face.

"I told you, it's in the truck."

"Keep him here," Kit said. "I'm going to check on Paizlee and Greg."

Kit sprinted on the pavement toward the house a hundred yards from the barn. He tore through the gate and onto the front porch. That's where he stopped, for another very large and dangerous-looking man was ushering Greg and Paizlee through the door at gunpoint. "Kit, he was watching through the window, and he thought he saw Andy pull a gun. Greg had just come in to check on me, and this creep pulled a gun on us."

"The sheriff's department is on the way," Kit said. "I'd like to know exactly what you men are doing here."

"They said they wanted to talk to you," Paizlee said as she rubbed moisture from her eyes. "So why don't they just do that and leave?"

"We're taking your brother to the jail in Nevada," Arturo said. "Now, you guys are going to get yourselves jailed as well if you don't quit attempting to block us from doing our job."

They were all standing on the porch now. Arturo motioned with his pistol that they needed to start walking. No one moved. "We're going out there to join Rick. Now get moving before someone gets hurt."

Kit finally turned and started walking very slowly toward the barn, hoping this would give the sheriff's officers time to get there. The others followed. When they had crossed the hundred yards to the barn, Arturo said to Andy, "Unless you idiots want someone to get hurt, put that gun away and let Kit go with us. I'll show him the warrant as soon as he gets to our truck."

Just then, sirens could be heard in the distance. Andy stubbornly continued to hold his gun on Rick. Arturo, just as stubbornly, pointed his at Kit. "The sheriff ain't gonna like you guys resisting like this. We came here peacefully and legally. I'm going to insist that you all be arrested," Rick was saying.

No one gave an inch. The sirens grew closer. Arturo began waving his gun around. "We have the authority to use whatever force we need to in order to take a fugitive into custody," he shouted. "The sheriff ain't gonna help you none."

Three separate sheriff's department vehicles flew into the yard and screeched to a stop on the pavement. The lead one was unmarked. The driver jumped out, his pistol drawn. It was Sheriff Marc Ledford, and his eyes were shooting flames. Andy lowered his gun. Arturo did not. "Drop that gun, mister," the sheriff ordered. Three deputies, also with drawn weapons, leaped from their cars.

The sheriff approached Arturo. "You've been given a lawful order. Drop that gun."

"Better do like the cop says," his partner said. "Ain't nothing he can do to us. We're here legally."

Arturo finally lowered his weapon, but he did not drop it. One of the deputies walked up behind him, reached around, and jerked the gun from his hand. "You guys don't know who you're messing with," Rick said.

The sheriff and his deputies, their guns trained on the two burly men, separated them from Kit and the others. "You all go in the house while we take care of these men," Sheriff Ledford said.

"Kit can't go. We're taking him in," Rick said from where he was now standing with his back to the barn beside his partner.

"We asked them for ID or at least a copy of the warrant they claim to have," Andy said as he tucked his gun behind his back. "They say it's in the truck, but we haven't seen it."

Arturo reached into a pocket, but before he could pull anything out, two deputies slammed him against the barn and put handcuffs on his thick wrists.

"Hey, that wasn't necessary," Rick protested, his face purple with rage. "He was just getting his ID for you."

"Check his pocket, Jason," the sheriff said to one of the deputies. He did and pulled a small .22 revolver out.

"That thing's legal," Arturo said. "My ID must be in the other pocket."

Sergeant Jason Anderson handed the little pistol to another deputy and then checked the pocket on the other side of the man's pants. It was empty; there was no ID there. "Secure Rick, and then we'll go see if they have a warrant in the truck," the sheriff said, his weapon still in his hand.

The deputies put the cuffs on Rick, searched him, pulled a gun from inside his pants and another from his right boot. Only then did Sheriff Ledford put his sidearm back in the shoulder holster inside of his jacket. He walked over to the burly guys' truck. He didn't see anything in plain view, so he had Rick and Arturo brought to him. "It's in the jockey box," Arturo said.

The sheriff checked, found a folded paper, opened it, and read for a minute.

"I told you it was legit," Rick said with a sneer. "Now get these handcuffs off of us. We'll be taking Kit back to Nye County."

"What is it, Sheriff?" Kit asked.

"A warrant for your arrest. It appears that the judge has revoked your bail," the sheriff said. Then, addressing Rick and Arturo, he asked, "Why was this in the jockey box instead of with you so you could show it to Kit in the first place?"

"We were afraid one of these guys would grab it and tear it up," Arturo said. "But you see it now. It's legal."

"What did I do now?" Kit asked desperately.

"We don't have that information," Rick said with a sneer. "The bail bond company gave us that warrant and told us not to lose it, to pick you up, and to bring you back to Nye County. And that is exactly what we will do."

"You men will be coming with us to my office," Sheriff Ledford said. "I still don't know who you are. You have failed to give us any proof that you are legitimate agents of the bail bond company."

"Take these cuffs off, and we'll show you our IDs," Arturo said.

"If you have it, you should have produced it already," Sheriff Ledford said. He turned to Sergeant Anderson. "Call a tow truck and wait here for it. These men are going with us."

"You're making a huge mistake, Sheriff," Rick growled.

"I don't think so. You produced no ID, and you are both carrying concealed weapons. We will be charging you with those offences and probably more. You are both under arrest," the sheriff said. He turned to his deputies. "Come on, let's put them in our vehicles, but search them again first. And I want the keys to their truck."

The keys were taken, but since no other weapons were found, the sheriff directed his officers to escort them to the sheriff's department vehicles. "Kit, you stay here. I'll get back to you," the sheriff said. "I'm going to check to see if this warrant is actually legitimate."

"Sheriff, you don't have to get a tow truck. We'll drive our truck and follow you to the jail," Rick said, sounding, for the first time, conciliatory.

"You'll do nothing of the sort. Sergeant Anderson," Sheriff Ledford said as he turned to the sergeant. "Make a complete inventory of their pickup before the tow truck takes it. And of course, if you find anything that's illegal, seize it."

Rick tried to argue more, but the sheriff was having none of it, and within five minutes, the two burly men were on their way to the sheriff's office in Fillmore.

CHAPTER NINE

I<small>T WAS ALMOST TEN</small> <small>O'CLOCK</small> when the sheriff finally returned to Kit's place and rang the doorbell. He came into the house when Kit opened the door. "Kit, it seems the judge in Nevada did revoke your bail."

Kit's gut churned. "What did I do?"

"Someone claims to have seen you on the Overmyer ranch, and one of the terms that was ordered when you were released on bail was that you would not go on that property," Sheriff Ledford explained.

"I haven't been there. I wasn't there the first time, and I haven't violated the order. I don't even know how to get there," Kit protested.

"I believe you, but for now, you are going to have to go. There's nothing I can do about it. I'm sorry."

Kit's face went dark. "Sam Overmyer and that crooked cousin of his are behind this. I just know it. He doesn't want me to race on Friday. They've lied again."

"I don't know about that, but you could be right," Sheriff Ledford said as Paizlee slipped from the room.

"Are those goons taking me tonight?" Kit asked. "They aren't guys I can trust. I might never make it to the jail with guys like that escorting me."

"No, they won't be taking you. They are not legitimate bounty hunters, and furthermore, they did not have any conceal carry permits on them. And that's not all. They had heroin and methamphetamine in their truck. One of my guys did a field test on it. That was enough to book them. The lab will tell us for sure. They're in my jail on several charges, including several felonies each."

"They'll bond out. After all, they work for the bail company."

"Actually, they don't. Someone pulled a fast one allowing them to come after you."

"That would be Sergeant Hodson," Kit said angrily.

"You may be right, but it's not going to be that easy for those two men. They even lied about their identities. We found out who they really are. Both are convicted felons and are still on parole. When we learned that, we added attempted kidnapping charges. They are not going anywhere, because there is now a hold on them. They will probably be going back to prison in Nevada unless we send them to prison here in Utah. I'll let the prosecutors work that out."

"So is someone else coming after me?" Kit asked.

"It will be a deputy from Nye County, and it is not Sam Overmyer's cousin. You'll need to come with me to my office, and we'll wait there for the deputy to show up," the sheriff said. "He should be there by around midnight or one o'clock. I'm sorry, Kit. You'll want to call your attorney."

"I'll do that, but I'm sure there's nothing he can do tonight."

"Probably not, but he will as soon as he can."

"Brandon, it's Paizlee Troxler," a very stressed voice came over the line as soon as Brandon answered.

"What's the matter, Paizlee?" he asked, trying to sound reassuring to her even though he had no idea what the problem was.

"They are taking Kit to jail again," she said. "You've got to help us."

"Why are they taking him to jail, and who are they?" the PI asked.

"Two rough-looking men came here and tried to arrest him. The sheriff has arrested them now for a bunch of stuff. Anyway, Sheriff Ledford said Kit's bail has been revoked. And I don't know why," she said earnestly.

"Okay, Paizlee, if the guys are in jail in Fillmore, who is taking Kit to Tonopah?"

"I don't know, but I'm sure the sheriff does. He's with Kit in the other room right now."

"Paizlee, tell me exactly what happened. Then I'll call Lawrence, and we'll go to work to get Kit out."

For the next several minutes, she told him the entire night's events. As she concluded, she said, "Kit just joined me. I'll put this on speaker so you can hear him too."

"Is that Brandon?" Kit asked.

"Yes, I called him," she said.

"Hi, Kit. Your sister has told me what's going on. However, she says she doesn't know who is taking you since the men who came after you are both in jail in Fillmore," Brandon said.

"A deputy is coming from Nye County. The sheriff is supposed to take me to his office and meet him there," Kit explained.

"It had better not be Sergeant Hodson," Brandon said.

"It's not. What do I do now? Hodson and Sam are behind this. Someone said I was on the Overmyer ranch again. Those guys lied again so I will be in jail and not be able to ride Kingfisher in the race in California."

"Those guys are bad news. Have you talked to Lawrence yet?"

"No, but the sheriff says I can call him before he takes me to Fillmore," Kit explained.

"Kit, let me call Lawrence," Brandon said. "And then we'll do whatever he thinks is best. You just be calm, Kit. We'll take care of this, I assure you."

"Thank you, Brandon," Paizlee said. "I didn't know what to do."

"You did right," he responded. "I'll keep you informed. Do you care if you get any calls in the middle of the night? Because that could happen."

"If it's you, I don't mind. Thank you."

As soon as the call from Paizlee ended, Brandon called Lawrence's cell phone. As it rang, he thought about Kit and Paizlee. They were good people. When this mess was over, he wanted to get to know them better. Actually, he admitted to himself, it was mostly Paizlee he would like to get to know better. He had been instantly attracted to her, something that had never happened to him before. He hoped he wasn't reading her wrong, because it sure seemed like she felt much the same.

His thoughts were cut off when Lawrence answered his phone. "Is there a problem, Brandon?" the attorney asked in his deep voice.

"Yes, a big one, I'm afraid. I just talked to Paizlee. She called me and was very upset. Bottom line, the judge over Kit's case in Nye County revoked his bond, and the bail bond company sent a couple of tough guys to arrest him," Brandon said.

"What are they claiming he did to justify revoking bail?" Lawrence asked.

"Kit is accused of sneaking around on Randall Overmyer's ranch," Brandon replied.

"That has to be bogus. Kit would never do something like that. He knew it was a condition of his release on bail," Lawrence said.

"Not only that—Kit says he has no idea where the ranch is even at. I mean, he knows it's in Nye County, but he says he's never even been in that county."

"I've never had a client who is as upstanding and honest as Kit Troxler. Don't you agree?" Lawrence asked.

"I do. He and Paizlee are bright, ambitious, and upright people. This is a setup crime if I've ever seen one," Brandon said.

"When did this trespass allegedly occur, Brandon?"

"Kit and Paizlee don't have any idea. But whenever it was, I'm sure I'll be able to prove where Kit was at the time."

"It's late, so I don't know that I can do anything tonight, but I think I need to go there in the morning. I can't let him sit in jail and worry," Lawrence said.

"There's something else to keep in mind," Brandon said. "Kit is supposed to have his horse in California Wednesday night or Thursday morning to prepare for the race on Friday. I'm planning on being there to help Kit make sure no one messes with Kingfisher."

For a moment, Lawrence didn't say anything. Brandon knew what that meant; he was in deep thought. "This smells of another dirty trick by Sam Overmyer and Sergeant Hodson," Brandon said finally. "With Kit in jail, he can't race, and I suspect that's exactly what Sam wants."

"Brandon, can you be in Tonopah by ten in the morning Pacific time? By then, I may have been able to do something with the prosecutor and the judge over the phone. If not, I'll be flying down as soon as I can."

"I'll leave early enough in the morning to make it by ten," Brandon promised.

"Keep me posted if you hear anything more. We really need to find out when this was alleged to have occurred."

"I'll get to work on that as soon as I get there," Brandon promised. "I'll talk to you later. I need to call Paizlee back and let her know what we're doing."

A young Nye County deputy picked Kit up shortly after midnight and headed back to Tonopah. The deputy seemed like a nice guy. He was not one of the officers who had been at Kit's ranch the day they arrested him. For the first few miles, they rode in silence, but finally the deputy said, "I'm Ari Short. I already know you're Kit Troxler. You're the guy that accused Sam Overmyer of trying to shove you over the rails."

"He almost succeeded. As it is, I nearly beat him after recovering my balance," Kit said bitterly.

"Yeah, I hear ya," Deputy Short said. He hesitated and then added, "Not a lot of people like Sam very much."

Kit asked, "What kind of guy is Sergeant Hodson?"

For a long time, Deputy Short didn't answer. When he finally did, he said, "Don't quote me, please. It could get me in a lot of trouble."

"I won't tell anyone. I mean, I have my own opinion. He's a crooked cop," Kit said.

"Do I have your word?" Ari asked. "And please, call me Ari if you don't mind, Kit."

"Okay, Ari. Yes, you have my word. Of course, Sam Overmyer and Sergeant Hodson will tell you my word means nothing. And by the way, I did not kill that horse of Sam's."

"I believe you. Sergeant Hodson is a first-class jerk. I don't like him, and I don't trust him. I hope you have a good lawyer, because he thinks he's got you nailed to the wall. He brags about it all the time."

"I do have a good attorney. So is my private investigator."

"You had to get a PI too?"

"My twin sister and I both feel like we have to do what it takes to beat those guys at their crooked game," Kit said. He was tired and bitter, and he knew it showed in his voice, but at this point, he didn't much care.

"I'm sorry, Kit. I can see how you must feel," Ari said. "I hear you have a great horse. Not from Sam or from Sergeant Hodson. I did a search on the internet. That black stallion of yours is said to be one of the fastest quarter horses in the West. Sam's was okay, I hear, but not in the same league as yours."

"Kingfisher is smart, he's fast, and he likes to win. He's a great horse," Kit told him.

"I see that you have a big race in California on Friday," Ari said. "Like I told you a second ago, I've been looking on the internet. Sorry if that bothers you."

"Not at all, but the timing of this bail revocation seems very suspicious," Kit said.

Ari looked over at him. "Are you saying that you think this was done to keep you from racing?"

"That's the kind of thing Sam and Sergeant Hodson would do," Kit said. "Somebody is lying. I've never been in your area in my life. I don't even know where Sam's dad's ranch is."

The two men seemed to have developed an easy camaraderie. At one point, Ari asked, "Are those handcuffs bothering you?"

"Of course," Kit said, "but at least you didn't put them on tight like Hodson did."

"Let me put them in front of you rather than in back."

That said, Deputy Short pulled to the side of the highway and stopped. "Here, let me see your hands."

A moment later, the cuffs were fastened loosely in front of Kit. "Thanks, that feels a lot better."

They continued to talk for a little while, but Kit was exhausted, and he started to nod off. "Hey, I'll shut my mouth and let you sleep," Ari said. "You look like you're about done in."

"Yeah, I haven't slept much lately. Sorry."

"Not a problem," Ari said.

Kit drifted to sleep.

"Hate to wake you," Ari said a little while later as he reached over and shook Kit. "It looks like there's an accident or something up ahead."

"Oh boy," Kit said, hating to wake to the nightmare again. "What time is it?"

"It's close to two thirty," Ari responded.

Ari's eyes were focused ahead as he slowed down. There was a pickup sideways across the road, blocking it. "I don't know what's going on here," Ari said without looking at Kit. "I didn't hear anything on the radio about an accident. You stay in the car while I check it out." The deputy grabbed his flashlight and stepped out of the patrol car, shutting the door behind him. Kit wondered briefly why no lights had come on inside the car. He decided it must be some kind of safety feature for officers.

CHAPTER TEN

Kɪᴛ ᴅɪᴅ ɴᴏᴛ ʜᴀᴠᴇ ᴀ good feeling about this. He tensed, thinking that if he had to, he'd flee from the car. He watched as Ari moved slowly toward the large pickup, his right hand on the butt of his weapon, his left hand shining his light about. He reached the pickup that was blocking the road and shined his light inside. Instinctively, Kit knew that he and Ari were both in serious trouble.

Kit had a feeling that he needed to get out of this car despite the officer's orders. He undid the seatbelt and then eased the door open, hoping the interior lights would not come on. He felt immense relief when they didn't. He was glad that his hands were cuffed in front of him. He could run a lot easier than if they'd been behind.

He crouched just low enough that he could see through the bottom of the window. Ari was still shining his light in the truck. A large man crouched behind the pickup where Ari couldn't see him. But Kit could see him as the lights of the patrol car illuminated him. He was dressed in dark jeans and a black tank top. He had a lot of tattoos. He turned his head, and Kit could see a narrow face with a long, hooked nose. A flash of something in his hand made Kit look closer. A pistol!

Kit had to warn Ari. He opened his mouth to shout just as Ari said, "Drop your gun or I'll shoot." But at that exact instant, flame flew from the barrel of the other man's pistol.

Ari fell in a heap, his pistol bouncing on the pavement. Ari had seen and recognized the threat. But he was too slow to save himself.

The big man didn't pay any more attention to the fallen officer. He was now looking toward the patrol car. Kit crouched low and headed for the edge of the road. There were brush and weeds there. He stepped into them, dropped to his belly, and began to crawl awkwardly, using his elbows and legs to propel him, desperate to get away.

"Kit Troxler. I know you're out of the car," Hooknose said, his voice as frightening as his face. Kit continued to crawl. He didn't dare look up for fear the gunman would see him.

"Give it up, Kit. I am not supposed to kill you, only shut you up."

Fat chance. He'd just shot a cop. He would not hesitate to shoot Kit. Kit had to get away. He could hear the big man as he moved around the patrol car. Then he was quiet. A moment later, he could hear the tap of boots as the man walked back toward where Ari lay. "I'll need your flashlight, Deputy. You don't need it now." The big man laughed and then began to shine the light in the general direction that Kit had gone.

"I won't shoot you if you give yourself up," Hooknose said.

Kit didn't dare chance it. At least for now, he thought he was out of sight. He wasn't making good time, but he was getting farther away. He had been crawling in a straight line away from the road. He veered to the right a little. He didn't want to end up back at the road, but he felt like he needed to change direction as a diversionary measure.

The minutes dragged by. Kit was not very far from the patrol car, but he panicked when he heard Hooknose begin to talk on the phone. "I need help here, Sam. He got away. And someone might be coming. I've got to get rid of the patrol car and hide my truck."

For a moment, Hooknose didn't say anything.

"I had to shoot the deputy, Sam. Now I've got to get rid of him and his car before someone comes along. I've been lucky to go this long without other traffic."

He was silent again for a moment.

"Hey, Sam! I had to, I tell you! The deputy would have said something to the sheriff. I'll put him in the trunk of the car. Then I'll drive it somewhere. You get out here fast. Kit can't get away."

Several thoughts went through Kit's mind. First, this was all Sam Overmyer's doing. Second, if the guy drove off in the patrol car before Sam got back to the road, maybe he could steal the truck and make a run for it. He stopped crawling and listened. Hooknose sounded rattled now. "I did not screw up. You and Vince did. If you guys hadn't insisted that those guys go after him when you knew they were convicts and that they were lying about their identities, I wouldn't have had to shoot the deputy. Now get out here and help me find this guy! This is your mess, Sam, not mine. And I will not go down for killing a cop. You and Vince had better take care of me."

More silence, then Hooknose said, "You do that. I'm about forty-five minutes from Tonopah."

That seemed to be the end of the phone call. A moment later, Kit could hear Hooknose grunting. Then the trunk of the patrol car slammed down. He took a chance and peeked up. Hooknose was getting into his truck. He started it and pulled it out of the traffic lane and then shut it off. Then he ran back to the patrol car. Ari had not shut it off, so all Hooknose had to do was drive it away. Which he did, in a hurry. He did not go toward Tonopah. Instead, he turned and drove back toward Utah, but he did not go far before turning south onto a little side road.

Wasting no more time, Kit jumped up and ran for the truck. To his dismay, the keys were not in it, and Kit knew nothing about hotwiring a vehicle. He had no choice but to go on foot. Instead of going north, in the direction he'd been crawling, he started jogging south, hoping that would keep Hooknose off his trail.

As he ran, he did what he'd been doing a lot in the past few minutes: he prayed. He also kept looking back up the road. A car was approaching from the east. That couldn't be Sam; he'd be coming from the west. Kit was already too far from the road to flag it down. Now he wished he'd stayed closer.

Then he realized he'd done the right thing, for the car pulled to a stop and Hooknose jumped out. Then the car took off again. He'd hitched a ride back to his truck. Hooknose started shining his light around again. He could not have gone far in the patrol car, for Kit had seen him turn off the main road. And very little time had passed. Kit, thinking sadly about Deputy Ari Short, headed east as quickly as he could go, trying to stay hunched over so he wouldn't be easily seen.

If the deputy was dead, there would be nothing he could do. But if on the off chance he was still hanging onto life, Kit might be able to help him. He just needed to find the patrol car. When he'd watched Hooknose turn off the highway, it was to the south, so at least he wouldn't have to cross the highway.

Brandon's cell phone was ringing. He rolled over in bed and grabbed it. He had not heard from Lawrence since their conversation last evening. He couldn't imagine why he would be calling at this time of night. He guessed it was him calling. He answered without looking at his screen. "It's the middle of the night," he said grumpily.

"Brandon, it's Paizlee. Where are you?" Her voice was frantic.

"I'm in bed," he said, staying calm in an effort to offset her obvious panic.

"Brandon, you've got to do something," she said. "Kit's in trouble."

"Woah, Paizlee. What are you talking about? We know he's in trouble," he said, still maintaining his calm but feeling a sudden sense of urgency.

"No, I mean his life is in danger," she said. The panic in her voice had intensified.

"I don't understand. Has he called you?" Brandon asked.

"No, but I know he's in trouble."

"How do you know that?" Brandon asked reasonably.

"It's hard to explain, but I can feel it," she said.

"Wait a minute now," he said. "I need more than that."

"Okay, so you know how Kit and I are twins."

"Yeah," he said.

"So ever since we were little, we sometimes get these feelings about the other one when there's danger. If one of us gets hurt or is about to, the other one knows it," she said. "We've never really understood it, but it's real. I can feel that Kit's in danger, and I think it's really, really serious danger."

"He's either in jail or almost there. What kind of danger could he be in?" Brandon asked reasonably, even as he sensed that Paizlee was telling him the truth, that she knew something.

"Please, Brandon, I just know it. You've got to do something," she pleaded.

Brandon pictured Paizlee's face. As strange as it sounded, he did not try to tell her she was wrong. He wanted her to have faith in him, not get angry because he made her think that whatever was happening was too farfetched to be believable. "I'll head toward Tonopah and I'll call the jail there to see if he's arrived yet. That's all I can do. I'll call you as soon as I know something."

"Thanks, Brandon," she said. "That's all I can ask. But please hurry."

He made the call to the jail in Nevada, but all he was told was that Kit had not been delivered there yet. He also thought about calling Lawrence but decided not to. Within a few minutes, he was on the road, driving faster than he should, not knowing what he might be driving toward but trusting Paizlee's feelings and knowing that Kit was not at the jail yet.

Kit reached the patrol car. The keys were in the ignition, but the engine was not running. He grabbed the keys and opened the trunk. Ari didn't look good. He touched his carotid artery and shook his head sadly. The young deputy was dead. He shut the trunk and looked at the keys in the dim light of a quarter moon. There was a handcuff key there. He used it to take the handcuffs off and then tossed them into the trunk with Ari's body. He noticed that Ari's cell phone was clipped to his belt but that his pistol was gone. Shuddering, he took the phone. At least he could call someone now. He'd left his new phone with Paisley so it couldn't be stolen again.

He slammed the trunk down and tried to decide what to do. Maybe he could drive the patrol car and get away. He slipped into the seat and inserted the key. Lights came on in the dash, but the car wouldn't start. Hooknose must have done something to the engine. Kit finally called Brandon Phelps. "Brandon, it's Kit. I'm using the deputy's phone. Luckily he left fingerprints on the screen. It took me several tries but I got it to open. Anyway, I'm in danger and need some advice."

"That's what Paizlee told me a few minutes ago," Brandon said.

"Yeah, she would know," Kit said.

"Tell me what's happening."

Kit told him as quickly as he could, but he kept looking back up the road. Hooknose's flashlight was shining back and forth a short distance to the north of the truck. It didn't look like Sam had arrived yet. He told Brandon that. "What should I do?"

"You say the car won't start?"

"It won't. The lights in the dash work, but the engine won't turn on."

"You are sure the deputy is dead?" Brandon asked next.

"Oh yes, he's dead," Kit said, his voice choking at the thought.

"Where is his firearm?"

"It fell on the road when he tried to get Hooknose to drop his gun but got shot instead."

"He probably has a shotgun and maybe a backup weapon in his boot," Brandon said.

"I'll look," Kit said. After searching, he spoke again. "I found the shotgun. I'm getting it loose now."

"Good. Make sure it's loaded, and see if there are spare shells."

Kit found that it was loaded and also found a box of 00 Buck shells, which he jammed into his pocket. Then he opened the trunk once more, shuddering at the sight of the dead deputy. But he did as instructed. There was not a spare pistol in Ari's boot. He reported that to Brandon.

"Okay, stay put while I make a couple of calls and see if I can get some officers headed your way."

A couple of minutes later, Brandon called again. "I don't think they believe me. You should be getting a call on his police radio any second now if you have the car on."

Kit turned the key in the ignition, and a moment later a female voice came on the air using the call number he'd heard Ari use when they left Fillmore. Kit grabbed the mic and said, "Ari's dead. A guy shot him. The car won't start. This is Kit Troxler. There are some guys after me. They want to kill me too."

"Who is after you?" the calm voice asked.

"Some guy with a hooknose and lots of tattoos and Sam Overmyer," Kit said, trying to keep from panicking as he saw another vehicle stop next to Hooknose's.

"That might be Herbie Dinkin. He's a dangerous man. But what makes you think this man, Sam Overmyer, is helping him?"

"I heard Hooknose call him and tell him to come out and help find me," Kit reported, his voice cracking as he spoke.

He heard a smile in the dispatcher's voice when she said, "That's what a lot of people call Dinkin. Okay, another dispatcher is on the phone with the sheriff. He says for you to stay with the patrol car until we can get someone there. Your PI just called, and he tells me you have the officer's shotgun. He also wants you to stay with the patrol car. Help is on the way."

"There are two of them now. I'm sure one of them is Sam."

"No, it's not. An officer just talked to his father. He says he's in bed asleep."

"Really?" Kit asked bitterly. "But someone is with Hooknose now."

"I understand. Use the shotgun only if you have to," the dispatcher said.

"Shouldn't I try to get away? Oh no, a pickup is coming this way now," Kit said.

"Stay calm. If you can, move away from the road, but keep the shotgun with you," she said.

"Okay, but they'll be here soon." His voice was quivering.

He left the car and slipped into the brush a short distance to the east but tripped and felt his ankle give way. He tried to keep walking, but it hurt terribly and would not support him. He did the only thing he could now. He sat down and hid in the heavy brush. Then he waited, his heart in his throat. He could see the lights of the pickup as it turned off the highway and drove right up behind the patrol car. Someone got out of the pickup, and Hooknose shouted, "If you can hear me, you would be best to give yourself up now. Killing an officer carries the death penalty, and I saw you do it."

So now he was going to be accused of killing an officer? How much worse could it get? He stayed quiet and waited, his heart nearly jumping out of his chest.

CHAPTER ELEVEN

KIT HAD NOT HEARD OR seen the lights of the second vehicle come this way. Suddenly, he heard a faint crackling of what he feared was Hooknose moving around, searching for him. He held the shotgun and prepared to shoot if he had to, wishing his ankle wasn't hurting so badly. The crackling stopped just a few feet from his location. A moment later, he heard a car door slam, and a second man tromped toward Hooknose and the patrol car. He realized that whoever it was had ridden here with Hooknose and left his vehicle up the road.

He could hear every word the two men were saying.

"Sam told us he couldn't come, that he was too far away. He said it was up to us now," Hooknose said.

"Kit's here somewhere," the other man said. "I'm sure."

"I don't know about that, Blaine," Hooknose said. "The little bugger is scared. He's probably running south as fast as he can."

"Or north," Blaine said. One of the men walked over to the patrol car and looked inside for a minute. "Dinkin, I think the kid's got Ari's shotgun! It's not in the car. He's been here!"

"That's bad. I should have taken it, but I had no idea he would get this far. So he did come here," Hooknose said. "We've got to find him. He can't be far. We may not have long. He may have called for help."

"Then let's go right now," Blaine said.

"Not yet. I've got a shotgun in my truck. I'll fire a few shots out into the brush. If he's close, who knows, I might hit him."

"You said Sam wants him left alive," Blaine said. "You said we've got to make it look like he shot the deputy and tried to get away."

"Too bad. Sam's not out here. It's up to me now, and I say he has to die!"

So even though Sam wasn't here, he had clearly been giving the orders. A moment later, Kit heard the unmistakable sound of a shotgun being racked. He ducked low to the ground only a second before Hooknose started shooting. Kit could hear the small BBs hitting the brush near him. He held his shotgun, ready to shoot if he got a target, but before he did, he felt his left arm go numb as some shot from the shotgun struck him. Another shot blasted the air, and this time, some of the tiny balls hit Kit's face. He fell flat from his crouched position.

"Did you hear that?" Hooknose asked. "It sounded like I hit him. Go see. I'll cover you."

"You go," Blaine said. "This ain't my fight."

"It is now," Hooknose said. "If he moves, you have your pistol. You know what to do."

"Sam ain't going to like this," Blaine complained, but Kit could hear him starting toward him.

Kit was in a bad position, and he knew it. But he struggled to sit up and hold the gun toward the approaching man. It was the little light from the moon reflecting from Blaine's pistol that alerted Kit to the fact that the man was almost to him.

"I see him," Blaine said. "He's still alive!"

"Then take care of him," Hooknose ordered with bloodthirsty coldness.

Kit raised the gun, and as he pulled the trigger, so did Blaine. Kit fell backwards in shuddering pain, and he felt blood oozing from him. He'd been hit.

Kit slowly faded toward unconsciousness as he heard Hooknose shouting, "You fool, Blaine." And then he began to curse. Kit didn't hear anything more.

Brandon's phone rang. He was driving as fast as he dared, knowing that Kit was somewhere needing help. A call from Lawrence a short while ago confirmed what he already knew; Kit never made it to the jail.

Brandon slowed down a little and verbally answered his phone through the Bluetooth. He assumed it was Lawrence calling with an update. But it was Paizlee's voice that filled his Bronco, panicked and frightened. "Brandon, Kit's been hurt really badly. He might die," she said.

Brandon didn't ask her how she knew, but he accepted what she said. "I'm hurrying as fast as I dare. And I'm praying for him."

"So am I," Paizlee said. "Our attorney called me. He said that Kit didn't ever make it to the jail. Where could he be?"

"I'll do everything I can to figure it out," Brandon promised without telling her that he'd already spoken to Kit. "He'll be okay," he said, trying to project confidence into his voice.

"I already know that he isn't," she said hopelessly.

"Paizlee, have faith," Brandon said. "I'll call you back in a little while."

He called the dispatcher again. "Your client talked to us on our police radio right after I talked to you," she said. "He told us that the guy who killed our officer was coming his way. I told him to get away from the car. We sent officers to the location we believe Mr. Troxler was. They found the deputy's patrol car. There's a lot of blood around but no bodies."

"So are you suggesting there was more shooting?" Brandon asked fearfully.

"Oh yes, for sure. Just a second. I have a call coming in. Stay on the phone."

He waited for three of four minutes before the dispatcher came back on the line. "Sorry to keep you waiting. There is a truck on the highway that is registered to a fellow named Blaine Ruley who is frequently in trouble. We believe another fellow by the name of Herbie Dinkin was the one who shot our officer. Mr. Troxler told us that it was a guy with a badly hooked nose. Some people call him Hooknose. He fits the description your client gave us. I'm sorry, but that's all I can tell you. I've got another call coming in." Just like that, the call was disconnected.

Brandon was devastated. He'd promised to call Paizlee back, but he had nothing hopeful to tell her. He thought for several minutes about what he should say to her. He needed to give her some hope, even though there was not a lot of hope available right now. It was almost certain that Kit was in the hands of a cop killer, something he did not want her to know.

His phone rang. It was the Millard County Sheriff, who introduced himself and then said, "Kit's foreman is worried sick. He told me who you are and gave me your number so I could tell you what I told Andy."

"Kit's sister called me a few hours ago. She's scared to death for Kit," Brandon said. "I talked to the dispatcher in Tonopah a short while ago. What she told me was not encouraging. Maybe they told you more than they told me."

"I'll tell you what I know. Then we'll both know all they are willing to tell us," Sheriff Ledford said. The only thing Brandon was told that he hadn't already heard was that there was a lot of blood out in the brush a short distance from a spot where it appeared a vehicle had been parked.

"I wish I hadn't let Kit go with that deputy," Sherriff Ledford said. "I should have waited until morning and then drove him there myself. There's no question that this whole thing was an attempt to get Kit killed. And even though Sam's father claims Sam Overmyer was home all night and Sergeant Hodson was on a transport to pick up a prisoner in California, I'm sure those two orchestrated the whole thing. I think they thought getting his bond revoked would not hold up so they decided on more drastic measures."

The two talked for another minute or two. Then, each promising to bring the other up to date on anything they learned, the call ended. It was just in time too, for Paizlee was calling again.

"Have you learned anything else?" she asked with a tremor in her voice.

"Nothing conclusive. The authorities are searching."

"Brandon. I've been praying nonstop since I talked to you a little while ago. I feel like he's hurt badly, but I'm almost certain that he's alive."

He had a hard time responding to her, but he tried for a moment longer. "Paizlee, you are a woman of great faith. Keep praying, and I will too."

Kit awoke to a great deal of intense pain in his abdomen and lesser pain on his face. He was in the back of a pickup truck. As he became more aware of his surroundings, he realized he wasn't alone back there. Next to him was the dead body of Deputy Short. There was also another body. It had to be the man who had shot him with a pistol at the same moment Kit shot at him with the shotgun. Kit was very weak, but he managed to turn far enough to determine that the man he knew only as Blaine was dead. *I killed him.* The very thought was almost more than he could bear. Tears flowed, and his whole body trembled with the horror of it.

The truck was on a terribly rough road, probably a long way from civilization. It stopped and then backed up a bit, turning as it did. When it stopped, Hooknose got out and looked into the back of the truck. He chuckled. Then he opened the tailgate and pulled all three of them from the back. When Kit hit the ground, the pain was jarring. But he managed to keep from crying out. He wanted Hooknose to believe he was dead.

Kit kept his eyes shut and lay as still as he could as Hooknose walked around the three of them, and finally, he said, "Well, Mr. Kit, dead men can't ride racehorses. Sam and Vince should be happy." With that, the killer got in his truck and drove away.

A massive search was launched in an attempt to find the missing officer, Kit, and the two outlaws, Blaine and Hooknose. Volunteers took to the sky in planes. Others drove their vehicles, and a few even went out on horseback.

Lawrence had his own plane. He'd flown since he was a young man. It was what he liked to do when he needed to get away from the intense pressures of his job. His wife didn't like to fly, nor did his legal secretary, Jenna Hubbard. He felt like he should put his other work aside and join in the search for his client simply because he could.

He came into the office at seven that morning, dressed in jeans and a polo shirt. "You don't look like you plan to work today," Jenna said with a smile. She was always early at the office.

"I'm going to take my plane up and join in the search for our client. I could use a spotter. Would you like to go?" he asked Jenna.

"You know better than that," she said with a frown.

"I know. What's Wiona doing today?"

"She was planning to help me a little later," Jenna said. "But knowing that girl, if you asked her, she'd join you in a heartbeat."

"I'll call her," Lawrence said. "I could use another pair of eyes."

"Hi, Lawrence," Wiona answered when he called. "Have they found Kit yet? I'm just sick worrying about him."

"Worrying won't help, but if you'd like to join me, you and I could fly down and search from the air," he said.

"Are you serious? I'd love to go."

"I'd like to be in the air within a half hour. You know where I keep my plane. Can you meet me there?" Lawrence asked.

"Yes. I'll hurry," she said. "We've just got to find him."

He ended the call, and with a smile, he said to Jenna, "I think your daughter has been struck by Cupid's arrow."

Jenna looked up from her desk. "You can say that again. Kit's all she talks about."

A half hour later, Lawrence and Wiona were winging south.

Brandon also joined in the search. He called Paizlee to let her know what he was doing. "I wish I could help," Paizlee fretted. "I'm crazy with worry. He's alive, I'm sure of it. But I'm scared that he will die if he isn't found soon."

"There are a bunch of planes going up to help now that it's light. I'm going to drive out on the road where the young deputy's patrol car was found," he said. "I talked to Lawrence earlier. By now he and Wiona will be on their way. He owns a plane and flies. I don't suppose you knew that."

"No, but that's great." Paizlee said. "Andy and Greg want to help too."

"I think the best thing you and the two of them can do is take care of the ranch," Brandon said.

"I guess, but I feel so useless," she responded.

"You are not useless," he assured her.

"I wish I were there with you," Paizlee said plaintively.

"I wish you were too," Brandon responded, and he realized how much he would like that. But for now, he needed to help find Kit.

Sam's phone woke him. "Hey, it's Herbie. Things didn't end well."

"What are you talking about?" Sam asked as he tried to get the cobwebs out of his head.

"Kit got the deputy's shotgun. He killed Blaine, but we got him too," Herbie said.

"Are you telling me you guys killed Kit?" Sam asked angrily.

"Self-defense," Herbie said. "He gave us no choice, and now Blaine is dead thanks to him."

For a moment Sam didn't respond as his brain tried to accept what he'd just heard. "Okay, I guess it couldn't be helped. Vince and I just wanted to talk to him before we took care of him. But you gotta keep out of sight, Herbie. The cops will be after you big time, and I don't think Vince can help much. I'll be in touch with you, and we'll meet up somewhere. Right now, I gotta make my dad think everything's okay."

"All right," Herbie said. "But you and Vince gotta help me."

"We've got your back, Herbie," Sam said.

CHAPTER TWELVE

RANDALL HAD BEEN WORKING SINCE daylight. He liked to work with his men when he could. To his amazement, Sam joined them a few minutes later. "Okay, Dad, what do you need me to do?"

Randall looked at his son for a moment, unsure why Sam wanted to help but grateful that he did. "Bruce and I were going to ride out to check the cows and the water, but if you wouldn't mind going with him, I could stay here and help a couple of the other guys exercise the colts."

"Sure, Dad, I'd like that. I'll get a horse saddled right now."

Randall shook his head. Was this really his son? Maybe he was turning over a new leaf. He'd been working out the best way to confront Sam about the things missing from the safe, but this new side of Sam made him rethink his plan.

An hour later, as he led one of his best colts back to the barn, he was surprised to see a Nye County Sheriff's vehicle coming down the lane at high speeds. At first, he assumed it was his nephew, which did not give him any pleasure. He very much disliked Vince. But as the Expedition drew closer, he recognized the county sheriff himself and one of his deputies. What in the world could they want?

Sheriff Nick Watson parked, spotted Randall, and got out of his vehicle, his deputy close behind. Randall tied the colt to a hitching rail and waited while they approached.

"Morning, Sheriff. What brings you men out this way?"

"We need to talk to your son," Sheriff Watson said, his voice very serious and his face dark. "Is he around?"

Randall felt a twinge in his gut before responding with, "Sam's out with my foreman on a horse checking some cows."

"When do you expect him back?"

"Not for several hours," Randall said. "What do you need to see him about?"

The sheriff and his deputy exchanged a quick glance, and then Sheriff Watson said, "We need to know where he was last night."

"He was here all night," Randall said, relief washing over him. If there was trouble, he could not have been involved. "You look stressed, Sheriff. What's going on?" Randall shifted his feet nervously and wiped some sweat from his brow with a bandana he pulled from a rear pocket of his jeans.

"A deputy was shot and killed last night. He was bringing Kit Troxler back to jail for violating the terms of his bail release," the sheriff said.

"Really? What did Troxler do?" Randall asked in shock.

"According to your son, he saw him on the ranch sneaking around. He was specifically ordered to stay off your place."

Randall felt faint. He removed his hat and rubbed his forehead again. His weak heart didn't need this kind of stress. "When did Sam see him here?"

The sheriff told him. Randall took a deep breath and, shaking his head, said, "That's not possible."

"Sam said it was," the sheriff said with narrowed eyes. "Why don't you think it was possible?"

"I don't think it; I know it," Randall said. "Kit was in Wyoming then."

"Or so he claims?" Sheriff Watson prompted.

"Sheriff, Kit and his sister and a private investigator met with me that evening in Wyoming. So I know he couldn't have been here. Are you saying that he was brought back to jail on Sam's say-so?"

"Actually, Randall, he didn't make it to the jail," Sheriff Watson said coldly. "Someone stopped him on the road several miles out of Tonopah, shot and killed Deputy Short, and also, we think, shot Kit."

Randall felt a jolt pass through him. "Let's go in the house and sit down where it's cool."

"No, we can talk right here," the sheriff said firmly. "Do you know a guy by the name of Herbie Dinkin? He's also known as Hooknose."

Randall was feeling sicker by the moment. "I'm afraid he's a friend of Sam's. Why do you ask?"

"That's who we believe killed Deputy Short. It seems Herbie ambushed Deputy Short and Kit. We are searching for him as well as another fellow by the name of Blaine Ruley. You may know him too."

"He's another friend of Sam's. I'm afraid my son doesn't keep the best of company."

"Yeah, that's right," Sheriff Watson agreed, anger and disgust in his voice. "We need to take Sam in. He lied to get Kit back in jail, and now we think Kit might be dead."

"Oh, Sheriff, I'm sorry. But I do know Sam was here all night." Randall could only hope that Sam was innocent of any involvement, but his pained heart told him differently.

"I will need to seize his cell phone. Does he have it with him?"

"I'm sure he does," Randall said, trying to suppress the pain. "He wasn't acting like himself this morning, Sheriff. Now I think I understand why."

"What do you mean, Randall?"

"Sam is lazy. I can't get him to lift a hand around here. But this morning, he came out and wanted to know what he could do to help. That's never happened before."

"Randall, I need to find him as soon as possible."

"Let me call my foreman," Randall said, "and find out exactly where they're at."

"Randall, do not tell Bruce why you need to know where he is," the sheriff said firmly.

"Okay. I understand. I'm so sorry about all this. But I can understand where you're coming from. Sam lied, and now you have a dead deputy and possibly a dead young rancher. I'll help you in whatever way I can," Randall said with almost overwhelming sorrow. "He's my son, but this is too much."

He called Bruce's cell phone number. As soon as Bruce answered, Randall said, "Where are you exactly?"

"Gee, let's see," Bruce said. After a moment, he explained his approximate location. "What do you need, Boss?"

"I've had something come up, and I need your help back here—yours and Sam's."

"Okay, Sam and I will head that way right now."

"Thanks, Bruce," Randall said. "Maybe I'll come out to meet you. I'll bring a four-wheeler."

"Sounds good, Boss," Bruce said.

Randall, sick at heart and feeling frighteningly faint, put his phone back in his pocket. "I've got several four-wheelers. Would you two like to ride out to meet Bruce and Sam?"

"I think we'd better," the sheriff said.

"Give me just a minute. My heart is weak, and I need to run take a couple of pills," Randall said.

"We can do this alone if we need to," Sheriff Watson said.

"No, I'll be fine in a moment."

He was already feeling better when he came back from the house. "Okay, we can go now." As they rode, Randall was having dark, troubling thoughts. Had Sam's racehorse not died, he would have been racing him in California later this week. He was pretty sure that Kit would have also been planning to ride down there. As much as he hated to admit it, he was certain now that Sam had found a way to keep Kit from riding. Jealousy was a terrible thing. And there was no question that Sam was jealous. Beyond that, lies did untold damage, and Randall knew that Sam had lied yet again.

With what he'd just learned, Randall admitted to himself that Kit Troxler had not caused the death of Sam's horse. He had no idea who had, but Sam had made up the story of seeing Kit that morning, the same as he had made up the story of seeing him again, a date upon which Randall knew Kit could not have been here on his ranch.

After a couple of miles, Randall could see Bruce and Sam riding toward them. He dreaded what was about to happen, but it had to. Sam had to be stopped. Because of him, a fine young deputy had died and possibly Kit Troxler as well. As hard as it was for him as a father, it was time to put an end to it.

The sheriff pulled to a stop. "We'll wait here till they reach us," he said to Randall and the deputy.

Sam, when he and Bruce were close enough to recognize the officers, reined his horse around and rode back the other way as hard as his horse would go. "Let's go after him," Randall said and started his four-wheeler.

"We've got to stop Sam," Randall shouted at Bruce a moment later. "Try to catch him. We'll try as well."

It was rough country out there, and the men on four-wheelers had a hard time going as fast as the horses did. Bruce, however, an accomplished horseman and former jokey, was gaining on Sam. The men on the four-wheelers kept going, but it was not easy. Bruce caught up with Sam. He rode up alongside him, but Sam suddenly swerved toward him and gave Bruce a shove, unseating him. Bruce managed to get his feet from the stirrups as he went off the horse, saving himself from being dragged.

He landed in a heap on the ground. Sam kept going. Randall and the officers were soon able to reach Bruce, who by then was on his feet and brushing himself off. "Are you okay, Bruce?" Randall asked.

"Yeah, but I could have been killed. What's the matter with that kid?" Bruce asked as he brushed himself off.

Randall watched Sam as he faded into the distance. There was no catching him now. Randall turned to Bruce. "Because of Sam, one of Sheriff Watson's deputies is dead, and there's a very good chance that Kit Troxler is too." Bruce's deeply tanned face went pasty. But he did not question what he'd just been told. "Sorry, Boss. I didn't think he would try something like that. I was going to grab his horse's bridle and try to stop him."

The sheriff was on his cell phone. His deputy walked toward where Bruce's horse had finally stopped. He caught him and started back. Sheriff Watson finished his call. "I'm sorry, Randall," he said. "But we're going to have to find Sam and arrest him."

"That might not be easy. He'll ride into the mountains. And I suspect one of his buddies, when he calls one, will meet him somewhere, and he'll be long gone," Randall said. "I don't know where I went wrong with him. When we get back, I'd like you to stick around for a minute while I check something in my house," Randall said.

"Sure. Just as long as it doesn't take too long. We need to get back to Tonopah," Sheriff Watson said.

It didn't take long after they went into the house for Randall to do what he'd put off doing simply because he hadn't wanted to face what Sam might have done. He opened his safe, reached inside, and pulled some things out. "I had a bunch of cash in here and a couple of valid credit cards that I wasn't using. Most of the cash is gone and so is one of the cards."

"Why would Sam steal from you? Didn't he have plenty of money?" Sheriff Watson asked.

"I closed his bank account, froze his credit and debit cards, and told him he would have to earn whatever he was willing to work for." Randall shook his head and sat down in a large chair. "I'm sorry, Sheriff. I hope you catch him soon, and his friends too."

Bruce came in, and, seeing Randall sitting there looking quite weak, asked, "Randall, your heart is acting up, isn't it?"

"I'm afraid so," Randall said. "I took some pills, but I think I'd better rest for a while."

"I'm terribly sorry, Boss," Bruce said.

"So am I," Randall said. "I'll try to get out and help in a few hours. I just need some time." He moaned. "Oh, what has Sam done? Those Troxler twins are truly fine people. I just hope Kit is not dead. If he is, I don't know if I can take it."

"Lawrence, I think I see something down there," Wiona said excitedly.

He banked his plane as he said, "Don't lose track of what you saw, Wiona. I'm going to fly lower." He turned the plane and flew it as low as he dared while Wiona continued to stare down.

"There! Right there!" she cried out.

"I see it now. Looks like three bodies. One of them has a uniform. Oh, Wiona," he moaned.

"Kit's got to be alive. He just has to be." She was unable to stop tears from coursing down her cheeks.

Lawrence didn't reply, as he was on his radio calling in the location. As soon as he finished, he said, "See if you can reach Brandon again." They had been coordinating with him and trying to stay close to where he was searching.

A moment later, he answered. "Have you found something?"

"Yes. Where are you? I'll try to get to them."

"I'll look for your plane, and you look for me," Brandon said. "Stay on the phone."

A minute later, Brandon said, "I see you guys. Lead me to where Kit is."

Brandon drove like a madman in the terribly rough terrain, but even then, Lawrence had to keep circling back to make sure they didn't lose each other. Finally, Brandon came over a ridge and spotted the bodies several yards off the rough track of a road, if it could even be called a road. He leaped from his Bronco and ran to them. There was no question that the deputy and the man he assumed was Blaine were dead. But as he knelt beside Kit, who was lying on his back, the hot Nevada sun burning his bloody face, he could see his chest slowly rising, then dropping back again. Into his phone, which was still connected to Wiona, he said, "Kit's alive. I need to see what I can do for him. Get a life flight helicopter on the way."

A former Navy Seal, Brandon was at home in situations like this. He began to check Kit very closely. He'd been hit by several shotgun pellets, some on his face, but fortunately, none of them had hit an eye. What worried him most was a nasty bullet wound in Kit's abdomen. It had bled a lot but was no longer bleeding, or he would surely have died by now. But it was extremely life-threatening.

He sprinted back to his Bronco, grabbed his first aid kit, a very large one with a lot of supplies an ordinary person would not know how to use. He laid a blanket over Kit, more to keep the sun from baking him than anything else. Then he folded it back to where he could see Kit's abdomen. He quickly cut away his clothing. Infection was already setting in. He cleaned the wound the best he could and applied disinfectant before bandaging it.

He gently rolled Kit partway over. He found what he had feared he would; the bullet had gone all the way through. The exit wound was nasty, and it also appeared infected. He ran back to his vehicle and grabbed another blanket. He laid it on the ground next to Kit and slowly, carefully, rolled him onto it. Then he repeated what he'd done in front. When that was done, he propped Kit on one side and began to clean the dozen or so small wounds from the shotgun.

Brandon was aware of Lawrence still circling overhead. He was relieved when he finally heard the distinct thump of an approaching helicopter. His phone rang. He took it from his pocket and looked at the screen. It was Paizlee. He answered. "Brandon, has anyone found Kit yet?" she asked.

"I'm with him. He's alive, Paizlee."

"I knew it. I knew it!" she cried. "Who found him?"

He explained briefly. "Paizlee, I'll call you back. There is a Life Flight helicopter getting ready to set down. I need to direct them."

"Okay, but how bad is he hurt?" she asked, her voice trembling.

"It's bad, but he'll live. I gave him a blessing. Keep praying like you have been."

CHAPTER THIRTEEN

KIT WOKE UP TO THE smell of antiseptics and the sound of beeping instruments. Someone was leaning over him. He felt gentle fingers easing one eyelid open. Light flooded in. Then the eye closed again. "Kit, I'm Dr. Rachel Jones. Can you hear me?"

Kit could hear her, but barely. He tried to speak, but his mouth hurt badly. He tried to open his mouth, but it felt as big as a sack of oats.

"Wiggle a finger on your right hand if you can hear me," Dr. Jones instructed him.

He managed to do that.

"You're in the hospital in Tonopah." At least he was alive, but his mind was fuzzy. He was trying to remember what had happened. She helped him again. "You were shot several times, but you are going to live. Wiggle a finger again if you remember that happening."

For a while, he tried to recall. Finally, a vague impression of someone with a crooked nose and lots of tattoos came to his mind.

"Do you remember yet?" she asked gently.

He wiggled a finger, but the memory was still fuzzy. He wanted to say something, but he simply couldn't.

"You have been hurt badly. But you will recover. We will be moving you into surgery in a few minutes. The surgeon is on his way. Do you understand?"

He moved a finger.

She sounded so nice. He wanted to see her and, after some effort, finally managed to open his eyes. She was younger than he had imagined. She smiled at him. "You can go back to sleep now. And don't worry. We'll take good care of you."

He faded again into welcome oblivion.

The next time Kit woke up, he was able to open his eyes. But he shut them quickly again, as it was too bright. He knew he was in a hospital, but he was still fuzzy over what had happened to him. A nurse hovered over him and asked, "How are you feeling?"

He hurt all over. "I guess okay," he lied, his words slurred but his mouth working.

"You're in recovery. Your surgery went well. The doctor will tell you more later."

"What kind . . . of surgery?" he asked, still slurring his words. He opened his eyes again and managed to keep them open.

She chuckled pleasantly. "Do you not remember getting shot?"

His eyes opened wider. "I got shot?" he asked dumbly.

"Yes, I'm afraid so, but you will have a complete recovery."

"Where did I get shot?" he asked.

"Somewhere in the desert east of here," she responded.

He thought about that for a moment. "No . . . where . . . on my body?"

"The worst was in your abdomen," she said. "But you'll be okay."

Kit was quickly becoming more alert. "The worst?" he asked.

"Yes. You also had a lot of shotgun pellets on your face, your neck, and your arms."

He stayed quiet for a long while after that as the nurse fussed around doing whatever it was that nurses did. He opened and closed his mouth a couple of times. Something didn't feel right. He began to feel with his tongue. He knew what his mouth felt like, or what it should feel like. He again felt with his tongue. Finally he figured it out. One of his top front teeth was badly chipped!

"Nurse," he said.

"Can I help you with something?" she asked.

"What happened . . . to my tooth?"

"Apparently one of the pellets from the shotgun you were shot with hit that tooth and broke it."

"Can it . . . be fixed?" he asked.

She chuckled. "You are coming out of the anesthesia just fine. I'll be able to move you to a room shortly."

"My tooth?"

She shrugged her shoulders. "It can be fixed. You'll probably need a cap."

"Did I swallow it?"

"I'm sorry, Mr. Troxler, but I honestly don't know. The doctor, during surgery, had to remove some pellets that were embedded in your skin, both on your face, your neck, and both arms. Count yourself lucky," she said. "You could have lost an eye or both eyes. You'll be fine."

He again grew quiet. He hurt, but he suspected he would hurt a lot more later on. Right now, he was drugged up. A fellow in scrubs stepped close to him. "Are you the doctor?" Kit asked.

"No, I'm a nurse. I'm just here to help move you to your room," he said.

Kit did not expect a greeting party. In fact, he hadn't really given it any thought. He was just now starting to recall what had happened to him. But his sister rushed to his side as they pushed the bed into the room. "Kit, I've been so scared for you. How do you feel?"

"I don't feel much but what I do is not fun," he said. He was able to talk better now. "How did you get here?"

"Lawrence gave me a ride in his plane," she said.

"What? Attorneys don't fly planes," he said.

"This one does," Lawrence said with a deep chuckle as he stepped over to the bed.

"What are you doing here?" Kit asked. "I thought lawyers were supposed to work in courtrooms, not hospitals."

"Kit, you are talking a little crazy," his sister said with a big grin.

"That's normal when a person is coming out of anesthesia," the nurse said. "Later, he might not remember what he said."

"That's good."

Another face appeared above him. Kit caught his breath. "Wiona?"

"Yes, it's me. And I look like me. But you sure don't look like you," she said with a huge grin.

"That's cause I've got a broken tooth," he said. "I liked that tooth. How am I gonna bite apples now?"

"You'll figure it out," Wiona said. She studied him for a minute. "I think you look quite cute, Kit."

"So do you," he said. Wiona smiled. Unlike his, her smile was gorgeous and her dimples deep. "How did you get here?"

"The same way Paizlee did. I flew."

Another face stepped into view. "Brandon," Kit said.

"It was Wiona who found you. It's good to see you."

"Where did you find me?" he asked.

"Down on the ground. Lawrence and I were in his plane looking for you," Wiona said. "Brandon was looking from the ground. After we found you, he followed the plane to where you were lying. He patched you up really well and gave you a blessing."

"So you didn't fly, Brandon?"

"No, well, yes, I sort of did. I mean, I drove awfully fast," he said.

Kit closed his eyes. A terrible memory was coming back. "Ari's dead, isn't he?"

"If you mean Deputy Short, then yes, he is," Brandon said.

"It's my fault," Kit said.

"No, don't blame yourself, Kit," Lawrence said. "It was Sam's fault and his friend Herbie, also known as Hooknose."

"Hooknose," Kit said. He squeezed his eyes tightly. "I'm remembering now. Ari told him to drop his gun, but he shot Ari down like he was nothing but a rat. Where is he?"

"We don't know, but the cops are looking for him and for Sam Overmyer," Brandon said.

"Sam lied when he said I came on his ranch again," Kit said. "He tells deadly lies."

"Yes, he does. I talked to Sheriff Watson, the sheriff of Nye County," Brandon said. "He told me that it was Randall Overmyer who figured out you couldn't have been on his ranch because the date Sam told everyone you were there, including the judge, was the very day we met with Randall in Wyoming."

"So he believes me now?" Kit asked.

"Yes, and he's convinced you could not have killed Sam's horse," Brandon said. "And he knows Sam lied about what he did to you at the race that started all this trouble."

Kit was having a hard time keeping his eyes open. But suddenly, he was wide awake again as another memory returned. "Did I kill Hooknose's, I mean, Herbie's friend?"

It was Lawrence who took over now. "Yes, in self-defense. It was Blaine who shot you in the abdomen. Herbie is the one who peppered you with shotgun pellets."

"But I killed a man. Oh no, I would never have done something like that. I'm so sorry. I shouldn't have shot him. I'll have nightmares about it the rest of my life. I hope God can forgive me."

"If you hadn't shot him, Kit, they would have finished you off. So don't let it worry you," Lawrence said. "You might also be interested to know that I talked with the prosecutor. He assured me that all charges against you regarding Sam's horse are going to be dismissed."

"We can be grateful for that at least," his twin sister said as she moved beside the bed and gently took hold of one of his hands.

To Kit's surprise and delight, Wiona stepped to the other side and held that hand. He looked at both girls, smiled, and said, "Thank you for all you've done for me." He could no longer keep his eyes open. But as he drifted off, he said with tears streaming down his face, "I killed a man. Ohh."

When Kit woke up again, it was because a nurse was there. She apologized but explained that she needed to check his vital signs. He nodded. "Did everyone leave?" he asked.

"If you're talking about Brandon and Lawrence, yes they did," Paizlee said. "I'm not leaving you."

"I'm not either," Wiona said.

While the nurse was still fussing around him, someone else entered the room. "You're the doctor that fixed me," Kit said.

"Yes, I am. I was assisted by Dr. Jones. My name is Dr. Ivan Sturgeon," he said.

Wiona with her quick wit said, "So when you operated on Kit, you were Dr. Ivan Surgeon."

He chuckled. "I get that sometimes. Let me tell you what I did to you, Kit."

"For him," Paizlee corrected.

"Yes, I guess you could say that," he agreed.

Dr. Sturgeon was probably a couple of inches taller than Kit with light brown hair and clear blue eyes. "You had some shotgun pellets in a number of places. I had to remove several that were embedded in your flesh, but you'll heal up okay. There shouldn't be too much scarring. The bullet to your gut was dangerous. I had to remove three short sections of your small intestine." He smiled. "I hooked it all up again though. It will bother you for a while, but eventually you'll be good as new. As for your broken tooth, you will need that repaired too. That will be up to your dentist."

"Thank you, Doctor," Kit said.

"It will be a few days before you can eat solid food, so don't expect to get out of here anytime soon," the doctor informed him.

They talked for a little longer, and then the doctor and the nurse both left, with a promise to keep a close eye on him. After he was gone, Paizlee and Wiona both approached his bed. Once again, his hands were in theirs. "Paizlee told me about how she knew you were hurt but also how she knew you were still alive. She says it's a twin thing. I think it's neat," Wiona said.

"I'm glad you're here, Wiona, but why are you?" Kit asked.

"Don't be dense, Kit," Paizlee said. "You two made a connection the first time you met. And don't deny it."

He had nothing to say to that. He just hoped it was really true. There was something about this red-haired girl that was special. He definitely wanted to get to know her better.

The three of them enjoyed a companionable silence for several minutes. It was finally Kit who broke the spell. "So, Paizlee, tell me this. Did you and Brandon also make a connection?" She blushed, and he grinned as much as his sore mouth would let him. "I thought so."

The next morning, Kit was surprised to see that both girls were at his bedside. "How long have you guys been here?" he asked.

"We haven't left," Paizlee said. "We both want to make sure nobody hurts you again."

"So you guys are my bodyguards," he said. His smile came less painfully this morning. "You both look really good."

"We brushed our hair, our teeth, and put on fresh makeup," Paizlee said.

"Just for you," Wiona added. "We can't have you looking at ugly faces, now can we?"

A thought slid easily through his mind as his eyes caught Wiona's. If there was a future for the two of them, he would never complain about all the trouble he'd been subjected to. Well, he might complain some, but it would have been worth it, for he would never have met her otherwise.

"Have you talked to Brandon?" Kit asked as his eyes transferred from Wiona's to Paizlee's.

She blushed again. "I guess we don't need him anymore. For that matter, we don't need our attorney either."

"You guys don't know those two very well," Wiona said. "I talked to my mother a few minutes ago. She told me that Lawrence is going to make sure you are justly compensated for your loss. And Brandon is going to keep investigating. They both want to find out who killed Sam's racehorse."

"Does it matter at this point?" Kit asked.

"Yes, it does," his sister said.

"He wants to find out all he can about Sam and his friends and, as he puts it, his enemies," Wiona added.

"But he told me that he won't charge us," Paizlee revealed.

"He has to," Kit said. "He has to make a living."

"He'll be okay, believe me," Wiona told him. "He's not a poor man."

"I still will pay him," Kit said with determination.

"You don't know Brandon," Wiona said with a dimpled grin.

"And you don't know me," he countered.

"I hope to though," she said with a twinkle in her eye.

That took the argument out of him.

An hour later, Doctor Sturgeon came in. He shooed the girls out with, "I need to check Kit's incision."

When he had finished, the girls came back in, followed by a tall, slender man in his mid-fifties wearing a uniform. "I'm Sheriff Nick Watson," he said. "Are you up to talking to me for a few minutes, Mr. Troxler?"

"I guess so," he said unenthusiastically.

"Do we need to leave?" Paizlee asked.

"Depends on who you are," he said.

"I'm Kit's sister, Paizlee, and this is our really good friend Wiona. She works for our attorney."

"Lawrence Heslop," Sheriff Watson said. "I've spoken to him on the phone. He sounds like a very efficient man."

"He is," Wiona said.

Kit spoke up, "Sheriff, I'm so sorry about Deputy Short."

"Thank you," the sheriff said soberly. "He will be missed, believe me. He had a bright future ahead of him."

"Was he married?" Kit asked.

"Engaged," the sheriff said. "Believe me, folks, my staff and I will not rest until we catch Herbie and Sam."

"What about Sam's cousin?" Paizlee asked with some determination.

"Yes, about him. I fired him a few minutes ago, and then arrested him. He's in jail as we speak. I've been worried about him for some time. I was hearing things, but no one could prove anything. Still, I never would have believed he was capable of planting evidence to convict an innocent man." The sheriff turned to Paizlee. "I'm sorry to have to tell you this, but I'll need testimony at some point from you about the evidence he planted in Kit's truck and the theft of those receipts from Kit's jockey box."

"I didn't actually see him put anything in there," Paizlee said. "I just saw him open the door and lean inside."

"That's all I need. A couple of my other deputies served a search warrant on his house just before I came over here. Your receipts, registration, insurance papers, and so on were in a drawer in his bedroom. That sinks him."

"I can't say I feel bad," Kit said. "So what do you need from me?"

"I want you to tell me all you can about the accusations that Sam and Vince leveled against you," he said.

It took close to an hour, and the sheriff recorded it all. "We'll catch Sam and Herbie, I promise you. They will both go to prison for the rest of their lives. Even though it was Herbie who killed Deputy Short, we can prove that Sam was an accessory. He will also be charged with murder, the same as if he'd actually been there. And if I can show that Vince was in any way involved in the events that led up to the death of Deputy Short, he will also go to prison for the rest of his life."

"That's good," Paizlee said with fire in her eyes. "Their lies really caused us a lot of trouble."

"For which I am sorry," Sheriff Watson said.

He rose to leave but stopped at the door. "You guys watch your backs. I wouldn't put it beyond the two of them to try to harm you more." With those alarming words, the sheriff left.

Not one time had anyone mentioned the race in California. Kit had thought of it a lot. But what was done was done. There were other races, and he hoped he would recover fully, for he was not about to give up on that exciting part of his life.

CHAPTER FOURTEEN

THE SHERIFF WASN'T THE LAST visitor to come to Kit's hospital room. Kit was shocked when Randall Overmyer walked in, his gray cowboy hat in his hand and his face sad. He set the hat down and faced Kit. "I'm sorry," he said. "I hope you can find it in your heart to forgive me someday."

"You didn't do anything to me," Kit said.

"I wish I could look at it that way, but I can't. I thought I was raising a son, but what I raised was a monster."

"Not your fault," Paizlee said. "We don't blame you."

"Thank you, but I blame myself. Somehow, someday, I will try to at least make it up to you two kids a little bit," Randall said. "Having said that, is there anything I can do for you right now?"

"I don't think so," Kit said.

"You were planning on buying some yearling bulls in Wyoming, weren't you?" Randall said.

"We were, but that will have to wait," Kit said.

"Because you spent your money on your attorney and PI." It was not a question. "Did you actually have some bulls picked out?" This time it was a question.

"Three of them. And the fellow was going to hold them for me for a few days, but I'm sure he's sold them by now. Anyway, that will have to wait. We'll get by without them."

"I don't see why it should have to wait," Randall said. "If you will give me the contact information, if they are still available, I'll buy them for you and haul them to your ranch. Please let me do that for you."

"Oh no. You don't need to do that," Kit protested.

"I think I do. And if those are already sold, I have a good eye for bulls. I'll find some you'll like. Please, it won't undo the hurt Sam caused you, that I let him cause you, but it would help me feel better."

"I don't have that information with me," Kit said, feeling increasingly uncomfortable, and yet also feeling like Randall was both sincere and to be trusted and that maybe it truly would help Randall feel better if Kit let him do this.

"Does your ranch foreman know which bulls they are?"

"Sort of. Andy wasn't with me when I went up to look at them. But I gave him pictures of them and copies of their registration papers. He has all the contact information on the seller, but still, you don't have to do this. I . . . we have no hard feelings toward you."

"Mr. Overmyer, I agree totally with Kit. We'll get through this and be okay," Paizlee said.

"You two are wonderful. And who is this young lady?" he asked as he turned his head toward Wiona, who was standing over by the window gazing across the room at Kit.

"This is a very good friend of ours, Wiona Hubbard. She works for our attorney, but right now she won't go back to work. She's being a pill." Kit managed a painful smile, and it brought Wiona to his side.

"That's right. I'm not leaving until you are. And I may be a pill, but you're just going to have to swallow it," she said with a grin as she stepped over and took hold of one of his hands. "Kit, would you take some advice from me?"

"Maybe," he said.

"Let Mr. Overmyer do this for you."

"Thank you, Wiona," Randall said.

Kit was still torn. "It's not his fault."

"That doesn't matter, Kit. He wants to help. Let him." Wiona smiled sweetly at him. Her smile melted his heart. "I don't give much advice to people, but I hope you will listen to me."

Randall took advantage of his unlikely ally. "Please, give me Andy's number, and I'll call him and make arrangements. I promise you won't go wrong. I know cattle. They have been my business, them and horses, for a very long time."

Kit caved. "Thank you," he said. "I'll give you his number, and you can enter it in your phone."

As soon as that was done, Randall said, "I'm sorry that you can't race that fantastic horse of yours this weekend. I have a feeling he would win if he were in the race."

"There's another race at Santa Anita Park in about three weeks," Paizlee said. "Kingfisher will win that one."

"Paizlee, are you crazy? I won't be able to ride that soon," Kit said. The two stared at each other for a long moment, and Kit discerned what she had on her mind. "No, Paizlee, you can't."

"Kit, you know I can. Andy can work with me to get me ready. I've raced a lot of times. I know, not in big races like this, but I know how. And I've worked Kingfisher out a lot. I can do this."

"Are you suggesting that you could be Kingfisher's jockey?" Randall asked, looking very surprised.

"Yes, I am," Paizlee said firmly.

"I can't let you do it," Kit said.

"Hey, brother, we own the ranch together. I can make this decision with or without your blessing. Three weeks. I'll bet by then you'll be able to go with us and give me last-minute advice," she said.

"Paizlee, no. It scares me."

Wiona squeezed Kit's hand. "I have some more advice for you, Kit."

"No offense, Wiona, but this is my sister. I'm kind of protective of her," he said.

"Too bad, buster. You're getting it anyway. If Paizlee says she can do it, I believe her. I think you should let her try."

"She's only ridden in minor races and never on a horse like Kingfisher," Kit continued to protest.

"Oh, I get it," Wiona said. "You're afraid she'll do too good and maybe want to take over as the main jockey." She smiled brightly. "Please, Kit, I think you should let her ride in the race at Santa Anita."

Kit closed his eyes. "I'm tired. You guys wear me out."

"I'm in no position to be giving you advice," Randall began, "but I will anyway. I think you should let her do it."

Kit did not open his eyes; he was in a lot of pain. But he knew Paizlee was right. She was a very good jockey. "Okay. Have it your way, sis. And thanks, Randall. You are a good man." In another moment, he felt sleep overtake him.

Brandon was in Nevada, and he was working hard. He was determined to learn all he could about Sam Overmyer, Herbie, and the disgraced Sergeant Hodson. The sheriff was being extremely helpful, and he had some of his deputies give Brandon some introductions to people in town.

Brandon had already talked to a lot of folks, and he was learning that Sam and his associates were not well liked by most people. Some were full of hatred. And most disturbing to Brandon was what one man told him, a man by the name of John Messler. He had at first been reluctant to speak with Brandon about Sam or Vince. After Brandon explained to him about Kit and what was happening to him, John changed his mind.

"Okay, I'll tell you a little about those two. But please, don't use my name if you speak to anyone about what I tell you," John said.

"Why?" Brandon asked.

"Because if it got back to Vince Hodson, my family and I would be in serious danger. Vince is a dangerous man," John told him. "Anyway, it's all old history, back to when Sam and I were classmates in school."

"I understand, and this will be only for me unless you decide otherwise at some point," Brandon said.

"Okay, so Sam's a small guy, always was littler than the rest of us. And he got bullied a lot. Now don't get me wrong, he usually brought it on himself with his big mouth. At any rate, when one of the bigger, and often older, kids got back at him in some way, they'd end up with black eyes or broken noses and such. Whenever that happened, whichever kid it was steered clear of Sam after that, and none ever dared tell what had happened to them."

"Let me guess," Brandon said. "Vince, his older cousin, got involved."

"That's what everyone believes," John said, "but no one really said much about it. There was one particular time involving a kid who was a year older than Sam and me. Sam said something about his sister that was really bad. I was there. I heard it. This other guy beat him—Sam—up pretty bad. I saw it, and so did some others."

"Did Sam's mother or father ever complain to the school about it?" Brandon asked.

"Not usually, but that time they did, and they were told that the kid would be called in. But he never came. He was found dead by his father." He went on to give Brandon some specifics.

"Suicide?" Brandon asked.

"That's how it was ruled. Rumors got around that he had some help from Vince, but no one dared tell the cops what they suspected, because we were all afraid of Vince. By then he'd been a deputy sheriff for three or four years, and he was getting a reputation as a cop no one wanted to mess with."

"So you honestly think that this boy was actually killed by Vince?" Brandon asked.

"Please, don't ever repeat this, but yes, I'm pretty sure of it, and so were some of the other kids," John said. "It eventually died down, and after that, Sam was untouchable. No one dared lay a hand on him."

That story, although impossible to prove, got Brandon thinking. It was very much on his mind as he entered a Tonopah bar a little later. Clark Drene was tending the bar. He hadn't been present the first time Brandon had been there seeking information, but this time he was. "Clark Drene?" Brandon asked.

"Who wants to know?" was Clark's response.

"I'm Brandon Phelps." He showed Clark his ID.

Clark studied it for a moment and handed it back. "Private investigator. What do you need to see me about?"

"I understand that Sam Overmyer comes in here a lot," Brandon said.

Clark's face darkened. "Haven't seen him since he caused a fight here a while back. It was a nasty one and people got hurt and my barroom got busted up. Course, that cousin of his, Sergeant Hodson, I believe, somehow slipped Sam out of here without the other officers noticing, and the whole thing was blamed on Bob Sims."

"Was Bob hurt?" Brandon asked.

"Yeah, and so was his wife. Sam was bragging about how he'd beat the Utah jockey in a race in Albuquerque. But Bob and his wife spoke up and said that they'd been at that race and told the crowd that Sam had shoved the Utah kid and that was the only reason he'd won. I didn't see it, but I can imagine Sam doing something like that."

"It happened, all right," Brandon said. "So I take it Sam got mad."

"Did he ever," Clark said. He went on to explain what happened after that. "Sam didn't get any blame. In fact, no one dared say what really happened because of Sergeant Hodson—his cousin. And like I said, Sam disappeared from the building. I've heard rumors that Sam has been protected by his cousin many times over the years and that he'd gotten him out of trouble and even avenged him, so to speak."

"Thanks for telling me this," Brandon said.

"I guess I had to. The sheriff needs to get rid of Vince. He lets Sam and his friends pretty much get their way."

"Then I guess you'll be glad to hear this," Brandon said. "Sheriff Watson has fired him and put him in jail to boot."

"Well, that's good to hear. But what did he charge him with?"

"Several things. The sheriff seems to think, and so do I, that Vince was somehow involved in the situation that got Ari Short killed by Herbie Dinkin," Brandon said.

"Vince and Herbie were pretty tight, that's for sure," Clark told him. "Blaine Ruley, the other guy that died that night, was also tight with Vince, Herbie, and

Sam Overmyer. Lots of rumors going around, but I think some of them may be true. Was that jockey from Utah being brought back to jail because he'd been snooping around Randall Overmyer's ranch when he wasn't supposed to be?"

"That's what Sam claimed. How do you know about this?"

Clark smiled. "I'm a bartender. I hear things when people don't realize I'm listening. And people in bars often have loose lips, and so rumors kind of spread here."

"I see," Brandon said, and he went on to explain most of what had happened and what he had learned. Clark nodded knowingly.

"Seems to me like Sam should be in jail too," Clark said.

"You're right, but the sheriff can't find him. Who knows, maybe Sam and Herbie are hiding out somewhere together," Brandon said.

"I wouldn't be surprised. But if this Utah cowboy didn't kill Sam's horse, who did?" Clark asked.

"That's what I'd like to know," Brandon responded. "So would the sheriff."

Clark rubbed the bar for a moment with a rag and seemed very thoughtful. Brandon waited. Finally, Clark looked back at him and said, "Bob Sims had to pay for the damage in the bar. That crooked sergeant saw to that. Bob brought me the money, but he was mad. I'm not saying he was mad enough to kill a horse but, well, just saying."

"Thanks, Clark. You've been a big help," Brandon said. "If you think of anyone else who may have been angry enough at Sam to kill his horse, let me know. That horse actually belonged to Randall Overmyer, and the sheriff and I both agree that we need to figure out who killed him. Here's my card."

"Just a second, Detective. This may not mean anything, but Bob's wife, Annie, is a veterinary assistant. I heard that the horse died of a large dose of insulin. Annie's an okay gal but, well, just saying. One more thing: I don't think Sam thought much of his horse. He knows, from what I've heard, that in a fair race, that Utah kid and his horse would have won that race easily. Just saying."

Brandon thanked Clark and left. Brandon got in his Bronco and started it, letting the air-conditioning kick in. He made some notes and then thought about what to do next. Clark had given him some things to think about. The guy kept adding just saying, but it seemed clear to Brandon that the bartender had given the matter a lot of thought.

He decided on a course of action, but first he wanted, out of courtesy, to talk it over with Sheriff Watson. It was nearly eight in the evening when he stepped into the sheriff's office. He was surprised the sheriff was still in. He mentioned that to him after he was ushered back to his office.

"My wife is used to my hours," Watson assured him. "I can't rest well until Herbie and Sam are in custody. Having a deputy murdered in cold blood is the hardest thing I've ever had to face, Detective. Deputy Short was a good man with a lot of potential."

"I can't even pretend to understand how it must hurt. I also want those guys brought to justice. If there's anything you can think of that I might be able to do to help, please don't hesitate to call me," Brandon said.

"I'll keep that in mind. You've been a big help already," Sheriff Watson said. "But tell me, how much longer is Kit going to be able to keep you on the job?"

"I'm on my own dime now. I guess I'm a little like you, Sheriff. I can't stop until I get to the bottom of this business with Sam Overmyer," Brandon said.

"I should let you know that Vince Hodson bonded out of jail this afternoon. He could cause you a lot of trouble if he decided to. I worry about Kit and his sister. I told them this morning that I feared for their safety."

"I've tried to tell them that too," Brandon said. "That's probably the biggest reason I'm still sticking to this case. With these guys on the loose, I want to be around so I can help out if I need to."

"You may be interested to know that Randall Overmyer went to see Kit in the hospital this morning," Sheriff Watson said.

"I didn't know that. That's a nice gesture on his part. I'm planning to go to the hospital in a little while to see Kit."

"He and his sister are fine people. We've got to help them through this. But tell me, Detective, is there something else you wanted to speak with me about?"

"Yes. I just spoke to a bartender by the name of Clark Drene."

"Clark is the owner of the bar. Did he tell you something that might help us?"

"He did, as a matter of fact." Then Brandon related his conversation with the bar owner.

"I had a feeling there was more to that fight than anyone would admit to me. I had other deputies there, but they all told me they didn't see Sam," the sheriff said. "Clearly no one dared point fingers at Sam Overmyer, including my own deputies. Their concern, I'm sure, was not Sam but Vince. I was stupid for keeping him on, but I couldn't find anything to fire him for. If I had, I would have done so sooner."

"That's all past, just history," Brandon said.

"But it's important history," the sheriff told him. "Kit did not kill that horse of Sam's, but someone did. I'm intrigued by Bob and Annie Sims. It sounds like they got the raw end of things that night, thanks to Vince."

"They paid for the damage in the bar like Vince ordered them to, but they were both very angry about it," Brandon said. "I think we should follow up on them. I was hoping you could tell me where Annie Sims works. I'd like to speak with her."

The sheriff told him. "Will you follow up with her and then get back to me? It would be very helpful to find out who actually killed that horse. It could tie in with my deputy's death and who might have been behind the order to kill Kit, or it might not. But I want to know who killed the horse. That's a loose end that needs to be tied up in my mind if nothing else. Annie certainly would have had the knowledge and expertise to do it and could have shared that expertise with Bob, although it sure would surprise me if it was them. But I long since learned that one should never fail to follow a lead just because of who it might be about."

Brandon stood up. "I'll go there in the morning. Right now, I need to get to the hospital and check on the Troxlers."

"Oh, that reminds me. Even though my department is spread thin with the manhunt for Sam and Herbie, I am going to keep a deputy posted outside his room for as long as Kit is in the hospital," the sheriff said.

"Thanks. That's wise. I'll get back with you later."

CHAPTER FIFTEEN

At that very minute, Sam and Herbie were conspiring as they sat beside a small campfire deep in the forest. "That rat, Troxler, has got to pay," Herbie said, shaking his fist angrily.

"And pay dearly," Sam agreed. "Thanks to him, you and I are both in a lot of hot water. He needs to feel the heat as well. Any ideas, Herbie?"

"As a matter of fact, I gave it a lot of thought before I figured out where you were probably hiding," Herbie said. "I still think you were right about him killing your horse. Now his horse needs to pay."

"If we can find him without anyone seeing us. The cops want us now," Sam reminded him. "And I don't think Vince can help us this time."

"They want me the most," Herbie said. "I had to kill a cop."

"That couldn't be helped, I'm afraid," Sam said. "You made the right call when he told you to drop your gun. It's just too bad that Kit didn't die too."

"I tried," Herbie said.

"I'm not faulting you. He won't be so lucky another time. But let's find that racehorse and kill it first." Sam laughed. "At least the hotshot won't be racing in California this week."

"Or for a long time. Maybe forever," Herbie reminded him. "I can't believe he survived. I thought he was dead, and I can't believe they found him and those other guys before the vultures and the coyotes did."

Sam shrugged and smiled. "It was pure luck. We'll get our revenge. But first we need some wheels. And this time, we won't hitchhike like you did getting up here after you hid your truck and your buddy dropped you off just outside the forest. That was smart, by the way," Sam added. "It wouldn't have been good for you to be seen in your truck."

"I can't be seen at all. I'll leave this area for good once we take care of Kit and his horse."

"Me too. This horse I have tied up here won't get us far. He can get us far enough, I suppose, but then I'll cut him loose. Maybe he'll find his way home. That should make my old man happy. We can ride until we find a campground. We'll find something suitable there," Sam said with a wink. "There are plenty of stupid people out there who would share a car with us."

Brandon pushed the door to Kit's hospital room open. He was glad to see that Kit was able to smile at him. Wiona smiled at him too. Paizlee did more than smile; she hugged him. He kind of liked that. For several minutes, the four visited. Finally, Brandon said, "I guess they're feeding you well, Kit."

Kit snorted. "If you call that stuff that's being pumped into me through a tube food. I don't even get to taste it. I can't actually eat until my intestines are healed so stuff can pass through them. I hope it won't be too much longer. I sure want some real food."

"I'm sorry about that," Brandon said. "Kit, would it be all right with you if I dragged these two out and got them something to eat outside of the hospital?"

Kit managed a grin. "Sure it would. They need some good food."

"The cafeteria here isn't that bad," Wiona said. "Anyway, Kit, you need someone to keep an eye on you. Remember, you're still in danger."

"There's a deputy outside the door, and he even has a gun," Brandon said dryly. "I think he can keep danger out for the hour it would take for me to take you two to dinner."

Brandon had to smile when he saw Wiona take hold of Kit's hand and say, "I'm not leaving. Paizlee, you can go if you'd like."

"Are you sure you two don't mind?" Paizlee asked.

"Why would we mind?" Wiona asked. "I'm not afraid to be here alone with Kit. I can handle him."

Brandon looked at the pretty red-headed girl. She seemed quite possessive of Kit. And Kit didn't appear to mind. "How is Lawrence getting along without your help?" he asked Wiona with a twinkle in his eye.

"He and Mom both said I should stay with Kit. Lawrence thinks I can do more good being here."

"Okay, then Paizlee, will you go to dinner with me?"

She blushed. "I would love to if it's okay with these guys."

"Go," Kit said. "Wiona and I'll be fine. But I have one favor to ask; Wiona probably wouldn't mind if you brought something for her."

"Yeah, that would be sweet. A pizza loaded with all kinds of goodies would be nice," Wiona said. "Or anything else would be okay too."

"We'll see what we can find. Paizlee, should we go?" Brandon asked.

"Sure," she said.

Wiona grinned mischievously. "So is that a date you two are going on?"

Brandon chuckled. "If Paizlee wants to consider it that."

"I do, and why don't you two consider yourselves on a date while we're gone," Paizlee said, grinning at Kit and Wiona.

"Sounds okay to me. Wiona, would you be my date for the next hour?" Kit asked.

"I would love that. You guys go now. Shoo," she said, waving a hand toward the door.

They left, both smiling. Brandon could hardly believe how lucky he was to have found this girl. He looked forward to getting to know her better. That was more than enough incentive for him to help find Kit's and Paizlee's enemies.

They found a restaurant that looked promising. "Hometown Pizza," Paizlee said. "That sounds good to me."

They took their time getting to know each other and simply enjoying the company as well as some exceptionally good pizza. As they were slowly eating their meal, Brandon said, "What I feel the worst about Kit getting hurt is that he won't be able to ride Kingfisher again this year. I was looking forward to watching him win this Friday." As he spoke, he didn't miss the sheepish grin on Paizlee's face.

"What?" he said.

"Kit's not the only jockey in the family. It's too late for the race Friday. But Kingfisher is also entered in another race in three weeks at Santa Anita Park in California. He will be there," she said.

Brandon's face darkened. "Paizlee, surely you jest?"

"Not at all. I've ridden all my life. I've even raced, but not with a great horse like Kingfisher," she said. "I can't wait."

"Paizlee, I don't think that's such a good idea."

She frowned at him. "Why not?"

"Well, you know, you could get hurt, and what if Sam and Herbie figure it out?" he asked as the pizza in his stomach began to take an unnatural course, an uncomfortable one.

"I can do this, Brandon. I've already talked to Andy. He's done a lot of the training with Kingfisher and Kit. He's all for it. He says he'll make sure the horse and I will both be ready."

"I don't know, Paizlee. But I guess if you really are a good rider, then what can I say? I do worry about those guys. What if we haven't caught them before that race?" Brandon asked.

"Then I'll hire someone to go along as security. Would you be interested in doing that? If not, maybe you can suggest someone," she said.

"You can't be talked out of this?" he asked, knowing what her answer would be. She and Kit hadn't kept that ranch going after losing their parents without being very determined people.

"Nope, I'm going to do it for Kit's sake and for Kingfisher's."

"Then I will be there, but you don't have to hire me. You can't keep me away."

Paizlee grinned. "I was hoping you'd say that."

"Hey, even if the cops and I manage to find Sam and Herbie before that, I will be there. That's a promise."

"Brandon. I like you—a lot. Thanks."

Randall Overmyer was up before the sun had risen the next morning. He'd called Kit's foreman, Andy, and had worked out some details. Randall and his ranch foreman, Bruce, were both heading for Wyoming as soon as they could get ready. He planned to stop on the way and pick up the information that Andy had on the bulls Kit had looked at. Randall had been in a dark place mentally for several days now, and he was worried about his weak heart. But doing this for the Troxlers had given him a huge boost. He wanted to do it, and he was determined to get them the best bulls that money could buy. And nobody knew good bulls better than he did.

Bruce met him outside the barn. "Boss, you won't believe this," he said. "That horse Sam rode away on was standing over beside the corrals when I came out this morning."

"You're serious?" Randall asked.

"Very. He still has the bridle and saddle on. The reins have been tromped on and busted, but the horse seems okay."

"I wonder if he got away from Sam or if Sam just let him loose. He surely knows that the horse would have headed for home and at least tied the reins loosely to the saddle horn before he let him go," Randall said. "I hope the horse didn't dump Sam up in the mountains and leave him up there injured."

"Boss, Sam knows how to ride. He didn't get thrown, and I'm sure the horse didn't stumble. I've felt his legs and checked him over thoroughly. He doesn't have a scratch on him," Bruce said. "I pulled the saddle off. He does have some nasty saddle sores. I treated them and put him in a stall in the barn where our guys can keep a close eye on him while we're gone."

Randall pressed on his temples and rubbed his eyes. "You're right, Bruce. What worries me now is why he let the horse go. I wonder if he's stolen a car or something."

"I'm sure he didn't walk out," Bruce said.

"It's too early now, but in an hour or two, I'd better call the sheriff and let him know that someone might be missing a car, possibly someone staying in a campground in the forest or someone passing through. It worries me now that I'm thinking about it."

"I'm sorry about what Sam has done to you," Bruce said.

"If he'd only hurt me, it would be okay, I guess. But what he's done to others . . . Somehow he's got to be stopped. I'd do it myself if I could," Randall said with a bit of anger in his voice. "What I can do is help those Troxler kids. If you will make sure the men know what to do while we're gone, I'll hook up the stock trailer."

Brandon checked at the hospital first thing that morning. He couldn't stop thinking about Paizlee Troxler. It worried him that she was so determined to race that big powerful stallion of theirs. And yet, he was proud of her as well. She was the kind of girl he'd been looking for ever since leaving the Navy Seals. They had enjoyed their little date. And from the looks on both Kit's and Wiona's faces, they had enjoyed theirs as well—as much as they could with one of them secured to a hospital bed by several tubes.

Another deputy was on duty outside Kit's room. "You're Detective Phelps, aren't you?" he asked.

"Usually people call me Brandon," he said with a smile.

"Okay, then you can go in. The sheriff said to be doubly careful about who goes in and out of this room. But he described you and said to let you go in anytime."

"I won't be long," he said.

"No problem. The sheriff did tell me to let you know if I saw you that Sam may have stolen a car from someone in the forest. He's doing some checking and will let me know if he's able to find out anything."

"What makes him think Sam's stolen a car?" Brandon asked.

"Sam's horse came back to the ranch—that's all. But I guess to Randall Overmyer's way of thinking, Sam would not have let the horse go unless he had other transportation arranged," the deputy said.

Brandon nodded. It made sense to him. He went into the room. No one was awake. The girls were sitting uncomfortably in a couple of soft chairs the hospital had provided. Kit was asleep in his bed. Brandon was almost overwhelmed by his feeling for these three. In a very short time, they had become like family to him.

For a moment, Brandon stood quietly and watched the three of them sleeping. He started to leave, being as quiet as he could, but suddenly Paizlee stirred. "Brandon," she whispered.

He signaled with his index finger for her to follow him. She rose gracefully from the chair and left the room with him. "Sorry I look like such a mess," she said when they'd left Kit's room and were far enough from the deputy that they wouldn't be overheard.

"Paizlee, you look beautiful to me," he said with feeling.

She met his eyes and smiled. "Thank you. You were going to leave without saying hello."

"I didn't want to disturb any of you. I don't know how you girls manage to get any sleep at all," he said.

"It wouldn't be so bad if the nurses didn't have to come in so often to check on Kit. Of course, I'm not complaining. I want him to have the best care possible," she said.

"Do you feel like going to the cafeteria?"

"Sure, I'd like that."

A minute later, they sat down and began to munch on some sweet rolls. "Paizlee, do you still plan to race?"

"I like you a lot, Brandon, but you are not going to talk me out of it," she said firmly.

"Just checking."

His phone went off, and he looked at the screen. "It's the sheriff," he said. "I'd better find out what he wants."

"Maybe they've caught Sam," Paizlee said hopefully.

"Maybe." But Brandon was afraid that was not what the sheriff was calling about.

CHAPTER SIXTEEN

"Good morning, Sheriff," he said as he looked at Paizlee's face. She seemed more worried than she had a moment ago. He sincerely hoped that the sheriff had good news.

"Brandon, did my man at the hospital tell you about the horse Sam got away on returning to Randall's ranch? Or have you been to the hospital yet?"

"I'm in the cafeteria with Paizlee," Brandon said. "Yes, he told me and what that could mean."

"I'm afraid Randall was right," Sheriff Watson said. "Two men generally fitting the descriptions of Sam and Herbie were seen driving out of a campground late last night in a dark blue Nissan Pathfinder. The couple who saw them was out for a late walk when the Pathfinder went by. Even though it was quite dark, they distinctly saw that the one guy had a hooked nose."

"Herbie," Brandon said bitterly. "So somehow Sam and Herbie got together up in the mountains. Why didn't the couple report the Pathfinder as being stolen?"

"It wasn't theirs. It wasn't until a deputy went there this morning that anyone knew it was gone. The folks who own the Pathfinder were staying on the opposite end of the campground from the people who reported seeing it go by last night," the sheriff explained. "They slept late this morning, but when the officer came around, they stepped out and noticed that the car was gone. It was another half hour before the officer talked to the other folks, and of course by then, he was no longer looking for a stolen vehicle but for someone who might have seen it leaving."

Brandon thought for a moment before he said, "So how many hours had the killers been gone before it was discovered?"

"At least six or seven," was the sheriff's answer.

"Why did they need to steal a car? Herbie had his, didn't he?" Brandon asked.

"I don't know that yet," the sheriff admitted. "Herbie would have been easily spotted in his own pickup."

"Have you searched Herbie's and Blaine's houses yet?"

"The two of them were roommates. They lived in a trailer house quite a ways out of town. And yes, we did search, but the only thing we found of any interest was some insulin and syringes."

"So one of them was diabetic? If so, do you know which one?"

"Blaine. As you know, his truck was left off the side of the highway out where my deputy was killed. There were also diabetic supplies in it, and they match what was found in Kit's truck," the sheriff revealed.

Brandon tapped his fingers on the table. His eyes and Paizlee's locked. He could see questions in her eyes, which he hoped he could answer in a little bit. "Follow me as I think out loud here."

"Okay," Sheriff Watson said.

"We know your former sergeant was close to those guys," Brandon said. "We strongly believe it was Vince who planted the syringe and insulin bottle in Kit's truck. If so, that likely explains where Vince got it from."

"That's what we think," the sheriff agreed.

"Okay, but I would think it unlikely that Blaine would have killed the horse," Brandon reasoned.

"That's true, Brandon."

"So I need to get to the vet's clinic this morning and have a visit with Annie Sims. She and her husband had motive since Sam and Hodson had both done them dirt," he reasoned.

"Would you get back to me as soon as you have a chance to talk to her? In fact, if you don't mind, maybe we ought to do that interview together," the sheriff suggested.

"That works for me. Where should we meet?" Brandon asked.

"Give me about twenty minutes, then I'll pick you up at the hospital. And, Brandon, you don't need to wait for me in the parking lot. I'd like to talk to Kit again, so I'll come to his room."

As soon as the call ended, Paizlee started throwing questions at Brandon, which he fielded quite well. The only thing he couldn't satisfy her on was one he didn't have a clue about. That had to do with where Herbie's truck was at.

They also talked about what they should do to make sure everyone stayed safe, including Kingfisher.

"We can't let those guys find him," Paizlee said.

"I am afraid they might try. Ordinarily, I would think that guys wanted for such serious crimes would be trying to get as far away as they could. But wounded pride and hatred often rob people of common sense."

"In the case of those two, they didn't have a whole lot of that to begin with," Paizlee said snidely.

After depositing their trash in a waste receptacle, they walked hand in hand toward Kit's room. It felt as natural as anything ever had to Brandon.

Wiona was sitting beside Kit's bed, holding his hand. She smiled sheepishly before asking, "Where have you guys been?"

"We've been in the cafeteria, planning how to keep everyone safe. Kit, how secure is Kingfisher?" Brandon asked.

"The man who owns the ranch where we're keeping him was one of our dad's best friends," Kit said.

"But can he keep him safe?"

"I don't know, to be honest. But I don't know what else to do with him. If Paizlee doesn't come to her senses and decide not to race him, we've got to keep him in shape and in training," Kit said. Then he frowned. "Has something changed?"

"I'm afraid so, Kit." Brandon then recapped for them his conversation with Sheriff Watson, who walked in just as he was finishing. "I've been updating Kit on Sam and Herbie," he told the sheriff.

"This is serious," Sheriff Watson said. "There's another thing that was just brought to my attention, and it could be a problem. Vince seems to have skipped town. No one knows where he may have gone."

"Not even his wife?" Paizlee asked.

"He's divorced, and his wife left town about a year ago, taking his two children with her. I have an officer trying to track them down right now. We'll see if she knows anything, but I don't hold out much hope on that. It was not a pretty divorce," Sheriff Watson said. "I wish I could have fired him then, but Vince is cunning, and I couldn't find grounds to do so. If she could have shown that he'd beaten her up, that would have helped. But she would never say anything like that. I think she was too scared of him to, like other deputies were. Just being mean to his wife was not something I could take that kind of action over. One thing about it, Vince was hired long before I became sheriff, so at least I can't take the blame for giving him a gun and a badge."

"What do you suggest we do?" Brandon asked.

"My first concern is to beef up security here at the hospital," Sheriff Watson said. "I have a lieutenant working on scheduling that. So you will see a larger police presence here shortly. At some point, I think it would be wise to move you, Kit, to a hospital somewhere else but not disclose the location. We'll need to visit with your doctor about that."

The mood in the room had turned very somber. "I'm sorry to sound so gloomy," the sheriff continued, "but these are some bad men we're dealing with. Brandon and I are going to go do a little work together. I suggest, no, I insist that you girls stay here with Kit. Don't leave the room without letting the deputies outside your door know where you're going, and then one of them will accompany you. I mean to the cafeteria or anywhere else in the hospital. It would be best if you didn't leave the hospital at all."

Brandon could see from their faces that shock had struck all of them. He realized that this room held some of the most important people to him in the entire world. It was strange how quickly that had happened. "You guys need to know that I will do all I can to help us through this mess. I care deeply for all of you," Brandon said.

"But what can you do?" Kit asked.

"Don't forget. Brandon was a Navy Seal," Wiona said.

"I've fought terrorists," Brandon added. "They are worse than even these guys because they were trained to wreak havoc. These guys are trying to figure it out as they go. I will get my head around it and see if I can't get out in front of them. I'll see you in a little while. But for now, I trust Sheriff Watson. He'll keep you safe. We will catch these guys."

As the sheriff and Brandon drove away from the hospital in his unmarked county SUV, he said to Brandon, "I didn't realize you had such a strong background."

"I've had some experience," Brandon said modestly.

They found Annie Sims hard at work at the veterinary clinic. Her hair was tied back in a ponytail. When she spotted them, she stopped what she was doing. "Sheriff, what can I do for you?"

"This is Brandon Phelps. He's a private detective who is employed by Kit and Paizlee Troxler," Sheriff Watson said.

"I hope you can do something for Kit," Annie said. "I know a bit about what he was accused of, and I know that anything Sam Overmyer says about anyone is probably a lie. His dad is a good man, but Sam is not. He and that deputy of yours, Sheriff, cost my husband and me a bundle."

"So I hear. Mrs. Sims, I fired Sergeant Hodson as soon as I found enough justification. Not only that, but I had him charged with a number of crimes."

"Good," she said with a clenched fist. "Does that mean he's in jail?"

"He was, but he's out on bail now."

Annie scowled. "He should have to stay in jail," she said bitterly. "I appreciate you coming here to tell me that."

"There's more," the sheriff said. "Are you aware that Sam Overmyer's racehorse was killed?"

"Everybody knows that," she said. "My boss went out there when Randall called. And before you ask me how he was killed, I know that too. Someone gave that beautiful animal a whole bunch of insulin." She shuddered, and a pained look crossed her face.

Brandon had been watching her closely. This woman might be tough, but he could see she had a soft spot for horses, and probably other animals as well.

"That's right," the sheriff said.

"My boss obtained the blood sample, which showed there was a large amount of insulin in the poor creature's body," she added. She shook her fists. "It makes me so angry. I heard Kit did it because Sam beat him in a race, but I find that hard to believe."

"I assure you that Kit did not do it," Sheriff Watson said. "It's a lie made up by Sam himself." He went on to explain to Annie why he knew that Kit couldn't have done it.

Suddenly, a sick look crossed the large woman's face. "Wait! Does this all have something to do with your deputy that was murdered by Herbie?"

"What do you think?" the sheriff asked.

She was very thoughtful for a moment and tugged at a stray lock of hair. "Bob and I have been really busy and haven't seen the news, but word gets around. Is it true that Kit was also shot?"

"Critically," Sheriff Watson said. "He is alive today because of this man right here." He nodded at Brandon.

"Sam is a terrible person," she said. She studied both men for a moment. "But I guess you guys know that. Where is he now?"

"We wish we knew. He and Herbie are both on the run."

Annie looked Brandon in the eyes and asked, "You are a PI and work for Kit, but what exactly is your interest in this whole terrible thing?"

"I was hired to help Kit Troxler clear his name," he said. "As I hear you know, he was cheated out of the win in that race by Sam."

"Yes, he was. Bob and I saw it. What can I do to help?" Annie asked.

"We are looking for whoever killed Sam's horse," Brandon responded.

Annie's eyes grew wide. "Are you thinking I did it?"

"Where were you that morning and the night before?" Sheriff Watson asked.

"I would never do something like that," she said, looking quite mortified. Then she traced her activities during the questionable hours. "Check with the bartender. Check with my husband. Check with our neighbors. Please, don't accuse me of such a terrible thing. Yes, Bob and I hate Sam. But we would never kill an innocent animal. I work here because I want to help animals, not destroy them."

She pled with her eyes. Brandon believed her.

"Can you think of anyone who might have been angry enough with Sam to do this to his horse?" the sheriff asked.

"A lot of people hate Sam, but I don't know who would do that to his horse. If I were angry enough to kill over what Sam and that deputy did, it would be Sam who's dead, not his horse." Her eyes shot fire.

"If you think of anything else, please let me know," Sheriff Watson said.

"There is one more thing. I saw Blaine Ruley buying insulin at the pharmacy one day. He must be diabetic."

"He was, but he's dead now," Sheriff Watson said.

"He was one of Sam's buddies. Surely it couldn't have been him." She paused. "Unless Sam did something to make him mad. Sam could do that, you know. You might consider Blaine, even though he's dead."

Annie was trembling, but it was with indignation, not guilt, Brandon thought. Once they had left the clinic, Sheriff Watson said, "That woman is innocent. And who knows, maybe Blaine Ruley could have done it. But we can't question him since he's dead. I'm not sure where to look now, Brandon."

"I'd like to take a look at the place where Herbie and Blaine lived," Brandon said.

"It's out of town a ways, but we can swing out there now if you want to," Sheriff Watson said.

The two men talked as they traveled to Herbie's trailer house. The death of Sam's racehorse remained a mystery.

"Sheriff, is the syringe that Hodson put in Kit's truck in your evidence room?" Brandon asked.

"It should be, unless . . ." Sheriff Watson paused and looked at Brandon.

"Unless it isn't?" Brandon suggested. "Unless Vince did something with it?"

"That's what I'm thinking. I'll look when we get back to town. Are you suggesting that if we ran some tests that we might be able to find proof that the syringe was used to kill the racehorse?"

"That's what I'm suggesting, Sheriff, although I'm not sure that's possible. And even if Vince put it in Kit's truck, that doesn't mean it's the one used on the horse."

"I'll look into it," Sheriff Watson said. "That should already have been done, but I guess I got too caught up in my deputy's death and didn't get around to it. I will now, if it's possible."

"This place is a mess," Brandon observed when they reached Herbie's trailer. There were broken-down cars and other junk scattered around in front of the place.

They got out and began to walk around. After finding nothing of interest, they drove back to town. Sheriff Watson called Brandon later with some bad news. "The syringe and insulin bottle are not in the evidence room. My evidence custodian can't explain what happened to it."

"Vince took it," Brandon said firmly.

"Most likely," Sheriff Watson responded. "But I can't prove it. Neither he nor anyone else checked it out. It's probably destroyed now."

Brandon was thoughtful for a moment. "Does he have any close friends in the department?"

"Why do you wonder?"

"Just a thought, but could someone who might take a risk for him for whatever reason have checked something else out and somehow managed to get the syringe and insulin bottle?"

"I hate to think it, but who knows? He could be paying one of the other guys off or even be blackmailing them some way. I'll look into it," the sheriff promised.

CHAPTER SEVENTEEN

A COUPLE OF SLOW DAYS passed. Things were getting both boring and tense in Kit's hospital room. Brandon had not turned up any serious leads on the killing of Sam's horse or the whereabouts of the wanted men. Paizlee, Wiona, and Kit were becoming extremely bored. Brandon worried about them. If something didn't happen soon, he feared that the camaraderie in the room could break down, and he didn't want to see that happen.

Then one phone call from Sheriff Watson stirred some excitement or, more accurately, angst. Brandon was taking a mid-afternoon break in Kit's room when the sheriff called. "Brandon, we found the stolen Pathfinder."

"Where?" Brandon asked before the sheriff could finish. The eyes of Kit, Paizlee, and Wiona widened with hope, even though they had no idea what Brandon had just been told.

"You probably won't believe this, but it's parked in the yard at Randall Overmyer's ranch."

"That's crazy, Sheriff. So those guys must be hiding out on Randall's ranch," Brandon suggested, already thinking that he might go there and help find them.

He could see questions growing on the anxious faces of his friends as they listened to his half of the conversation.

"No, it's pretty clear that they came and left because Sam's Dodge pickup is gone," Sheriff Watson said.

"Sheriff, I'm in Kit's room at the hospital right now. I just put my phone on speaker. Would you repeat what you just told me so the others can hear it?"

As the sheriff did that, Brandon could see the boredom drain away in the faces of his friends. Then the sheriff went on. "Randall and his foreman are still out of state. They're due at the Troxler ranch with Kit's new bulls late this afternoon. I called him to tell him about Sam's truck. Randall's beside himself."

Kit was feeling a lot stronger. In fact, they were finally allowing him to eat some soft food. His new best friend, Wiona, had stuck with him day and night, and he liked that. On the other hand, worries over the danger they were all in and the danger Kingfisher might be in weighed heavily on his mind. Even though the news broke the boredom, it made him extremely restless.

Kit waited for the sheriff to conclude his stunning call. Then he said, "I need to go home."

"Kit, the doctor doesn't even want you moved to a hospital closer to home yet," Paizlee said. "He did say this morning when I talked to him out in the hall that he had talked to someone at the hospital in Fillmore. He said they will take you whenever he feels like it would be safe to move you."

Brandon had been leaning against the wall, listening and thinking. He voiced his biggest concern over the possibility of Kit being moved by saying, "Kit, Sheriff Watson has been great to us by providing beefed-up security. I don't know if Sheriff Ledford in Millard County would be able to provide the same level of security. But if you'd like, I'll call him and see what he says."

"Thanks, Brandon. That would be great," Kit said.

Brandon did not voice another idea he had, since he didn't know if it could be pulled off. Instead, he pushed himself away from the wall and said, "I've got a few people I want to talk to today, then I'll be back."

Paizlee followed Brandon out of the room, but she did not proceed farther than a few yards down the hallway, where she remained under the watchful eyes of the deputies posted there. She clung to Brandon's arm for a moment. He smiled at her, gave her a brotherly peck on the forehead, and said, "Sometime this will be over, and you and I can get to really know each other."

"I can't wait," she said. But she had more on her mind. "Listen, so far Kingfisher has been safe at Norm Smith's place, but Norm called me just before you came in. I didn't want Kit to worry more, so I didn't tell him what the call was about. But you have to know. Norm said there's been a big silver Dodge pickup driving slowly by the lane to his place a couple of times early this morning. He wondered if he needed to worry. I wasn't sure then, but now I am. There's a lot for him to worry about. I didn't know Sam had his truck back."

"Oh my, Paizlee! That could be Sam's truck. Give me Smith's number, and I'll call him and Andy," Brandon said as his mind shifted from what he'd been going to do to a new idea that began to percolate in his mind. "I'll let you know how it goes."

Paizlee returned to the room, and Brandon hurried out to his Bronco. It was oppressively hot, but that did not particularly bother him. He was used to weather even more extreme than this in the Middle East. He pulled out his phone as he leaned against his truck and placed a call to Norm Smith.

As soon as Norm answered his phone, Brandon introduced himself and then jumped in. "Paizlee Troxler just told me about your earlier call about a silver Dodge pickup."

"Yes, but she didn't seem to worry any more than usual," Norm said.

"Now she is worried, and so am I," he said. He explained about Sam Overmyer's truck having been taken from Randall's ranch in Nevada.

"Okay, I'm worried now too," Norm said. "I guess I'll just have to beef up the security around Kingfisher, but honestly, I'm not sure it's a good idea to keep him here now. Those guys must have an idea that I have Kingfisher here, or they wouldn't be in the area."

"We don't know for sure that it's them, but we have to assume it is. I tell you what I'll do," Brandon said. "I'll call Sheriff Ledford and have him put an all-points bulletin out on the truck and the men. They're wanted for murder in Nye County. I'll also call Andy Boyse, and he and I will talk about a possible solution for the immediate future."

"Thanks, Detective," Norm said. "Keep me posted, please."

Brandon made a call to Sheriff Ledford, who said, "Thanks for your call, Detective. I suspect you're calling about the same thing Sheriff Watson of Nye County called about earlier."

"Probably. Those men are now in a large silver Dodge Ram. It's been seen passing by in the area of Norm Smith's ranch," Brandon said. "I just talked to Smith. He's worried sick about that expensive horse of Kit's."

"As am I," Sheriff Ledford said. "An APB has been sent out, and everyone is on the lookout for those guys and the truck. I know the man Sheriff Watson called Herbie killed one of his deputies and nearly killed Kit Troxler."

"That's right," Brandon agreed. "It sounds like you're on top of things."

"It's stretching me thin, but we're trying. I'll send someone out to Norm Smith's place right now and follow up with him. Do you have anything else, Detective?"

"I do," Brandon said, and then he talked to him about possibly moving Kit from the hospital in Tonopah to the one in Fillmore.

"Sheriff Watson also spoke of that," Ledford said. "I don't know how I'm going to handle the security on that. I may have to call on some of my fellow sheriffs to send me some help."

"Thanks, Sheriff. We don't know if we're going to move him or not. I'm going to call Andy Boyse now and make sure he takes extra precautions at Kit's ranch as well," Brandon said, then ended the call.

"Detective," Andy said as soon as he answered Brandon's call. "I just got a call from Paizlee. She is worrying herself to death."

"So you know that Sam Overmyer and one of his wanted-killer friends are likely in your area in Sam's silver Dodge Ram?" Brandon asked.

"Yes, and I just barely called and talked with Norm Smith. He told me he'd just talked to you. Anyway, we're thinking maybe some other ranchers in the area might be willing to help out and that we could shift Kingfisher around from place to place until this is over," Andy said. "By the way, I'm expecting Randall Overmyer here in a few hours with the new bulls. The ones Kit had picked out were sold already, but it sounds like Randall spent a lot of time looking and finally found some excellent ones."

"My next call will be to him," Brandon said. "He already knows about Sam's truck being taken from his ranch, but I want to see if he has any advice on how to proceed."

Then Brandon hung up and got in contact with Randall. The rancher's suggestion surprised Brandon.

"I think Kingfisher might be safer at my place than here in Utah," Randall said. "I'm wondering about loading him as soon as I deliver Kit's bulls and hauling him to Nevada with me."

"You would do that?" Brandon asked.

"Yes. Sam has no future with my ranch, and I have no other children. But I do have plenty of money," Randall continued. "If the sheriff would help me arrange for a number of private security people, we could guard Kingfisher on my ranch and help protect the kids while Kit is hospitalized."

"You just read my mind," Brandon said. "Not about moving Kingfisher, but about hiring private security. And I know how to go about that. If you really want to do this and can afford it, I'll arrange the security, and it will be the best available."

"I can easily afford it, but how will you do that?" Randall asked skeptically.

"I am not the only former Navy Seal around. And there are lots of Army Rangers and others as well," he said.

"But surely it would take days to round up some of your old colleagues who would be able or willing to drop what they're doing and come help me," Randall said.

"One phone call is all it'll take. One of my closest friends from my Navy days runs an agency that provides protection. His firm is in LA, and I'll bet he could have a team to your place by late tonight."

"Are you sure?" Randall asked. "That sounds too good to be true."

"I saved his life once, and we've been very close since then. He would drop anything he's doing to help me. And he and his men and women are some of the best operatives in the world."

"I'll pay whatever it costs, Detective. Make sure he knows that," Randall stressed.

"I'll make the call right now, and then I'll let Andy Boyse and the rancher who is currently keeping Kingfisher know what we want to do. I'll also talk to Kit and Paizlee so they can give their stamp of approval," Brandon promised. "I'll have Andy call you directly so the two of you can work things out. The only other thing we need to worry about is making sure you aren't followed or harassed along the way. You can leave that up to me too."

Randall chuckled. "There is more than one way to get to my ranch from Fillmore. Bruce and I will map one out and let you know. And one more thing, Detective; I'm sure Kit wants his horse kept in training and in shape. Bruce is a former jockey and a very good trainer, just like Andy is. I don't know what plans he has to race Kingfisher, but I suppose he could hire a jockey if he wants to use him later this summer. I know a couple of good ones that I could arrange for."

Brandon did not want to disclose that he had a jockey located. He would prefer that Paizlee would agree to let them hire someone, but he had a feeling that was not likely to happen. It wouldn't hurt to try though. "Let's keep that in mind. I'll get back to you."

Brandon walked into Kit's hospital room. All the arrangements had been made. Now he needed to let Kit and Paizlee know what, with their approval, was going to happen. Paizlee ran to Brandon and gave him a hug as he stepped into the hospital room. "I don't suppose those guys have been caught yet."

"I'm afraid not. But they're being hunted, and hundreds of cops are on the lookout," he said. "Now let me tell you what we would like to do." He explained what he'd discussed with Randall, Andy, Norm Smith, and his friend, Karl Shutter. "Kit, Paizlee, do we have your blessing?"

"Why would Randall do that for us?" Kit asked doubtfully. "He's already done far more than I could have ever asked for in buying those bulls for us."

"Because he likes you two and his own son has caused all this heartache and pain you've been through. Put yourself in his shoes," Brandon suggested. "What would you do?"

Kit looked at his sister. She nodded and said, "I think we should let him do it if he really wants to. And then I could start riding Kingfisher and be ready for the race in a few weeks."

"Paizlee, Randall and I talked about this. He knows some really good jockeys you could hire," Brandon ventured.

She scowled at him. "You don't think I can do it, do you?" she asked with a pout. "That makes me want to even more. I can do it, and I will."

Brandon had upset her, and he didn't want her mad at him. So in an effort at appeasement, he said, "You can prove it to me right there on Randall's ranch. Would you do that for me?"

She studied his face for a moment; hers was hard and determined. Then she broke into a grin. "It's a deal," she said. "And if I find out Kingfisher is too much for me, which I don't think I will, then I'll back out." Without giving Brandon a chance to respond, she turned to Kit. "I say we should let Randall help us."

"Let's do it then," Kit agreed.

That was all Brandon needed. "You guys won't regret this. I'll give Karl the go-ahead."

Wiona had sat quietly, watching and listening during the entire exchange. "There's one thing that really worries me," she said.

Everyone looked at her.

"What's that, Wiona?" Kit asked.

"Brandon said that Randall and Bruce are going to find an alternate route to make it less likely that Sam and his friends will know where he's going," she said. "But we shouldn't underestimate them."

"Okay, so I'll ask Karl to provide them with an escort," Brandon suggested. "It will be several hours yet before Randall gets to Fillmore with the bulls. It would give Karl time to rush someone up to Fillmore as well."

"That's good, but it's not enough," Wiona said stubbornly. "Remember, I work for Lawrence. He has defended some pretty bad people, and the one thing my mother and I have learned from him is that serious criminals are always plotting and planning ways to keep doing what they do best. They want to get off for what they got caught for, but they don't want to change their lifestyle."

Kit watched her. "What are you getting at, Wiona?"

"First, just because Sam's got his truck back, that doesn't mean they'll use it to try to find Kingfisher when they discover he's no longer with Mr. Smith, and they will discover that," she said.

Brandon agreed. "You're right, Wiona. They'll steal and do anything to prevent people from recognizing them. But Karl's men are trained very well in this sort of thing. Did you have something more in mind?"

She grinned. "If he can arrange it, I'd like to fly with Lawrence, and we could keep an eye out from high in the sky."

"But how would you know what you're seeing?" Paizlee asked with a raised brow. "It could be dark by the time they get Kingfisher loaded and ready to leave. Then again, they may have to wait until early in the morning. Randall and Bruce are sure to be very tired."

"The trick would be to simply watch for anyone who follows, and alert Randall so he could take some kind of evasive maneuvers," Wiona said. "That could be done after dark if it comes to that."

"I'm not sure I follow you, Wiona," Kit said.

"If anyone we see were to follow Randall, we could simply watch to see if he continues to be followed," she said.

"And you could let Karl's people know," Brandon said. "They could stop whoever it is and, ah, neutralize them if needed. Good thinking, Wiona. But why don't you let me call Lawrence."

"I was hoping you'd say that," Wiona admitted. "But I want to ride with him if he can do it."

"If he can't, and I believe he will make every effort to work it out, then I suspect my friend Karl can arrange a plane," Brandon said. "Are we all together on this?"

It was a big step, but they all agreed, and Brandon retreated from the room to call Lawrence and set the plan in motion.

CHAPTER EIGHTEEN

SAM AND HERBIE WERE NO longer driving Sam's Dodge Ram, but it was close by. They stayed in a small motel room in Utah County, plotting and planning. They did not want to be too close to Fillmore until they were ready to take action. The Ram was parked around back, out of the sight of prying eyes. They were discussing what to do about the Ram, as they both knew it was likely to be something the cops would be watching for. They needed to figure out how to get to Kingfisher. They were pretty sure he was being held at a place owned by a rancher named Norm Smith. They'd driven by his place a couple of times very early that morning. The guy had a large horse barn, the kind that would be best for keeping a racehorse. It was the only place with a barn like that anywhere near the Troxler ranch. It also had a small racetrack, a practice track. They could return there after dark and find the horse, if it was there, and deal with it.

Both men stewed with anger and blamed Kit for all their troubles. They were determined to get their revenge, but they needed money. Sam had tried to get some using the credit card he'd stolen from his father's safe, but it was frozen. He couldn't believe his father had already figured out that he'd been in the safe.

He still had a few hundred dollars of the stolen cash left. Herbie had some money, but they needed more, and they were intent on getting what they needed. They finally settled on a plan. They assumed that the missing Ram had been noticed. Just in case the cops were looking for it, they decided to leave it parked where it was so they could avoid detection until they could move on to the next step of their deadly plan.

They had ditched their cell phones and bought some cheap burner phones quite some time ago. Using one of those, Sam called Vince Hodson. Vince was as angry as they were, and like them, he blamed Kit Troxler for all his troubles, including the fact that he'd gotten fired and charged with various crimes. "We need your help now, Vince," Sam said. "We can't get to that horse of Kit's without different wheels."

"That's for sure," Vince agreed. "What do you need me to do?"

"My truck is parked behind a motel we're holed up in," Sam said. He gave him the address. "I'll leave the signed title and the keys under the floor mat on the passenger side of the truck."

"I'm in the clear right now. I'm out of jail on bond, and there is no way I'm going back," Vince growled. "So this had better work."

"Hey, Vince, that truck has a clean title," Sam said. "You won't have a problem trading it in. Just make sure you get enough cash and an older car to keep us going for a while. When you've made the trade, let us know what the car is and then leave the keys and cash in it, and you can go. But don't go too far. As soon as we get those wheels and the cash, we're heading back down to Fillmore. We're going to take care of that horse tonight. We think we know where it is."

Randall had hoped to load Kingfisher and be on his way before it was fully dark. But he'd blown a tire on the stock trailer, and it had taken an extra couple of hours before it had been fixed. So by the time he pulled into the yard of Kit's ranch, it was late. Andy met him, and they unloaded the bulls. "Those are nice ones," Andy said. "We sure appreciate you doing this."

"It's the least I could do," Randall said. "Where's the horse?"

"He's back here. Norm Smith got really nervous, so he and I brought him back a while ago," Andy said.

"I don't think it would be safe for Bruce and me to head to my place tonight. We're both too tired, and I don't want to take a chance on having an accident and injuring Kit's horse. Is Kingfisher safe for tonight?"

"I hired a couple of guys to stay up all night in the barn, and Sheriff Ledford said he'd keep a deputy here as well. I wish our old dog hadn't died. All we have now is a small pup, and he's no help as a guard dog," Andy responded.

"I know what you're saying. I'm without a dog right now too. That's never good on a cattle ranch, but I haven't found a good replacement yet. Anyway, we'll run into town and get a room. We'll be back by daylight."

"Would you like to leave the trailer here?" Andy asked.

"No, it'll be fine," Randall assured him.

"I'll see you at daybreak then."

Randall hadn't attempted to hide his truck and horse trailer when he'd parked it beside a motel in Fillmore. Sam recognized it immediately as he and Herbie—both dressed in black—drove slowly up the street. They each carried a knife and a pistol. "I wonder what my dad's doing here," Sam said.

"Maybe he's helping Kit now."

"Helping him how?" Sam asked.

"I don't know. Maybe he's going to take Kingfisher someplace where he and Kit think we can't find him," Herbie suggested.

"Maybe," Sam conceded. "I don't want to go through the trouble of finding out where. We're probably right about where Kingfisher is now, so my selfish old dad won't need his truck and trailer to move him. Let's give him something else to do. Let's flatten all his tires."

"Hey, good idea," Herbie agreed with a big grin.

"You take the right side, and I'll take the left. If anybody comes by, duck out of sight until they've passed," Sam said.

"But what exactly are we going to do?" Herbie asked.

"Use your knife, you idiot. Slice the tires on both his truck and the trailer," Sam said.

Chuckling, the two fugitives hurried to complete the destruction. A couple of minutes later, they were back in the car Vince had obtained for them, an old rusty Chevy Impala. They quickly drove away. "Now to take care of Kingfisher," Herbie said. "You have Blaine's insulin and syringe, don't you?"

"In my pocket," Sam assured him.

The two men found that the yard at the Smith ranch was unguarded. Earlier, they'd seen men wandering around, which was part of what made them think they'd found where Kingfisher was being held. Leaving their old Chevy hidden alongside the road in a clump of trees, they slowly worked their way to the ranch. It was the middle of the night, and it was very dark. Without the aid of a small flashlight, they might not have been able to find their way.

A yard light stood between the house and the barn. They saw no other lights, so they stuck tightly to the very edges of light. They stayed several feet apart with Sam in the lead, moving cautiously. They did not see any of the men that had been there earlier, but they both knew they could still be around. Eventually, they found a small door that led into the barn from the back and stepped inside.

They had not considered a dog—not having seen any earlier. That was a mistake. A growl in the darkness was the only warning they had before Herbie was attacked. He screamed as the dog tore at his right arm, shredding it. He beat at it with his left hand. "Sam, help me!" he shouted.

Sam, coldhearted as a man could be, left Herbie to fight the dog. He found a light switch and flooded the barn with light. He hurried deeper into the barn, checking the stalls one at a time. It didn't take long before he realized there were no horses. None!

Cursing, he headed for the exit where Herbie was down on the ground with the dog still tearing at him. Only now did Sam attempt to help his comrade. He kicked at the dog. Then he pulled out his knife and stabbed. The dog yelped and jumped back, letting go of Herbie.

"Let's go," Sam said urgently as he stuck his bloody knife back in the scabbard on his side.

"Help me up," Herbie said weakly. "I'm hurt bad."

Sam grabbed his left arm and pulled him to his feet. Herbie was indeed in a bad way. His face was torn to shreds, and blood poured from both arms and legs. He even had blood coming from his throat. But he stumbled along beside Sam, even dragging on him, as they fled along the edge of the light. Finally, after they found the security of darkness, Sam let go of him. At that same moment, Sam heard someone shouting. Footsteps pounded from the house toward the barn. Herbie slumped to the ground with a groan of pain. He was too big a man for Sam to carry, so Sam did what cowards always do; he fled and left Herbie where he'd fallen. A short while later, he was safe inside his motel room, his mission to destroy Kingfisher a failure and his partner lost to him.

He called Vince, waking him up. "Kingfisher wasn't in the barn," he announced to his cousin.

"But you said he was at the Smith ranch," Vince said. "Now what are you going to do?"

"I don't know," Sam said.

"Okay, you, Herbie, and I need to get together, I guess. You guys don't seem to be able to handle this by yourselves," Vince said angrily. "Nothing's changed. All your life I've had to look after you and fight your fights. I can see I'll have to do it again. We've got to find that horse. Kit has ruined my life, and he's going to pay."

"Ah, about Herbie," Sam said as he heard a siren on the street outside the hotel.

"What about Herbie?"

"I lost him," Sam said.

"What do you mean, you lost him?" Vince asked.

"A dog got him."

"Where did you leave him?"

"He's at the Smith place. He collapsed, and I couldn't carry him."

Vince groaned. "Did you know your dad is here in Fillmore?"

"Yeah. Herbie and I flattened all his tires. I think he was going to do something with Kingfisher for Kit," Sam said.

"Well, at least you did one thing right. We both need to sit tight for now. We can't be seen. I'll call you later," Vince said. "I've got to think."

Brandon had joined his friend Karl Shutter, and the two of them had driven together to Fillmore in Karl's vehicle. They'd stayed in the same motel as Randall Overmyer and were both up and ready to go when Brandon's phone rang. It was not yet light outside.

"Brandon, this is Randall. We've got a problem that will delay us this morning."

"What kind of problem?" Brandon asked.

"All the tires on my truck and trailer have been slashed," he said, sounding rather calm under the circumstances. "It had to have been Sam. No one else would know my truck and trailer."

"So he's close by?" Brandon asked.

"He is or was," Randall agreed.

"I'll come out and take a look." Brandon put his phone back in his pocket and told Karl what had happened.

Together, the two men stepped outside and walked around the side of the motel to where Randall and Bruce were standing beside the crippled truck and trailer. Brandon's phone rang again.

"Detective Phelps, this is Sheriff Ledford. We believe we have the man who killed the deputy in Nye County."

"Herbie?" Brandon asked. "Where is he?"

"He's been flown to Provo on a medical helicopter. We don't think he'll make it. He was torn up pretty badly by Norm Smith's dog during the night. Smith found him lying beside the road not far from his house," the sheriff reported. "He had lost a lot of blood and was unconscious."

"He was alone?" Brandon asked.

"We doubt it," the sheriff said. "We also found Norm's big dog in his barn. It had been stabbed but is alive and at the vet's. Herbie did not stab it. He has a knife on him, but it's clean, no blood. Someone else did."

"So Sam stabbed the dog," Brandon concluded. "Kingfisher wasn't there, so at least they didn't harm him."

"He's safe at Kit's ranch. I just talked to Andy. Those men you detailed there for security told Andy it has been a quiet night," Sheriff Ledford said. "I think we need to have Mr. Overmyer load the horse and get on his way. I just spoke with Lawrence Heslop. He's already picked up Wiona Hubbard in Tonopah and is flying here to keep an eye on Randall as he moves the horse."

"I'm afraid it'll be a while before that can happen," Brandon said. He explained about Randall's slashed tires.

"That will take a long time to fix," Sheriff Ledford said.

"Too long," Brandon agreed. "Let me make a call and see if we can use Kit's truck and trailer instead."

Brandon called Paizlee, who sounded drowsy. He explained things to her after she seemed awake enough.

"Kit's asleep," she said. "I'll tell him when he wakes up. Just go ahead and use our truck. Andy has the keys. And Brandon, please be careful."

"Always am," he said. "That's how I got to be so old." He chuckled. "I'll see you in a few hours."

The town was waking up. A pickup truck drove past, followed by an older sedan, an Impala. Brandon turned to Randall. "We'll use Kit's truck."

"Okay. Bruce will stay here with my truck and get the tires replaced, then drive back to my place later," Randall said.

"Then you'll need to come with us out to Kit's ranch," Brandon said. "I'll call Andy so he'll be expecting us. Perhaps he could drive Kit's truck and you could ride with him so that he'll know where to go."

"All right. Let's get that horse to my ranch," Randall said.

"Vince, I just drove past my dad and Bruce and a couple of other guys. They're all standing around Dad's truck and trailer looking stunned." Sam laughed. "They don't seem to know what to do."

"Find someplace where you can keep an eye on them," Vince said. "I want to know exactly what they do."

"Okay," Sam agreed. He parked the Impala up the street and watched. He saw his dad and a couple of men get in a shiny black SUV with California license plates. As they drove off, he dialed his cousin and told him what was happening.

"Follow them," Vince said, "but don't let them see you."

"I've got it," Sam said. "Oh, a deputy sheriff just stopped by Dad's truck." Sam pulled onto the street. "He's talking to Bruce."

"Don't worry about them. Just figure out where your dad's going," Vince told him. "And don't try anything stupid."

"Where are you?" Sam asked.

"I'm close. I can see you. That's good. Now don't get too far behind, but make sure you see where they're going," Vince said. "Once we know, then we'll figure out what to do."

CHAPTER NINETEEN

"THEY WENT TO KIT'S RANCH, Vince," Sam reported. "Those fools took the horse back there. I'll get to him tonight."

"Think about this, Sam," his more intelligent and cunning cousin said. "If they have him there, I would be surprised if they don't have security as tight as Fort Knox. Just lay low and watch for them to come out with the horse after a while."

"How can they do that?" Sam asked. "It's going to take hours to replace the tires on Dad's truck and trailer."

"Maybe they'll wait hours before they leave," Vince suggested. "Or maybe they'll use Kit's truck and trailer."

"I hadn't thought of that," Sam admitted.

"Keep watch. Let me know if Kit's truck and trailer come out of there. If it does, then your job will be to follow them. I'll come too, but I'll stay farther back."

"I've got it," Sam said. "And I'll also watch to see if Bruce brings my dad's truck in after a few hours. We have nothing but time on our hands."

"That's all you've ever had," Vince remarked snidely. "I used to have a job. Two jobs, actually. The second one was keeping you out of trouble. You have no idea the risks I've taken to help you. Someday, I'll tell you about the most risky one, not counting this thing that's going on now."

Sam bristled at the jab and went silent. An hour later, he perked up. As soon as he could see that Kit's truck was headed north on the interstate, he again called Vince, even though he was still smarting from what Vince had so clearly implied earlier. It wasn't his fault Vince had gotten fired. No. Everything was Kit Troxler's fault.

Vince took his time answering his phone. "I've been listening to the local news on the radio, Sam. You and Herbie messed up big time last night, and now Herbie is dead."

"He died?" Sam asked. "It was just a dog bite. He should have been able to crawl away and hide."

"He died!" Vince repeated. "It was more than just a dog bite. That dog must have torn him to pieces. If he could have gotten away, he'd have called you. I hope you're happy."

"Hey, it ain't my fault," Sam whined.

"Well, it sure isn't mine!" Vince shouted through the phone. For a moment, neither of the cousins said anything. Then Vince went on. "I guess there is one good thing about it. It will take some of the heat off of you. I mean, you know, you didn't kill a cop, but he did."

"Yeah, good point," Sam said. Without giving time for Vince to come up with anything else, Sam quickly added, "Kit's truck and trailer are headed north on the freeway."

"North?" Vince asked.

"Yep. Maybe they're taking him to Wyoming or Idaho," Sam guessed.

"Or anywhere else in the country," Vince retorted. "Keep him in sight. I won't be very far behind you."

The route that Randall and Andy took was a long and roundabout way to get to Randall's ranch. Riding with them was one of the security men. Brandon rode with his former Seal buddy, Karl, and they went out ahead of them on the planned route to watch for any kind of trouble. Another vehicle, this one an old pickup truck, with a new and powerful engine and the best suspension money could buy, followed close behind Kit's truck and trailer. Farther back were two agents in a white sedan. Lawrence Heslop and Wiona Hubbard flew overhead.

Eventually, they began to travel in a westerly direction. Two hours into the trip, as they were winding on a less-traveled local road in the western part of Utah, Brandon's secure radio beeped. "Brandon, it's Wiona. I keep seeing an old-looking blue sedan. It's about a half mile behind Randall and Andy. I've looked through the binoculars, but I can't really see what the driver looks like."

"When did you first notice it?" he asked.

"It was just after we left the interstate. We keep circling around up here, and when I saw it for the third time, I thought I should let you know."

"Good work, Wiona," Brandon said. "I'll have Karl's guys check it out."

Karl, who had listened with Brandon, said, "We'll start back toward the horse trailer, Brandon. I'll let my men know about the potential problem." To the agent in the truck with Randall and Andy, he gave an order to have them stop and wait until further notice. To the men in the old pickup trailing the horse trailer, he gave orders to close in on Andy and provide close protection and backup to him and Randall, explaining that they were heading back their way.

To his operatives in the white sedan, he said, "Intercept the blue car when you see it." After that he spoke to Lawrence and Wiona in the plane. "Let us all know when our men get close to the car you spotted, Wiona."

"Okay," she responded, "but we have to circle around and around up here. Lawrence can't fly as slowly as you guys are driving."

Sam saw a white car coming up behind him at high speeds. He made a fast call to Vince to tell him about it. Then he stuffed his phone into his pocket and watched as the car drew ever nearer. He slowed down, thinking maybe whoever it was would fly past him. He felt a rush of panic as they pulled right up alongside him on the narrow road and slowed to match his speed. There were two men in the car.

The passenger, a musclebound man, signaled for Sam to pull over. Instead, Sam slammed on his brakes, turned as fast as he could, and sped back the way he'd just come. They were soon right on his tail again. He weaved back and forth in an attempt to keep them from passing him again. Panicked, he reached out of his window with his pistol and fired a shot. The car backed off for only a moment, and then it approached again. He fired two more quick shots and laughed when he saw steam pouring from the front of the car. He sped up, leaving the other car behind.

Suddenly, his car shuddered. Then his rear window blew out. He could see in his mirror that one of the men in the now stationary vehicle was firing a rifle. He tried to drive faster, but his car began to shake and pull to the left. He tried to keep it on the road, but he couldn't. The car ran off the road and into a large bunch of brush. Sam bailed out of his car, looking at the back end to see what had caused him to lose control. His left rear tire was shredded.

Cursing, he sprinted away, ducking low. He took a fraction of a second to look back. The two men did not pursue him, but one of them was taking careful aim, and a second later, another shot rang out. Behind him, his car blew up, and flames engulfed it. What was up with those guys? Who were they? He hadn't done anything to them.

They did not attempt to fire again, and Sam got back up on the pavement and ran for all he was worth. Before long, his lungs were burning. He felt close to passing out. But before he did, a car stopped.

Vince leaned out of the window. "Get in!"

Sam barely shut the door before the car spun around and raced east. "What was that all about?" Sam asked when he finally got his breath back.

"It looks like Kit has spent money on some hired killers," Vince said. "We've gotta get away from here and ditch this car."

"They couldn't have got a good look at this car," Sam reasoned. "They were too far back."

"Didn't you see the airplane?" Vince asked.

"What airplane?"

"One circled right over you when you jumped out of your car. Look back there. You might be able to see it," Vince ordered.

"Yeah, I see it. It's coming right up behind us," Sam shouted.

Vince stopped the car and bailed out. "Get out, Sam. We're going to shoot at that plane. Maybe we'll get lucky and shoot it down. It's flying pretty low."

Wiona had been keeping the rest of them apprised of developments as they occurred below them. Lawrence banked the plane as he drew near the car on the ground, the one that had picked up the driver of the destroyed blue car. "They're out of the car," Wiona shouted, watching through her binoculars. "They've got guns. They're shooting at us!"

Lawrence sped the plane up and moved out of the range of their pistols before saying, "I think they hit the plane, but everything feels okay. I need to be sure though." He chuckled. "Such fun. Beats the courtroom any old day. I've never been shot at before."

Wiona reported what had happened in a quavering voice. "It looked like Sam had been in the car that got blown up, and I think it may have been Vince who picked him up. I didn't get to study them for very long before they started shooting. But I've seen both their pictures, and I think it was them."

Karl's voice came on the radio in response. He was urgent and firm. "You guys back off. Don't take any more chances. Fly back toward us."

"I wonder if those guys are okay," Wiona said as they flew over the car the two agents had been in. They were standing outside the car.

"They look fine," Lawrence said. "This is a good straight stretch of road here. I'm going to set this old bird down."

Wiona tensed, made sure her seat belt was secured, and closed her eyes. This was not fun. She'd been shot at! The plane had been hit. And now they were going to land on a road! She shuddered. She opened her eyes to see the road rushing up to meet them. She quickly shut her eyes again and leaned forward.

She felt the plane slowing.

"Piece of cake," Lawrence said. "I just hope there's nothing seriously wrong with the plane. Wiona, open your eyes. You're missing all the fun."

She kept her eyes closed, her fists tightly balled, and waited for . . . she wasn't sure what. A few moments later, she felt the plane touch down, bounce back up, then touch down again, and finally slow to a stop. Only then did she open her eyes. They were safely on the ground.

With a chuckle, Lawrence said, "There, Wiona, that wasn't so bad, was it? Let's get out. I want to check the plane over. I'm pretty sure we got hit at least once."

It took a moment for the tension to drain away. Finally she did as instructed and climbed down to the road. She stepped away from the plane, off the pavement to the soft shoulder of the road. Lawrence was still chuckling. He walked over to her, put an arm around her shoulder, and hugged her gently. Then he said, "I'm sorry I frightened you. I've always wanted to do that."

She found her voice. "Do what?"

"Land on a country road where planes aren't supposed to land," he said. He stepped away from her. "Let's see if there's any damage."

They began to examine the plane. "Is this supposed to be here?" Wiona asked when she spotted a small hole on the underside of the right wing.

"Ah, so we did get hit. It looks like it just missed the fuel tank," he said. "We can be glad for that."

"What fuel tank?" she asked.

"The one in the wing," he said. "This plane has two tanks, one in each wing."

"Wouldn't that have blown us up?" she asked, trembling.

"I don't think so, but maybe. Glad it didn't." Lawrence chuckled again. "We're fine, Wiona, and so is Kit's horse. We did our job."

"I guess we did, didn't we?" she said as the fright wore off. "But those guys got away."

"I'm sure Brandon already has cops looking for them. We are safe to get the horse to Randall's ranch now."

Wiona looked around. "We're in the middle of nowhere," she said. "There can't be many cops close by in this empty place."

"Probably not," he agreed. "But someone will catch them sometime. Gee, if the cops didn't ever catch the bad guys, you and your mother and I would all be out of a job."

Just then, the large black SUV that was driven by Brandon's friend Karl Shutter stopped just short of the plane. Brandon and Karl jumped out. "Is everything okay?" Brandon asked with concern on his face.

"We're fine," Lawrence said. "Wiona and I just had a little fun, that's all."

Wiona pointed at the bullet hole she'd found. "He thinks this is fun," she said, trembling again.

The men hurried to where she and Lawrence were standing and looked up. "That's a bullet hole," Karl said. "We need to take this very seriously."

"Sure is a bullet hole there, but it didn't get the fuel tank," Lawrence said with a grin. "And it didn't interfere with the flaps. There may be one or two more holes though."

Brandon shook his head as the two former war buddies helped search for more bullet holes. The plane, it turned out, had been hit twice, but no serious damage was done.

"Okay, we'd better go talk to my men. Their car is out of commission. Then we need to get that horse to safety," Karl said urgently. "My guys in the pickup will stay behind the trailer the rest of the way."

"I'll wait here until you're sure everything's okay," Lawrence said. "Then, even though I think we've scared those two off, Wiona and I will fly on to Tonopah with you and keep watch again. She saw them with the binoculars after they jumped out of their car. She's pretty sure it was Sam and Vince." He paused for a moment. "You will go up with me again, won't you, Wiona?"

"Hey, you know what cowboys like Kit say, don't you?" Brandon asked in a teasing voice.

"What's that?" Wiona asked.

"When you fall off a horse, the first thing you do is climb right back on. That way you don't have time to work up a fear of riding. Same thing applies to airplanes."

"Okay. I'll get back in," she agreed, putting on a brave face.

"Kit's going to be so proud of you," Brandon said, grinning, and he followed Karl to his SUV.

"Don't tell Kit," she said. "I will do it myself when we get back. I don't want him to worry."

"Okay. If you say so," Brandon called back to her.

Arrangements had to be made for someone to come out and pick up Sam's burning car and the other disabled one. The men who'd ridden in the damaged car were left to explain to the cops a very sanitized version of what had happened, and the rest of the party finally headed to Randall's ranch.

Lawrence took off from the narrow road like he'd done it a hundred times before. And soon he and Wiona were circling around above the truck and trailer with its expensive cargo, Kingfisher. Karl and Brandon again took the lead while the two agents in the old pickup followed behind. The rest of the trip back was uneventful. By evening, Kingfisher was safely tucked away in Randall's barn with a host of security agents making sure Sam and Vince didn't show up later and cause any more damage.

CHAPTER TWENTY

"Hey, Wiona," Kit said with a grin as she walked into his hospital room that evening, followed by Lawrence and Brandon. "Looks like you got Kingfisher down here without any problems."

Paizlee, who was hugging Brandon, looked over at Wiona. "Like you asked, we didn't tell him. So you go ahead."

"Tell me what?" Kit asked as he sat up straighter and winced in pain. "He is here, isn't he?"

Wiona grinned at him. "Kingfisher is at Randall's ranch, and he's safe, but there was a little bit of trouble as we were bringing him."

"What happened?" Kit asked, concerned.

"Nothing serious," Wiona said as she squeezed his hand and looked adoringly into his eyes.

"Wiona, what aren't you telling me?" he asked with his eyebrows scrunched.

"Well, Sam and Vince got away again. At least we think it was them. Pretty sure, actually. Anyway, they followed us, and there was some shooting, and one of Karl's cars was hit. But the guys are okay. One of them hit Sam's car with something pretty powerful after he'd left it and ran off on foot into the brush. It blew up."

"Wow. Those guys sure must hate me," he said. "That sounds like a lot of trouble. I'm glad you have all arrived safely."

"Tell him the rest, Wiona," Lawrence said with a bit of a chuckle.

"Oh yeah," she said in a teasing voice. "Lawrence had a lot of fun. He landed on this little narrow highway with his plane. It scared me, but it turned out okay."

"Tell him why we landed, Wiona," Lawrence said a little sternly.

Wiona shuddered then. "Well, you see, Kit, those guys shot at me and Lawrence in the plane. And they hit it twice. We landed so we could make sure there was no serious damage."

"Oh, Wiona!" Kit said in alarm.

"Hey, it's okay. Like they say, all's well that ends well," she said with a grin. "It really was a hoot."

Kit took a moment to consider what he'd been told. Then he said, "And you got in the plane again after a scare like that, or did you ride with Karl and Brandon in a car?"

"When you fall off of a horse, what do you do?" she asked.

Kit nodded. "I get it. I get back on. I'm proud of you. Now, you guys, I want to know everything that happened."

So they told him.

Anger and hatred have a way of cankering the soul. Evil men become more evil when revenge, whether it is justified or not, is what they seek. Thus it was with Sam Overmyer and his cousin, Vince Hodson. Nothing mattered to them as much as exacting the revenge they felt Kit Troxler had coming to him. They attributed the death of their friend Herbie to Kit. They blamed the loss of Sam's racehorse on Kit. They blamed Sam's estrangement from his father on Kit. And finally, Vince's job loss was also blamed on Kit. They took no responsibility for having done anything to contribute to their own downfalls.

They had no idea where Kit's horse, Kingfisher, had been taken, but they intended to figure it out. Unfortunately, they couldn't ask someone since they were wanted men, and one slipup could land them both in jail. That was to be avoided at all costs. So they schemed.

"I have an idea," Sam said as they sat in a recently stolen pickup at a rest area along I-15, north of Fillmore.

"Let's hear it," Vince said.

"I think we need to see where they take Kit when he's discharged from the hospital. Wherever he is taken is probably where we'll find Kingfisher," Sam reasoned.

"The problem with that is that we are both too well known in Tonopah," Vince countered. "We can't go there and just see for ourselves."

"Then we need to figure out a disguise," Sam suggested.

"I'm sure we could do that, but I know of another way," his cousin said.

"Let's hear it, Vince."

"A couple of the officers I used to work with did some really stupid things. I know what they did, but they don't know that I know," he said with a sinister smile.

"Are you suggesting blackmail?" Sam asked.

"I am. I could let their secrets be known without having to expose myself to do it. They would be shaking in their boots right now if they knew that I know what they did. Since I lost my job, thanks to Kit, I have nothing to lose by letting their highly illegal acts be known," Vince said.

"I think it sounds like a great idea," Sam said, smiling at the thought of getting someone else to do their spying for them. "Might they also be persuaded to act on your behalf in doing damage to Kit's horse or his home or his sister?"

"Oh yes. I think that can be arranged. And I also have some associates who aren't cops who have a lot to lose if I reveal their actions."

"Who exactly do you have in mind? Do I know them too?"

"You know one of my cop friends. He's a deputy I worked with," Vince said. "The other one is a Las Vegas cop who is the brother of the deputy you know. Their names are Kirby and Mickey Fry. And if word got out what they did, they would fry."

"I know Kirby, but I don't know where he's from."

"They grew up in Los Angeles but drifted to Nevada after they were both out of high school. Kirby landed a job with my department, and Mickey went to work with the Las Vegas Metropolitan Police Department."

"What did they do? Little things or something big?" Sam asked.

"If you think of bank robbery as big, then yes, it is big."

Sam's eyes popped wide. "No, not something like that? I can't believe any cops would have robbed a bank. That would have been too stupid."

"Believe it. And here's the beautiful part, Sam. I have proof."

"What kind of proof?"

"It happened like this. Several months back, I was at a party with the two of them and some other fellows we know. Everyone got plastered. And everyone got talking big. I had a feeling about what kind of thing was coming, so I hid a little recorder in the room and then told them I had to go. I did leave, but I came back later to retrieve my recorder and listen to it. I was about knocked over by what I heard.

"One of the guys who isn't a cop made a dare to the others," Vince continued. "He bet they wouldn't dare rob a bank. At first they all just kind of laughed at the idea, but he kept prodding them. Finally, Mickey and Kirby got to thinking about how much money they could make. Cops aren't well paid, you know, and they can always use a little extra cash."

"But rob a bank? No way!" Sam said.

"Yes!" Vince said, his eyes glistening as he remembered what his friends had planned and carried out.

"They actually did it?"

"Yep. They did. After I left that day, I guess they decided they wouldn't tell me. And none of them ever did. Mickey and Kirby and some of the non-cops were the ones who actually planned to go in and rob the place. Another non-cop was to be the driver of the getaway car."

"Vince, this seems awfully farfetched to me," Sam said. "Wouldn't they be recognized?"

"They didn't do it in Nevada. No, it went down clear up in San Francisco, and they decided on the specific bank that night. I got it all on my handy little recorder. So I went up there on my own and watched the thing go down from across the street. I videoed everything I saw them do. All of them had their faces covered, and they used notes to make their demands," Vince said. "But I could tell by what they wore which guy was which."

"I can't believe they never figured out that you knew what they did," Sam said.

"This is the beautiful part. I always figured that if I needed them to do something for me, like I need them to now, that this would be my leverage. And I do have a lot of leverage, Sam. You see, some guy in the bank tried to be a hero, and he was shot and killed. So it's not just a bank robbery I can turn them in on. Murder too."

Sam was thoughtful for a moment. "That's really bad. But if you somehow turned them in, wouldn't they wonder how you knew? If they wondered and told the cops, couldn't you be charged with not stopping it once you knew what they were doing?"

"I suppose there's a small chance of that, but they wouldn't think of it since they'd be so busy trying to dig their way out of trouble."

"Do you know how much money they got?" Sam asked.

"I do. Kirby accidentally let me know that they had a meeting planned back in Vegas a few days later. The meeting was set on a day I was supposed to be on duty in Nye County. I think they did that so I wouldn't try to crash their meeting since we were, after all, buddies. Of course, Kirby didn't actually say that they would be talking about the holdup and all, since I wasn't supposed to know anything about that. And if I hadn't known what they'd done, I'd never have been able to guess why they were getting together without including me."

"So I guess you don't know what happened at that meeting," Sam said.

"Actually, I do," he bragged. "I managed to fake an illness and got three days of sick leave. I bought a listening device in Vegas that would work through most walls. They planned to meet in a hotel room in Vegas. They had rented it a couple of days before. I don't know why, but it was a day or so before Kirby left Tonopah. Without realizing it, he slipped and mentioned the room number but not what they planned to do. I figured I knew, so I went down and rented the room next door under a fake name. I had to pay a few extra bucks to get the room I wanted, but it worked out. Anyway, I set up my little device. I heard it all quite clearly through the wall. And in answer to your question, they stole nearly a million dollars. Quite a haul, wouldn't you say?"

Sam didn't argue with that. "Let's get on it then."

"Just a minute, Sam. Let's consider all the angles here. One of the guys who robbed the bank owns a couple of drones he uses to video things," Vince revealed. "That could be useful to us. I've been thinking; how do we know for sure that Kingfisher is no longer on Kit's ranch?"

"Duh," Sam said. "I watched them take him away, and we followed them for a long time before we ran into trouble."

"You didn't tell me that you actually saw Kingfisher when they loaded him," Vince said.

"Well, no, I didn't actually see them load the horse," Sam admitted.

"You also didn't actually see him inside the horse trailer, did you?"

"No, but I could tell there was a horse in there," Sam argued.

"In other words, we don't know that this wasn't all a ruse to try to make us think he was gone so we would leave him alone. I think the first thing we need to do is take a look at Kit's place with a drone. And even though I could blackmail my friend on this, I think I can get him to help us without actually having to resort to that," Vince said thoughtfully. "I'll keep the blackmailing for when we need it more. I'll see if I can reach him. If he says he can't do it, then I might have to let him know that I know about the robbery and the murder. Either way, if Kingfisher isn't there, then we'll find a way to put pressure on someone to tell us where they took him. And I would be willing to include your dad in those we pressure. You don't object to that, do you?"

"Certainly not," Sam said coldly. "He turned against me. So he can't blame anyone but himself for whatever happens to him."

"Good. So first we need to find out how soon Harry can have a drone in Fillmore."

"Harry is the guy with the drones? What's his last name?" Sam asked.

"Harry Murray. He's from Henderson. He's a daredevil. He does all kinds of crazy stunts," Vince said.

"Wait. I know that name," Sam said. "Doesn't he do motorcycle jumps, crazy dangerous ones?"

"That's the guy. He's the one that came up with the idea of robbing the bank in San Francisco. As I've thought about it, I came to the conclusion that Harry had the bank robbery thing in mind a long time before that party. You see, he was the one who suggested which bank to rob. I think he'd scoped it out already," Vince said. "He's a bit crazy but a good friend."

"Then call him," Sam said.

As it turned out, Harry Murray was more than happy to help. And he agreed to do it for only expenses. "I owe you, Vince, for helping me fly this drone a few times, and you didn't charge me. This is the least I can do since the cost is minimal." Sam and Vince had the money to pay him with some of what was left from the proceeds of the sale of Sam's Dodge Ram.

"How soon can you help me?" Vince asked him on the phone.

"Will tomorrow work? I don't have anything going on for a couple of days. Where do you need me?" Harry asked.

"Do you know where Fillmore, Utah, is?" Vince asked him.

"Been through there on I-15 dozens of times," Harry said.

"That's where we need you."

"You said you need to take a look at a ranch from the air?"

"That's right, Harry, and this is not something I want broadcasted. It needs to be kept totally quiet. You can handle that, can't you?"

"You know me well enough to know that I keep my mouth shut," Harry said, sounding just a little hurt.

"Let's pick a place to meet, and it needs to be really discreet."

"Yeah, I'll bet. I've heard about the trouble you and your cousin are in," Harry said. "If I can help out somehow, I'd be glad to do it. And while we're at it, I can give you a few more pointers on running my drone."

"That would be great. By the way, who's been talking to you?" Vince asked.

"Kirby, of course. He told me you'd been fired and what your sheriff used as an excuse," Harry said. "Kirby said you were treated badly. He says you didn't do whatever it is the sheriff accused you of. He says it's all because of a crooked jockey from Utah."

"You know quite a bit," Vince said. "And it's all true. The ranch we need to look at is owned by Kit Troxler, the jockey you just mentioned. He has caused me and my cousin no end of trouble."

"Then let's meet," Harry said. "This sounds like fun. And you know how I like fun."

They decided on a location for the next day at noon.

CHAPTER TWENTY-ONE

BRANDON HAD PICKED UP PAIZLEE and was taking her out to Randall's ranch. She was, she'd said, going stir-crazy. He had hesitated until Kit said, "Seriously, Brandon. She doesn't deserve to be cooped up here like this every day. Let her go see Kingfisher and even take him out for some exercise."

"Are you sure that's a good idea?" Brandon had asked even as he honestly looked forward to some time alone with Paizlee. He'd wanted to get to know this girl better since the very first day they'd met.

"What can happen?" Paizlee had asked lightly. "I mean, I'd be with the toughest and meanest guy I've ever met. If you can't protect little ole me, then who can?" And with that, she'd rolled those sparkling, light-blue eyes of hers, and he'd given in.

"Randall has a nice ranch," she said when they reached the ranch and looked over the yard and fields beyond. "I can't imagine why Sam wasn't willing to do his part here. I mean, this could have all been his someday." She waved her hand in a broad, sweeping gesture.

"I guess he just doesn't have the love of the land and of the animals that you and Kit do," Brandon responded.

Randall walked toward them, a big smile on his face. "Welcome, you two," he said. After giving Brandon a hearty handshake, he reached out, took Paizlee in his arms, and hugged her.

Brandon watched her reaction to the hug from a man whose son wanted her and her brother dead. He liked what he saw.

"You have no idea how much Kit and I appreciate what you're doing for us," Paizlee said. "You are a wonderful man."

Randall beamed for a moment, and then sadness clouded his intelligent brown eyes. When he spoke, it was with a catch in his voice. "Paizlee, not once in Sam's adult life has he ever said anything that kind to me. You and Kit are more than welcome here anytime. I mean it. You have brightened up my life, and I badly needed that. Come on. Let's go have a look at that gorgeous stallion of yours. I think he's lonely."

One of Karl's men watched them with an expert eye. He looked around, alert to any sign of danger. Brandon did the same, but he saw none. The two men nodded at each other, and then Randall led the way into the barn, a barn that was every bit as nice as the one the Troxlers owned in Millard County. Brandon was impressed. Kingfisher was not the only horse in there, and as they walked down the alleyway past the stalls, Randall spoke to each horse as they poked their noses through to see him. He patted heads with genuine affection.

Even though Paizlee was anxious to see Kingfisher, she admired every equine head they passed. Brandon could both see and feel a bond developing between the rancher and the young woman as she spoke kind words about his horses.

Kingfisher whinnied, his magnificent head poking out of the window in his stall when Paizlee approached. She ran the last few steps and patted his forehead with affection, kissing him quite tenderly on the face. "I'm going in, Randall."

He nodded. "I'd expect nothing less."

She opened the stall door and stepped inside, shutting it most of the way behind her.

Brandon had been around horses some in his life and enjoyed riding, but what he saw as he and Randall stood looking into the stall was beyond his life's experience. Paizlee threw her arms around the big stallion's neck, pulling his head down, and then she hugged him tightly, standing there without saying another word, just keeping her head against his shiny, black coat. For several minutes, she didn't move, and the horse stood there like he was enjoying receiving the show of affection as much as Paizlee was enjoying giving it.

Randall appeared to be deeply touched.

"I'd say she's missed him," Brandon said.

Randall nodded and, while keeping his eyes on Paizlee and Kingfisher, said, "That girl loves that horse. I've never witnessed anything like it on my ranch. It does my heart good. And I suspect her brother feels the same way she does."

"He does," Paizlee said from inside the stall. She stepped back and surveyed Kingfisher as he nuzzled her neck with what could only be termed as affection. She then began to inspect him, lifting each of his feet in turn, looking at them closely and then putting them gently back down. She patted his muscled rump, then slid around the back of him and continued on the other side. It was a good fifteen minutes before she finally patted him on the head again, planted an affectionate kiss, and left the stall.

Her eyes were glistening. "He looks so good, Randall."

"Honestly, Paizlee," Randall began, "I've owned and ridden a lot of horses in my life. I know horses like a dentist knows teeth. But I've never seen a finer stallion than this one. He's truly magnificent. Should we catch him?"

"Oh yes, please, let's do," she said.

"We brought your gear down with us," he said. "It's all here in my tack room."

Brandon simply stood out of the way as the rancher and the young horsewoman caught and saddled the stallion. They put a racing saddle on him, something that seemed like nothing to Brandon. It was small, light, and the stirrups were slender. He followed Randall as Paizlee led Kingfisher out into the bright sunlight. "Where do you exercise your horses?"

"Just follow me," Randall said and led the way past the barn. They soon came to a well-groomed track beyond a thick stand of trees. Brandon opened the gate, and Paizlee led the horse in. "I won't be too long. Watch me, if you will, and tell me if you see anything that's not quite right with him. If he feels okay today, I'd like to put my regular racing saddle on him tomorrow and give him a good run. Today, I'll just get a feel for him." She put on her racing helmet and adjusted the strap. She turned toward Brandon, who was standing a few feet back, near Randall. Karl's man also stayed near, ever watchful, a reminder that danger could easily lurk close by.

"So what saddle is that?" Brandon asked.

She grinned. "It's an old practice saddle."

Brandon was amazed at Paizlee's ease and grace as she accepted Randall's offered hand, putting one foot on it and then swinging effortlessly into the saddle as he lifted her. She set her boots quickly into the stirrups. Kingfisher was a truly beautiful specimen of a horse, but Brandon could say the same for the girl who was now on the horse's back.

"Do you have your phone with you?" she asked.

"I do," he said as he dug it out.

"Would you mind taking a couple of pictures of us to show Kit? And when I come past here in a little bit, we'll be going at a pretty good clip. Not full on, but fast. I'd like you to video us as we pass. I want to let Kit take a look."

"I'd love to." Brandon began taking pictures right then. He wanted them for himself as well as for Kit. This girl was stirring his very soul.

She started off, walking at first. "Look at that horse, would you?" Randall said as he moved away from them. "He's prancing. He can feel it. He wants to run. A true racehorse likes nothing better. But she's in control. That girl is amazing."

After a little bit, Paizlee let him trot. Then they began to slowly lope. Even as they got farther and farther away, Brandon could see what Randall had pointed out; the black stallion wanted to run.

Brandon hadn't noticed Randall's foreman approach them, because he'd been so busy admiring Paizlee and Kingfisher. It was only when Bruce spoke that Brandon noticed him. He chided himself. Some protector he was. He needed to be more alert and not let himself get so caught up in Paizlee.

Bruce, who had a set of binoculars around his neck, said, "Boss, I've seen some good horsemen in my day, but that girl, when she swung up on that magnificent animal, became one with him. I could see it. I would guess Kit is just the same. What beauty. What a horse."

"You're right," Randall said. "That horse was bred to run, and that girl was born to ride."

Brandon watched them as they spoke with each other. Both were smiling. Not any of the hatred, anger, and spite that Sam possessed showed anywhere in these two men. He felt like bringing Kingfisher here had been the right decision.

Together, the three men watched as the horse and rider started around the bend at the far end of the track. At that point, Bruce lifted his binoculars to his eyes. "He moves like a true champion, Boss," he said with a smile on his face.

Brandon strained to see them at that distance. He let his eyes slip for a moment and glanced back at Karl's agent. He appeared relaxed, but Brandon could tell he was watching everywhere almost at once. He raised a small radio to his mouth, and Brandon heard the agent say, "Is everything okay down there, Don?"

He didn't hear the response, and he felt himself tense. Only when the agent lowered the binoculars and nodded at Brandon did the tension ease. Karl's men were doing their job. He was glad they were here because one never knew what Sam and Vince might try next. Danger could easily lurk anywhere, and those men, like Brandon himself, were trained to see and feel it before tragedy occurred.

He looked back at the track and gasped. Paizlee and Kingfisher were coming toward them at an incredible speed. She was leaning forward, almost to his neck, and the magnificent horse came thundering toward them so fast it took his breath away. He lifted his cell phone and began to video. Brandon could scarcely keep the phone on them with how quickly they rode.

Then they were around the next curve and taking another lap. Bruce surprised Brandon when he suddenly let out a loud yelp followed by delighted laughter. Karl's agent was on his phone again. Paizlee was in good hands with Karl's experienced agents.

"Boss, did you see that?" Bruce shouted as both hands pumped the air.

"Yes," Randall said calmly. "What a beautiful sight. I can't imagine what it must look like when he runs full speed."

"Are you honestly saying that wasn't full speed?" Brandon piped up.

"Oh no, not nearly. She's holding him back, Brandon. I can't wait to see what he will do tomorrow," Randall said just as Brandon's phone began to ring.

"Hello," he said.

"Brandon, this is Andy," he heard Kit's ranch foreman say. "I think we have a problem. There's a drone flying overhead. That's never happened before on this ranch."

Instinctively, Brandon looked up. The Nevada sky was clear and hot. The only thing he could see up there was a soaring eagle out looking for a morning snack. He continued to survey the sky as he said to Andy, "I don't like the sound of that."

"I wonder if it's someone looking for Kingfisher," the foreman said.

"If so, they won't find him there," Brandon said with a measure of relief.

"Whoever is running that thing will probably be persistent," Andy said.

"How long has it been since you first spotted it?" Brandon asked.

"About five minutes. If it comes closer, would you like me to try to get a picture of it on my camera to show Karl and his agents?"

"Yes, please do that. I fear that it will only be a matter of time before they bring a drone here too," Brandon said. "That's got to be the work of Sam and Vince, although I can't imagine how they could pull that off."

"I'm sure it is. Has Paizlee seen Kingfisher yet?" Andy asked.

"Oh my, Andy. She's on him as we speak. I am blown away, both by that magnificent horse and by Paizlee."

"He's the best I've ever worked with, Brandon. And let me tell you this; Paizlee is not quite up to Kit's ability yet, but she is very, very good," Andy told him.

"I'll say. Send me a picture if you can and let me know when the drone leaves," Brandon said.

After ending the call, Randall returned to watching Paizlee. She was thundering toward them once again. A few hundred yards out, she began to slow Kingfisher down. By the time she and the horse reached them, she was walking him. Bruce met her and said, "Miss Troxler, I am very impressed by both you and that horse. That's probably the finest horse I've had the privilege of knowing, and as a former jockey, I've known some good ones. Let me walk alongside of you as he cools down and, if you don't mind, give you some of my observations."

"Thank you. I'd like that, and you can call me Paizlee."

Brandon, with a grin on his face, turned away and walked back to Karl's agent. "I'm Brandon Phelps."

"Hey, it's good to meet you. Karl talks about you all the time. He says he'd like to get you on the team but that you seem to enjoy what you're doing too much to change," the agent said. "My name's Santos Garcia. I was an Army Ranger, and I'm the team leader of the crew on duty here on the ranch today."

"It's good to meet you too, Santos," Brandon said. "I appreciate how observant you are."

"That's what we're trained to do, as you know," Santos said, even as he continued to look around. "Karl says you saved his life. He has nothing but good things to say about you."

"He would have done the same for me. He's a good man and a wonderful friend. You know how it is, Santos. That's what we signed up for. I'm sure you've saved a few lives yourself," Brandon said.

Santos nodded. "You had a phone call and started searching the sky. What's that about?"

Brandon filled him in on the phone call from Andy Boyse. "I'm sure it's no coincidence," Brandon said. "These guys have apparently stepped it up a notch."

"I'll let our team know, and I'll call Karl, unless you want to," Santos said.

"You go ahead," Brandon said.

"Either Karl or I will let you know what we need to do."

"Thanks, Santos," he said and walked back to where Randall was still watching Bruce and Paizlee as they walked Kingfisher around, cooling him off.

"That girl can ride," Randall said. "I figured she'd be good, but she's more than that. She's truly a gifted rider, and she loves it."

"Even I could tell that," Brandon agreed.

"Is everything all right?" Randall asked, shooting a glance at Santos.

"Does Sam know anyone who owns and flies drones?" Brandon asked.

A dark look passed over Randall's face. "I don't know who all he knows. But if he doesn't, I'd think that maybe my nephew does."

"There's a drone flying above the Troxlers' ranch," he said. "I wanted to make sure Karl's people knew about it," Brandon told him.

Randall shook his head sadly. "I'm glad Karl's people are here. Sheriff Watson would never have the resources to counter what Sam and Vince are apparently willing to do to stop this horse from racing. Sam's horse was a good one, but he and Kingfisher are not even comparable. I promise you, Brandon, that I will do whatever it takes to protect those kids and their horse."

"I know that, and I appreciate it," Brandon said. "So do they."

Together, Randall and Brandon walked toward Paizlee and Bruce. She had dismounted and was beaming. She let Bruce take the reins and hurried to Brandon. He hugged her. "I had no idea."

"About what?" she asked with an innocent look on her face, her brows knit but her eyes shining.

"About the way you can ride. I don't doubt for a minute that you'll do fine when you race him in California in a few weeks," he said. "I'm impressed, both by you and by Kingfisher."

"Isn't he wonderful?" she said.

"Both of you are," he responded, and even though he would not have thought that it was possible, the beaming face that was looking into his beamed even brighter. His heart melted.

CHAPTER TWENTY-TWO

"WE'LL NEED TO BRING IT down from time to time, as you know," Harry had said. "But I have plenty of batteries on hand here. And just to be on the safe side, since this isn't how I usually use this drone, we'll change the site we launch from every time we send it up for a half hour."

They sent the drone up three times, the last one being a little before dark. "Unless they kept that horse in the barn, that one you guys are looking for is not at this ranch. What's next?" Harry asked as they were packing up.

"I guess nothing for now. But we do need to find out where he was taken," Vince said in frustration. "Once we have an idea where he is, we may need you again."

They dismissed Harry the next morning, and the cousins sat down to once again consider what they should do. "There are more races coming up in California. Perhaps they're considering taking him out there somewhere," Vince said as he rubbed his chin thoughtfully.

"Do you seriously believe they would race him again?" Sam asked. "Kit can't ride. We know that. So who would they get to ride him?"

"I'm sure there are jockeys who would ride a horse like Kingfisher if they were asked to and paid well," Vince said. "But realistically, we wouldn't really know where to start to find him. At some point I'm sure we can find out if he's been entered in any races, and if he is, head there and do whatever it takes to stop him."

"Vince, I've been thinking about those pals of yours who robbed the bank and killed a man. I think we should use one or two of them to find out what we need to know," Sam said. "My father knows where Kingfisher is at. I'm sure of it. And so do Kit and his sister and that ranch foreman, Andy whatever his last name is."

Vince suddenly chuckled. "If those guys can rob a bank, they can kidnap someone for us."

"My father?" Sam asked. "That would serve him right."

"I was actually thinking of Andy, Kit's foreman," Vince responded. "We'll make him tell us where they took Kingfisher."

The two men considered it for a minute, and then Vince said, "Let's get Harry back here. He can do it for us." He called Harry's number.

"Did you decide you need me to fly my drone for you again?" Harry asked Vince when he answered.

"Yes," Vince lied. "How soon can you be back here?"

"A couple of hours," Harry said. "Just remember that I don't want to take any chances of getting caught. I wouldn't want to lose my license or get my drone grounded. As you know, this is a very expensive one, more advanced than most."

"You will be fine," Vince promised as he smiled slyly at his cousin. "You can count on it."

Kit was slowly walking the hallways when Brandon arrived at the hospital the next morning. Wiona and Paizlee were right with him, one on each side. Two of Karl's agents were also walking with them, one in front and one behind. Both were alert and prepared to act at the least provocation.

Brandon joined them and said, "Hey, Kit. Looking good."

"Thanks. I'm doing a lot better. They're letting me eat real food now."

"Is this the first time you've been walking?" Brandon asked.

"No, Wiona and Paizlee have been making me do this for a couple of days. It's getting easier now," Kit said.

"Don't let him blame us," Wiona said with a grin. "We're just following the doctor's orders."

"I admit it's good for me," Kit said with a feeble grin. "Hey, so Paizlee did well yesterday, huh?"

"I'll say. She really can ride," Brandon replied.

"I'm going to ride him again in a while," Paizlee said. "I'm impressed with Bruce. He knows what he's doing. He's a good trainer. He says he wants to put a stopwatch on me today to see how fast Kingfisher can do one lap on Randall's track."

"I'll be there watching," Brandon promised.

"Me too," Kit said.

"Woah, Kit," Paizlee said in alarm. "You can't leave the hospital. We'll video it for you."

They turned and headed slowly back toward Kit's room.

"I'm serious," he said. "I'd be okay for a few hours. We'll talk to the doctor. I need the fresh air, and if I could see Kingfisher, I'm sure it would give me a mental boost."

"It's not just your current state of recovery that concerns me," Brandon said. "You've got to remember that Sam and Vince are somewhere plotting against you."

"Didn't you guys say they were in Utah yesterday, flying a drone over the ranch a couple or three times?" Kit asked.

"Someone was, and Karl is dealing with that for us this morning, sending a couple of his operatives to check things out. But just because they may have been there yesterday, that doesn't mean they couldn't be here today," Brandon said.

"These guys here will take care of me," Kit said, pointing at the agent in front of him. "They're good. I trust them, and I trust you, Brandon."

"I don't know, Kit," Wiona said. "I don't think you should rush things."

"I'm tired of being babied," Kit snapped in an unusual show of anger.

Wiona's face went red. "Do you want me to go back home?" she asked. "If you don't want me here, I'll leave."

"I'm sorry," Kit said. "I didn't mean you or Paizlee. I meant this whole hospital thing. I like having you here. I really do."

"But if I baby you . . ." Wiona began.

"You don't," Kit said. "I didn't mean that. You're great company. But please, will you support me in this? I want to watch Paizlee ride Kingfisher today. I'm sure we can convince the doctor. I mean, I guess I wouldn't care if he made us take a nurse along."

"To baby you?" Wiona asked, but she was grinning now.

"If that's what it takes, then yes," he said firmly.

Brandon, experienced as he was in dealing with people who were anxious to get well and back into action, decided it might be a good thing for Kit. "Let's see if we can convince the doctor."

Once Brandon was on board, it didn't take long for Wiona and Paizlee to agree. Convincing the doctor proved to be a little more difficult, but Brandon was a great persuader. Dr. Sturgeon finally agreed on the condition that a nurse accompany them at their expense and on her own time to make sure an IV drip was kept going. It was set up for one in the afternoon.

Brandon, it was decided, was to take Paizlee out earlier and then return and accompany Kit and Wiona. He, of course, would be providing extra security with Karl's men. He left the others in the hospital and went out again to make a phone call he didn't want the others to overhear.

His call was to Sheriff Watson to inform him of what they had planned. The sheriff was fine with it.

As they talked, Brandon asked, "Sheriff, how much do you trust your other deputies? I'm hoping that Hodson was the only rotten apple in the bunch."

"I hope that too, but I am nervous, to be honest. One of my guys was pretty tight with Vince, and I've heard that he's been complaining that I was too hard on him."

"Do you mind telling me who that deputy is?" Brandon asked.

"No, but don't repeat it to anyone. It's a young fellow by the name of Kirby Fry. His brother Mickey works for the Las Vegas Metropolitan Police. I met Mickey once, and something about him didn't sit right with me," Sheriff Watson said. "But again, all I have is a feeling."

"It's been my experience that one unhappy person in any organization can cause widespread discontent," Brandon said as he made a mental note to see what he could learn about the Fry brothers.

"I don't do anything that could get me in trouble with the law," Harry protested. "I'll fly my drone for you again, but asking me to kidnap someone is stupid. I don't do stuff like that." He was angry and so was Vince.

The two glared at each other with building fury. Sam, who had stayed out of the discussion so far, piped up. "Vince, it's time to use the ace you have up your sleeve."

Vince glanced at Sam and nodded. "If you never do anything that could get you in trouble with the law, why did you guys rob that bank in San Francisco? A man was killed there. That makes it murder."

Harry's face went pasty white, and he started to stutter. Finally, he denied it, even though he had given himself away. "I don't know what you're talking about."

"Sure you do," Vince said. He named the other men. "I can prove what you guys did, and I guess I'm going to have to do it."

"You're nuts," Harry said. "I would never do something like that."

Vince's smile was enough to turn a man's toes up. "You have a choice, Harry. Either you get out there to that ranch and grab the foreman and bring him here to us, or you can kiss this old world goodbye."

Harry, daredevil, man of many feats, started to babble. "I gotta go home now," he managed to say. "I won't kidnap anybody."

While he and Sam had been waiting for Harry to return, Vince had arranged the video and audio recordings he had loaded onto his new phone in case he needed them. Without another word, he pulled out the phone, worked with it for a moment, and then shoved it in front of Harry's petrified face, a look that was foreign to the daredevil. Long before it had come to an end, Harry closed his eyes and hung his head.

"That's you in the getaway car," Vince said. "I'd know that shirt anywhere."

Harry shook his head but couldn't get his mouth to work.

"Here's a picture of the man we want. Go get him. Bring him back to this little dump of a motel, and then you can go home," Vince said. "And your secret will be safe, unless . . ." He trailed off and didn't specify what he meant, but he was sure Harry could figure it out.

Five minutes passed. Harry made no move to get up from his chair. Vince started the recording of the session he'd taken after the robbery, the one he took through the wall of the hotel rooms. He turned the volume up and let it play. That finally did it.

"I'll get him," Harry said. "But you gotta get rid of that stuff then."

Vince shook his head. "I might need your help again or help from the other guys. And I would suggest you don't let them know what I know."

"You got my word," Harry said with a trembling voice.

"Not good enough. Give me your phone." He held out his hand, but Harry did not surrender it. Vince hit him in the chest so hard and so fast that Harry didn't even have time to react. He crashed against the wall and slid to the floor. Vince helped him to his feet. Then he emptied the man's pockets. "We can use this cash," he said. "And we'll keep your keys and wallet for now. You can use our car. We may need that drone of yours that's out there in your fancy pickup if you screw up this little assignment."

It was another five minutes before Sam and Vince finally ushered Harry out the door. At the last second, Vince handed him a pistol. "You might need this." They watched until he was in the car they had stolen and was on his way before they both burst into laughter.

"Think he'll get Andy for us?" Sam asked after the two had their laughing fit under control.

"He has no choice," Vince said. "And then when Andy tells us where the horse is, we'll decide what to do about the two of them. One thing's for sure, we can't let Andy or Harry tell anyone what we know."

"So we'll . . ." Sam began but couldn't go on.

"That's right. Are you up to it? This is your mess we're cleaning up, you know. We will do what we have to do. I've done things like this to help you out before."

"Sure," Sam said, but his face had gone pale.

Harry Murray was a daredevil and had always prided himself on his courage. But it eluded him now. He was scared. He had never expected his friend Vince Hodson to be like he was this morning. He would never have imagined that Vince would turn on him like this. If he got this Andy guy and took him back, what would happen then? If he failed, what would happen? In either scenario, he didn't like what he thought the answer might be. Harry the daredevil was feeling real fear.

He was just pulling into the ranch yard, which he was familiar with from having seen it on the video feed from his drone, when he saw the man he was looking for. He had just stepped out of one of the outbuildings near the large barn. Harry stopped but kept the car running. The man he believed was Andy approached him. He was so focused on his intended victim that he failed to notice two men close in on the rear of the car.

He found just enough of his missing courage to open his car door and get out. He cleared his throat and said, "I'm looking for Andy Boyse."

"I'm Andy. What do you need to see me about?"

"You need to come with me," he said as he produced the pistol.

"What's the gun for?" Andy asked.

"Drop it," a deep voice behind him said.

Harry spun in a panic and started wildly pulling the trigger. He barely even saw the large man before he returned fire. Harry fell against his car as pain pierced his chest, then bounced to the ground, still firing his pistol without a target. The last thing he knew was the gun being jerked from his hand.

"Ever seen this guy before, Andy?" the operative, the large man who Andy knew as Dave Washington, asked.

Andy, shocked by the sudden violence, shook his head. "No."

"Watch for others," Dave said to his partner. "Surely he wouldn't try something like this all by himself."

As the second operative watched for others, even glancing periodically into the sky, Dave knelt beside the would-be kidnapper. Andy watched and slowly shook his head.

"He's gone, and there is no ID on him." Dave stood up, pulled out his phone, and dialed.

Andy finally shook off the shock but felt his knees tremble as he thought about what this man had intended to do. How could something as peaceful as racing horses lead to something like this? Then he listened as Dave spoke into his phone.

"Karl, we've had trouble here. I had to kill someone."

Dave listened for a moment, and then he said, "He tried to kidnap Mr. Boyse at gunpoint. When I told him to drop the gun, he turned and started firing at me." Dave listened again before saying, "No sir. He has no ID. I'll call you back after I check the car. Do you want to call the sheriff, or should I? That works for me, Boss." He ended the call.

CHAPTER TWENTY-THREE

BRANDON HAD BEEN STANDING WITH Karl outside Kit's hospital room after leaving Paizlee at Randall's ranch in the capable care of Karl's operatives. He had just turned to enter the room when Karl got a call from his operative in Utah—Dave Washington. Even though Brandon could hear only one side of the conversation, he had a pretty good idea what had happened. After Karl, whose face gave nothing away, had spoken with the sheriff in Millard County, he knew exactly what had happened.

"These guys are out of control," Karl said. "The dead man has no ID on him. Andy is fine. But are you sure you want to take Kit out to Overmyer's ranch?"

"Let's explain what just happened and let him decide," Brandon said.

They explained. Wiona looked very concerned.

"I am not going to let Sam Overmyer decide what I do or don't do," Kit said firmly. "Besides, if that just happened at our ranch, those guys couldn't possibly be here. We're going."

"Are you sure, Kit?" Wiona asked.

"Absolutely. Are you with me on this?"

She didn't hesitate before saying, "Of course I am, Kit. Let's go watch your sister ride."

After two hours had passed and Harry had still not returned with Andy, Sam started to get nervous. "What do you think happened?"

"Either he got scared and ran or he botched it somehow," Vince said. "My guess is that he ran."

"What do we do now?" Sam asked.

Vince smiled. "We need some eyes in the sky."

"We have Harry's drone."

"We sure do. Let's go give it a try."

They drove out of town, down a side road, and then into a desolate area, the same location they'd used the day before. From there, they sent the drone aloft. Its video feed was working perfectly. Having previously operated this very drone, Vince soon had it aloft. He kept it high and made it quick, using the coordinates he'd helped Harry use the day before. Within a few minutes, Kit's ranch appeared far below the drone.

It took only a few moments to realize what had happened. There was a hearse there, a bunch of sheriff vehicles, and the car they had sent Harry off in. Vince didn't waste any time. He brought the drone back, landed it, put it away in Harry's truck, and they drove away.

"What do you suggest we do now, Vince?" Sam asked.

"Nobody will know us in Harry's truck. So let's go to Las Vegas and lay low for a day or two while I have the Fry brothers see what's happening with Kit. When he gets out of the hospital, I want to know where he goes. I have a feeling he will lead us to that horse of his," Vince said. "We'll get that horse yet, and then I think we should take care of Kit and his sister as well. They've caused us so much trouble that we have no choice now but to make them pay for it."

Brandon watched as Kit hobbled slowly toward the big black horse, a grin on his face. He was using a cane to walk, and the nurse walked beside him holding the IV bag. Wiona was right there with him. There was no doubt that the young cowboy was in pain, but he was bravely trying to hide it.

Paizlee, who was already dressed to ride, stood beside Brandon, watching her brother intently. Bruce led Kingfisher from the barn and walked him toward the small cluster of people. Randall stood a few steps away from the barn door, watching with interest.

Kingfisher reared and whinnied at the exact moment Kit called out his name. The nurse grabbed Kit's arm, looking wildly about her. Kit said something to her, and she calmed down some.

"Will he hurt Kit?" Brandon asked.

"No, he's just excited to see him." Paizlee glanced briefly up at Brandon's face, her eyes shining. "You would be surprised at the bond that develops between a horse and a human, at least a human whose love the horse can sense."

Kingfisher pranced back and forth as Bruce clung tightly to the lead rope. Kit held out his hand as he got close. "Are you glad to see me, big guy? I've sure missed you." The nurse stood as far back as she could, holding the IV bag aloft. Wiona stayed just a step behind him.

Brandon was aware of Paizlee taking hold of his hand, but she did not take her eyes off her brother and Kingfisher. The horse stopped and seemed to shiver in anticipation as Kit touched his forehead and whispered to him. Then the superb animal simply stood there, his proud head lowered to where Kit could reach the top of his head and scratch him behind his ears.

Brandon watched in wonder. There was no doubt about the affection between the two. Finally, releasing his hand, Paizlee joined Kit, Wiona, and the nurse. She stroked Kingfisher's neck while Kit whispered something Brandon couldn't make out. Paizlee smiled at whatever he said. It was clearly an intimate moment between the twins and the horse they both loved.

Kit laid his head against Kingfisher's neck as Paizlee slowly walked around him, looking him over carefully, keeping her hand on him. Pretty soon she'd circled him. For several minutes, the two stood with the horse between them, but finally Kit patted the big neck one more time and stepped back beside Wiona.

"Let's see how he does, Paizlee," he said. Then he spoke to the nurse. "I know it made you nervous, but thanks for letting me get close to him."

They all began to walk toward the track. Brandon offered to bring his Bronco and let Kit ride, but Kit said, "I'm doing okay. I want to walk."

It was not a short walk, but Wiona stayed right with Kit, and the nurse trooped diligently along on the other side of him. Brandon dropped back a few steps and joined Randall, who was shaking his head. "That boy, that girl, and that horse." He didn't say any more, but from the tone of his voice, Brandon knew Randall was moved by what he'd witnessed.

Bruce and Kit passed the trees and on through the gate to the track and then were talking intently as the rest of the group caught up. Karl and his operatives were spread out, keeping watch all around them. Kit finally went back through the gate. "We'll watch from out here, Wiona," he said as he steadied himself against the sturdy, white wooden fence.

Randall had stopped a few yards back. Brandon looked back to see Randall hurrying toward the barn. He wondered what was going on, so he watched nervously. When Randall came back out, he smiled to himself. Randall was carrying a canvas folding chair.

Bruce led Kingfisher around for a couple of minutes before he stopped next to Paizlee and offered her his hand for her foot. She stepped in and then swung gracefully onto Kingfisher's back and put her boots in the stirrups. She leaned forward and patted Kingfisher's neck. Bruce gave her some more instructions. Then she walked the horse onto the track and headed around it. After a couple hundred feet, she let him begin to trot, then far down track, she eased him into a slow lope.

"See the way he's pulling on the reins?" Kit said to Wiona, who was kneeling next to the chair Randall had brought for him. "He's telling Paizlee that he wants to run."

"Paizlee looks so at ease on him."

"She is. She knows what she's doing."

In a short while, they went around the far end of the track. As they approached again, Paizlee was letting him run faster. Just before the horse and rider reached the point where Bruce was standing, holding a stopwatch, he shouted, "Let him run!"

It took only a second for the black stallion to reach what Brandon assumed must be his top speed. Paizlee was leaning almost onto his neck. She seemed so much like she was part of the horse, that, like the day before, Brandon was amazed. It was a very short time before the horse was thundering toward them again. Kit shouted in joy. "Go, Kingfisher! Faster, boy! You can do it!" He was out of his chair, holding onto the fence with both hands.

To Brandon's complete amazement, he could actually see the horse pick up speed and run faster than he could have ever imagined. He streaked past Bruce like a freight train, and Paizlee didn't attempt to slow him down until he was coming around the far bend for the third time. By the time they reached Bruce again, she had him down to a slow lope.

"He isn't even winded yet," she shouted. "He's amazing!" Pretty soon, she had him slowed to a walk and approached Bruce again. "How did he do?"

Bruce was shaking his head and looking at the stopwatch as if he couldn't believe it. She jumped gracefully from Kingfisher's back.

Randall approached Bruce. "Let me see that." He looked at the time. His eyes grew wide, and a big smile covered his face. Then he took the reins from Paizlee, who stepped over and looked at the stopwatch. Her eyes popped open in shock.

Kit, who could hardly stand the suspense, had passed through the gate, practically pulling his nurse along. Wiona was beaming beside him. Bruce and Paizlee met him just a few feet from the fence, and Kit looked at the stopwatch. "Oh my!" he shouted. "I knew he was fast, but that is unbelievable."

"The last horse I clocked in that half mile was Sharpshooter," Bruce said. "I thought he was quite fast, but Kingfisher just beat his time by twenty seconds. I've never seen a horse run so fast."

Paizlee's eyes shone brighter than Brandon had ever seen them. "Kit, it felt like he could have kept up that pace forever. He didn't even get winded. It was so exciting!"

Randall let Bruce take Kingfisher, and Bruce continued to walk him.

Randall walked up to Kit. "Young man, you have one mighty fine horse there. I hope you guys will let me go with you the next time you race."

"You've earned it," Kit said. "I . . . we owe you so much."

Randall's face sobered. "You don't owe me anything. There is nothing I won't do for you two. I'm just so sorry for the pain my son and nephew have caused."

"Believe me, Randall, there are no hard feelings. We feel blessed to have gotten to know you."

"The blessing is all mine," Randall said with a catch in his voice. "Bruce will work with you, Paizlee, and with Kingfisher. As amazing as today's speed was, he and I are both convinced there is still more speed in that horse. We'll condition him and work with him. By the time you decide to compete, I don't think there is a quarter horse in the West that can beat him."

"Brandon, I hate to admit this, but I think I need you to bring your Bronco over here," Kit said. "It's tiring, but nothing could have done me more good than to see what we all just witnessed."

"Tell me something," Brandon said. "How fast do you think he was running?"

"If you're talking miles per hour, thirty or so," Kit said.

Back at the hospital, Kit was glad to get back in bed. The excursion to Randall's ranch had been mentally invigorating but physically tiring. Brandon and the two operatives had brought Kit and Wiona back to the hospital, but Paizlee had chosen to stay at the ranch for a few hours and spend time with Kingfisher. She also felt a pressing desire to help Randall in some way.

She had offered to clean his house, and at first, he said it wasn't necessary, but when she'd insisted, he'd accepted. "This place hasn't had much of a woman's touch since my wife died. My sister, Vince's mother, comes out occasionally, but she is not in good health, so she can't do much. And lately, since Vince has been acting worse than he ever has, she has come out less."

Brandon drove back to the ranch, leaving Kit and Wiona alone, except for the men who stood diligently outside the door, keeping watch. The doctor came in and checked Kit over carefully. "I think that was good for you," he said. "You're healing faster than I would have thought possible."

"Prayers have helped," Kit said, looking fondly at Wiona, who he knew was praying for him constantly.

"Prayer does help," Dr. Sturgeon agreed. "Now, you let your nurse know if you need anything."

Wiona sat beside the bed and talked quietly with Kit until he drifted to sleep. Then she sat back and pulled up the scriptures on her phone and began to study.

Lawrence Heslop had just been hired on what looked like a very difficult case. He stepped from his office and spoke with Jenna Hubbard, his secretary. "I hate to have to do this, Jenna," he said, "but I'm going to need Brandon to come back and do some investigation for me on this new matter."

"I need Wiona again too," Jenna said. "I'm falling behind. I've hated to have to bother her because I get the feeling that she likes to be with her cowboy. I suppose I could bring in some temporary help, but it would take too much time to bring someone new up to speed."

Lawrence smiled. "Karl Shutter and his employees have things under control in Nevada. I'm sure Brandon could come help me for a while. I also think it would be good for Wiona and Kit to have some time apart. I'll have Brandon bring her up with him first thing in the morning."

"I'll call Wiona and tell her," Jenna said. "She's told me several times that if I need her, she would come."

With that settled, Lawrence returned to his office. Jenna picked up her office phone and rang Wiona's number.

"Hi, Mom," her daughter said. "I just stepped into the hallway. Kit's sleeping. We've had quite a day."

"Tell me about it," Jenna said. She listened and could hear the enthusiasm in her voice and the deep feelings her daughter was developing toward Kit. After a few minutes, she said, "I hate to do this to you, but Lawrence's slow time is over." She told Wiona about the difficult new case he had taken on. "He's going to need Brandon. It's quite complex."

Wiona didn't need to be told that Jenna would need some additional help too. "I'll come up with Brandon. I'm sure you're in need of my help, aren't you?"

"Very much so. Would you be willing to do that?"

"Of course," Wiona said. "I hate to leave Kit, but Paizlee is here, and Kit is doing much better. He'll understand."

"You like him a lot, don't you?" Jenna asked.

"I do, Mom. But a little time apart might give both of us time to think about how we feel and what the future holds. When is Brandon going back?"

"Lawrence would like him to come back in the morning," Jenna said. "He's calling him now."

"Then I'll be with him. Honestly, I could use the break. This hospital is wearing on me, and I could use some sleep in my own bed rather than in a hospital chair. I'll see you tomorrow."

Vince was driving Harry Murray's pickup south on I-15. He was careful to stay within the speed limit, something he'd never done even when he was a deputy sheriff. Sam was dozing. They'd made the decision to go to Las Vegas where they could easily hide out while they decided their next move.

Money was not a problem now. Harry had been carrying a large amount of cash, and they had withdrawn a bunch of money from his accounts in Cedar City, then ditched the cards. He also had Harry's phone, but he had a disturbing thought.

"Sam, we gotta ditch this phone," he said, waking his sleepy cousin. "At some point, they'll figure out who Harry is, and when they do, they can use his phone to find us."

Vince tossed it out the window and then used his burner phone to dial a number he knew by heart. It was the cell phone number of his former colleague Kirby Fry. When Kirby answered, Vince identified himself. "Are you on duty or off?"

"I go on at six. I have the dreaded shift. How are you doing, anyway? I still can't believe the sheriff treated you like he did. You've worked hard and been loyal to him. He knows I feel that way, but he isn't giving an inch," Deputy Fry said.

"I'm getting along. Sam and I have been keeping out of sight since Sam has a warrant out for him. At least, we assume he does. His dad was as rotten to him as Sheriff Watson was to me. Sometimes we think we know someone and find out we don't," Vince said.

"Is there anything I can do to help?" Kirby asked.

"If you're willing, there is something I need to know," Vince said.

"What is it? You've been a good friend, and it's not the same working for the sheriff since you left. I'll do whatever you need."

"My problems and my cousin Sam's have all been caused by the guy who killed Sam's racehorse, Kit Troxler," Vince began smoothly.

"Yeah, I'm aware of that situation," Kirby said.

"Well, Kirby, I need to know if Kit is still in the hospital in Tonopah or if he's been moved. He also has a twin sister. I'd like to know if she's down there. I'd also like to know, for Sam's sake, what his father is up to these days," Vince told him.

"That'll be easy. I'll get back to you when I find out," Kirby promised.

"Thanks, man. I'll make it up to you," Vince lied. "I have an unlisted number now, a burner phone, so I'll call you back. You won't have to worry about calling me."

"Was that Kirby Fry you were talking to?" Sam asked after Vince hung up.

"Yep, and he's going to help us. I didn't even have to threaten him."

CHAPTER TWENTY-FOUR

PAIZLEE TOOK A FEW MINUTES' break from cleaning to check on the race in California she was planning to ride in. It was a little less than three weeks away. She was both excited and nervous about it. She hoped Kit would be up to going. She really needed to have him there both for moral support and for advice.

After checking on a few details and confirming everything was set, she went back to work. She'd started with Randall's kitchen. He'd kept things in better shape than she'd thought he would. But the floor needed to be mopped, and everything was dusty. She got it looking good and went to work in his living room. She vacuumed, dusted, straightened, and soon had it in tip-top shape.

Brandon and Randall came in, and she asked if it was okay if she did his laundry. "My goodness, Paizlee," Randall said. "You're a hard worker. I'd like to pay you for all the cleaning you've done. My laundry is way behind. I'll sort it for you and then, if you don't mind, I'll let you wash and dry it."

She smiled at him. "Randall, you've already paid me. Those new bulls and these security guys have cost you a lot. Please, just let me do this. And if you'd like, I'll fix dinner for you both in an hour or two."

"If you can find something to fix it with, that would be great. I need to get some groceries either tonight or in the morning," Randall said. "And if you don't mind, it would be nice if Bruce could eat with us too. I'd like to talk a few things over with the three of you. There's meat in the freezer and some potatoes that I think are still good in the basement. Sorry, but I don't have any milk. I do think there are some rolls in the freezer as well. I try to stock up from time to time, but like with my laundry, I've kind of let it slip lately," he said. "I'll get my laundry together. Also, my bedding hasn't been changed forever, I'm afraid. And Sam's room is a mess," he said. "I'll get his stuff as well. I'm quite sure he won't be back." He had a catch in his voice.

"Just show me what to do, and I'll take care of it." She and Brandon followed Randall back to his large bedroom and helped him strip the bed. Together, they gathered up his dirty clothes and the washcloths and towels from the bathrooms.

When they got to Sam's bedroom, she and Brandon tore the bedding off while Randall gathered up a bunch of dirty clothes. Randall's bedroom had been quite orderly. Sam's was a reflection of his personality—a total mess. As Randall walked out with an armful of laundry, Paizlee said to Brandon, "I hope Randall doesn't mind me doing this."

"I'm sure he's grateful," Brandon responded. "You sure get a lot done fast."

"My mother taught me well. I'll always be grateful for that. I love Kit dearly, but if I didn't do his laundry, he'd never have anything clean to wear."

Randall came back in. "Would you pile Sam's stuff over there on that desk, if you can clear his junk off? I guess I'll need to go through his room and clean it out." His voice broke. "This is so difficult. Sam's mother and I tried hard with him, but he was rebellious from the time he was little. I think I gave him too much, and he came to expect it. I'm at fault, I suppose, for the way he turned out."

Paizlee stopped what she was doing. "Randall, you are a wonderful man. Don't blame yourself."

"I try not to, but it's hard," Randall said. "I love that boy so much, and I tried to tell him so, but I cannot remember a time when he ever expressed love to his mother or to me. My wife was a small woman, and Sam says he got his size from her. He hated her for it. Oh, I shouldn't go on like this. There are two more bedrooms on the second floor and more in the basement. We had always thought we'd have a large family, but it didn't happen."

"Maybe tomorrow I'll clean them too," Paizlee said.

"That would be nice. You and Kit will need rooms of your own when he gets out of the hospital until it's safe to take Kingfisher back to your own ranch," he said.

"You don't need to—"

Randall interrupted. "Please, it will be nice to have some company here for a while."

"Thank you," she said.

"And, Paizlee, why don't you make a bed up for yourself now. You don't need to spend all night in that hospital room. We'll make sure you get safely back and forth. But you could use some rest, I'm sure."

At dinner that night, Brandon broke the news to Paizlee that he was going to have to return to Salt Lake the next morning.

"I'll miss you," Paizlee said, "but I understand. What about Wiona?"

"They need her too," he said. "She'll be riding back with me in the morning."

"Brandon, with Bruce and me, my hired hands, and Karl's men, we'll keep Paizlee and Kit safe. You just go do what you have to, and we'll take care of things here," Randall promised.

The four of them talked about Kingfisher's training for several minutes. "I'm sorry to have to deprive Andy of the fun of working with him," Bruce said. "But it's a great privilege to be able to help you with such a fine horse. Do you have an idea when you plan to race him?"

Paizlee hesitated just briefly and then decided she had to trust these men. Randall picked up on the hesitation. "Paizlee, you have my word that no one will learn of your plans from the two of us. Believe me, we want Kingfisher to excel, and we want you and Kit to as well."

"Okay," she said. "I'll tell you." And she did.

"Not quite three weeks," Bruce said, rubbing his chin. "We can have him ready. But I'll need you every day between now and then."

"I'll be here," she said. "Except we don't work him on Sundays."

"I respect that," Bruce said. "That gives both of us a break too." He grinned. "It takes a lot to get me excited these days, but I am."

"We just can't let Sam and Vince know," Randall said, dampening the mood slightly. "Even then, when we are down there for the race, we'll have to be doubly on our guard."

"Yes, we will," Bruce said. "No one but you, Paizlee, Kit—when he can— and I are to handle him. We need to instruct those operatives of Karl's to keep folks out of the barn. I don't even want any of our hired men in there taking care of the other horses and stalls unless I am with them."

"I'll clean Kingfisher's stall," Paizlee said.

"Maybe I'm being paranoid. I think I can trust my men, but I know that people can be bribed or blackmailed. I can't keep my guys here at the ranch all the time. They need to be able to go to town on their days off," Randall said, his brow wrinkled in thought. "Bruce, would you put a lock on Kingfisher's stall? Make it a strong one. Then only you, I, and Paizlee will have keys."

"We should give a key to the security men," Brandon suggested. "Those men know how to keep things secure and how to keep secrets."

Randall nodded. "I see your point. Yes, a key for them, but only one."

Paizlee started to clean up after dinner, and Randall began to help. "I can do this, Randall," Paizlee protested.

"But I'm used to cleaning up after myself," he said.

"I know. I was impressed with how good the kitchen looked. But I need to earn my keep," she said.

"And I'll help," Brandon volunteered.

"Okay, you two, if you insist," Randall said with a grin. "In that case, why don't you help me make a list of what we need from the grocery store, and I'll go in this evening and stock up."

"Sure. If Paizlee isn't here when you get back, you'll know that we've gone to the hospital to see Kit," Brandon said.

"That'll be great. Then will you stay here tonight, both of you? I have plenty of room," Randall said.

"It may be late, but yes, we'll do that. Right, Paizlee?" Brandon asked.

"I guess so. I do need to be here to fix some breakfast and to take care of Kingfisher's stall," she agreed.

"You'll be busy," Randall said. "Bruce will set up a schedule for Kingfisher's training, and he will need you to help as much as you can. If I'm asking too much, you just say so."

She shook her head. "I can handle it. I'm used to hard work."

"You have no idea how good it is to have someone so willing to help. Sam would never even rinse off his dishes. You are a gem," Randall said with a ring of sincerity in his voice.

As soon as the grocery list was complete, Randall left. Brandon and Paizlee cleaned the kitchen from dinner, and then they, too, drove to town, with one of Karl's men following. Karl and Brandon were determined to be extremely careful.

Deputy Kirby Fry was thinking about the favor Vince had asked of him. This was normally a boring shift, unless there were bar fights, but there hadn't been many of those lately. So he drove around, not sure what to look for to help Vince. Well, there was one thing, he thought, and he swung by the hospital.

As it was, he didn't even need to go inside to check, for he saw Randall Overmyer's truck in the parking lot. There was no doubt in Kirby's mind that Randall was there to see Kit. Randall had come in to see Kit the evening Kirby had pulled a security shift there. He decided to wait and see where Randall went after he left.

He didn't have to wait long before Randall came out. He was talking to a man Kirby had seen there that same evening. The two of them walked to Randall's truck, talking. Then they shook hands, and the stranger went back in the hospital. Kirby couldn't help but notice how the man he didn't know looked around constantly. Part of the security that had been arranged for Kit, he concluded. He could tell Vince when he called that Kit was still in the hospital.

Kirby followed Randall at a discreet distance when he left the hospital. Randall drove to a grocery store. When he came out, he was pushing a cart full of groceries, which he put in the back seat of his truck. He returned the cart, something Kirby never did.

Randall headed north in the direction of his ranch. Kirby could see no reason to follow him. So instead, on a whim, he went back to the hospital, parked where he could see the front entrance, shut his car off, and waited. If the man he'd seen with Randall earlier came out again, he'd see which way the guy headed.

It turned into an hour's wait. He got no other calls, so he hadn't seen any reason to leave. Finally, the man came out, and with him was the pretty girl Kirby knew to be Kit's twin sister. The two were holding hands, talking and laughing. Yet, even then, the man never quit looking around. His eyes fell on Kirby's car and stayed there for a moment. Kirby couldn't help but squirm.

But the man and Kit's sister kept walking. Kirby got out of his car and looked across the parking lot. They got in a tan Ford Bronco and headed out. They were soon driving north. He followed them, curious. He planned to find out where they were going. He just hoped he didn't get any calls or get distracted in some way.

Santos Garcia took his job with Karl Shutter's agency very seriously. He'd followed Brandon and Paizlee from the ranch to the hospital. It was his habit to notice anything unusual as he fulfilled his duties. Tonight, he'd been bothered by a county sheriff vehicle that had come to the hospital twice, but the deputy had never gone inside.

His concerns had risen substantially when the officer had followed Randall Overmyer from the hospital. He'd radioed the officers on duty inside that he was going to be leaving for a few minutes and had requested that they make sure Brandon and Paizlee didn't leave until he got back.

Randall went to the grocery store. The officer had waited there and again followed him when he left. While Randall had been in the store, Garcia had gotten a pair of nighttime binoculars out and examined the patrol car. He'd jotted down the unit number and the license plate number.

Randall had driven north, and the deputy had followed him until he'd gone a couple of miles beyond the Tonopah city limits. Then he'd turned and driven back to the hospital, where he had once again waited in his car. When Brandon and Paizlee had come out, he'd stepped out of his car and watched them until they got in Brandon's Bronco. He had followed them since then.

Agent Garcia radioed both the men at the ranch and the ones in the hospital to inform them what was happening. Then he continued to follow, awaiting instructions from his supervisor at the ranch.

It was not his supervisor who radioed him back. It was Karl Shutter himself, calling on their secure phone. "Santos, Brandon is aware that he's being followed. He's going to turn east shortly. If the deputy still follows him, you do the same. Let Brandon lead him for several miles. If he still follows, then I'll need you to take some action to distract him," Karl said.

"Like what?" Agent Garcia asked.

"You can outrun anyone in that car you're in. Pass him and do something to attract his attention, and then if he pursues you, lead him on a long and wild chase," Karl ordered. "That car of yours is deceptive, as you know. He'll think he can easily catch you. That will be his mistake. Make sure you keep an eye on the map on the dash. Don't let yourself drive on a dead-end road. Don't let him get too close, and don't let him catch you either. After you're far enough away, lose him and then go back to the ranch and change your license plates. I've already sent another car your way to assist Brandon if he needs it."

"I got it, Boss," Santos said.

"Did you by any chance get the officer's license plate number or the unit number of his patrol car?"

"I got both." He recited them to Karl.

After a moment, Karl said, "Brandon has turned. Did the deputy follow?"

"Yes."

"Why don't you give it another four or five miles. If he's still behind Brandon at that point, then you know what to do. Let me know how it goes. And avoid gunfire at all costs," Karl ordered. "But don't let him come toward Randall's ranch."

"I'm on it," Santos said.

Deputy Kirby was feeling pretty smug. As long as he didn't get another call, he'd figure out where the Troxler twin and her companion were headed. The Bronco had signaled and then turned right onto a road Kirby knew. He followed. So far they'd gone four or five miles. He looked in his rearview mirror.

A car was coming up on him at high speeds. He swore and pounded his fist on the steering wheel. He expected the car to slow down when the driver realized he was behind a marked sheriff unit.

The car was an older gray sedan with dings and dents. It shot past Fry at an extremely high rate of speed, probably all that old car could do. Then it turned off onto another road and headed south. Fry thought about pursuing him but then changed his mind. He kept following the Bronco.

To his surprise, a short while later, bright lights shone again in his rearview mirror, and the guy didn't dim them. The same old car pulled past him, but as it went by, the driver presented Deputy Fry with an obscene gesture, then sped past. That was too much. Fry's anger stoked, he hit his lights and siren. He was soon closing in on him. That guy was going to jail.

Fry thought he was about to catch him, but then the guy turned south and sped up. Fry sped up too until he was again closing in on the old car. But once again, the car turned, this time back to the west. The road they were on was not paved, and both cars slowed down. But Fry was determined to stop the guy if he had to run him off the road.

Once again, he closed in on the reckless driver. And once again, the car took a different road, sliding as it turned. They were heading south again. A couple of miles later, the car again changed roads, heading east. Every time Fry thought he had him caught, the car would speed up and then change roads at the next intersection.

What was this guy doing? Suddenly, the car ahead slowed, and then it made a quick sliding turn and drove straight back at him. He frantically pulled to the right as far as he could to keep from getting hit head-on. The old car went by, and he could see the crazy driver laughing at him.

Fry slammed on his brakes and tried to turn, but he was going too fast and slid off the road. He tried to pull back on but got high-centered. Cursing, he got out to see what he could do to get back on the road. After inspecting and trying to maneuver the car as best as he could, he eventually realized he was not going to be able to get the car back on the road by himself, and he called for assistance.

Fry was angry, but he was also embarrassed. He should have been able to catch that banged-up old car. When he was asked by the dispatcher to describe the car he'd been chasing, he lied. He told her it was a red Corvette with Nevada plates. In reality, he had no idea what the plates were, but no way was he going to admit that he was outrun by a beat-up old car.

CHAPTER TWENTY-FIVE

BACK AT THE RANCH, BRANDON Phelps waited for Agent Garcia. When he arrived, the two chuckled together before Garcia said, "I'm pretty sure he ran off the road. From the last I saw of the lights, the patrol car had not moved. I'm sure he's fuming."

"And trying to figure out how to explain himself to the sheriff in the morning," Brandon said.

"Yes, and that," Garcia agreed.

"The real question is what he was up to. Tell me how you got onto him," Brandon said.

The two men talked as they walked up the steps to the large porch at the front of Randall's house and sat down in some wicker chairs under the light. Randall came out and joined them. "I take it from what Paizlee said that you guys had some trouble tonight," he said.

"Well, maybe." Brandon summarized what had occurred. "You see, it may be nothing, but I'm thinking that it isn't. The big question in my mind is why a deputy sheriff would be following first you and then me. Surely they have more to do than that."

Randall ran a hand through his thinning hair. "I suppose Vince has some friends in the department. Could he have talked one of them into doing this to try to find out where Kingfisher is?"

"That's what I'm afraid of," Santos said. "He seemed determined to follow Brandon. It took me two attempts to make him mad enough to chase me."

"I don't like this," Randall said.

"It's almost inevitable, I'm afraid," Brandon told him.

"Hey, I've said it before, Detective. I don't care what it costs. I intend to keep that horse and those guys safe."

"I'll let Karl know," Brandon told him.

The men talked for a while longer.

"You'd better get some sleep, Brandon," Randall said at last. "You have a long drive ahead of you in the morning. And I would guess that Lawrence will have you working as soon as you get there."

Brandon nodded. "He certainly will. I've been lucky he's been able to spare me this long. I do get other clients from time to time, but the bulk of my work lately has been for Lawrence."

"Paizlee has a bed ready for you in a downstairs room. She'll be sleeping upstairs. And she says she'll make us some breakfast in the morning. She's a good one, that girl," Randall said. Then he grinned. "She kind of fancies you, Brandon."

"I fancy her too, but I'm also a realist. Our lifestyles are a world apart. I don't see this friendship I have with her being anything more than just that, a friendship," Brandon said wistfully.

Deputy Kirby Fry was still waiting for someone to come pull him back onto the road when his cell phone rang. He looked dismally at the screen, hoping it wasn't Vince. He didn't want to talk to him while he was in such a foul mood. Thankfully, it was his big brother, Mickey, who worked for the department he hoped to someday work for—the Las Vegas Metropolitan Police Department.

"Hey, quick question for you, Kirby," Mickey said. "I was supposed to meet Harry Murray tonight. We had some really hot dates lined up and tickets to a show on the strip with dinner afterward."

Kirby interrupted him. "You didn't call just to make me jealous, did you?"

"No, I didn't. We haven't gone yet. Harry was supposed to meet me at my apartment, and he didn't show up. That's not like Harry."

"You did try to call him, didn't you? Harry always has his phone with him unless he's doing some crazy stunt."

"I've tried and tried, but his phone is going to voicemail."

"What are you calling me for? It's too late for me to take his place on the date, and anyway, I'm on duty."

"I wondered if you'd heard from him. I'm worried something's happened to him. You know what dumb stuff he's always doing. I wasn't aware he had some kind of stunt set for today, but maybe he got involved in some last-second thing," Mickey said.

"This is kind of farfetched, but could he have gotten himself arrested for something?" Kirby asked. "You know how he is."

"Yeah, I do know, and that's what worries me."

"He wouldn't flap his jaws to get out of trouble if he's in a jam, would he?"

"I don't think so," Mickey said, "But I can't be sure. He was only the driver in that little adventure he talked us into up in San Francisco. He could finger us and try to keep himself out of it, I suppose, but I can't see him doing that."

"I wonder if Vince might have asked him to do something for him. I'm doing Vince a favor right now," Kirby said. "He's really in a jam, you know. And the sheriff here treated him like a clod of dirt for no reason at all. Oh, and he told me he's using a burner phone. He wouldn't give me the number."

"Then maybe I'll give Sam a call," Mickey said.

A few minutes later, while Kirby was still waiting for another officer to come pull him back onto the road, Mickey called him back. "I didn't get an answer from Sam's phone."

"Vince said he'd call me back, but he hasn't yet," Kirby said.

"What did he want you to do?" Mickey asked.

"You know that guy from Utah who caused so much trouble for Sam, the one who accused him of cheating to win that race in New Mexico?" Kirby said.

"Yeah, I know who you're talking about. And then he killed Sam's horse, the sleaze ball. And didn't he cause a bunch of trouble that ended up getting one of your fellow deputies killed?" Mickey asked.

"That's him. Vince wants to know where his horse is so he can even the score."

"Are you sure? That sounds risky to me. Isn't it still in Utah?" Mickey asked.

"That's the problem. He doesn't know where it is. He asked me to find out if Kit was still in the hospital here, which he is. He has some expensive bodyguards, tough-looking guys, looking out for him now. I guess Kit knows he's poked a hornet's nest."

"Okay, Kirby, when he calls you back, would you have him call me? Something is definitely wrong. I've checked with my department. They have no record of Harry being in an accident or anything like that. If something has happened, it wasn't in Las Vegas, or I could find out."

"Sure. I'll let him know to call you. I wish I was there to take his place with the hot chicks," Kirby said wistfully. Kirby could see lights bobbing in the distance, coming toward him. "Hey, I got a call. I gotta go," Kirby lied.

Kirby, after a lot of irritating kidding from the officer who pulled him out of the ditch, was finally able to head back to Tonopah. He still had a shift to finish. It was about ten when he got another call. This time it was Vince. He came right to the point. "What have you learned for me, Kirby?" he asked.

"Kit is still in the hospital, and some hired goons are protecting him there," he said. "I saw Sam's dad too. He'd been in the hospital visiting the troublemaker."

"That'll make Sam's day," Vince said. "Is that all you've learned?"

"So far. I've had a really busy shift, but I'll keep trying to learn more. I did see Randall Overmyer go to the store though. It looked like he bought a bunch of groceries."

"I suppose that's normal. He probably doesn't get into town that often," Vince reasoned.

"That's what I figured. Hey, my brother called. He'd like you to call him."

"What does he want?"

"He had a double date tonight with Harry Murray and some hot chicks."

"Kirby, what in the world does his dating life have to do with me?" Vince asked curtly.

"Murray didn't show up for the date, and Mickey can't reach him on his cell phone," Kirby told him.

"I can't help him with that. It's not my job to keep track of Harry," Vince said, sounding angry and frustrated.

"I don't know what to tell you. Just call Mickey," Kirby said, starting to get angry himself. He hadn't had a good night, and having Vince growl at him was not helping.

"Okay, but I don't really have time for this," Vince said. "I'm rather busy." He ended the call.

Kirby looked at the phone in his hand for a moment before he put it down. He felt like asking Vince what he was busy doing, that he didn't have a job so he should have plenty of time. But he didn't want to get the guy riled, so he kept his thoughts to himself. He had a shift to complete, and he was going to look around the area for the rest of it and try to find the creep who had run him off the road. If it hadn't been for that guy, he reasoned, he might have been able to give Vince some helpful information.

Vince grumbled angrily to Sam. "I'm sure not going to tell Mickey that the fool got himself killed. He doesn't need to know that you and I have seen him."

"That seems simple enough to me," Sam said. "Just call him and tell him you have no idea where Harry is."

"I guess I can do that," Vince agreed. So he dialed Mickey's cell phone number and waited while it rang. When Mickey finally answered, Vince identified himself.

"How come you changed your number, Vince?" Mickey asked.

"The sheriff had no business firing me. I was doing a good job, but since he did, I figured there was no way I was going to let him or the prosecutor's office or anyone else get a hold of me and demand that I come testify in court. I have three or four cases pending. But that's not my problem anymore. So I changed phones. And I am not giving out the number to this one," he said.

"I can't see what good that will do you," Mickey said. "They know where you live."

"I'm not going to stay in Tonopah," Vince said. "I'll sneak in some night with a rental truck, and me and Sam will load my stuff."

"Where are you moving to?" Mickey asked.

"I don't know yet, but it will be where they can't find me."

"Vince, just a little advice from a friend; you can't just ignore the charges I've heard the sheriff brought against you. You need to get an attorney and fight them," Mickey said. "Clear your name, and then you won't have to leave."

"No, I don't think so. They aren't going to find me. And the charges he made up against me are bogus and not serious enough to worry about when I don't show up," Vince said. "They'll just forfeit my bond and be done with it. Anyway, Kirby said you wanted me to call you."

"Yeah, I was wondering if you've heard from Harry," Mickey said. He explained why he wanted to know.

"Nope, I haven't heard from him," Vince lied.

"Would you try to call him?" Mickey asked. "Maybe he's embarrassed for standing the girls and me up and is ignoring my calls. He would probably answer you."

"Sure, Mickey, I can do that. I'll get back to you."

"Don't be long. I gotta tell those girls something."

After about five minutes, Vince called Mickey back. "His calls go to voicemail. I tried a couple of times. I'll keep trying."

Mickey, sounding worried, said, "Okay, thanks, Vince. Let me know if you do get a hold of him."

Vince smugly promised that he would.

While Vince had been on the phone, Sam had been fuming about his dad apparently being friendly with Kit Troxler. His dad had really treated him, his own flesh and blood, badly. He was trying to think of a way to get back at him. He got an idea, and it made him smile.

"What are you so happy about?" Vince asked.

"I was just thinking about Dad," Sam said.

"I don't see how that could make you happy," Vince said.

"What makes me laugh is that I just thought of something that we could do, with the help of Kirby Fry, that would cause my dad some real trouble," Sam said.

Vince looked at him suspiciously for a moment. "Let's not attract attention to ourselves, Sam. But tell me what you're thinking of doing, and I'll decide if we should do it or not."

"We should have Kirby put a bomb in an innocent-looking package and in Dad's truck. That package would blow up, and Dad would be out a truck."

"Wait a minute. That could kill your father," Vince said doubtfully.

"I don't really care at this point," Sam said.

Vince laughed. "That would be kind of funny. But I don't know if we should use Kirby."

"Do we care? I mean, you could put the guy away for life with what you know. I think we should try it," Sam said. "Anyway, he would think it was something I had of Dad's that I wanted to return and couldn't do it for fear I'd be seen. He wouldn't know it was a bomb."

"When it went off, he would," Vince argued.

"Just let him know what you know about him and the robbery and murder in San Francisco, and he wouldn't dare say a word."

"That's true, I suppose, but there must be a better way to do it," Vince said doubtfully.

"Listen, man, Dad has become friendly with Kit Troxler. Maybe after the bomb he would quit being friendly to him."

"I wonder what he even helps Kit for," Vince said thoughtfully. "And we know he does. I'm sure he helped him hide his horse."

"Who knows," Sam said. Then suddenly he pumped his fist as a thought hit him. "Vince, I'll bet Kingfisher is at Dad's place."

For a moment, Vince looked shocked, but slowly, a smile lit his face. "Yeah, maybe you're onto something. We have that drone of Harry's locked in the back of his truck. I wonder what its distance is. I mean, how close would we have to be to spy on your dad's ranch? I think it can reach pretty far, but we need to know for sure."

"We could go out in the desert and experiment," Sam suggested.

"We'll do that in the morning," Vince said decisively.

"Let's do it," Sam agreed. "But I still want to blow up Dad's truck."

"It would take us a little while to prepare a bomb. And then we've got to figure out a way to get it to Kirby," Vince said.

"We can check out the drone in the morning and then get on the internet and figure out how to make a bomb in the afternoon," Sam said.

"We could do that, but I am still wondering about having Kirby deliver it. For one thing, you and I both know your dad always locks his truck when he's not in it. And Kirby would have to wait for him to go to town again."

"I'll bet that wouldn't be long. If he's coming in to see Kit at the hospital, all he'd need to do is watch for the truck. And who says it needs to be in the cab? It could just be left in the back, right behind the cab. Dad always has all kinds of stuff back there. He wouldn't even notice it until it went bang."

"It shouldn't be too hard to build one," Vince said.

Sam went on thinking. "Hey, I have a better idea!"

"What now?" Vince asked suspiciously.

"I wonder if we could just drop it in the back of the truck with the drone," Sam said.

"I'm not sure how we'd do that. I don't think this drone is designed to carry something that could be dropped like that," Vince argued.

"Okay, how about this," Sam said. He was on a deadly roll with his thinking, and he was getting excited. "We could fasten the bomb to the drone and then fly it into his truck. I don't think it would need to be too heavy."

"That's true, and the drone is designed to carry things, just not to drop them with precision. Harry and I did drop a gallon of milk once on a friend's house as a joke, but we nearly missed."

"Let's do it."

"But we need the drone to look for the horse first, don't you think?"

"Okay, so let's do the drone surveillance first and then bomb the truck, if we can hit it. No, wait," Sam said as he felt his excitement accelerate. "Let's bomb his house."

Vince looked at him for a moment, and Sam could tell by the spark in Vince's eyes that he had him thinking. "Sam, what if someone were in the house when we bombed it?"

"Who would be in it?" Sam asked. "If it's Dad, I really don't care."

Vince shook his head. "No, I was thinking that someone could be staying there."

"Like who?" Sam asked.

"Well, if Kit's sister is hanging around, maybe your dad is letting her stay there. That's another reason to take a quick look with the drone," Vince said. "And if we killed her, I think that the sheriff would call in all the help he could get and look for us."

"Why for us?" Sam asked. "It could be anybody."

"Sam, think about this for a minute. I'm a cop."

"You were a cop," Sam corrected.

Vince went on as if Sam hadn't reminded him of that. "You would be the first person they looked for. And I would be the second. And something that serious wouldn't just be dropped when they failed to find us right away."

That thought jolted Sam. "Okay, but what if Kingfisher is at our ranch?"

"Your dad's ranch," Vince corrected, getting back at Sam.

"Okay, Dad's ranch," Sam said. "If he's there, if we can figure that out using the drone, then we could bomb the barn and kill the horse. That's what I really want to do."

"And several other horses and maybe a person or two," Vince said.

"We could watch with the drone and make sure no one is in it and that Kingfisher is, and then we could fly the drone right into the barn," Sam said. He was determined to create some serious damage. Revenge was like an unquenchable fire in his mind.

"Now you're making sense," Vince said. "We can do that, but we will have to have plenty of power in the bomb we build and then hope it will burn what it doesn't blow up. And then we'll have to leave, go a long ways away where we can't be found."

"Let's do it," Sam said, pumping his fists. "Dad and Kit will pay for ever messing with me."

CHAPTER TWENTY-SIX

Constant vigilance was maintained at the Overmyer ranch, especially around the house, the barn, and the practice track where Kingfisher had his daily workouts. There was never a letup at the hospital either. Operatives brought Paizlee in to visit Kit every evening. Kit was restless with Wiona gone, and he desperately wanted out of the hospital.

His boredom was broken each day when his foreman, Andy Boyse, called to give him updates on his ranch and to ask for advice. It was also broken at least twice a day with sweet calls from Wiona.

Finally, just four days after Wiona and Brandon had gone back to Salt Lake, Dr. Sturgeon approved his release from the hospital. Kit was taken by two teams of operatives to Randall Overmyer's house. He was able to walk around the yard and spend time sitting on the deck. He took a special interest in Kingfisher's training. Bruce was extremely pleased with how training was going, and Paizlee was getting more confident each day.

The day following Kit's release from the hospital, he was sitting on the deck, reading a book, when he heard a buzzing sound in the air. He stood up and walked to the edge of the deck, where he soon spotted a drone circling in the air.

Karl himself had come up from California the day before and was overseeing the protection efforts in person. He ran to the deck where Kit stood. "If that thing has a camera in it, then whoever is operating it probably knows you are here and that Kingfisher is as well. Bruce is heading for the barn with him now, but I'm afraid there's nothing more we can do except keep an even closer watch."

"I'm going to go to the barn and have a look at Kingfisher," Kit announced.

"I'll walk with you," Karl said. It was slow going, but Karl, ever alert, stayed right with him.

"Can anything be done about that drone?" Kit asked.

"My men are setting up some equipment over there that, if we have to, could take it out," he said, pointing into the center of the yard. "Unless I perceive some danger, though, I can't risk doing that, as it could be perfectly innocent."

Kit's face darkened. "You and I both know it's not. Someone is flying that thing in order to spy on us and my horse."

"I'm sure you're right, but all we can do is increase our patrols," Karl said. "We will keep you and your horse safe."

"Okay, I'm depending on you," Kit said.

"I expect nothing less," Karl replied. "I'm going to go over and make sure that little heat-seeking missile launcher is ready, but again, I hope I don't have to use it. I could use a rifle, but this little missile is a guaranteed hit if I have to use it."

"I'm going in the barn," Kit said, and he walked through the door just as Randall did.

Randall shook his head. "I hope that isn't my son spying on us," he said. "But at this point, I wouldn't put anything past him." Then he switched to a different topic. "Kingfisher will be ready for the race, Kit. He looked great today. Bruce and Paizlee only brought him in because of that drone."

"I sure do appreciate all you're doing for my sister and me. Someday, I'll try to repay you for all your effort and expense."

"Kit, you don't owe me a thing. So don't worry about it," he said just as they reached where Paizlee was rubbing Kingfisher down. Bruce was cleaning his stall. Kit began to help Paizlee as best as he could, grateful for such a wonderful horse.

Sam and Vince were getting angrier and more dangerous by the hour. Sam was jumping up and down and pumping his fists with glee. "They're in the barn. Let's fly that drone into it right now."

Vince, who was at the controls, looked up at him. "They will all most likely die if we do that."

"Serves them right," Sam said coldly. "I'm sure you've never killed anyone, but look at what they've cost you and me. We can kill them and then get out of the country."

Vince nodded. "Actually, I have. You remember that kid who hanged himself after he'd beaten you up?"

"Yeah, what about him?" Sam asked.

"He didn't do that himself. He had help," Vince said coldly.

"You killed him?" Sam asked, taken aback.

"You say these guys had it coming. Don't you think he did?" Vince asked.

"Yeah, actually, I do. Thanks for doing that for me, Vince. Now let's do this. We didn't go to so much trouble making a bomb not to use it."

Without another word, Vince brought the drone around again and started it once more on a path to the barnyard. "Are you sure, Sam?" he asked. "In a minute it will be too late to change our minds."

"Why not? We'll be out of here, and there is no way anyone can possibly figure out it was us who blew them up," Sam said. "Nobody caught you when you hung that loser. And you told me that there is no way for anyone to trace where that drone came from or who was operating it after it blows up."

"That's true," Vince said. "Okay, let's go for it. I'll direct the drone so it will hit just above that big door they all just went through. That will be the end of them. Then we're out of here."

Kit and Paizlee had finished rubbing Kingfisher down and let Bruce take him to put him in the stall. They walked toward the big door where the sun was shining brightly into the barn. "There's that drone again," Kit said. "It's coming right this way."

They watched it for a few seconds. "Surely it's going to start going up again now! They must be trying to get a close-up of us. Kit, this is scary. Will Sam never give up?"

The drone continued to come, its speed seeming to accelerate, and it was getting closer and closer to the ground. Kit had overdone it today and was getting weak. He leaned against the door frame. He looked over to where, across the large yard, Karl was kneeling behind the small missile launcher.

"I wonder if . . ." he started to say when suddenly, a small missile was launched.

In what seemed like a minute, but was really seconds, the missile sped toward the drone. There was a huge midair explosion that shook the ground. The blast was so strong that it knocked the twins to the floor of the barn. The flash of the explosion was almost blinding. The missile and the drone were blown into thousands of tiny pieces that drifted to the ground between the barn and Karl's missile launcher.

Randall came running up to Kit and Paizlee. "Are you two okay?" he asked as he dropped to his knees beside them.

"I think I'm bruised, but I'm fine," Paizlee said. She was also feeling some pain in her face, but she ignored it over her concern for her brother. "Are you okay, Kit?"

Kit was not okay. He was writhing with pain on the ground, holding his stomach with both hands. "What in the world was that?" Randall asked, his voice desperate.

"The drone blew up," Paizlee said. "It was heading for the barn, for us. Karl hit it with a missile."

"I'll call 911," Randall said frantically and grabbed his phone.

Kit struggled to sit up, but Paizlee gently pushed him back to the floor. "Don't, Kit. Just lie still. Randall is calling for help."

"I'll be okay in a minute or two," Kit protested just as Karl Shutter and Dave Washington reached him. "I'm just dazed a little. What happened, anyway?"

"There was a bomb on that drone," Karl said, his face contorted with anger. "I think whoever is behind this was trying to blow up the barn with your horse and you guys in it."

Karl and Dave examined Kit.

"An ambulance is coming and so are some officers," Randall said.

"Help me up," Kit said.

"No, you stay put," Dave, the big, confident operative said. "I know what I'm doing. I want to make sure you're okay."

Paizlee, who was pale and trembling, had gotten to her feet and was watching, ignoring her own pain in her concern for him. "I can see some blood."

"We've got this," Karl said. "Kit will be fine."

"But the blood," she protested.

"It's not from his old wound. A tiny piece of shrapnel hit him in the chest, but it's not serious," Karl said. The two men had removed Kit's upper clothing and could plainly see a small piece of metal piercing his chest just below the collar bone. There was a burned spot around it. "It was hot when it hit him," Karl explained.

Paizlee felt lightheaded, but she did not turn her eyes away until Randall said, "Paizlee, look at me."

She did.

"You have a couple of small pieces of shrapnel in your forehead. It just missed your eyes. You have some burns too."

"Really? I knew something was wrong," she said.

"Let me see," Karl said as he stood up and left Dave to care for Kit.

"I felt something, but I didn't think I was hurt," she protested. She lifted a hand toward her forehead, but Karl caught it before she could touch the metal.

"Don't touch anything. I'll take care of it. You sit down over here against the wall," Karl said as he gently steered her that way.

Randall, joined now by Bruce, stood in shock. "I can't believe Sam would do this. He and Vince meant to kill all of us and the horses."

"We don't know that," Bruce said.

"I know it!" Randall said angrily. "I can feel it in here." He touched his chest. "Someone has to stop those guys."

Once Kit was attended to, Karl gathered everyone together. "I have a rifle in my SUV. I'm going to fire a shot from it."

"Why?" Randall asked, arching his eyebrows.

"Because I don't want the police or anyone else to know that I fired a missile. We will hide the apparatus in my vehicle. We'll claim I shot at the drone with my rifle and got lucky and hit it. Does anyone have a problem with that?"

Randall spoke quickly. "Karl, you saved our lives. Your secret is safe with me. How about the rest of you?"

Everyone agreed. "Thanks," Karl said. "What I did in using it was justified. I may have hit it with a rifle, but that would not have been easy, as fast as the drone was flying. Anyway, I don't want people knowing that my operatives and I have that capability."

A minute later, he fired a single shot from his rifle and then walked back to his SUV and leaned it against the back door. He rejoined the others. "It won't take much to convince the sheriff and his deputies that I hit it with my rifle."

When the sheriff and a host of other officers arrived, no one questioned how Karl had managed to stop the drone from hitting the barn. The sheriff briefly looked at Karl's rifle. He bounced the empty shell in his hand, and said, "Amazing shot, Karl. You saved a lot of lives today."

Sam and Vince were in Harry's car, fleeing from the remote spot where they had launched the deadly attack. They had left the controls to the drone behind in their haste to get away. They didn't want to take any chance of being found with them in the stolen pickup and didn't think they would be easily found way out there.

"We got 'em," Sam said gleefully.

"Yes, we did," Vince agreed. "Now we gotta get out of this state. No one will know to look for Harry's pickup for a while."

"Are we going to LA?" Sam asked.

"Yep, to the great melting pot of America where no one will find us." Vince laughed. "We'll hole up there for a few days and then leave the country. Kirby and Mickey think they pulled a great one in San Francisco. What they did was nothing compared to what we just did. Wow, what a rush."

Brandon had just walked into Lawrence's office following some shocking news about Lawrence's latest client when his phone began to ring. He looked at the screen and was surprised to see it was Paizlee calling. "Hey, Paizlee," he answered lightly.

"Brandon, they tried to kill us! They almost did. Kit is on the way to the hospital again," she said, and then she stopped as if to take a breath.

"Calm down, Paizlee. First, are you okay?" he asked.

"I'm okay. But they took Kit to the hospital," she repeated.

"Is he badly hurt?" he asked as Wiona left her desk and ran to his side, her face white.

"I don't know," Paizlee said. "We both got hit with some shrapnel, but I'm afraid that Kit's stomach was hurt again when we both were blown to the floor."

Brandon, a man not easily rattled, said calmly, "Tell me what happened, Paizlee. Do I need to come right now?"

Paizlee didn't answer.

"Brandon, this is Karl. I just snatched Paizlee's phone away. Everyone will be just fine. Kit is on the way to the hospital out of an abundance of caution, but he was not seriously injured. Paizlee had some very minor injuries, but she is okay. Everything is secure here. Let me explain what happened."

"Okay, let's hear it," Brandon said. "I'm going to put my phone on speaker. Lawrence, Wiona, and Jenna are all with me now, and I don't want to have to repeat anything."

Karl then recited the events of the past hour.

"My case here is over," Lawrence said when Karl had finished. "The client that had us so busy was murdered last night. The cops are looking for the killer, but I no longer have to defend him. Brandon, Wiona, and I are going to fly down as soon as we can get free here."

"In that case, I'll have someone pick you up at the airport," Karl said.

The call ended. "I've got to see Kit," Wiona said, wringing her hands and sobbing.

"You will," her mother told her calmly. "You run home and pack."

"I'll take her," Brandon said. "I have what I need in my Bronco."

"I'll meet you two at the airport," Lawrence told them.

They had not yet arrived at Wiona's mother's home, where Wiona was also living, before Brandon received a call from Sheriff Marc Ledford of Millard County. "Brandon, have you got a moment?"

"Yes, Sheriff. What's up?"

"I just learned from the medical examiner the identity of the man who was killed at Kit's ranch. His name is Harry Murray. He's a daredevil, stuntman kind of guy from Las Vegas. He was reported missing. He also has a couple of very high-tech drones."

"So do you think that was who was snooping at Kit's ranch with a drone?" Brandon asked.

"Yes, but I'm sure he had help," Sheriff Ledford said.

"I'm sure I know who," Brandon replied. "What about his car? Have you found it?"

"It's a pickup truck with an enclosed bed. It's gone. There is now only one drone at his place outside of Vegas. I have a feeling that Sam Overmyer and Vince Hodson took both the pickup and the drone," he said.

"Sheriff, I'm flying down to Nevada with Lawrence Heslop in a little while. Have you heard what happened there?"

"No, did those guys figure out that Kingfisher was at the Overmyer ranch?" Sheriff Ledford asked, alarm in his voice.

"They did. Let me tell you what happened just a short while ago," Brandon said. While he talked, he reached Wiona's home. She jumped out and ran inside while Brandon recited to the sheriff what he had just learned from Karl.

"What will they try next?" Sheriff Ledford asked. "These men have turned into deadly killers. Does Andy Boyse know about this?"

"I have no idea," Brandon responded.

"I'll make sure he does," the sheriff said.

Karl's number-two man, Dave Washington, picked Lawrence, Brandon, and Wiona up from the airport a few short hours later. The first stop they made was at the hospital, where Kit had again been admitted for observation, although Dr. Sturgeon couldn't find anything seriously damaged from the bomb attack and his old wounds were still healing nicely. Wiona insisted on staying with him.

Leaving her and a couple of Karl's operatives to protect Kit, the others drove to the ranch. It was one large crime scene. Sheriff Nick Watson was running the investigation, but he explained that due to the use of a drone, investigators from the Federal Aviation Administration were on their way. However, Sheriff Watson explained that due to the power of the blast, the drone essentially disintegrated.

Deputy Kirby Fry was one of the officers at the scene, having been called out to assist that morning even though he was still on the night shift. As he was working there, he got a call from his brother, Mickey, who was on duty in Las Vegas. "Kirby," Mickey said, "we just learned that Harry Murray is dead. That fancy pickup of his is believed to be in the hands of Sam Overmyer and our friend Vince. No one has any idea where they are."

"I know where they were," Kirby said after a moment of thought. "They used Harry's drone in an attempt to blow up Randall Overmyer's barn with several people and horses inside." He gave what details he knew to Mickey. "So I'm pretty sure those two are on the run in Harry's truck."

"You said Vince had you doing him a couple of favors," Mickey said. "Did he mention anything about this to you so you would be expecting it?"

"Nope, not a word," Kirby said.

Sam and Vince were kicked back in a motel near Los Angeles, drinking beer and watching the news on TV. They were hoping to hear something about the barn and its human and equine contents being blown and burned to bits. They had ditched Harry's pickup several hours ago and were using a car they had stolen.

The newscast they had been waiting for finally came on. They both began to curse when it was reported that the drone, carrying a bomb, had been blown out of the sky by a high-powered rifle. Nothing was said about who used the rifle. Not that it mattered. They had failed in their deadly attempt at murder and mayhem.

After letting the bad news sink in, Sam said, "I want to check with the racetracks in the state. I'm sure there is a race coming up. If so, I'll find out if Kingfisher is signed up to race. If he is, we can still defeat Kit and Kingfisher."

An hour later, Sam had found the information he sought. With a wicked gleam in his eye, he said, "Get this, Vince. Kingfisher is racing at Santa Anita Park in Arcadia the week after next."

"Who is riding him, I wonder," Vince said.

"Well, if you remember, the video from the drone showed Kit's sister on Kingfisher at my dad's track. I wonder if she's good enough. I can't imagine she is. If not, then I'm sure Dad will hire a jockey for them. He seems to have kicked me out of his family and adopted them."

"Either way, we've got some plans to make. We can't mess up again, Sam. This might be our last chance to even the score."

CHAPTER TWENTY-SEVEN

THE PAST FEW DAYS HAD been quiet. Kit was much improved, and Kingfisher and Paizlee were almost ready for the big race at Santa Anita Park in Arcadia, California. There had been no word of Sam or Vince, meaning that they were both still on the run somewhere. No one relaxed, for those two were likely to be planning more trouble, especially after their latest murderous attempt had failed.

After an extensive search, law enforcement officers had found where the drone had been operated from. Fingerprints that matched both Sam and Vince had been found on the abandoned equipment. That was a bit of a surprise, as it would have seemed like Vince would have been more cautious than that. At any rate, warrants were issued. Sam and Vince were wanted by both local and federal authorities for a multitude of serious state and federal felonies.

The pickup that had belonged to Harry Murray was located in a mall parking lot in Los Angeles. No usable fingerprints were found after a quick check of the car. It could only be assumed that it had been stolen by the two fugitives, which led to the assumption that they were in the Los Angeles area. This was of grave concern to Kit, Paizlee, and their friends since the upcoming race was in Arcadia, a scant few miles north of where the car had been found.

On a Monday evening, just four days before the Friday race, a group was gathered in Randall's living room. They were discussing the upcoming race and trying to make a plan to keep the horse and rider safe. The group included Kit, Paizlee, Brandon, Wiona, Lawrence, Hank, Dave, Randall, Bruce, and Andy. Lawrence had flown Andy down from Fillmore just that afternoon since he was going to be involved in the event at Santa Anita Park.

"Can anyone find out who is racing in a particular race?" Karl asked as they began the process of setting up security for when they raced Kingfisher.

"Pretty much," Kit said. "It isn't always known well in advance who the jockey is going to be, but the horse has to be officially entered."

"Do you think Sam and Vince would assume that Kit is going to ride him, Paizlee?" Karl asked.

"Not necessarily," Paizlee said. "Surely they know how badly he was injured thanks to them."

"Would they think it would be you?" he asked.

"I don't know. With that drone, they may have seen me on Kingfisher on the track," she responded. "But we weren't running him all out like we have on some days."

"Sam will think you are not capable of riding in a real race, Paizlee," Randall said. "He doesn't think women are good for much. He always treated his mother horribly. So my guess is that those guys will think we are hiring a jockey."

"I told the race organizers that I would probably be riding when I signed Kingfisher up, but I also told them that could change," Paizlee said.

"Why did you do that?" Brandon asked. "After all that's happened, are you beginning to think that it might be too dangerous?"

Paizlee scowled at him. "No, I was just being reasonable. What if I got hurt during the training? Then someone else would have to ride."

"Are you really sure you want to do this, Paizlee?" Brandon asked with concern in his voice.

"Yes, I am. And you are not going to talk me out of it. The only way I would not ride is if Kit was able to, and he can't. So that's that."

Brandon smiled at her. "Sorry, just making sure."

She smiled back, and the tension faded.

"Let's talk about what kind of things we need to be prepared for," Karl said. "I'm not familiar with horse racing, so I don't know when or how someone could cause injury or do some kind of damage to cause a horse to lose a race or not even be able to run."

"There are lots of things we have to prevent," Paizlee answered. "For example, if someone slipped in and gave Kingfisher a large drink of water right before the race, he would start out okay but fade away partway into the race."

"Why is that?" Brandon asked.

"It adds weight, and it also sloshes around in their stomach, causing them to be a little sluggish," Andy explained.

"What else do we watch for?" Karl asked.

"Someone could slip the horse some kind of drug in a sugar cube or in the feed or even with a syringe that would cause them to perform below their capabilities, far below in many cases," Bruce said.

"I won't ask what kind of drugs, because I'm sure the list would be very long. Is this something that would happen in their stall?" Karl asked.

"It could," Andy put in. "Or it could happen when we take him out for a workout. Or it could happen any time after the horses are being led out to begin the race. What we have to do is make sure no one is able to make contact with Kingfisher from the moment we arrive with him at the race grounds until he is taken to the starting gate."

"I see. So I will need a list of who exactly is authorized to have contact with him," Karl said.

"Those of us in this room," Randall said very strongly. "No one else, unless it is a race official or a veterinarian. Even then, we would need to have at least two of us who are very knowledgeable right with them at those times."

"Why would a veterinarian need to see him?" Karl asked.

"Possibly to draw blood for testing. Some people have been known to give their horses something to boost their energy or otherwise improve or diminish their ability to run," Andy said.

"We have reason to be particularly concerned, so we will not want to allow anyone near Kingfisher without establishing their identity and their right to be there," Bruce said.

"If a vet was to draw blood, and that will probably happen, then we just need to watch and make sure he doesn't do anything fishy," Randall put in. "And under no circumstances is a vet to be allowed to give him a shot. If one even looks like that is about to happen, we would want you or your operatives to remove that person promptly."

"Would a legitimate veterinarian do that?" Dave Washington asked, speaking for the first time.

"A lot of folks can be bribed or blackmailed," Randall said, narrowing his eyes. "And that is exactly what I would expect Sam and Vince to attempt."

Karl nodded. "Anything else?"

Kit spoke up next. "We need to make sure no one gets near our racing gear. A small cut in a bridle rein or the cinch on the saddle, or who knows what, could cause a calamity and destroy our chances of winning."

Karl, Dave, and Brandon were taking notes.

"So in a nutshell," Karl said, "we must guard against anyone getting near the horse or the gear."

Everyone nodded their agreement.

"What about another jockey during the race?" Brandon asked.

"If Paizlee senses anything out of the ordinary with any of the other jockeys, she will need to keep Kingfisher from getting near that horse during the race," Kit said. He gave Randall an apologetic look.

"That's what happened with my son," Randall said. "He tried to unseat Kit, and in doing so, Kit couldn't make up all the lost time even though he was able to regain his balance. Is my understanding on that correct, Kit?"

"Yes, that's exactly what happened. Sam won't, of course, be riding in the race on Friday, but there are other jockeys who might be bribed to try something sneaky," Kit told the others.

"I will instruct my men and women to try to find out all they can about any other jockeys they can identify," Karl said. "And we will be watching each one whenever we get a chance. Paizlee, if one of us sees something of concern before the race, you will hear about it immediately. Once you are out of the gate, you're on your own, I'm afraid."

"Have pictures of my son and nephew been circulated to the authorities at the park?" Randall asked.

"They will be. I haven't mentioned this before," Karl said, "but I have a woman on my staff who is an amazing artist. We are preparing a number of pictures, both hand drawn and computer generated, that will show what the men would probably look like with a number of different disguises."

"What kind of disguises?" Paizlee asked.

"Adding beards, moustaches, glasses, and different styles of clothing. They could change their complexions, get haircuts, or wear wigs. My artist is trying to think of anything they might do and provide us with drawings of both men with the different looks," Karl said. "Each picture, when I get them distributed, will be numbered. Those two will almost certainly be at the race somewhere, and I want my people and all of you to be able to recognize them no matter what changes they've made to their appearances to try to throw us off."

"You may all be thinking about the drone that nearly killed some of you. We don't know if they have another drone. So we will also be watching for one," Dave said.

"If we see one, what can you do? I don't think you would want to try to shoot it down in the city," Bruce said.

"No. If we see one, we'll alert the proper authorities. I will make sure the local police and the park security officers know that a drone could be used. Because of the tight regulations regarding them around the park, I don't really think they will try that again. But we will be prepared if they do," Karl said.

Brandon's face, usually so unreadable, looked concerned. "Paizlee, after hearing all this, I've got to say that I don't think you should ride."

She shook her head and glared at him for a moment. "I trust all of you to keep me safe and Kingfisher and our gear untampered with. I will be alert and ride to the best of my ability."

"Which says a lot," Kit said. "Paizlee rides as well as I do."

She looked at her brother with a half-smile on her face. "You know that's not true, Kit. But I will do my very best. All of you should quit worrying about me and worry instead about what someone might do before the race."

"Which is all we can reasonably ask," Randall said.

"Paizlee," Brandon began again.

"Brandon," she said as she shook a finger at him. "Please don't. I can do this, and I am going to."

"Okay, I know when I'm beat," he said with downcast eyes.

Karl lightened the mood with a laugh. "I know this guy. He isn't easily defeated. I would not be alive today if he was someone who gave up easily. I've seen him in the most dangerous of circumstances, and never did he back down if he could conceive a way to defeat the enemy. You, Paizlee, must have some amazing power to be able to get him to admit that he's been beaten."

"I am beaten," Brandon repeated. "I'm not happy to have to admit it. But you'd better believe, Kit and Paizlee, that I will do everything within my power to make sure nothing goes wrong. You have my word."

"And you have mine as well," Karl added. "But keep in mind that though we are very good at what we do, mistakes can be made."

"We understand," Kit said.

"You can count on the best effort of every man and woman we assign to this operation," Dave said. "Like Karl said, we are not infallible, but we are very, very good. So when do we leave for California?"

"Wednesday morning," Bruce said. "That means we have just two days to finish preparing Kingfisher."

"Is everyone in this room going to be at the race park?" Karl asked.

They all indicated that they were. Even Lawrence said, "I wouldn't miss that race. And if I can be of assistance in keeping a preventive eye on things, please count on me. Wiona is going to fly to LA with me, and to make the trip easier on Kit, I'd like him to fly too. I have plenty of room," Lawrence said. "And I have a rental SUV waiting for us at the airport."

"I think I should ride with whoever is pulling Kingfisher's trailer," Kit said with a slight shake of his head.

"Kit, please, ride with us. There will be plenty of people watching out for your horse," Wiona said with a pleading look in her eyes.

His eyes met hers. "Okay, if that's what you think is best."

"I think it's best too," Paizlee said. "I'll ride with Brandon. We'll be following closely behind the trailer."

"Bruce, Andy, and I will take turns driving my truck, which will be pulling my horse trailer with Kingfisher inside," Randall said.

Karl spoke up again. "I want Dave to ride with you men. He'll watch for trouble and react to anything that he perceives is amiss."

No one had to verbalize how competent and skilled Dave was. He was also well liked by all of them. "I would appreciate that," Randall said.

"Santos Garcia and I will be in the lead vehicle with two operatives right behind us in another one," Karl announced.

"What about the others who have been assisting here?" Randall asked.

"They will leave in the morning, a day ahead of us, and scope out the race ground as well as the hotel rooms we have arranged. They and others currently on another assignment in LA will provide protection and be eyes and ears for us at the park and track, at the hotel, and on the route between," Karl explained.

"It sounds like you have thought things out very well," Randall said. "I appreciate everything you have done and are doing."

"You're welcome," Karl said sincerely. "Now, do any of you have any questions?"

No one did, so they adjourned the meeting.

Sam was excited when he ended his call. "He's still going to be racing at the Santa Anita Park on Friday," he told Vince.

"That's only a few miles north of here," Vince observed. "Who is the jockey?"

"They wouldn't tell me," Sam reported. "They said it has not yet been confirmed."

"Probably a hired jockey then," Vince concluded. "We have some work to do. First, we need to disguise ourselves. We'll cut our hair, dye it, buy fake beards and moustaches, and get a new wardrobe that is different from what we usually wear."

Sam had no argument. They'd discussed this a lot since they had arrived in LA. He mentioned the next step, which they had only loosely discussed. "Then we need to go to Santa Anita Park and scope it out. We need to figure out where security might be, where the horses are stabled, and get a look at the track itself."

"And we need to see if we can figure out what other jockeys are racing and which horses they are riding," Vince suggested. "I suppose you know which race Kingfisher is in that day."

"He'll be racing at about three in the afternoon. There are three races before and one after."

"All right. Let's give each other a haircut," Vince said.

CHAPTER TWENTY-EIGHT

MICKEY AND KIRBY FRY WERE both angry. Mickey had spent some time on the internet and had learned that there were upcoming races at Santa Anita Park. "I'm going to call the police in Los Angeles," Mickey said. "I'll tell them I'm sure Sam and Vince are there and that they plan to disrupt the race."

"But we just think they're there," Kirby said doubtfully.

"No, we know it. We were notified here in my department by the LAPD that Harry's pickup has been located in the parking lot of a mall. They took it in, processed it more thoroughly, and finally were able to identify four partial prints. They matched Sam's," he said. "I can't believe they would be stupid enough to not wipe the truck down more thoroughly or to wear gloves anytime they were using it. Vince has been a cop for a long time. He should know better."

"Sam doesn't. Do you know when the race is?" Kirby asked.

"Yes, I've been working on that. Kingfisher, that's Kit's horse, is signed up to race at about three o'clock Friday afternoon. Those guys will be there, and they will get arrested," Mickey said. "I hold them personally responsible for Harry's death."

"Vince was supposed to call me again, but he hasn't. I could have told him that I saw Randall Overmyer's truck going through Tonopah pulling a horse trailer. There were at least four people in the truck. One of them was Paizlee Troxler. Randall was driving. Randall's foreman was in the back seat with Kit's sister, and there was a large man sitting next to Randall in the front," Kirby said. "I guess Vince doesn't care to know that now, or he'd call."

"Yeah. Well, I'll talk to you later. I'm going to call the LAPD and tell them to look for those guys in Arcadia," Mickey said. He laughed as he ended the call.

"Well, cousin, I guess we're as ready as we'll ever be. Every time I look at you, I almost wonder who you are. No one will ever recognize us now," Vince said to Sam with confidence.

"Don't you think we should get back to the racecourse? I think they'll be coming this afternoon with Kingfisher. They'll want time to familiarize him with the track and to do a workout or two on him," Sam said as he looked at Vince's shaved head and full beard. "No one will know you or me. We can move around there with ease."

"I agree. Let's watch the news for a bit, then we'll go," Vince said.

They saw the news a short while later and were shocked to see their pictures on the TV screen. The newscaster, a man by the name of Jerrod Gallagher, said, "These two men are from Tonopah, Nevada. They are Sam Overmyer and Vince Hodson. They have warrants out for their arrests from Utah, Nevada, and California. The sheriff of Millard County, Utah, wants them in connection with the death of a Las Vegas man by the name of Harry Murray, a fairly well-known daredevil and stuntman from Las Vegas. Murray's pickup truck was found in the parking lot of a mall, and it is believed to have been driven there by Overmyer and Hodson. A call from an officer in Las Vegas a short while ago alerted the police to look for them in or around Santa Anita Park in Arcadia."

Sam and Vince were both stunned. "How could they know all that?" Sam asked.

Vince shook his head. "Keep listening."

What they heard next enraged Vince.

"A police officer in Las Vegas who claims to be a close friend of the late Harry Murray told police here that the men are planning to disrupt a race at Santa Anita Park on Friday where a horse from Utah by the name of Kingfisher is slated to run. That horse is owned by twins Kit and Paizlee Troxler, who own and operate a cattle and horse ranch in Millard County."

The newscast gave further details of Kit being shot and nearly killed by an associate of the two men and of a drone that had allegedly been stolen from Harry Murray being used in a failed attempt to murder several people on a ranch belonging to Sam's father in Nye County, Nevada. The story was quite detailed. "Both men are presumed armed and extremely dangerous," Gallagher concluded.

After stomping about the hotel room for several minutes, cursing and telling Sam what he would do to Mickey and Kirby if he ever saw them again, Vince finally calmed down. "That does it, Sam," he said. "It's time to let the police in San Francisco know what those guys did. I'm going to do that right now."

"Can't that wait?" Sam asked. "We need to get out to Santa Anita Park. We might get a chance to take care of Kingfisher this afternoon."

"No, it can't wait. I want to discredit Mickey. When they get copies of what I have, no one will believe him anymore, and maybe it will take some of the heat off us. Let's let this story cool while I put the heat on those guys. Right now, cops will be all over Santa Anita Park looking for us."

"They won't know us even if they see us," Sam reminded him.

"We wait, Sam," Vince said firmly. "I'm calling the San Francisco police right now. It's my turn to get some revenge. We have plenty of time to take care of Kingfisher."

Paizlee called Kit when they were still over an hour from Arcadia that Wednesday afternoon. Kit reported that it was sunny with a breeze in Arcadia that seemed to be keeping the smog at bay.

"The drive so far has been uneventful," Paizlee said. "But Dave says that the closer we get to LA, the more chance there is of those guys trying something."

"That's probably true. So you guys need to be careful," Kit said. "We're at a hotel now. I've been resting, but we will leave as soon as you reach Arcadia. I want to be there to see Kingfisher when he's unloaded."

"Brandon says there are not only a lot of Karl's men waiting for us but also a large number of Santa Anita Park security people and Arcadia officers," Paizlee announced. "He just got off the phone with Karl, who has been talking to one of his guys at the park. It sounds like the cops are more interested in this than they would normally be because Sam and Vince are wanted for so many crimes now. You know that guy who was killed on our ranch in a shootout with the cops? Karl told Brandon that his pickup has been found in LA and that a couple of Sam's fingerprints were found in it."

"I hope they catch them soon," Kit said. "Be watchful. I'll see you in an hour or so."

"Karl is sending more of his people to help escort us," Paizlee said. "See you soon."

Kit lay back on the bed. He was a bit sore, but nothing worse than he had expected. Lawrence and Wiona each had separate rooms next to his. Karl's man, Santos Garcia, was in the room with Kit, but he kept going out, checking whatever he checked, and then returning with a report.

Santos currently sat on a sofa in the far end of the room, talking on his secure phone. Kit turned the TV on. He was sick of TV after all the days he'd watched it while in the hospital, but he decided to watch it for a while anyway. He switched from channel to channel.

Suddenly Garcia stood up. "We need to see the news." He told Kit which channel to turn to. "There is some breaking news about a Las Vegas cop and his brother who is a Nye County deputy."

Kit found the channel. The newscaster, who identified himself as Jerrod Gallagher, said, "This breaking news is just in. The bank robbery and murder in San Francisco a few months back has been solved. An anonymous caller contacted the San Francisco PD a little while ago and told them who was responsible for the murder. He backed it up by sending pictures of the robbery taken from somewhere close to the bank. But that isn't all. He also sent audio recordings of the suspects discussing it with each other following the robbery."

Kit was sitting up now, intently watching the newscast unfold.

"The voices on the recording called each other by name. One of them was Harry Murray, the daredevil who died in a shootout in Utah and whose pickup was found in LA. Another was a police officer from Las Vegas identified as Mickey Fry. A third was Mickey's brother, Kirby, a deputy sheriff in Nye County, Nevada." Gallagher went on to name the other suspects.

"We are told that law enforcement moved rapidly and that all of the suspects are in custody. In an interesting twist to this story, a source inside the Las Vegas Metropolitan Police Department revealed that Officer Mickey Kirby was the officer who'd reported to the LAPD that Sam Overmyer and former Deputy Sheriff Vince Hodson were planning to make some kind of an attack on a horse and its owners at the races on Friday at Santa Anita Park."

Kit looked at Santos, who was still intently watching the TV screen. He said nothing, but he was very puzzled. He didn't like what he heard next.

"This development has cast serious doubt on the information provided about Overmyer and Hodson. The authorities in both Los Angeles and Las Vegas are cautioning that Officer Fry may have been lying all along."

He went on to recap the earlier story about Sam and Vince and confirmed that the fact still remained that Sam's fingerprints were found in the truck that had belonged to one of the robbery suspects, Harry Murray, who had died in a shootout in Utah.

Gallagher then turned to other news, and Kit shut the TV off. "Agent Garcia," Kit began, "does this mean that the police and you guys will not give us as much security as was planned?"

"I can't speak for the police, but if anything, we'll step up our efforts. Karl had called me on the phone just before I had you turn to the news channel.

He's not sure what the cops will do, but he said to assure you that we are with you guys all the way."

"Thank you," Kit said. "I wonder if Paizlee knows."

"You can count on that," Santos said. "Karl was going to call Dave as soon as our call was over."

"I think I'll call her if that's okay," Kit said.

"Of course it's okay," Santos responded. "I'm going to step out in the hallway again and do a little surveillance. Karl is sending us another agent to stay in the hallway. I'll be going with you to the park when you go, but he will be here to make sure no one messes with your room or Lawrence's and Wiona's."

Santos stepped out into the hall. While Kit was on the phone with his twin sister, there was a knock on his door. He tensed, hoping that Agent Garcia was close by. He got off the bed and made his way to the door. "Hang on, Paizlee," he said. "Someone is at my door."

"Be careful," Paizlee said in alarm.

"I will be," Kit promised. He felt immense relief when he heard the deep, unmistakable voice of Lawrence Heslop.

"Kit, it's Lawrence and Wiona. Would you mind if we come in?" he asked.

"Paizlee," Kit said into his phone, "it's Lawrence and Wiona. I'll call you back in a bit after I see what they want." He opened the door and stepped aside as the two of them entered.

"We were thinking maybe you could use some company after the news we just heard," Lawrence said. "You didn't by any chance hear it as well, did you?"

"I did. This is getting confusing. I don't know who the real bad guys are. Apparently another Nye County deputy is as crooked at Vince Hodson," Kit said as he shut the door behind them.

"I just talked to Brandon," Lawrence said. "I already told Wiona this, but the security operatives are going to come right to our hotel here in Arcadia, and we'll all travel together to Santa Anita Park."

"That sounds okay to me," Kit said. "I want everyone to be safe."

An hour later, he and the others all arrived at the stables safe and sound. There were still a lot of police officers there. There was also an undisclosed number of operatives, in plain clothes, from Karl's protection agency. Bruce and Andy, the two foremen who had worked with Kingfisher, led him from the horse trailer.

In addition to the residual effect of the bullet that had torn up his insides, Kit's gut also ached with apprehension. Wiona and Agent Garcia walked beside him, following the horse. Right behind them were Paizlee and Brandon. In the lead were Karl and Dave and other agents whom Kit didn't know. He was impressed with how alert they all were. He also kept looking around, recalling in his mind the different looks his two enemies could have taken in disguise. He saw nothing to alarm him.

Kit was relieved when Kingfisher was settled in a strong stall in a huge barn. He and Paizlee stood inside with him for several minutes, petting and speaking softly to him. The big black stallion seemed quite at ease, despite other horses neighing and stomping in nearby stalls. "I think I should stay with him tonight," Kit said to Brandon and Karl when he and Paizlee finally left the stall.

"Kit, you've only been out of the hospital for a few days," Wiona protested. "There are a lot of people here to help with him. You don't need to be here."

"He's my responsibility," Kit said stubbornly. "I'm staying here."

"In that case, we'll both stay," Paizlee said. "He's my responsibility too."

"You guys can do what you like," Karl said, "but my people and I have accepted responsibility, and we take it very seriously. I think you should rest in a hotel room tonight and be here to stay with him all day tomorrow."

"We will have to be working him tomorrow," Bruce reminded them. "Paizlee, you will need to be rested and ready to spend some time on him."

"I agree with Bruce," Andy said. "Let Karl's people take care of Kingfisher during the night."

"Paizlee, maybe they're right. You need to be rested tomorrow. I'll stay with him. I can get some pillows and a blanket, and I'll be just fine," Kit said.

"But like Wiona said, you have not been out of the hospital for very long," Paizlee persisted.

"If you want to stay here, Kit, I'll stay with you," Wiona volunteered.

"You don't have to do that," he argued.

"But I want to," she responded.

"Then I'd like that," Kit said.

"Let me stay with the horse, and you two both get some rest tonight," Brandon said, entering the debate.

Kit and Wiona both stubbornly resisted.

"In that case, I'll stay late and return early," Brandon relented.

Finally, it was agreed. But for the rest of the evening, the entire group stayed close. Brandon and Lawrence left for a time to pick up pizza and drinks for everyone and blankets and pillows for Wiona and Kit.

Other men and women not in their party also hung around the barn until quite late, mostly employees of the horses' owners. Kit couldn't help but eye each of them with some degree of suspicion. But as the evening grew late, fewer and fewer hung around. Mixing with them were some of Karl's people who were dressed to not stand out. Karl had made sure that each of his operatives was known and familiar to Kit and Wiona.

From time to time, uniformed police officers patrolled the stables in pairs, as did park security officers. After his bad experience with Vince Hodson, Kit wasn't entirely comfortable with the cops. He studied each of them carefully, comparing them to the various disguises Karl's artist had produced to show how Sam and Vince might look. He was convinced that those guys would be around. It worried him and was the main reason he wanted to stay with Kingfisher.

Karl provided Kit with a secure phone that he could quickly alert the operatives on if he saw anyone or anything suspicious. And Karl promised there would always be a couple of them constantly on the move within the large barn.

Somewhat reassured, Kit and Wiona made themselves a place to relax beside Kingfisher's stall. The two of them decided to take turns sleeping. They were each diligent when it was their turn to keep watch.

CHAPTER TWENTY-NINE

Wiona had the first scare. She poked Kit and whispered as he woke. "That guy," she said, pointing, "keeps walking by us. Just a few seconds ago, he peeked into Kingfisher's stall. I pretended to be asleep. Then he walked on past and is standing down there just leaning against the wall holding a black bag. And I don't know where Karl's guys are or the security officer that was supposed to be on watch. I haven't seen them for a little while."

Kit also felt something was wrong. Karl's men had been close by most of the time, and they had seen the security officer regularly. He watched the guy by the wall for a moment. He was a small man, maybe five foot six. He had dark hair that fell almost to his collar and covered his ears. Kit sent a quick message to both of Karl's operatives, explaining his concerns. Neither he nor Wiona had seen the guy before. Due to his small size, Kit assumed he could be a jockey, but what was he doing in here with a black bag? Only authorized people were allowed in the barn and stable area.

The operatives did not respond to the message. Kit's healing gut twisted.

"I'm scared," Wiona whispered.

"It's probably nothing. Let's pretend we're asleep and see if he comes our way again," Kit suggested softly. He was not nearly as unconcerned as he tried to make Wiona think he was.

Without moving his head and by opening his eyes only a slit, Kit kept peeking at the man who appeared to be watching them. Finally, to Kit's dismay, the fellow started walking toward them. In one hand, he held the small black bag, which he reached into. Kit prayed for help from Karl's men, but he still hadn't had a reply to his text. As he prayed, a strong feeling came over him that if the stranger was bent on mischief, he and Wiona were on their own. Wiona, close beside him, was breathing heavily. He could feel the fear emanating from her. He shivered.

The stranger stopped by the door to Kingfisher's stall. When he began to slide it open, Kit peeked up at him. In the man's right hand was a syringe. To Wiona, he whispered, "I've got to stop him," and he leaped to his feet, ignoring the pain in his gut.

He stormed through the gate just as the man was about to insert the syringe into Kingfisher's hip. "Stop!" he commanded.

The stranger jerked his hand back and looked straight at Kit in the shadowy light. "I'm a veterinarian," he said. "The owner of this horse asked me to come give him a shot, that he's acting ill. He got me out of bed. Said it couldn't wait."

"The owner? Who is that?" Kit asked as his whole body tensed, ready for violent action. He was aware of Wiona, who had moved into the stall with him. The stranger still held the syringe, but he slowly placed the black bag on the floor of the stall.

"I'm not good with names, but he paid me to give him a shot," the stranger said. "I'll need you two to step out in case this horse kicks."

"Who paid you?" Kit insisted.

"I told you I don't remember the name. But he was a big man with a shaved head and a black beard, and he wore glasses. Now step back."

Kit pictured in his mind a couple of the artist's renditions of how Vince might look. It had to have been him who hired this little man to do his dirty work. "What's your name?" Kit asked.

"I'm Dr. Board. Now move. I need to give this horse a shot."

"Put the syringe down," Kit ordered as his anger continued to build. "I own this horse. Get out of this stall."

The man moved quickly and thrust the syringe toward Kingfisher's shoulder. Kit, despite the pain, moved swiftly, grabbing the offending arm and jerking it back. The man did not drop the syringe. With his free hand, Kit struck him on the side of the head. The faux veterinarian spun around and tried to hit Kit, but Wiona was right there. She struck at his fist, deflecting the punch.

Kit pulled harder. Wiona grabbed the man's other arm and held onto it, even as the man swung her against the wall of the stall. Kingfisher jumped back and snorted. The man twisted and struggled, but the two of them held onto his arms. The man attempted to turn the syringe on Kit, but he jerked the man's hand violently. The syringe missed Kit but stuck into the man's neck. Whatever was in the syringe entered the stranger as his hand involuntarily pushed the plunger in his struggle to free himself from Kit and Wiona.

He screamed, and Kit and Wiona both jumped back, letting go of his arms. Wildly, the stranger grabbed the syringe and pulled it out of his neck. Kit pushed

Wiona out of the stall door and followed. Gentle, sweet Kingfisher had taken all he was going to of the disruption to his night. He slashed with both front feet at the intruder, knocking the man hard against the wall of the stall.

"Stay out here," Kit said. "I can't let Kingfisher kill him."

He stepped into the stall again as the big stallion continued to tromp on the intruder. "Kingfisher, no," he commanded. The horse, upon hearing his voice, ceased his stamping and turned toward Kit. "It's okay now, big fella," Kit said soothingly as he reached out and touched Kingfisher's neck.

He petted and talked softly for a moment, and he could feel the tension easing from the big horse's body. "Wiona, can you pull this guy out of here?" he called out. "I need to keep Kingfisher calm."

"I'll try," she said, a quaver in her voice.

Kit continued to soothe Kingfisher as Wiona crept timidly back into the stall. She grabbed one of the man's legs while watching Kit and Kingfisher.

"You're doing great," Kit said. "Kingfisher is calm now. Pull the guy out of here."

She tugged, and the man's body started to slide across the stall floor. As soon as she and the body were out of the stall, Kit said. "I'll be out in a moment. Leave the gate open a little bit."

He put his hands on Kingfisher's cheek. The beautiful stallion lowered his head, and Kit was able to put his arm around his neck. There, with his head against the smooth black hair of his glossy coat, he continued to speak softly. Finally, he backed away. "That's a good fella," he said. "It's okay now."

Kingfisher threw his head and whinnied. Other horses answered his whinny. He looked at Kit, stepped close to him, and rested his head gently on Kit's shoulder. Kit patted his head for a moment. "I need to see if I can help that guy." He stepped back, and as he did, he noticed the syringe lying on the floor near the black bag. He bent and picked them both up, gave one last affectionate pat on Kingfisher's forehead, and stepped out of the stall. He placed the bag on the floor, sat the syringe on it, and then shut the gate to the stall and latched it securely.

Wiona was on her phone. She had pulled the man into the center of the aisle. He was not moving. "We're both okay, Brandon, unless Kit tore something loose inside. I'm going to have a lot of bruises, but nothing is broken, even though the guy slammed me against the wall. The guy fought us hard until he accidentally stuck himself with the syringe."

She listened for a minute on her phone as Kit knelt beside their attacker. His head was bloody from the damage inflicted by Kingfisher's hooves. He didn't seem to be breathing, and Kit couldn't find a pulse.

"Kit, Brandon's coming. He's calling Karl. He can't imagine where Karl's men are," she said. "And he's getting the cops and security officers to come as well. He said to do what you can for the guy but not to let him get away."

"He won't get away," Kit said soberly. "I think he's dead."

Wiona gasped. "Is he really?"

"I can't find a pulse, and he isn't breathing."

"Ooh," Wiona said as she looked at the man she'd dragged from the stall. "His head!"

"Yeah, I think he made a huge mistake. Are you okay? He banged you around in there pretty hard."

"I'm sore, but he didn't break any bones. How are you, Kit? You look kind of pale."

"I'm hurting too. But I don't think I did any damage to my gut. I hope not," he said.

Kit's phone buzzed. He answered it.

"Kit, have you seen my guys yet?" Karl Shutter asked.

"No," Kit said. "I texted them when we first saw this guy, but they didn't answer. They've been close by all night until this guy showed up. I'm afraid he did something to them."

"I'm on my way, and so are more of my people. The cops should be there before we are. Are you or Wiona hurt?"

"Nothing bad. He wasn't a big guy, but he was determined to do something to my horse. I couldn't let him," Kit said.

"How bad is he? Brandon told me that Wiona told him that he stuck himself with his syringe," Karl said.

"Kingfisher kind of worked him over too. I'm pretty sure he's dead."

Karl moaned. "I guess it's good you two stayed there. But it's not like my guys to fail like that. I'll be there shortly. Don't move the body, and don't touch anything."

"I picked up the syringe and the guy's little black bag and brought them out of Kingfisher's stall. I was afraid he might damage them."

"That's good. Just leave them for now. Do you have any idea who the guy is?"

"No, but the description he gave of the man who he said hired him, who claimed to be the owner of Kingfisher, kind of fits one of the pictures your artist drew. It had to have been Vince Hodson."

Just as the call ended, two policemen and two security officers ran into the building, guns drawn. They put them away as soon as they saw the body on the floor and Kit and Wiona holding each other. One of them confirmed what Kit had already determined; their attacker was most certainly dead.

Kit and Wiona told them what happened. One of the policemen and one of the security offers went in search of Karl's missing operatives and the missing security officer. The others continued to question Kit and Wiona. They were asked if they needed an ambulance. They said they didn't.

Pretty soon, Karl Shutter, Dave Washington, and Santos Garcia arrived, followed shortly by Brandon and Paizlee. Karl listened with a tight face to an officer who announced that his missing men and the security officer were alive but unconscious. Each had a dart in his neck—they had been tranquilized. They were all being taken by ambulance to a hospital. A search of the black bag revealed the source of the darts.

There was a small dart gun and more darts in the bag. It appeared that the darts were loaded with a tranquilizer that, according to Karl, had caused the operatives to lose consciousness almost at once. That was later confirmed by the doctors who treated them. All three were expected to recover fully.

Also in the bag was a mostly empty insulin bottle. Randall Overmyer, who had arrived only moments before, remarked, "That was how Sam's horse was killed. Now I'm wondering if Sam himself might have been behind that. I know he grumbled that even though he won the race in Albuquerque, which he cheated to do, that he was disappointed in his horse."

Kit couldn't help but agree, but he did not say so, nor did anyone else. They just let the idea sink in. Perhaps at some point, the truth would come out.

As a precaution, Kit and Wiona were both checked over at the hospital. Scans of Kit's gut did not reveal any damage. As soon as they were allowed to leave, they both went to the hotel and cleaned up. But Kit was determined to get back to Kingfisher as quickly as possible, and Wiona wouldn't let him go without her. When they returned, they found Paizlee in the stall with Kingfisher.

The body of the man identified as Elmer Board had been removed. He was not a real veterinarian but did have some fake ID on him. He also had a driver's license that showed who he really was. Mr. Board was a local bad guy with a long criminal record. The false ID had allowed him to be admitted into the stable area by park security, and he had apparently made the attack with the dart gun very quickly on Karl's operatives and the security guard who had been inside the barn shortly after being admitted.

Though an intense search of the area was conducted by the police, no one found Vince or Sam. But they were somewhere in disguise. Brandon stated what was on everyone's minds. "It didn't take those guys long to find someone who would do their dirty work for them. We should expect them to try again in some way."

Later that day, Kingfisher was taken out to the track and given a good workout with Paizlee on his back. He was in top form, certainly none the worse following the attempt on his life during the night. If Vince and Sam's hired crook had succeeded, Kingfisher would have been just as dead as Sam's horse.

As for Karl's men and the security officer, they all regained consciousness in the hospital. They had each been alone and had seen the attacker, but he had shot a dart at each of them before they could react. That, Karl explained, was uncharacteristic for his men. This Board guy must have been highly efficient with the dart gun.

They came into the stable, apologized to Kit and Wiona, and promised that it would not happen again.

"I'll have four of my people here tonight," Karl said. "But I hope you guys will go home and get some rest."

"Not a chance," Kit said stubbornly.

"If Kit stays, I'm staying too," Wiona added.

Karl shook his head. "I guess I can't blame you. I'm glad you guys didn't get the dart gun treatment as well."

"We pretended to be asleep," Kit said. "I guess we didn't look like much of a threat."

As the hours passed and Elmer Board didn't report back to Sam and Vince, they became more worried that he'd failed. Sam finally called the park and asked if Kingfisher was still going to race the next day and was told that he was.

"I guess it's on to our next plan," Sam said angrily. "Kit must lead a charmed life. But we'll win yet. Let's go back to the park. Our disguises worked great."

"Let's change them a bit out of the abundance of caution. Elmer seemed like someone we could rely on to get the damage done," Vince said. "But since he wasn't, we should assume that he gave our disguises away. We need a different look before we show up there again." He slammed his fist down. "I should have done it myself."

Sam looked at him. "That wouldn't have worked any better."

Vince glared at him. "Oh yeah? It worked on your horse just fine, and I didn't get caught."

"Wait, Vince, are you saying you killed my horse?" Sam asked as his face flushed with sudden anger.

"Yeah, I was trying to help you again, so don't get all bent out of shape," Vince said. "You could never win with him, and I thought that your dad would get you a better one. Don't tell me that wasn't a good idea."

Sam simply stared at him. "So all this time," he said finally, "it wasn't Kit or someone he hired. And it was you I saw sneaking around? Vince, I can't believe you would do that."

"That's right. I made sure you saw me but not close enough to know it was me. Sam, I did it because of what Kit was saying about you. I always defended you. I did this for you. And Kit is still the one to blame for all our troubles," Vince argued.

"You had no right," Sam shouted. "You should have at least asked me first."

"Would you have let me?" Vince asked.

"No, but still, I can't believe you would do that and then blame Kit."

"I did it for you, Sam. So calm down. We've got more important things to deal with now."

"I suppose you're right," Sam agreed after a couple more minutes of arguing. "But I still say you should have told me first."

"Of course I'm right. I'm always right, Sam. And it was best the way I did it. You should be thanking me, not getting angry. Now, get over it. We need to focus on what we have to do. We need to be able to mingle with jockeys and owners and even security people. You know jockeys don't make much, and I'm sure the security people are way underpaid. With Harry Murray's money, we can afford to make an offer to someone who won't turn us down," Vince said. "We can't afford to fail again. We have got to get our revenge. Kit and his sister and your father have done us way too much damage to ignore."

Sam shook his head. "You killed Sharpshooter," he said as if still in shock.

"Yes, and you owe me for doing it. You owe me for lots of things, Sam. I even killed a guy because of what he did to you, at great risk to me. I killed your horse for your sake, at great risk to me. Now get over it, and let's get to it."

Sam continued to sulk, but an hour later, he got back to what he knew had to be done. Soon, in new disguises, the two men returned to Santa Anita Park. They began to mingle. And within a couple of hours, they'd found someone who, for a hefty price, would assist them in accomplishing their goal. Even though they actually saw Sam's father, Kit, and a pretty red-headed girl standing in the sunlight outside of the barn that housed the racehorses, neither Randall nor Kit paid any attention to them as they passed.

They were feeling pretty good about themselves. Kingfisher was not going to win any races the next day. They were confident of that. And no one would have any idea that they were behind the calamity they had designed.

CHAPTER THIRTY

WIONA TUNED OUT THE CONVERSATION between Kit and Randall and watched the people who occasionally strolled past. Suddenly, with a jolt, she realized she may have seen a couple of men walk past who resembled the portraits prepared by Karl's artistic operative.

She had small copies of the pictures in her pocket. She pulled them out and studied them for a moment. Surer than ever of their identity, she put all but two of the pictures back in her pocket. Then she urgently interrupted Kit and Randall.

"Hey, guys, I might be wrong, but I think I may have just seen Sam and Vince. A couple of guys that looked a lot like these pictures I'm holding passed by a little while ago. I got these out and studied them. I think we should spread the word. Maybe someone can catch them if we hurry," Wiona said.

Kit did not question her, nor did Randall. Kit got on his secure phone and called Karl. "Sam and Vince are in the park," he said. "Wiona saw two guys that fit two of your pictures just a little while ago."

"What are the numbers on the pictures?"

"Seven and thirteen," Kit responded.

For a moment, Karl didn't respond. "Okay," he said finally. "I've got them in my hand. Where did she see them?"

"We are standing outside the south side of the barn getting some sun," Kit said. "Randall and I were talking, but Wiona saw them stroll past."

"Okay, I'll put out word to my people, the cops, and park security. You guys let the rest of your gang know, and maybe we can catch them before they do more damage. If any of you see them, don't approach them, but let me know where they are. And one more thing, Kit: don't you guys go looking for them. If you happened to run into them, they might attempt to do something to you right then. Make sure your people let us do the searching."

"I can't believe my father is here with Kit. Talk about a traitor," Sam said. "We should go back there and bash some heads."

"There are too many people around, Sam," Vince cautioned him. "We don't want to create a stir that could ruin the plan. Be patient. We need to bide our time."

"I guess you're right," Sam reluctantly agreed.

"You know I'm right. And neither your dad nor Kit seemed to recognize us."

"I don't think they even saw us," Sam said. "They were busy talking and didn't look up. The redhead might have seen us, but I don't even know who she is, so she for sure wouldn't know who we were."

"We've done well this afternoon," Vince bragged. "We can't lose now."

About fifteen minutes passed before Kit got another call. "I guess it wasn't them," Karl said.

"Who was it, then, and how do you know?" Kit asked despondently.

"One of the security officers knows them. He said they are decent guys and are from right here in Arcadia. He even told me their names and that they were friends of his. Good catch, nonetheless," Karl said.

Kit thought for a moment. "Is there any chance the security guy is lying? Sam and Vince paid that guy, Elmer Board, last night to do what he did. They won't give up."

"A fair point, Kit. I'll check his background. I have his name. In the meantime, I'll bypass him and the other security officers and ask my people and the police to keep looking," Karl said.

"Thanks," Kit said.

A few minutes later, Brandon and Paisley joined them beside Kingfisher's stall. "Karl called me. He told me your concerns about the security officer. I'd like to think someone in his position couldn't be bought off, but then Vince was a cop and he was crooked. I would like Paizlee to stay here with you guys while I join up with Dave. The two of us and all of Karl's people but two—who will stay here at the barn with you guys—are going to circulate throughout the entire park. We'll check everywhere."

"Those guys don't know me," Lawrence said. "And they owe me for damage to my plane. I'm going to go look around myself." Kit argued, but Lawrence was adamant and away he went.

After Brandon and Lawrence left, Paizlee, Kit, Wiona, Randall, Bruce, and Andy waited.

Karl checked the background of the security officer who claimed to know the two men Wiona had seen. He was fairly new and had no serious criminal history, but Karl also learned he was a big spender, gambled a lot, and was deep in debt. That aroused his suspicions, so he went one step further in his inquires. He searched for the two men the officer had claimed to know, and they weren't listed in any databases—they did not exist. The officer had lied, and Karl had to know why.

The head of security for Santa Anita Park, a retired police major by the name of Byron Ingram, was a stern, large man in his late fifties who still used his former title. His keen blue eyes gazed at Karl as he spoke, giving nothing away about what he was feeling. Karl outlined his concerns very clearly while Dave watched the major closely. Dave was well known among those he worked with for possessing the ability to accurately read people's faces.

When he had finished, Major Ingram ran a beefy hand through his full head of short, white hair. Karl glanced briefly at his second-in-command. The two made eye contact, and Dave made a negligible shake of his head; Dave had not been able to read anything from the major's face.

"This is a serious accusation you're making, Mr. Shutter," Major Ingram said. "I understand your concerns about the safety of your clients and their horse. That was certainly manifest when that foolish man weaseled his way past my people, disabled yours and one of mine, and came close to killing a very valuable horse. But I have never had a complaint like this lodged against Officer Vern Considine."

"I understand he has a decent record, but how do you explain the fact that the two men he named appear in no databases?" Karl asked.

"I can't explain it, but maybe Officer Considine can. I'll have him come in," the major said. "Maybe he can explain things to the satisfaction of you two men."

While waiting for Officer Considine to arrive, Major Ingram asked Karl and Dave about their backgrounds. When they had finished, he said, "I'm very impressed. But I hope you are wrong about Officer Considine."

Moments later, Considine entered the major's office. He was a slender man of about six feet in his mid-twenties. Karl immediately sensed that the officer was nervous. He kept swallowing and looking around. His prominent Adam's apple kept bobbing up and down.

"Sit down, Considine," Major Ingram said. "I think you know who these men are."

Without meeting anyone's eyes, he mumbled, "Yeah, we met."

"I understand you were shown some pictures a short while ago. You say you know the men."

Considine swallowed, his eyes blinked rapidly, and he looked quickly around the room. Karl glanced at Dave, who nodded. This guy was nervous.

"I would like you to tell us more about these friends of yours," the major said with a perfectly straight face.

"They, ah . . . I, ah . . . they aren't exactly friends, just guys I know," he stammered.

Those keen blue eyes of Major Ingram's studied the officer's face, but not once did the officer meet the major's eyes. The bobbing of the Adam's apple increased, as did the incessant blinking.

"Tell me how you know them," the major said.

"Ah . . . well . . . ah . . . I met them in a bar, you see. We played a few rounds of pool," the officer said.

Karl glanced at Dave. A tiny nod told him that the major was, as Karl himself suspected, having a hard time believing his officer.

"How often have you been with them?" Major Ingram asked.

"Oh, ah . . . maybe twice," he answered. Sweat was beading on his forehead.

"Where do they live?" the major asked.

"I, ah . . . I don't . . . don't really know."

"Then why did you tell Mr. Shutter that they lived in Arcadia?"

"I, ah . . . I just . . . you know, assumed. I mean, like, you know, that's where I met them." This man was lying through his teeth.

Karl spoke up. "When I talked to you, you seemed very certain that they lived in Arcadia. Why are you saying now that you don't know?"

"I, ah . . . I—"

Major Ingram interrupted him sharply. "Quit saying ah. Quit stuttering. Are you lying to me, Officer?"

"I, ah . . . no . . . I wouldn't do that," he said.

"Look at me!" Major Ingram suddenly thundered so loudly the windows of his office rattled.

He did, but only for a fraction of a second. The major's face was dark and his brow creased. His mouth clamped tight. He turned to Karl and nodded. Karl took that as permission to question him.

"Tell me, Officer, when did you first meet these men? What did you say their names were?"

Officer Considine didn't even stutter this time. He simply failed to respond.

Karl pressed him. "You told me their names without hesitation earlier. But now you don't remember? Think about it. When did you first meet them?" Karl gave Considine a chance to respond, but when he did nothing but blink, swallow, and sweat, he went on. "You met them today, didn't you? Possibly this morning or early this afternoon."

"I, ah . . . I don't remember for sure."

The major broke in sternly. "I told you not to say ah. I meant it. Officer, I am going to have you take a polygraph. You know, a lie detector test. I am going to set it up right now."

The tall, thin man seemed to shrink. His eyes began to water. The major looked steadily at him. "Look at me!" he thundered again.

It didn't happen. Considine's eyes continued to dart around. The major turned to Karl and Dave. "I am going to give him a polygraph. I am an experienced polygraph operator, and I have my equipment in that closet behind me. But while I set it up, you two may ask him whatever you like."

Karl said, "Let me alert my operatives and the police and security that the two men are the ones we are after. Then I will ask him a couple of things." After a couple of calls, he turned to Considine. "You are deep in debt, Officer. Did you get that way gambling?"

"I'm, ah . . . ah, no," he stuttered.

"You are going to do very poorly on a lie detector. You have been lying since you came in the room. I didn't ask you if you are in debt. I did my homework before Agent Washington and I came in to speak to your boss. So tell me what I asked. I know you gamble. Is your debt from gambling?"

"Ah . . . maybe a little bit. I, ah . . ."

"Quit that, Considine!" the major said very loudly. He had yet to get out his equipment. He was simply observing Karl and Dave.

"You are also a big spender, aren't you?" Karl asked.

"I, ah . . . don't think so," he said. There was no outburst from the major. Apparently he had given up on making Considine quit saying *ah*.

"How much did those two men whose pictures we showed you pay you to say you knew them?" Karl asked. "Maybe you could empty your pockets for us. I'd like to see how much they gave you."

This time, Considine actually looked at his boss. "I don't have to do that, do I?" he pleaded pitifully.

"I think it would be a good idea. Right here on my desk," the major said, thumping a thick index finger in front of him.

Considine shook his head. "No," he said flatly.

"You either do what I just said to or you are fired. I am tired of the games. These men you are protecting are killers. Put everything from your pockets on the desk."

"I need to . . . ah . . . go now."

"Empty your pockets!"

Considine shook his head.

"Gentlemen," Major Ingram said. "Why don't the two of you give him a hand there."

They did that, lifting him from his chair. Considine struggled. But Dave was a very strong man. He held him while Karl emptied his pockets. He had a comb, a pair of nail clippers, a handkerchief, a ring of keys, a cell phone, a wallet that contained a driver's license, some credit cards, a couple of receipts, and twenty-eight dollars in cash. He also had some loose change. Following that, Karl pulled from his front left pocket a large wad of hundred-dollar bills.

The major counted the bills one at a time. He ended up with one thousand dollars. "Okay, tell us what these men asked you to do in exchange for this money," Major Ingram said, showing him the pictures that Wiona had earlier identified.

Considine slumped in his chair. "I, ah . . . ah . . . was supposed to say I knew them if anyone asked."

"Is that all?" the major asked.

"They told me that if I saw anyone bothering a jockey by the name of Kit that I was to ignore it. They said Kit was a troublemaker. They said if his horse, Kingfisher, placed high in a race tomorrow that I should report that he cheated."

"I guess we won't need the polygraph after all," the major said. "I am very disappointed in you. Thank you, gentlemen, for bringing this unfortunate matter to my attention."

The major radioed all of his officers on duty and reinforced what Karl had already alerted them to. "The men whose pictures you were shown earlier and told to look for," he said, "are wanted across three states. Find them and bring them in. But be careful; they are dangerous men, and you should consider them armed. They are the ones who set up the attempt to kill one of the racehorses in our care last night."

He put down his radio and made a phone call. Shortly, a pair of uniformed police officers came in.

"Arrest this man," the major said. "He is as of this minute fired from his employment. Mr. Washington and Mr. Shutter will give you a statement, and then they will need to leave. They have been most helpful, but they have a horse and a couple of jockeys to protect."

Vince and Sam were not found that afternoon or evening, and the security for the horse and his owners was increased. The next day, at three o'clock in the afternoon, Kingfisher, with Paizlee Troxler as jockey, was due to race in the main event of the day.

CHAPTER THIRTY-ONE

Kit and Wiona, despite beefed-up security at the stables, stubbornly refused to leave and spent the night next to Kingfisher's stall. There were no further attempts to harm the horse that night. Fortunately, they did get some sleep, though they were both very tired as the morning dragged on.

There was a lot of activity in the barn and surrounding area as horses racing in earlier races came and went. Paizlee and Brandon had joined them at around eight in the morning. Shortly after, both trainers, Bruce and Andy, were also there. They all persuaded Kit and Wiona to go to their rooms at the hotel and get some rest so that they would be alert and rested for the three o'clock race.

They were, of course, taken there by a pair of Karl's operatives. Both, in their respective rooms, were soon asleep with the men standing guard in the hallway.

Sam and Vince had been shocked when they had spotted Officer Considine being escorted to a police car in handcuffs by a couple of uniformed officers the previous afternoon. Having failed again in their attempt to cause trouble for Kit and his horse, Sam and Vince had left the park. They were determined to succeed as the hour for the race drew ever closer. They knew what they had to do, and they set about doing it. They entered the park with their disguises altered again, both confident that they would not be recognized. With their pockets full of more of Harry's money, they strolled purposefully through the crowds at the park.

Vince had done some research the previous evening. He'd discovered that one of the jockeys who was to ride in the race with Kingfisher was in a bad way financially, every bit as bad as Considine had been. They went looking for him, eventually found him, and pulled him aside.

Santos noticed two men talking to one of the jockeys who was to ride in the three o'clock race. Karl had done research on all the jockeys and all the owners and trainers for that race. He had sent all of his operatives pictures of each on their cell phones and told them to keep an eye on them. Brandon also was given hard copies to distribute to each of the folks involved with Kingfisher.

Santos had also studied the pictures Karl's artist had created. The men with the jockey looked like they could match a couple of the pictures. Unfortunately, there were a lot of people in the park, and many were milling around. He wasn't close enough to the jockey to be sure about what had occurred before the men he suspected moved away from him. He shoved his way through the crowd and reported on his radio what he'd observed.

"Try to keep the guys in sight," Karl said. "Which picture numbers did you think they resembled?"

"Ten and fifteen. They are shoving their way quickly through the crowd." He gave their location in the park, and Karl ordered other operatives to converge on that area.

"What about the jockey?" Santos asked. "I can't keep track of him too."

"You know who he is, right?" Karl asked.

"I think I do," Santos said. "I'll know him if I see him again."

"Okay, we'll let him go for now. We want to catch these other two and find out if they are our suspects," Karl said. "I'll alert security and the police."

A minute later, Santos had managed to get a little closer, but then the two men split up. He radioed that information to the other operatives and followed the taller one, the one he believed to be Vince Hodson.

Santos was almost certain now who the men were, for the tall one kept looking over his shoulder. Having apparently realized that he was being followed, he began to run. Santos radioed his position and the direction Vince was going as well as the last location he had on the small man he believed to be Sam Overmyer.

"I have Hodson in sight," Dave reported. "He's coming toward me." A moment later, he radioed again. "Santos, he's swerving away from me."

"I'm almost to him."

A third operative reported that Hodson was now in sight and coming in her direction. The three operatives closed in on him. Vince apparently failed to suspect the third operative, a woman by the name of Joana Shirk, a former marine. When she was almost to him, she shouted at him. "Stop right there, Vince."

He looked right at her, and then he simply charged toward her with his head lowered. Santos and Dave were almost to him.

"People, get back!" Dave shouted. "This man is a killer."

The crowd reacted in a panic and pushed away just as Vince reached Joana. He apparently thought he could simply run her down and go on past. He was sorely mistaken. She was standing still, and when he reached her, she moved swiftly to the side and, with a lightning-fast move with one leg, took his legs out from under him. He fell on his face, but there was a pistol in his hand.

"You're dead, lady," he said as he sat up.

Garcia reached him just then. "Drop it!"

He looked briefly back, and when he did, Joana jumped to the side and pulled a weapon. Dave had also closed in. "Vince, drop it," he said. "You can't get away."

Vince swung his pistol in Dave's direction, and Joana fired. Instead of a bullet striking Vince, electricity jolted through his system—Joana had fired a Taser, and it struck right over the man's heart. He fell back, and Dave disarmed him. Within seconds, two police officers and a park security man ran up. The security officer and one policeman began moving the crowd back farther.

Dave turned Vince on his back, and Santos slapped a pair of handcuffs on him. "Watch for Sam Overmyer," Dave said as soon as Vince was secured. "He could be coming to help his cousin." He then frisked Vince and pulled out another gun from his boot and a large knife hidden inside his pants. He also pulled out a cell phone.

Sam was nowhere near. He'd abandoned his cousin and fled. In fact, he was hiding in the stolen car in the parking lot, a car that he and Vince had arrived in that morning. He tried to call Vince, but the voice that answered the phone was not Vince's.

"Sam, this is Agent Dave Washington. Vince is in custody. You can't get away. All the exits are now blocked. You might as well give yourself up."

Panicked, Sam ended the call. Without Vince to tell him what to do, he felt helpless. Vince had always been there for him. So he stayed in the car, ducked out of sight, and hoped for the best. But in the next few minutes, he managed to calm down and thought of a way to get out of the park. He heard a car moving just outside of his. He poked his head up, saw a young woman driving the car in his direction, and made a quick decision. He leaped from his car just as the woman reached him. He held his gun toward her. She froze and stopped the car. He approached. "Stay in the car and unlock your doors," he shouted.

She looked at him, fear in her eyes.

"Now," he said. "Or I'll kill you and take your car."

She unlocked the door, and he jumped in the backseat. "I'll be lying down back here. Leave the park and don't let anyone know I'm here, or you're dead."

The woman didn't speak, but she did as he said. She slowed at the exit, and he heard her say something to the officer about her baby being really sick, that her babysitter had called in a panic, and that she needed to get home right away.

The officer told her to hurry, and she drove out of the park and onto an adjacent street. After they had gone a few blocks, Sam sat up. "That was good thinking about your baby. That lie might have saved your life. Pull over and get out."

She started to cry and told Sam that her baby really was sick, and she had to get home.

"Just get out. I need your car. And leave your purse. I don't want you using your cell phone."

She did, and he drove off in her car, leaving her sobbing on the sidewalk. Sam drove the stolen car to the hotel and parked it in the back between other cars, and then he hurried into his room. He was on his own now, but Kit would still lose. He and Vince had made sure of that. He decided to sit right here in the hotel room and watch the race on TV. He could laugh his head off when Kingfisher failed in the race, as he was confident he would. And then he'd leave LA.

Vince had refused to speak. He admitted nothing. He even denied being Vince, and he had no ID on him showing otherwise, but there was no doubt who he was. So he was hauled off to jail. The continuing search for Sam was thorough, but even though they found a stolen car in the large parking area with thousands of other cars, Sam had somehow managed to get away. The car was towed to be checked later for fingerprints and any other evidence that could be found in it.

Kit's nerves were on fire. Kingfisher and Paizlee were almost ready to go. Bruce had walked Kingfisher to the saddling area and was beginning to saddle him. Paizlee was wearing the dark blue colors that Kit had worn in Albuquerque. Brandon put an arm around Paizlee's shoulder. "Watch the other jockeys, but keep a close eye on number fourteen with the striped yellow jersey. We think he may be the one that Santos saw talking to Vince and Sam. He'll be on a tall gray mare, the only gray in the lineup."

"I see the mare," Paizlee said, "but I don't see number fourteen."

"He'll be here. He'll probably show up beside his horse around the same time you go in there. Be careful, please," Brandon said.

"Kingfisher and I have trained hard. We can do this."

"Another jockey, probably fourteen, might try something," Kit said urgently.

"But they don't know for sure or what was said, Kit. Santos admitted he wasn't close enough to see if any money changed hands. They were probably just trying to get information from him. We don't even know if they knew he was a jockey," Paizlee said.

"Okay," Kit said. "But remember, you are far more important to me than winning this race. If you have to lose to stay safe, you do that. There will be other races."

In Paizlee's eyes, Kit saw the gleam he knew would be in his own if he were riding. She desperately wanted to win, and he was afraid she'd take whatever risks she had to in order to ride Kingfisher to the finish line ahead of the other eight horses.

"We can win this, Kit. Then the next time he runs, you can ride, and you can win," Paizlee said with a smile. "I'll be okay."

Kit knew his sister. She was determined. "Get in there. And be careful. I love you, sis."

"I love you too, Kit. Pray for me. The Lord will help us."

He choked up and didn't respond. Brandon walked with her into the ring. For a moment, she petted the big stallion, and Kit could see her talking to him, just like he would have done if he'd been riding. Then Bruce helped her onto Kingfisher, and in a moment, looking every bit a jockey, his twin sister was ready.

Kit spotted number fourteen on the gray mare. He was just a couple places away from Kingfisher when the horses were led into the starting gate. Kingfisher was prancing and throwing his magnificent head. Kit's heart swelled with pride. Kingfisher was ready for this; he was anxious to run, and there was no doubt he would give it all he had.

Sam was tense but smiling as he watched the racehorses being led into the starting gates on TV. A flush of anger wiped the smile away. He should have been racing out there. He was born for it. He was a better jockey by far than either Kit or his sister. And it was indeed the sister who was on the horse.

The camera swung slowly from one horse to another. He watched with interest as number fourteen and the gray mare he was mounted on were led in. He and Vince had given that guy a lot of Harry Murray's money. He'd better do his job. If it were him on the gray mare, Sam knew he could do it. He only hoped number fourteen was half as good a jockey as he was.

A smile again crept onto his face. There was not only the money, but there was also the threat that Vince had made just as the jockey had walked away. "You screw up, and we'll hunt you down. You won't live to race again," he'd said. Sam had seen the sudden fear in the guy's eyes.

CHAPTER THIRTY-TWO

THE GATES OPENED, AND THEY were off. Paizlee had never felt so alive in her life, and the big stallion beneath her was feeling great. He flew out of the gate and quickly took the lead, but Paizlee remembered the instructions she'd gotten from Bruce and Andy. She held him back just a little and let a couple of the others move ahead of her.

The strength and speed of Kingfisher was to be saved until they were closer to the end. Let others think they are winning, she'd been told. Then let Kingfisher do his thing. She was also watching for the gray mare with number fourteen mounted on her. The gray had also started very fast out of the gate. Research that Kit had done a little earlier told them that the gray was a very fast horse. And of course, the jockey was probably not to be trusted.

Paizlee settled Kingfisher in at fourth place and kept him close to the ones in front of her who were running in a pack. One of them was the gray mare. Paizlee could feel in the reins that Kingfisher wanted to pass the others, but she held him back, content with where she was at the moment. After they passed the first turn, the gray mare dropped back until he was running right beside her. The jockey looked over at her and grinned. It was not a nice grin. It was full of malice, and her heart took a little tumble. He was the one. She let Kingfisher move ahead. Then she glanced back briefly.

The jockey on the gray mare had his quirt going, and his mount once again came alongside her. She held Kingfisher back just a little, but the gray mare continued to stay beside her. The jockey moved her closer to Kingfisher, and suddenly, he swung his quirt, and had Paizlee not seen it coming, it would have struck Kingfisher right on the head. Now she was angry. She knew she had to get away from the gray mare. The two horses ahead were riding close to the fence.

There was no way she could go inside of them, so she swung wide, but when she did, jockey fourteen moved his gray mare over until she actually collided with Kingfisher, smashing Paizlee's leg. Kingfisher reacted by slowing down. The gray mare then surged around the two leading horses and took the lead herself. Paizlee could not afford to get any further back, and she urged Kingfisher to speed up, ignoring the throbbing in her leg. She could feel his powerful muscles as he surged forward.

There was often something between a good jockey and much-loved horse that made it so they could communicate as if they were one. She felt that. Kingfisher felt that. She urged him silently to speed up. He responded.

Kingfisher easily passed the other two and caught up with the gray mare. Number fourteen looked over his shoulder and saw her coming. He moved away from the rail. She knew what he wanted. He wanted her to try to pass on the inside. She had been told not to do that under any circumstances. So she simply followed until they rounded the last curve. Then she urged Kingfisher ahead, staying wide.

Number fourteen saw her come alongside and once again moved his mare over. He waited until Kingfisher was even with the mare's neck, then he swung the quirt again, and even though Paizlee tried to steer wider, it connected with Kingfisher's face. The big stallion went wild for a moment, making it hard for Paizlee to stay on. Once again, the gray mare pulled alongside them, and the rider tried to hit Kingfisher with his quirt again. But this time, Kingfisher simply bolted ahead, and the quirt hit Paizlee on the leg, the opposite one of the one that had been smashed earlier. Pain shot through her along with a healthy dose of righteous anger.

She had to make Kingfisher move faster or the other jockey would try again. It took little urging to get her horse to speed up. She leaned forward on his neck, tapped him with her quirt, and shouted, "Now, Kingfisher! Give it all you have!"

Kingfisher responded, and then Paizlee took a chance and glanced over her shoulder. The gray mare had fallen a couple of lengths back. Her jockey was working the quirt for all he was worth, but it appeared she didn't have any more speed to give him. Kingfisher, on the other hand, literally flew down the middle of the track. Paizlee continued leaning forward as far as she could and urged him on, feeling that she was one with him.

She saw the finish line coming up. It was like Kingfisher knew something great was happening. At that point, Paizlee didn't think she could have slowed him down if she'd wanted to. He ran like he'd never run before. It was exhilarating. Paizlee didn't even feel the pain in her legs. She simply rode this amazing racehorse.

Kit was shouting, and Wiona was screaming. The crowd roared as Kingfisher swept past the finish line a good ten lengths ahead of the gray mare. The third-place horse was several lengths behind her. Kingfisher slowed down, and finally, Paizlee turned him back. She had only trotted a hundred feet when she saw the gray mare charging right for her. The gray's jockey was using his quirt for all he was worth.

Kingfisher himself sensed the danger, and as Paizlee leaned forward, he leaped to the right and then, in a moment, was in full stride. The gray horse and rider clipped Paizlee's leg as she passed, but in another moment, they were safe again. She slowed Kingfisher once more, but the gray mare and number fourteen had turned and were headed for them again.

The third-place horse's jockey, seeing what was going on, managed to head the gray mare off. By then, there were men running onto the track and shouting at jockey number fourteen. He tried to run one of the officials over, but the man stepped aside just in time and grabbed a rein, pulling it out of the jockey's hands but then let it loose, unable to hold on. The gray mare was wild with fright at that point and charged into the fence, sending the rider off and over the fence, where he landed in a heap of tangled arms and legs. His career was over.

Kit stood with Paizlee in the winner's circle. "That guy was crazy," he said, referring to number fourteen. "You should have seen the gray mare's owner. He would have beaten that jockey to a pulp if security officers hadn't intervened. The jockey was bruised badly from his fall, but he only suffered one broken bone, his right arm. The mare, once she was caught and calmed down, seemed to be okay."

"Where's the jockey now?" Paizlee asked.

"The police arrested him," Kit said. "He will be taken to a hospital to be treated, and then he's off to jail."

"I heard over the loudspeakers that his horse was disqualified because of what he tried to do to Kingfisher and me," Paizlee said.

"That's right. You're limping," Kit observed. "Are you okay?"

"My legs are hurting, but I'll be fine."

Then they had to stop talking while a wreath was placed over Kingfisher's head, and they were given the winner's trophy and congratulated heartily. Both of them were on a high from the dramatic race.

Later, they went to the stands following Bruce and Andy and accompanied by a trio of Karl Shutter's operatives. They watched the last race before deciding to find something to eat. While they gathered at a restaurant in the park, Brandon told them Karl would join them shortly but his other men and women were still keeping a close guard on Kingfisher.

Randall congratulated Paizlee on an amazing ride and once again apologized for the trouble his son and nephew had caused. "Hey," she said with a grin. "It's all good. We won."

"I'll say it's good," Bruce said. "I learned from one of the officials that Kingfisher set a quarter-horse track record this afternoon. And he did that despite being run into and quirted on the face."

Lawrence said he'd have to be there the next time Kingfisher raced. "I think I'm hooked," he said with a deep laugh.

"It is kind of catching at that," Andy said. "You know, I knew we had a good horse the day Kit's dad brought him home as a yearling. But I didn't know then just how good he really was." He turned to Kit. "By the way, did you know that your dad put a million dollars of insurance on him?"

"We both knew," Paizlee said. "But we don't ever want to collect on it. We just want to keep racing him."

Kit turned to Randall. "We owe you a huge debt. You've got to let us repay you."

Randall shook his head. "I wanted to do it, but there is something you could do for me, if you're willing."

"Anything," Kit said.

"I have a couple of top mares. Would you consider giving me a chance to get a couple of colts out of Kingfisher?"

"Of course," Kit said just as Karl joined them.

"So what happened when they questioned that crazy jockey?" Brandon asked.

"He confessed that two men, whose names he didn't know, had paid him to make Kingfisher lose. He said he would never have done it, but the taller of the two told him if Kingfisher won, they would find him and kill him. I think fear of that threat drove him crazy, and that's why he did that stupid stuff after the race was over."

Randall frowned. "Now they need to catch my son. He started all this. It can't go on."

At that very moment, a half dozen police officers met at the motel where Sam was believed to be holed up. A report had earlier been made by a woman who had been forced at gunpoint by a man meeting Sam's description to take him out of the park. Then he kicked her out of the car. She reported it stolen once she found a phone. Sam had made her leave hers in the car.

It was the GPS of her phone that led them to the motel where they were now preparing for the arrest. At that point assignments were given, and then they took their places. Two officers knocked on the motel door. There was no response, but someone could be heard moving about inside. Using a key provided by the motel management, one of them unlocked the door and kicked it open and then jumped back.

A bullet whizzed out the open door and into the wall opposite. The officers dropped down, and one of them peeked in, keeping low. He spotted Sam, who was at the far end of the room. Sam pointed the gun, and the officer fired at the same moment Sam did. Both the officer and Sam went down. The pistol slipped from Sam's hand.

Two officers who had been waiting nearby rushed in while the other one at the door pulled his wounded partner away from the door. Sam tried to reach the gun, but an officer kicked it out of his reach, and then the injured outlaw was cuffed and searched.

The bullet that had been fired at Sam had hit him in the right hip. The officers worked to stop the bleeding as others called for an ambulance for both Sam and the wounded police officer, who had been struck in the shoulder by Sam's bullet.

Sam, though injured, cursed Kit, shouting at the officers that it was all Kit Troxler's fault. He continued to blame Kit for all his trouble and resisted, kicking and fighting for all he was worth, until he was finally subdued by a paramedic who gave him a tranquilizer.

Karl's phone rang, and he answered it. He listened for a couple of minutes, and then he asked, "What is the address of the hospital?" A moment later his call ended. Karl turned to Randall. "Sam is in custody, but he was injured and has been taken to a hospital."

He then explained about the arrest and how it had gone down, according to the officer who had called him. "I'm going to the hospital. Brandon, will you go with me?"

Brandon agreed but said, "Let me guess—they found the car at the hotel by using the GPS on the lady's phone."

"Actually, Sam had taken her phone into his hotel room. So it led them right to him," Karl said.

"I hope he admitted what he'd done," Randall said.

"No, he resisted arrest in the worst way. He actually shot and wounded a police officer before he was subdued. Even then, all he could do was curse Kit. Apparently it was really quite an ugly scene."

"Brandon, Karl, do you think they'd let me talk to him at the hospital before we head back to Nevada in the morning?" Randall asked.

"We'll make it happen if you want us to," Lawrence answered for them. "I have a little pull—even clear down here in California."

Later that evening, Randall, accompanied by Kit and Paizlee, entered the hospital room where Sam was being treated and held under heavy guard. Randall felt that his son owed them an apology. He didn't know if he'd get it or not, but he was determined to make him face them. Lawrence, good to his word, had pulled strings and gotten the hospital visit approved.

Kit felt terrible at the look of pain in Sam's father's eyes as he approached him in his bed. Randall, his voice full of emotion, said, "Sam, you need to apologize to Kit and Paizlee."

Sam looked at his father with hatred shooting from his eyes. "For what? It was all Kit's fault."

Randall shook his head. "You know, Sam, you're in a lot of trouble. I would think that you would want to act better now. Maybe a good lawyer or two could keep you from having to spend the rest of your life in prison. Why don't you just admit what you've done?"

"Kit . . . killed . . . my horse," Sam said.

"Sam, I may not have been a good father, but I'm not as dumb as you seem to think I am. I know you killed your horse and why," Randall said.

Sam eyed his father suspiciously. "You don't know that."

"Why don't you tell me about it," Randall suggested.

Sam looked at him and then threw daggers from his hate-filled eyes at Kit and Paizlee. He looked back at his father. After a moment, he turned his head away from his father. "Sharpshooter was a dud," he said quietly. "I would have sold him and bought a new one, but I knew you wouldn't let me do that. But I didn't kill him. It was Vince. He admitted it to me yesterday. I really did think it was Kit. Vince figured that if Sharpshooter died you'd replace him with a faster horse. He should have known better. You're so selfish. The only one who's ever watched out for me is Vince. You never did. I have nothing more to say to you. You ruined my life. Now get out, all three of you. I never want to see you again."

CHAPTER THIRTY-THREE

THE NEXT EVENING, AFTER KINGFISHER had been safely returned to the Overmyer ranch, Paizlee and Wiona fixed a celebration meal. Randall, both ranch foremen, Lawrence, Brandon, and, of course, Kit, were all there.

After a good meal, they all helped clean up, and then Randall invited them into his living room. "I have some things I want to say to you, Kit and Paizlee, and I want the rest of you to hear it."

They were soon comfortably seated in Randall's spacious living room. Randall got right to the point. "I am going to leave this ranch to you, Kit and Paizlee."

"You can't do that," Kit protested in shock.

"That's not fair to you," Paizlee chimed in.

"I'm not a young man, and these past few weeks have taken a toll on me. My heart is bad, and I don't think it's going to keep ticking for many more years. I have no heir now, but you two have become closer to me than my own son ever was. I'll be getting in touch with my attorney on Monday and have him create a new trust for me leaving my ranch to you. Please, don't argue."

"But we already have a ranch," Kit said, arguing anyway.

"And there are two of you. You'll both marry one day. One of you and a spouse could take care of this place, and the other one and a spouse could take care of your Utah ranch," he said. Then he smiled fondly at the two of them. "Now my old ticker really is bad, but I'll be darned if I'm going to let it give up on me until I've got a couple of really good foals out of my mares and your stallion."

Absolute silence reigned for a good five minutes. Wiona finally broke the silence with a grin. "I could probably learn to be a cowgirl if someone I know would teach me."

Kit went red, but all he did was smile.

"I've been thinking about working out of Las Vegas if the circumstances were right," Brandon added. "And I could still work for you, Lawrence. Maybe I could get you to teach me to fly." He shrugged his shoulders. "Who knows, maybe I could even learn to ride a horse and herd cows." He paused and looked fondly at Paizlee. "Like I said, if the circumstances were right."

Paizlee went red, but all she did was smile.

ABOUT THE AUTHOR

CLAIR M. POULSON WAS BORN and raised in Duchesne, Utah. His father was a rancher and farmer, his mother a librarian. Clair has always been an avid reader, having found his love for books as a very young boy.

He has served for more than forty years in the criminal justice system. He spent twenty years in law enforcement, ending his police career with eight years as the Duchesne County Sheriff. For the past twenty-plus years, Clair has worked as a justice court judge for Duchesne County. He is also a veteran of the U.S. Army, where he was a military policeman. In law enforcement, he has been personally involved in the investigation of murders and other violent crimes. Clair has also served on various boards and councils during his professional career, including the Justice Court Board of Judges, the Utah Commission on Criminal and Juvenile Justice, the Utah Judicial Council, the Utah Peace Officer Standards and Training Council, an FBI advisory board, and others.

In addition to his criminal justice work, Clair has farmed and ranched all his life. He has raised many kinds of animals, but his greatest interests are horses and cattle. He's also involved in the grocery store business with his oldest son and other family members.

Clair has served in many capacities in The Church of Jesus Christ of Latter-day Saints, including full-time missionary (California Mission), bishop, counselor to two bishops, Young Men president, high councilor, stake mission president, Scoutmaster, high priest group leader, and Gospel Doctrine teacher. He currently serves as a ward missionary.

Clair is married to Ruth, and they have five children, all of whom are married: Alan (Vicena) Poulson, Kelly Ann (Wade) Hatch, Amanda (Ben) Semadeni, Wade (Brooke) Poulson, and Mary (Tyler) Hicken.

They also have twenty-six wonderful grandchildren and two great-granddaughters.

Clair and Ruth met while both were students at Snow College and were married in the Manti Utah Temple.

Clair has always loved telling his children, and later his grandchildren, made-up stories. His vast experience in life and his love of literature have contributed to both his telling stories to his children and his writing of adventure and suspense novels.

Clair has published over forty novels. He would love to hear from his fans, who can contact him by going to his website, clairmpoulson.com.